HER
Burning
LIES

BOOKS BY PAMELA FAGAN HUTCHINS

DETECTIVE DELANEY PACE SERIES

Her Silent Bones

Her Hidden Grave

Her Last Cry

Her Forgotten Shadow

PATRICK FLINT SERIES

Switchback

Snake Oil

Sawbones

Scapegoat

Snaggle Tooth

Stag Party

Sitting Duck

JENN HERRINGTON SERIES

Big Horn

MAGGIE KILLIAN SERIES

Live Wire

Sick Puppy

Dead Pile

KATIE CONNELL SERIES

Saving Grace

HER Burning LIES

PAMELA FAGAN HUTCHINS

bookouture

Published by Bookouture in 2025

An imprint of Storyfire Ltd.
Carmelite House
50 Victoria Embankment
London EC4Y 0DZ

www.bookouture.com

The authorised representative in the EEA is Hachette Ireland
8 Castlecourt Centre
Dublin 15 D15 XTP3
Ireland
(email: info@hbgi.ie)

ISBN: 978-1-83618-400-3
eBook ISBN: 978-1-83618-399-0

To all the amazing people who worked to contain the Elk Fire in Wyoming's Bighorn Mountains in 2024, especially the crews who prepped our home and the area around it.
And to my beloved husband, for giving me the opportunity to write in France and explore Europe for a year, thanks to his job and his hard work.

ONE

Genevieve Martine wedged herself into a closet, pulled the crooked door shut, and held the iron knob shut with both hands. She peered out between the boards. Her heart was hammering against her chest, and it took every bit of her self-restraint not to whimper. What she really wanted to do was scream for help, but where they were, no help would be around to hear her. Any sound would draw the wrong kind of attention.

She drew a shuddering breath through her nose, then almost gagged. She knew well the stench of death—*lanmò* in her native Creole, where her father would throw entrails in a pile as he butchered goats for the market. She never lost her revulsion for flies, maggots, and the unrelenting assault on her young nose as searing heat and her father's neglect did their work—until he would open the gate and let the village dogs clean up at day's end.

What is in here with me?

She pressed a hand over her mouth. Her dry, parched mouth. Her feet were bare. Were they touching something dead? Was the hem of her ridiculous gray dress dragging in decay? She thought of her attacker. Their familiarity with the old stone house. Had they brought someone else like her here? A low moan vibrated her fingers. She shook her head. She couldn't bear to think she might be in the closet with someone who had been... been... been... and now Gennie was here... and what were they going to do to her?

No. They will not kill me. I will survive this like I have everything else!

But even if she survived, the fire raging across the grasslands was coming for her. Since yesterday it had been spreading, cornering livestock, sending families fleeing from its path, over-taking wildlife. The firefighters couldn't get control of it, and the skyline was all billowing white and gray smoke that burned her eyes and seared her throat. She couldn't outrun a wildfire. Not barefoot and without a vehicle. If she got the chance, she would look for a watering hole or stock tank for the cattle. Lowering herself into water might be her only hope, if she wasn't boiled alive.

Suddenly, two beady eyes were boring into hers from the other side of the crack in the door. And then something terrifyingly odd happened. Snakes slithered out of the eyes and through the cracks, coming at her.

She let out the scream she'd been holding in. "Maman!!!!" She screamed so raggedly that her cries scraped her throat raw. Screamed until she was lightheaded and gasping for air. Screamed so loud she almost believed her mother back in Haiti —dead and buried five years now—would hear her far, far away in Wyoming and rise from the grave to save her youngest daughter.

Almost.

Then the doorknob jerked out of her hand. She stopped screaming and faced her attacker. What frightened her most wasn't their stature or the terrible sword they carried, thinner and longer than the fighting machetes used back in her homeland. It was the impassive, unfeeling stare. Like Gennie was nothing more than a roach to squash under a shoe.

Gennie had a brief flash of memory. Her mother defiant as her father rained blows on that beautiful face, hands down to shoo her children away. She had fought all her life to protect Gennie and her six sisters and one brother from the brute. *Oh, her strength.* The heart of a creature three times her size.

I will be like her.

Gennie clenched her hands, digging broken fingernails into calloused palms. Maybe Maman had arisen to save her after all.

Then another face filled her mind's eye. Red and scrunched from the effort of crying. A miniature version of Maman. *I will return for you.* She had promised. She had meant it. Tears welled in her eyes.

But first I must fight.

Before her, the figure grew, shooting up taller and taller and becoming a terrible dragon when it reached its full height. *This can't be real!*

She screamed again, but this time she raised her fists, just as she'd seen her own mother do on the night she died. The night Genevieve fled her home forever, only to end up in this new hell.

The smell hit her again. The awful, putrid smell. A horrible compulsion came over her to turn from the monster and figure out what was dead on the floor behind her.

What it was, she would never know, though. The dragon reached for her. She punched outward, connecting with flesh, but the grasping fingers still came. They jerked her out of the closet and away from who or what had lain dead at her feet.

Deputy Investigator Delaney Pace bounced her knee and bit her tongue. Between Gabrielle—Delaney's semi from her ice road trucking days—and the trailer behind it loaded down with supplies, her adopted daughter Carrie was commandeering a full, heavily laden eighteen-wheels. The two of them had struck a pact in the spring that Carrie would apply to colleges during the summer if Delaney gave her driving lessons. They'd each kept their end of the bargain, with school starting now in two weeks. It turned out that Carrie had great driving aptitude, but she was young and inexperienced.

Maybe a fifty-vehicle fire relief convoy isn't the best choice to road test her?

"Stop staring at me so hard. I know what you're thinking," Carrie said.

Even though Carrie was wearing clear safety glasses and a red bandana over her face, Delaney could still hear her clearly over Gabrielle's engine and the road noise. The girl had a voice that carried. She kept her hands at ten and two and eyes on the road, though. Sharp eyes that missed nothing. Long, straight hair, dark at the roots and faded from her latest temporary color wash from purple to a grayish lavender. She barely looked substantial enough to turn the steering wheel.

Delaney lifted her own kerchief. "How's your following distance?"

"Appropriate. Forty-foot tractor-trailer equals four seconds—"

"Or more."

"Or more of following distance."

Delaney clocked it off a fence post. Over four, not quite five seconds. "What's it look like in your side mirrors?"

"Like that yahoo didn't take driving lessons from you. He's crowding me a little."

Their own trailer was loaded with bales of hay. Delaney hoped the truck behind them wasn't carrying water, which would increase his stopping distance because of its weight. "Tap your brakes a few times to flash the lights at him."

"I did. He's not buying what I'm selling."

"People are anxious to get there."

On either side of the road, black ground smoldered. The smoke seared Delaney's throat and irritated her eyes and nasal passages. Wildfires had been devastating Kearny, Sheridan, Johnson, and Campbell counties for nearly a week. The fires had burned the pastureland for livestock. Water sources had been reduced to sooty puddles. Exhausted firefighters and beleaguered ranchers needed fresh food, clean clothes, water, electrolytes, veterinary items, fencing materials, and a replenishment of their fire suppression tools, equipment, and supplies.

The community was riddled with anxiety, and Delaney understood it all too well, having spearheaded a gargantuan fire relief effort a few years before for a large swath of the Midwest. Those fires had moved fast and were hard to contain, with heat so intense they would ignite grass in front of the fire line, especially when, as now, it was extremely dry and combustible. She still had nightmares of hundred-foot-tall flames, fire racing across Kansas prairie at seventy miles per hour, firefighters killed protecting people who refused to evacuate, cattle that shouldn't have survived the flames but did, and the ranchers who cried as they mercifully ended the lives of suffering animals.

That fire had taught her that the trick was not to wait until people asked for help. Getting in front of their needs was critical, just like getting in front of a fire's progression was critical. She'd started organizing the community to meet those needs as soon as the fires had started, which she considered a task adjacent to her job as a deputy. Temporary Kearny County Sheriff Leo Palmer—the man who had been her partner, her best friend, and almost something much more until recently—had lodged no objections to her using work hours to get it done, even as he focused on marshalling other law enforcement resources to aid in evacuations and road closures, strategized with community and incident leaders in the response, and placated the public's voracious and understandable demand for information.

Leo. For the millionth time, the kiss she'd planted on him a few months before—during a cold, driving rain in a macabre mountain cemetery filled with plastic flowers and homemade tombstones—distracted her from the moment. It had been an earthquake, shaking her psyche to its depths. For a few days afterwards, she'd almost given in to her feelings. *And his pheromones.* But she'd come to her senses. Been jerked to them by Alcohol, Tobacco, Firearms, and Explosives agent Clark Applewood. He'd told her Leo had gone behind her back and released their prisoner Igor Salazar to the feds, because Salazar was a confidential informant in a case with national security implications. The feds believed that trumped the fact that he was a serial kidnapper and abuser of young girls. It had turned out Apple-Pie misled her, but she hadn't learned that until she'd doused the blaze between her and Leo with a cold bucket of fortuitous reality. She couldn't risk everything on a relationship—or whatever it had almost been. Leo was her boss and running for sheriff. She needed her job. And she had to protect Carrie and Kat—her niece-turned-daughter—from emotional upheaval in their already tumultuous lives.

The thing with Leo had tumult and emotion written all over it.

She'd dodged the bullet. Stepped back from the brink. All the time she would have spent with him she'd invested in her daughters and on hunting for her mother.

Then why can't I get that kiss out of my head?

Siri announced their next turn a mile away. Less of a turn and more of a destination, really. The convoy was offloading near an old stone farmhouse on a property the fire had already cleared. One of the trailers was carrying nothing but a forklift and a front-end loader for that job. Smaller vehicles would take loads directly where they were needed most.

"Talk me through your turn and parking," Delaney said.

Carrie's response was quick and dry. "Go slower than a giant sloth scratching its butt."

Delaney wasn't going to quibble over semantics. Or let Carrie see her smile. "And?"

"Downshift the shit out of this bucket of bolts."

"Watch how you talk about my girl."

"Beware of the bumps. Don't crowd my buddies. Park facing out. Use the eyes in the back of my head." Carrie had already let off the gas and was now downshifting and applying the brakes. She eased into a turn.

"Stay in the center. There are ditches on either side."

"Relax. I'm all over it."

"That's exactly what I don't want you to be."

"Ha, ha, ha." Carrie swung to the right to make room for an arcing turn to the left, aiming for a position to park facing out with sufficient room between them and the vehicle in front of them.

Delaney relaxed a fraction. Then, just as Carrie turned back to the left, Delaney looked in the left side view mirror. A pushy driver was cutting them off to park nose-first in their space. "Brakes!" she shouted.

"What?!" But Carrie braked. Unfortunately, she forgot to push in the clutch. The tractor jerked and stalled. The other driver rushed past on the left, only a few feet away from their front bumper. He was driving too fast, and the bumps were rocking his trailer from side to side. Carrie flipped him off and shouted, "Asshole!"

Delaney agreed, but she shushed her. "You always have to expect something like that to happen."

"Now I don't have room to park."

"But I do. Let's switch."

Carrie crawled over and Delaney went under as they exchanged seats.

Carrie smacked a fist in one palm. "He's not going to like what I have to say to him."

Delaney restarted the tractor, put on her hazards, and backed up to make room. "He's not going to hear any lip. We're here to help people and animals. Not settle scores." She executed the turn and parked next to the other truck. *But I'll find the right time and place later.*

"Fine." Carrie's tone was grudging. Delaney loved seeing the spark in her. Despite a former and much older boyfriend kidnapping Carrie and her twin brother then shooting and burying them in the badlands, Carrie had somehow escaped the grave. But the same evil man who killed her brother had murdered her mother, too, and made a second attempt on Carrie. Delaney had worked the case and brought Carrie into her little family at its conclusion—Carrie's father was still living but had relinquished parental rights. Some people might have been beaten in her shoes, but Carrie was emerging from the dark times with strength and a fighting spirit.

The two of them exited Gabrielle. Delaney headed for the trailer of heavy equipment. She was proud of Carrie, which gave her a pang of missing Kat. Kateena—Delaney still called her that in her head, even though that name was now forbidden in favor of the cooler nickname—was spending the day with the sheriff's department's true boss, their admin, Clara Eckhardt. Clara had been a rodeo star forty-plus years before and was now Kat's mentor in the girl's quest to become a champion barrel racer. The two of them were helping move horses displaced by the fire to safe locations, as part of a volunteer group.

"What do I do now?" Carrie said from behind her.

"Stay out of the way while I get the cats herded. After we unload, we'll make another trip."

"Cool. It's um, really hot and smelly out here. Can I sit in the cab?"

"Sure."

The heavy equipment trailer was parked nearest to the farmhouse. Delaney trudged over the charred ground. She could picture the inferno that had swept through a day or two before. Some of Delaney's scariest memories growing up in Kearny had started with someone in her dysfunctional family shouting, "Fire!" The Paces had homesteaded together on the ranch she occupied now—her father, a victim of patricide at the hands of her brother in front of Delaney's very eyes when she was only eleven, her free-spirited mother who had disappeared shortly before his death, and her ultra-religious, ultra-strict grandparents, who abdicated responsibility for Delaney to a succession of foster homes after their son died. Delaney had joined the sheriff's office at the urging of a deputy who had mentored her as a teen, but a few years later she'd run away from the town and its painful memories of her youth to drive big rigs. The isolation and constant moving on the open road served as her self-administered therapy for nearly a decade.

But then she learned Kateena needed her. She came back to Kearny to care for her. She returned to the sheriff's department.

And she was soon reminded of the reality of fires in northern Wyoming on summer days when humidity dropped to single digits. A single spark could go on to burn hundreds of thousands of acres. From lightning. A cigarette. Overheated vehicle brake lines. Mismanaged campfires. Even prescribed burns gone awry.

She reached the equipment trailer. The driver was nowhere to be seen. She went to the trailer's roll-up door. It was still padlocked shut. *We're wasting time.*

"Delaney!" It was a familiar woman's voice.

Delaney turned with a warm smile for the woman in baggy jeans with long brown hair scrunched into a messy bun which showed its streaks of light gray. "Shirleen."

Shirleen Hancock was a social worker. Her lean body spoke of a life lived hard, with scars crisscrossing her collarbone, and eyes that were never shocked and always empathetic. Surprisingly beautiful eyes, actually, with big, dark pupils like midnight pools. Because of their professional lives, Delaney had dealt with Shirleen frequently over the last few months. The two no-nonsense women had hit it off from the get-go. Their interactions had driven home how tightly woven poverty, substance abuse, and mental illness are with crime.

"Hello, Delaney," Shirleen said.

"Thanks again for being part of this."

Shirleen had insisted on helping out with the relief convoy. Delaney had paired her up with another driver. Luckily, Shirleen was tall and strong—nearing fifty, Delaney would guess—and thus a help instead of a hindrance. Relief work wasn't for wimps.

"Absolutely. This fire is bad for all of us. It's going to make things hardest on those in our community who already had it rough. In other words, my clients," Shirleen said.

Delaney didn't disagree.

A high-pitched scream from nearby interrupted them. Without hesitation, Delaney ran toward it, in time to see the missing driver burst out the farmhouse door and fall to his hands and knees in the char. He vomited just before Delaney reached him.

She stopped beside him. "Jake, what is it?"

He heaved again, then wiped his mouth. Delaney could hear others gathering behind her. Jake Hemmler pointed at the house and shook his head. Another retch overtook him. *Whatever this is, it can't be good.* Dead cow? Deer? *Please don't be a person.* No one had been reported missing. Not that Delaney had heard about.

She patted her waist. She wasn't in uniform, so she wasn't wearing her duty belt. She felt naked without it. But she wasn't defenseless. Her Staccato was tucked in a waist belt with an extra clip of ammo and her multi-tool.

She stepped inside and turned on her phone flashlight. The house was old. From the early 1900s, she guessed. Mostly open space with what appeared to be a bedroom or storage room off the back.

Footsteps sounded behind her on the dirt floor.

"Stay outside," she said, hand up, but not turning around.

The front room was clear, so she went into the smaller room. A closet door stood ajar. But it wasn't the unusual sight of a closet in a house this old that stopped her cold.

A gasp. Carrie's voice. "What's wrong with her? And what's that thing sticking out of her stomach?"

Delaney recited words of comfort in her head without consciously summoning them. *Though I walk through the valley of the shadow of death, I will fear no evil.* Psalm 23:4.

It was a woman—anchored to the dirt floor by an enormous sword through the midsection and looking very, very dead.

THREE

Leo turned off the blue and white lights strobing from his sheriff's department truck. Luckily, he'd been mere minutes away when dispatch had requested backup for Delaney. He eased into a parking spot where he hoped his truck wouldn't get smushed. Hailing from California only a little more than a year before, he considered his truck to be on the large side. Here amongst the big rigs, it felt Lilliputian. Smaller trucks, still bigger than his, buzzed between the behemoths, beds filled with supplies offloaded from the giant trailers.

Delaney did this. His emotions made his face feel warm. It was impressive—and needed. Even though she'd ended things between them before they'd barely started, he was proud of her.

Carrie met him as he emerged from his truck with his crime scene kit. "Hey, Leo. She's in the house with the, um, body. It's, like, super gross but sad."

"You saw the body?"

Leo knew how protective Delaney was of her girls. Having his sister Adriana and nephew Freddy living with him wasn't the same as adopting two teens, but he could understand how Delaney felt. He was living under the shadow of the Bajeños and the threat they posed not just to him but to everyone he loved. He felt like he'd aged a decade in the months since his former Drug Enforcement Agency handler, Special Agent Natalie Amin, had warned him the Bajeños were on to him, from when he was working for the San Diego police department undercover with the Mexican cartel as an IT specialist. *I wish I'd said no way in hell to that assignment on day one.*

Now they knew he'd been undercover, but the DEA didn't think they'd learned his real identity. It was too late to cover any tracks if they had. Over the summer, he'd invested in sophisticated security for their home and hired a discreet bodyguard to monitor whether anyone was following Adriana and Freddy. The only good thing to come from Delaney rebuffing him was that it might keep her under the Bajeños radar, if they found him. So far, he didn't think the cartel had followed him to Wyoming. *But what do I really know for sure?*

Carrie said, "Delaney told me to stay in the truck, but she forgot to handcuff me to the steering wheel."

"Are you okay?" he asked, concerned. Carrie had a history of trauma. Life-altering trauma.

She shrugged, but her face was pallid. "What're you gonna do? My new mom's a cop."

"You're going to stay in the truck now, though, right?"

"I mean, it's too late."

"But it's a crime scene. We need to prevent contamination—keep people out."

Her face brightened. "I can help with that."

His other deputies—plus many city, county, and state law enforcement officers and even feds—were busy helping the beleaguered area and its residents as roads were closed, evacuations were ordered, and people and their animals and businesses were displaced. Crime scene techs, the coroner, and the county forensic pathologist were on their way, but he had no one else. He could use a hand.

"Thanks. You're deputized. No one comes in without Delaney's or my permission."

She gave him a crisp salute. "10-4."

He left her at the door and went inside. The interior of the little house was dark save a single shaft of light. His eyes, irritated by the smoke and adjusted to the daylight, were useless. "Delaney?"

"Back here," she said. "I'm alone, except for the victim." Her tone was the epitome of professionalism, which was worse than if it had been hostile. He missed their banter and camaraderie. He missed her. "Sorry it's so dark. The windows are boarded up."

He turned on the powerful beam of his duty flashlight and shone it toward her. She was standing in a doorway. Eerie shadows obscured her face, but her cats'-green eyes glowed back at him. Even in jeans, work boots, and a WYO Rodeo T-shirt, with wild tendrils of hair escaping from her braid, and a look of serious concern on her face, she was mesmerizing. An ache of longing had him struggling to remember what he had been about to say.

He swallowed, then recovered. "Has anyone been in here besides you?"

"Jake Hemmler. The guy who found her body. He managed to unload his lunch outside instead of in here, at least, but he ran through like a rabid elephant. And Carrie snuck in, but she stayed right on my heels until I shooed her out."

"I've got her guarding the entrance. I'll get the scene roped off, then join you."

"Good call. I decided to focus on the primary site for a few minutes, but I was thinking about the extended scene. We need to relocate the aid operation. Not that it will do much good. All these people and vehicles have probably already destroyed any outdoor evidence."

"We could get lucky. I'll take care of it."

Her head bobbed, looking disembodied in the light. "Talk to Lucas Planter. He drives a yellow rig. He'll know what to do."

"Got it."

"I didn't anticipate a death scene, so I don't have my gear."

"Take my kit. All I need is the tape."

They moved toward each other. As he neared the center of the house, the smell of death replaced the smoke. The presence of the victim pulled at him like a magnet, stronger the closer he got to her. He'd called Delaney on his way to the scene, and she'd given him a thorough description. Very thorough. He dreaded seeing the body. Before Wyoming, he hadn't handled any murders. Even after a year of unprecedented violent death in their sparsely populated county, he still had the same reaction every time—a deeply personal sense of obligation to bring justice to the deceased. The younger they were, the stronger the feeling. Women impacted him more than men, too. Maybe that made him a little bit sexist, but he felt what he felt.

He removed the crime scene tape from the bag and handed it over. Her hand brushed his as she took it. The hairs on his arm rose.

"Thanks. Anyone else coming?" she asked.

"Sugar and Trey will be here as quickly as they can. The coroner is on his way. Dr. Watson may beat them all." He retreated toward the hazy smoke-filled light of the door. "I'll be back soon."

"See you."

Outside, he gulped in deep lungfuls of acrid air. He scanned the area. It was buzzing like the inside of a beehive.

"What are you looking for?" Carrie said from her position leaning against the outside wall of the house.

"A yellow truck."

Carrie pointed. "Lucas. And you call them tractors. Or semis. Or big rigs."

"Gotcha." Delaney had already explained this to him more than once, but it was hard to break a lifetime of habit.

"His tractor is near the entrance, but that's Lucas over there. The big guy in the old-timey coveralls." She pointed.

Leo frowned. The guy in the Levi's denim overalls *was* big. Tall, muscular, and with the kind of belly that would make Leo want to sleep with his shoes on instead of having to lean over to take them on and off. He was holding a clipboard—*wouldn't a tablet be more useful?*—and waving his arms around like he was directing traffic. Which Leo guessed was exactly what he was doing. "Is he friendly?"

"He treats me like I don't exist, but he's nice to Delaney." She waved a hand around. "All the guys are."

Of course they were. "All right. Thanks." He strode toward the larger man.

Lucas and the people around him stopped talking and turned to watch Leo's approach. When Leo had first moved to Wyoming, he'd stopped conversations because he'd found it difficult to shed his Californian vibe. From his Reef Swami casual boots to his too-kempt beard, it was clear he wasn't local. Now he blended better but had the same effect for a different reason—he was running for the permanent job as sheriff of Kearny County, having held the role temporarily after the last two sheriffs had died in office. Local politics was akin to a religion in the area. That didn't make him a god, but it did make him the subject of a lot of scrutiny and debate.

He raised a hand in greeting. "Good afternoon. I'm Sheriff Leo Palmer, and I'm looking for Lucas Planter."

The big man grunted. "You found him."

Leo extended his hand.

Lucas eyed it for a slow three count before shaking it.

So, he's not voting for me. Leo smiled anyway. "You've heard a dead body was discovered in the house over there?"

"We've heard."

The other people around him were nodding. Leo recognized social worker Shirleen Hancock among them, but otherwise, they were strangers to him.

Leo said, "Unfortunately, that means this whole area is a crime scene, and we need you to relocate the aid effort."

Everyone and everything grew very still.

Lucas's expression didn't change. "We're in the middle of saving lives."

"Which is much needed and appreciated. I just need you all to move to an alternate location, as quickly as possible."

Lucas shot a look at another man, who raised his eyebrows. Lucas returned his gaze to Leo. "Crime scene? So, it is a murder."

"It's premature to speculate about the cause of death, but circumstances are such that we will be investigating all possibilities."

Lucas guffawed. "Damn, Sheriff. You got that political speech down pat. We heard the circumstances were that it was a body with a sword through it."

Of course—the guy who discovered the body is talking about what he saw. Leo's jaw spasmed from clenching his teeth. "Deputy Investigator Pace said you're the one to make this relocation happen."

Lucas's eyes narrowed. "I am, but I'm no miracle worker. This is my grandpappy's place. He's doing hospice."

"I'm sorry to hear that."

"It's not like I've got access to more properties near to where help is needed."

An older woman half Lucas's height spat chewing tobacco then said, "I got a place. Or my dead husband had one. I ain't never done nothing with it since I hate anything to do with that basspole, but I expect it'll suit our purposes."

Lucas turned with a grin. "That's generous of you, Betty."

"Black Bear Betty to you. It's about five miles up the road.

The J Bar H. There's a big sign by the gate. I need to go get it ready, but that won't take long."

"Half an hour?"

"If that."

"I'll spread the word."

"Thank you, uh, Ms...." Leo couldn't get the name to pass his lips. He knew the woman as Elizabeth Jurgenson, although he was aware of her nickname. He'd never met her, but earlier that year, she'd been charged with first-degree murder in Sheridan County. Those charges had later been dropped. Thanks to a mutual friend in Trish Flint with the National Forest Service, Leo had helped the hot shot defense attorney who defended Ms. Jurgenson on an information technology issue unrelated to the case. Jenn Herrington.

She spat tobacco juice on the ground. "Black Bear Betty."

Leo nodded. "Nice to meet you. Thanks again." He turned back to Lucas. "You, too, Mr. Planter. I'll leave you to it and get back to work myself." He touched the bill of his ball cap. "Stay safe, everyone."

Return sentiments were expressed by everyone except Lucas Planter.

Leo walked back toward his truck, making mental notes for the investigation plan he'd be drafting on his tablet as soon as he grabbed it out of the vehicle. It started with two witnesses.

Lucas Planter. And Jake, the guy with the big mouth who'd found the body.

Leo secured the perimeter of the house and an extended area beyond it, where there were no people or vehicles. It was all he could do until the trucks, trailers, and heavy equipment vacated. Just as he finished, a white Cadillac Escalade parked beside his truck. Tiny Louise Watson climbed down from it. She smoothed her black slacks—he'd never seen her wearing anything else—and straightened a surprising hot pink blouse. Rumor had it that she had been involved in a long-term relationship with Sheriff Fentworth Coltrane, upon whom Leo had been foisted by the DEA after they'd accused him of getting too close to the cartel. It had been Leo's observation that Dr. Watson seemed to be grieving after Coltrane's death. Just in the last few months she'd begun to dress in brighter colors and seemed brighter herself.

Leo wound the excess tape back onto the roll. "Dr. Watson, thanks for getting here so fast. I was just about to head into the scene myself."

"You're welcome. The coroner called me. He has a conflict and blessed me handling things." In Wyoming, coroner was an elected position which handled all deaths, with the forensic pathologist called in only if necessary. Dr. Watson and the coroner in Kearny County had a great relationship, and he willingly handed off any cases that would potentially be subject to criminal investigation. She lifted her sunglasses up her forehead. "Talk about a scene." She waved her hand at the vehicles.

Engines were firing and a few of the tractor-trailers had already begun to line up at the entrance to the property.

"They're leaving soon."

Dr. Watson nodded, her mouth in a straight line but approval in her features. "Lead the way."

They both greeted Carrie on their way into the house.

"Dr. Watson's here, Delaney," Leo said.

"Louise!" Delaney's voice was warm and welcoming, contrasting with how she'd greeted him. It stung a little.

"Hello, my dear. Have you solved the crime yet?" Louise said.

"No. But I've marked potential evidence. There are a few footprints." Delaney pointed the flashlight at the floor. Numbered little yellow stands had been erected in a few spots. "Watch your step."

Leo said, "Lucas has the convoy moving out, except for your, uh, rig."

Delaney groaned. "Shoot. I hadn't thought about Gabrielle. I can't have Carrie drive home alone."

"Is it full of supplies?"

"Probably."

Carrie poked her head in, obviously eavesdropping on everything being said in the house. "Jake unloaded it."

"Good. Well, Leo, how about you put up the tape with Gabrielle inside it, then let us out later?"

"That will work," he said.

Dr. Watson stepped off in front of him. Leo made his way behind her, fighting the urge to shut his eyes. Dirt, rocks, and debris crunched under his boots. The engine noises outside seemed to fade, creating a cocoon of silence. He put his hand under his nose as the smell hit him again.

"Oh, my." Dr. Watson stopped.

Leo nearly bumped into her. Over her head, he could see the victim clearly now. It was a sight that would be seared in his memory forever. A big sword and a small woman. The sword was as unusual as it was jarring, with an ancient look to it. Middle Ages, maybe? Slightly roughhewn and fairly plain, but exuding an air of nobility. The woman was on her back with her hands loosely around the blade. Her hair was fingernail short, and her skin was dark. Black. She was dressed in a plain gray dress, boxy and long—too warm for the season, in his opinion. There appeared to be dried blood on her dress and midsection, which made sense, given her impalement. Her face was turned to the side, as if looking away in humiliation. Besides the entry point of the sword, he didn't see obvious areas of injury or bleeding, or signs that she'd been burned by the fire.

"The fire didn't get her," Delaney said, reading his mind as always. "Because the house didn't burn."

Dr. Watson settled herself by the body. She dipped her

head and mouthed words. *Praying.* When she was done, she donned gloves from her pocket. Leo slipped on a pair as well.

"I wonder if the killer expected the fire to get rid of the body?" Leo moved to the side for a better view.

Delaney said, "She's in a structure of rock with a tin roof and dirt floor. Even though there's some wood, these grassfires move so quickly that I think it just swept by."

"Then either they didn't know the house wouldn't catch, or they didn't care."

"Or they killed her before the fires started."

"Hey, you guys?" It was Carrie. "There are some news people out here. They parked too close, and they want to come in."

Leo raised his voice. "Tell them I'll be out soon and that I said I'll arrest anyone inside the tape and tow any vehicle that's not out on the road."

"Okay. I'll try."

Dr. Watson sighed and put a hand on the dead woman's arm. She gently squeezed it, then released it. "Extremely low humidity and high temperatures. That shortens the duration of rigor mortis, which this woman is past."

Delaney squatted beside the doctor. "How long would you have expected it to last out here normally?"

"Starting three hours after death and lasting thirty-six hours. Roughly."

"So, a day and a half normally. Less than that in this case. What does the shortened rigor mortis mean for us?"

"Just that we can't know when she was killed. It could have been less than a day and a half ago. Or longer. I won't know anything for sure until I get her in the lab, but I'd say it is extremely unlikely she died more than two days ago."

Leo had the movements of the fire memorized. "The fire was all over this area two days ago."

Delaney looked up at him. "That means there's no way the killer didn't know about the fire."

Leo chewed the inside of his lip. "Maybe they were in a hurry because of it. Made mistakes."

Delaney sighed. "That were either burned up or crushed by tires."

"Unless they made those mistakes in here."

"How much of a hurry were they in, though, if they took the time to kill her like this?" She gestured at the sword.

Dr. Watson paused in her scrutiny of the body. "Kill her like this? You mean with the sword?"

"Yes."

The doctor shook her head, which slid her wire-rimmed glasses down her nose. "The sword isn't what killed her."

"How do you know that?" Leo asked.

"She wasn't alive when it entered her body. If she had been, there would be blood splatter up onto the blade. There's not. Gravity was the only force left on the flow of blood. There was no heartbeat to pump it out. It pooled. See?"

Leo leaned in. The blade was basically clean. "Then what killed her?"

Dr. Watson shrugged. "We shall see when I get this young lady back to the morgue. I'd like to call her by her name." It was one of the things Leo respected about Dr. Watson. She never dehumanized her patients. Always treated them with respect, as individuals. "Any identification or idea who she is?"

Delaney clucked her tongue. "Nothing I could find. And you've seen her fingertips, right?"

Dr. Watson turned the woman's hands over and held her flashlight up to them. "Yes. Burned off."

Leo moved to where he could see the woman's face. He stared. A shudder ran through him. He'd seen her before. And not so long ago.

He was supposed to be meeting her for coffee tomorrow.

He cleared his throat. "I—uh—I think might know her."

FOUR

"You think you know her?" Delaney didn't like the stab of jealousy in her midsection.

Leo made a sound like he'd swallowed a ball of yarn. "We'd been talking online, if it's who I think it is. The hair is different, though. We haven't met in person."

The jealous stab twisted painfully. A few months before, Leo had been dating online quite a bit. She hadn't seen the signs of it recently. The incessant notifications and texting. Sightings of him around town with a stream of women. Not since their moment on the mountain, anyway. She tried to keep her feelings out of her voice, off her face. "You haven't stopped with the dating apps?"

He lowered his voice. "I tried dating someone I know. It didn't work out."

Dr. Watson stood, removed her gloves, and said, "That's my cue to finish this at the morgue. You two can discuss which one of you messed up that thing that should have been perfect between you." She left quickly without another word.

Delaney closed her eyes, waiting for an empty room. It was clear Louise believed something had happened between her and Leo. Was that the general consensus? The chill between the two of them had raised eyebrows. From inseparable to siloed, collaborative to strained politeness.

She rocked back to sit on her heels. "Leo..." She trailed off.

His cheeks were red, and he made air quotes with his fingers. "You haven't stopped with the dating apps?"

She winced. "I'm sorry. I shouldn't have said that. But please don't air our history in front of Louise." *I nearly slip and say something too personal a hundred times a day.* It was getting harder lately. More charged instead of less. Was it for him, too? She held up her hands. "I'd like a retraction."

He readjusted his ball cap. "Yes, please. Let's walk this whole thing back."

She stood, nodding, relieved but sad for some reason, too. "Great. We need to just figure out who this woman is."

"I think—"

Carrie poked her head in. "One of the reporters is trying to interview me and she's shooting video. Totally uncool. Oh, and your crime scene people are here. So is Clint Rock-Below."

Delaney growled and barreled across the house. Reporters harassing Carrie was not okay. She stopped at the door and put a hand on her daughter's shoulder. "I'll take care of it."

Sugar Kukh—Sugar Cookie to her friends—marched in laden down with equipment, her counterpart—a recent addition from Cheyenne named Trey Jenson—hustling behind her. The two crime scene techs made for a visually interesting team. Trey looked like a Millennial replica of the Marlboro man, with a luxurious mustache and slouchy cowboy look sans cigarette, only his jeans were pressed and his moisturized skin less rugged. This week, Sugar's rainbow hair tips were reminiscent of the colors in her new neck tattoo. Always cutting edge for rural Wyoming, she'd stepped her style risks up a notch after a profile in the state's primary online news source had made her regionally famous. They were lucky to have the two of them.

Kearny was able to afford their own small crime scene team due to the discovery of rare earth minerals in the county. Most of the rest of the state relied on Cheyenne's state unit.

Clint Rock-Below entered the house last. The state police officer grew more distinguished and handsome every year, from his prominent features and dark coloring to his dive-on-in dimples. He'd recently cut his traditionally long hair. It was taking Delaney some time to get used to it. Born and raised on the nearby Crow Reservation which had also been hit hard by the fires, he was providing aid in the area. "Hey, everyone. I was nearby and heard what happened."

Leo glowered. "Rock-Below." Delaney and Clint had gone on a few dates, and Leo was not a fan.

"Hello, everyone. Watch for the evidence markers," Delaney said.

Sugar squatted down to unload a backpack. "I was thinking of playing Whack-a-mole with them."

Delaney smiled at her. "Somebody left the sugar off the cookie today."

Trey snorted. "Tell me about it."

Carrie said, "The reporters, Delaney?"

Delaney needed to send them packing. "Get in the truck. I'll be out to deal with them in a second."

Carrie's voice switched to full whine mode. "I don't want to get in the truck. It will be too hot."

Delaney said, "Run the air con."

"And the cell service out here is balls."

"Uh-uh. No vulgarities."

Clint snickered. "We've got Delaney 2.0 it seems."

Delaney narrowed her eyes at him. "Bite your tongue."

"About how much longer?" Carrie said.

From behind her, Leo said, "We should let Sugar and Trey do their work. I need to finish securing the scene. After that, you and I should meet back at the station, Delaney."

"I can help you with the scene, Leo," Clint said.

Delaney would have to leave the relief work to Lucas and the team. Murder trumped almost everything. "I just need to drop Carrie at the house and grab my gear. Say, an hour?"

Carrie bounced up and down on her toes, then froze. "Who'll guard the door?"

Trey flexed an unimpressive bicep. "I brought the muscle."

Sugar shook her head. "I brought the sawhorses. We'll block it off. That will slow them down at least."

Trey walked into the back room and moaned. "Sweet baby Jesus, there had better be a reservation in hell for the monster who did this. The poor girl."

Sugar followed him and clapped a hand to her mouth, head whipping from side to side. After a moment, she regained her composure. "If that doesn't motivate you to search for evidence until you're bleeding from your nail beds, nothing will."

Delaney couldn't have said it better.

Clint folded his arms across his chest. "It's the kind of thing that makes me want to remove the badge and go hunting the old-fashioned way."

Sugar gave a shuddering sigh. "That sword. It looks…"

Leo said, "Medieval?"

"Expensive. People drop real coin on cosplay and comic cons, you know? Some of my friends have spent a whole paycheck on their outfits for this week."

Delaney had only the vaguest idea of what cosplay was and no idea what comic cons were.

"The Renaissance Festival?" Clint asked.

Delaney had seen ads for a Renaissance Festival to be held at the local arena. Kat and Carrie were both planning to go. The idea was ludicrous to her. Talk about cultural appropriation—the Renaissance was a European thing, and a very old thing at that. A cultural, artistic, economic, and political rebirth from the fourteenth to seventeenth centuries in a region that already had hundreds of years of established communities, states, and governments. The United States was two hundred and fifty years old and founded in the homeland of nomadic people with only oral history. Wyoming itself had only become a state in 1890. To her thinking, a Renaissance Festival in Kearny was just an excuse to play dress-up, drink beer, and eat turkey legs.

Sugar was nodding. "Yeah. And the victim looks like she's dressed for it, ya know?"

"What's her costume, though?" Carrie said. Delaney had almost forgotten the girl hadn't gone to Gabrielle. "All my friends are going as, like, bar wenches or Maid Marian."

Sugar shrugged. "I'm not sure. But it's cheap fabric. Like something that would come with a warning to keep away from open flames."

A blinding light filled the room, reaching into the corners, searching for something salacious. *The reporters in pursuit of click bait.*

Delaney advanced on them, arms waving to ruin the shot. "Vultures out, now. Carrie, let's go."

The videographer and the other reporters hesitated but Delaney, Carrie, Clint, and Leo exited anyway, which pushed them back. One woman stood out from the others in a poufy blonde helmet of hair, thick camera-ready makeup, and an honest-to-God fuchsia-colored skirt and jacket over a pearlescent silk blouse—with high heels. In rural Wyoming.

Voices shouted over one another. "Sheriff, Sheriff, can you give us a statement?"

"No comment," Leo said.

A woman's voice carried over the others. "Will this take your attention away from the fires threatening people's lives and livelihoods?"

Delaney hustled Carrie toward Gabrielle, bristling.

"Will you consider your opponent's request that you withdraw due to the massive number of murders since you took the job? In his opinion, you're failing the community you are paid to serve and protect." It was the woman's voice again.

Delaney's fists balled. No one was going to get away with cheap shots at Leo with her around. She whirled, getting an eyeful of fuchsia, and marched to the blonde, entering a cloud of cloying perfume mixed with industrial-strength hairspray. The videographer backed up a few steps.

"Will you consider a request to scurry back to your home market and leave our county in peace? Around here, that wardrobe is a visual assault."

The videographer snickered and kept shooting. Leo was standing behind him, eyes sparkling, a smile curving his lips. *Oh, his lips.* Delaney found herself smiling back at him, unable to tear her eyes away from his. Then he and Clint walked together to the edge of the existing tape line and began stringing a new barrier.

Delaney turned to face the camera straight on. "Now that the relief trucks have relocated, the sheriff is cordoning off more of the scene along with one of our brothers from the state police. All of you need to move yourself and your vehicles behind the tape. Anyone caught on the wrong side will be prosecuted." She looked at an imaginary watch on her wrist. "Starting now."

FIVE

The girl hated it when her uncle came to visit. It had started with the way he began looking at her after she started junior high. It was creepy. He stared too long when her parents weren't in the room. It didn't matter what she was doing, his eyes were on her. They didn't watch her face either. He looked at particular parts of her. Parts that made her want to cross her arms over her training bra to hide her chest. To sit on her bottom so he couldn't see it.

Then he had started touching her more often. Her arm. Her shoulder. Her knee. Then her waist and her side. It was yucky. He was a grown-up, and he was her uncle. Her dad was always saying "family before anything," which is why any time his baby brother fell on hard times, her parents would have a fight, and then Uncle Rick would show up with his rucksack and sleep on their couch until "something came along."

So, she didn't tell her parents. She was always getting in trouble with her dad anyway, for not doing her chores right or for spending too much time with the horses and not enough helping her mother.

Then it got worse. Uncle Rick started saying things that

made her uncomfortable. About how pretty she looked. How fast she was growing up. All the boys who probably wanted to kiss her. How jealous he would be when she got a boyfriend, since he'd never had a girlfriend like her.

It was too much. She told her mother about it while they were picking worms off the tomato plants.

Her mother tsked and didn't pause her work. "Do you hear how silly you sound? Most girls would be tickled pink to get compliments like that. I sure would have been at your age. You've always been Uncle Rick's favorite. It would hurt his feelings if he knew the things you're saying about him. What you think about him," her mom had said, her thin lips puckered in disapproval, which was her usual expression. Thin lips, thin nose, thin face. Long skinny fingers and toes. Not a single bit of excess flesh. She reminded the girl of the dogs that chased rabbits around tracks that she'd read about in books. "Not to mention how your father would react."

"Don't tell Dad or Uncle Rick! Please!"

Her mother sighed. "I'm not going to. I wouldn't do that to them."

On that day—*the* day—as soon as the girl heard his truck pull up in front of their house, she ran out the back door to the stable and her horse. Bip had cut his leg. He was recovering in a stall, and he wasn't happy about it. She hurried straight to him. It made her feel better just to be around him. His head was already over his stall door.

"Hey, boy."

He nickered at her and bobbed his nose.

"I know you're bored."

He was the only horse in the stable. It had four stalls, and it felt empty and forlorn with only him in there. She'd lobbied with her mom to convince her dad to bring in at least one more horse to keep Bip company. Horses were herd animals. It was very hard for them to be without a buddy.

She slipped open his stall door. A person buddy was better than nothing. Once inside, she leaned against his shoulder. Bip wasn't a pretty horse—rangy and tall with a narrow butt and bony hips—but he was smart and sweet. She stroked his warm sorrel neck to calm her own nerves. *Maybe Uncle Rick is just dropping by. Maybe he'll be gone when I go back in the house. Maybe I won't even have to see him.*

"Let's give you fresh straw, buddy."

She grabbed a pitchfork and shoveled the dirty straw into a wheelbarrow. Bip watched with interest. She dumped the full barrow into the manure heap outside then returned with a load of fresh straw, which she spread in a thick layer on the stall floor. It smelled fresh. Clean.

"That's nicer."

In the tack room, she filled a bucket with the tools and supplies she needed to tend to Bip's wound and give him a proper grooming. She stuck a few treats in her pocket. Bip was no dummy, and he had a keen sense of smell. He was full-blown whinnying as she made her way back.

"Hold on." She laughed. "I'll give you a cookie in a second."

A hand encircled her arm. She yelped and dropped her bucket.

"Hey, kid. You didn't even come say hello to me," Uncle Rick said.

She kept her eyes off his face. The heavy mustache that bounced over his tobacco-stained teeth when he talked. The dark eyes, almost black. The big pores in his skin and the gap in his eyebrow from a barb wire scar.

She hated that face.

She tried to pull her arm away. He gripped it tighter. So tight it hurt. "I'm taking care of my horse. He's injured."

"Your mom said you've been complaining about me to her."

An icy cold dripped from her scalp down the inside of her face.

"She told me she set you straight." He chuckled and with his other hand, he cupped her chin and lifted it until she was facing him. "It isn't my fault you're so dang pretty, you know."

Her mind raced for what to do. Her parents weren't on her side. She was small for her age—fourteen—and Uncle Rick was a man. All she could come up with was to beg. "Please let go of me."

And to her surprise, he did. "Show me this horse of yours."

Her hand was shaking so hard that she had trouble unlatching the stall door.

"I used to work for a vet. Bring him on out and let's take a look."

She clipped a lead rope to Bip's halter and walked him out.

Uncle Rick took the lead from her. He tied Bip to a D ring on a hitching post. It was where she saddled the horse when she rode him. Uncle Rick put a hand on the horse's shoulder and stroked the length of his back as he returned to where she was standing. "He'll be all right here."

Then faster than she could blink, he whirled her around, so her back was to him, putting one arm around her waist, the other over her mouth. He whispered in her ear. "You already know it won't do you any good to tattle or scream."

No, she screamed against his hand. He was right. It didn't do any good. He shoved her into Bip's stall. *No*, she screamed in her head. And then the tears came, but they didn't do any good either.

SIX

Delaney couldn't help smiling as Clara Eckhardt slung a purse over her shoulder. Her friend's bag was bigger than her torso, but the former rodeo star and current sheriff's department administrator was more wiry than thin. Delaney wasn't sure she could best her in an arm-wrestling contest. She was absolutely certain the sheriff's department would descend into chaos without her.

Clara patted her heart. "Thanks for your help, Kat. True horsemanship is about far more than riding well. You helped lots of horses today. Once you truly learn what it means to care for them, it changes the person you are in the saddle. You're on your way, kid."

After bringing Kat home, Clara had stuck around to chat. Since Clara had started working with Kat, she'd become part of their unorthodox family. The group had migrated into Delaney's bedroom, where she was in the final stages of getting ready to go into the station.

Kat dove under Clara's arm and squeezed her. "It was so sad. All the horses that were hurt and hungry and didn't have a place to stay. They're lucky you and Mark had room for them." Clara and her husband lived on his family ranch.

Clara smiled. "I'll see you tomorrow. If you have a ride?"

Delaney buckled her duty belt. "Between Carrie and me, we'll make sure she's there."

"Maybe Carrie can stay over and do a little riding."

"Uh, you know me and horses. But thanks." Carrie had tried riding several times. It was hard to say who enjoyed it least, her or the horse.

"Yes, I do." Clara smiled and waved. "I'll let myself out. Goodbye to some of my favorite ladies, then. See you at work, Delaney."

A chorus of goodbyes rang out as Clara departed.

Delaney opened her gun safe, into which she'd placed her gun as soon as she and Carrie had gotten home. She checked her magazines, tucked them and the Staccato into her holster, and shut and locked the safe. "Are you two sure I'm not going to regret leaving you here instead of with Skeeter at the Loafing Shed?" Skeeter Rawlins was the private investigator who moonlighted as a child minder and chauffeur. Or was it the other way around? He could often be found hanging out at the Pace family bar, the Loafing Shed, which Delaney was overseeing in trust for Kat until the girl reached twenty-one.

Carrie was stretched out on Delaney's bed. Kat moved to her wobble board. Building balance and strengthening her core had become an obsession in her quest for rodeo greatness. She'd gotten pretty good at the board. Delaney had tried the thing a few times when the girls weren't around and had landed on her butt.

Kat squatted, arms extended like she was holding reins. Dudley, her black and white French bulldog, was jumping up and down in front of her, barking. The dog was not only noisy, he smelled like he needed a bubble bath. Kat talked over him.

"I'm going into eighth grade. I'm old enough to babysit. Carrie's a senior. We're not babies."

"But you're my babies. My Kitty Kat and my Carrie Berry." Delaney used the nicknames they both claimed to hate.

Boing, boing, boing. Bark, bark, bark.

She tried to ignore the dog and continued. "Sometimes you make less-than-optimal decisions when you're together."

Boing, boing, boing. Bark, bark, bark.

And it's good to have Skeeter around when my job brings less than desirable people into your orbit. Things had been quiet on that front lately, thank goodness.

Boing, boing, boing. Bark, bark, bark.

She waved her hand at the canine menace. He was possibly the world's cutest animal in the black and white tuxedo that nature had given him and that his belly strained to escape. But he could get on a nerve. "Can you make that dog shush?"

"Right." Kat laughed.

Carrie sat up. "Speaking of less-than-optimal decisions, was Leo talking about you and him when he said he tried to date someone he knew, and it didn't work out?"

Kat jumped off the wobble board. "You're dating Leo? But what about if Freddy and me ever get together? You know I like him! That would be so... so..."

Delaney felt a flicker of panic. "Kat! I'm not dating Leo. Carrie, quit being an eavesdropper and a rabble-rouser."

Carrie narrowed her eyes. "I wasn't eavesdropping. I was helping. And you were talking about airing your history. And Dr. Martin said—"

"Carrie, I was never dating Leo. Stop." She angled a death glare at her older daughter, away from Kat's accusatory gaze. She mouthed, "Later."

One corner of Carrie's mouth quirked up. "Oh, I get it. You were talking about a case."

A little of her tension eased. "Correct."

"Sorry."

"That's okay." Delaney turned to Kat. "Are we good?"

"I guess." Kat shrugged. "What's for dinner?"

"How about I meet you guys at the Loafing Shed?" Delaney faced the vanity mirror with a brush in her hand. She set it down. A weed whacker would have been more effective. The wind had gotten it good.

Kat hopped back on her board. "Cool. It's barbecue chicken night. Skeeter is helping Mary make it on the grill."

Mary Galvez, the manager of the bar, had resurrected the kitchen and licensing for food service. The menu and patronage were slowly building, and Mary had big plans. Earlier that summer, she'd convinced Delaney as trustee to finance a patio addition. They'd moved the displaced parking to the side of the building and installed more floodlights for safety. Delaney had to admit that the outdoor seating and retractable awning were quite inviting. Mary would have to hire more staff soon.

"Can I bring a friend?" Carrie said. "Victoria?"

Delaney pried her hopeless hair into three sections and plaited it into a low braid. "If that's code for 'can I have a friend over while you're gone, Delaney?' then the answer is no. If that is sincerely 'can my friend Victoria meet us at the Loafing Shed?' then the answer is yes." She secured the braid with a band then applied some lip balm. "Now, don't do anything that endangers your lives or will result in one or both of you grounded. Again."

"Bye," Carrie said.

"Yeah, bye, *Mom*," Kat added.

Delaney waggled a finger at her. "Save whatever you were going to ask for after buttering me up with the M word until I see you at the Shed."

· · ·

Delaney took the chair in front of Leo's desk. Something had changed in that moment when he'd smiled at her after Delaney had stood up for him with the reporter. Something that had followed them into the office and was growing stronger by the second. She was sweating. Her mouth was dry. A piece of her wanted to scream in frustration at her weakness, but a bigger part wanted to weep softly and crawl into his lap, wrap her arms around his neck, and never let go. Kissing him again would be good, too. *I thought I was past this.*

"Everything okay with your girls?" he asked, his voice thick.

He feels it, too. "As of twenty minutes ago, yes. I've learned never to underestimate how quickly that can change."

"Seriously. Freddy has been even more challenging for Adriana since Ashley broke up with him. He's unpredictable. A danger to himself and others, even when he's not moody."

"Oh! I didn't realize they'd split up." Kat was going to lose her mind over this news.

"About two weeks ago. She's at a summer camp, and I think he's been trying to keep it quiet, hoping she'll change her mind."

Delaney made a zipping motion over her lips. "And Adriana is good?" The small talk was like getting reacquainted after a long time apart. A little awkward, but necessary.

"Having trouble at her job. She's not much for sticking to anything. Jobs, friends, men. Something always comes up. She has never equated that *something* to herself, but... there is a common denominator."

Leo had told her once that Adriana's husband had been on borrowed time in their marriage before his death. "Your house isn't sounding very peaceful."

An odd look crossed his face. "That's putting it mildly."

She tilted her head and waited for him to elaborate. Leo had seemed preoccupied lately. She'd assumed it was the rift between them. But now she wondered if it was something more.

He cleared his throat. "Okay, I've had time to pull up everything I could find on the woman I believe is our deceased." He turned his laptop screen toward her.

The shift was abrupt. *How is it that he pulled back faster than me this time?* It was the right thing to do, though. After a low-crime summer in the county, today's events would throw them back into the hyper-focus and long hours of a murder investigation, right in the middle of the wildfire. "Tell me what I'm looking at."

"Jenny Martin. It's her profile. What do you think?"

"She's very pretty." *And young.* Her dark eyes were a flattened oval—they looked sleepy—and her black hair was long, full, and wavy. Too much for her small features, but still pretty.

"No, I mean do you think she's our victim?"

"She could be. Impossible to be certain but this is a good place to start." Delaney scanned the profile. "Do you have her phone number or contact info?"

"No."

"Do you know if this is her real name or where she lives or works?"

"No. We've talked online, but nothing she's said is verifiable."

Delaney wanted to see those messages. Only she really *didn't* want to see them. She lowered her voice and kept her tone light. "Who knows if the person you were talking to is the woman in this picture? Or even a woman at all."

He grimaced. "True enough. But I assume, based on past experience, that she's the person who would have showed up for coffee tomorrow."

He'd liked her enough to make a date. It hurt. "Or still might. If we can't verify her identity before then, you'll need to go. If nothing else, it's a wellness check."

He stared into her eyes until her insides flipped over, then finally cleared his throat. "Maybe I can send Drew." Drew Knowles was their newest deputy, only a few months past his training in Douglas, coming off a job for the railroad in Torrington. He was a hard worker and fun to be around. Based on their attrition rate in the last year, Leo had already hired another deputy who would start the training program next week.

She loved the idea of sending Drew, for wholly unprofessional reasons. "Makes sense. That way we can focus on the case." *And not your dating life.* She typed JENNY MARTIN, KEARNY, WYOMING into her search engine. "I got nothing."

"Yeah, I tried that. Why don't I work on searching variations on the first and last name?"

"I can check missing persons for people matching our victim's description and look for similar cases. And I'll try to get a warrant for her information from the dating app, although it may be premature."

"Thanks." He pushed his tablet across the desk to her. "I'll send you a copy of the preliminary investigation plan. We can keep it updated through the Cloud."

Delaney didn't bother explaining for the millionth time that she worked better off the back of an envelope with a dull pencil. But his investigation plan—as always—looked pretty darn good for the scant information they had. When she'd finished reading she scrolled through pictures she'd taken at the scene.

She turned her phone toward Leo when she'd found the one she wanted—the sword. "Sugar said it looked expensive. What do you think?"

"Big. Heavy. A two-handed grip. I don't know enough history to be sure, but I get a medieval vibe."

She nodded. "I'd add not homemade. Sugar mentioned cosplay. And something called a comic con."

Leo pointed to the line in the plan where he'd written COSPLAY. "You have no idea what those are, do you?"

"And proud of it."

"Comic cons are conventions that used to revolve around

comic books but have expanded to include all things sci-fi and fantasy. Even a little beyond. Famous actors and writers attend to engage with fans. There's a ton of different ones now that go by different names but generically as comic cons. And fans often dress up in homage to their favorite characters. Think costumes, hence *cosplay*."

"Playing dress-up."

"Yes. But for grown-ups."

"It's not just for Halloween anymore."

"Nope. And Sugar may be onto something. There's a cottage industry now around these conventions. People drop serious money on their costumes."

"Which could include medieval swords?"

"Oh, sure. Think *Game of Thrones*."

"Didn't watch it."

"How about *Vikings*?"

"Of course I've heard of the Vikings. They're a football team in Minnesota."

"No, the show." He sighed. "Just trust me. Medieval is big. But it's not just conventions. We've even got a Renaissance Festival starting here tomorrow."

Delaney pushed tickly hairs away from her face, tucking them behind an ear. "It doesn't feel like a Wyoming kind of thing. Is this all our new out-of-state residents bringing their culture with them?"

"Maybe. But it's also possible Wyomingites will love it." He groaned. "Half the town probably got costumes for it. I wonder how many got swords?"

"But that's Renaissance. You do know that the Renaissance came after the Middle Ages, right?"

"No one likes a stickler."

She threw up her hands. "Hey, details matter."

"*Anyway*, there will be a lot of medieval costumes in town."

"And Renaissance ones."

He shook his head, smiling. "If you want to be a stickler, historians differ on when the Renaissance started, by hundreds of years. So, who's to say precisely whether something is purely medieval or purely Renaissance?"

This banter—she'd missed it. "Bottom line is our killer may be into cosplay and conventions or festivals—one of which is in our town—and we need to find the groups that outfit these wackos with their expensive toy swords."

"Or, in this case, their expensive and very real swords."

Delaney hated that he put it that way. She hated even more that he was right.

His phone rang. "It's Sugar."

"Put her on speaker. Please."

He nodded. "Hey, Sugar. You've got me with Delaney."

Sugar's voice sounded smug. "I've got an engraved crucifix on a broken chain ground into the dirt outside at the crime scene, courtesy of me."

Delaney sat bolt upright. She'd been so sure the fire and the tractor-trailers had obliterated any evidence. Could the crucifix be related to their case? A real lead?

SEVEN

After hours at her computer, Delaney was bleary when she entered the back door of the Loafing Shed. She'd accomplished a lot, though. Their probably-not-enough-cause warrant for the dating app had been sent to the judge. The missing persons reports she'd scoured and pulled a few possibilities from, although none were as close a match as Leo's date.

Her search for similar cases—in the surrounding seven-state area, where she'd focused on murders of women whose fingerprints were burned off with swords at the scene, and with a side search adding in just those crimes perpetrated against young women of color—had opened a window on a world of truly sick behavior. None of the cases were an exact match, but some were promising. She'd built a file and would study them more closely later.

She'd even updated Leo's investigation plan, albeit grudgingly, and smiled again at the addition of the engraved crucifix. Sugar said the fire had destroyed any fingerprints and DNA, but she and Trey were getting it cleaned up to see if they could read the words etched into the metal.

Now, the clink of glass and cutlery over laughter and loud

conversation welcomed her into the bar. The yeasty smell of old beer, the worn wooden floors under her black tactical boots, the humid air—it felt like home, down to her daughters' voices over the din. How many times in her life had she slipped in this door holding her father's hand? Until the day he'd been stabbed to death in this hallway, she'd been his shadow, on the dirt racetracks of Wyoming, around their family ranch, and in this bar. She touched the medallion at her sternum reflexively. Cheap and heavy, it read "Eastern Wyoming Dirt Track Champion." A souvenir of one of her dad's wins. No matter how many years passed, she couldn't enter this place without the painful memory of his death or the familiar longing for his presence.

She passed the bathrooms. A paunchy body nearly knocked her over as it exited the men's room.

"Delaney! I was just about to call you." It was Skeeter with his perpetual goofy smile. Lately, between his burgeoning skip trace and background checking business and increased sitting engagements for Juan Julio, Mary's three-year-old son, he was a busy guy.

"About?"

"Hot-off-the-press news about your mother."

And just like that, the sound in the bar was muffled by a loud rushing noise in her head. An "Oooooh" escaped her lips. The hallway tilted, and she caught herself by a hand on the wall.

Nothing about her mother was hot off the press. The woman had run away more than twenty years before. Delaney could barely remember adoring her, since she'd hated her for so much longer. Her grandparents had done nothing but spout venom about Fabiola Pace.

Fabiola.

Ethereal moonbeam dancer and green-eyed, anklet-wearing bestower of kisses. Delaney had believed her dead until her brother had told her otherwise. Then, after months of fruitless searching, she'd accepted that Liam's declaration was nothing more than another attempt to hurt and manipulate her. Because if Fabiola had been alive when Delaney was a teen being passed off to worse and worse foster homes, she would have come back and rescued her. Any decent mother would have. Delaney knew that more than ever now that she had two daughters.

Ipso facto, there was no way Fabiola Pace could be of this world.

"You okay, boss?" Skeeter put a hand under her elbow.

"Just dehydrated and hungry. What's the news?"

"I talked to an old geezer who used to be friends with your grandpa. Everyone around town kept telling me he was the one who'd know what went on in your house, but it's taken me months to track him down. He moved out of state and into an old folks' home in a little town where one of his kids lives. You know, the kind of place where the booze is rationed, and everybody has one of them Clappers in their rooms?"

"An assisted living center."

"Yeah. One of them. They sound like hell to me." He nodded, seeming lost in thought.

Impatience crackled inside her. "Skeeter?"

"Sorry. Anyway, Jethro Peters—that's his name—swears your grandparents convinced your daddy to send her off with a religious cult."

Delaney felt her forehead tighten into and lift her brows. "Send her off? What do you mean by that?"

"The impression he gave me is that it was kinda like sending her off to rehab. You know—against her will."

Delaney shook her head so hard it felt like her brain was slamming into her skull. "My dad wouldn't have done that. He loved her." *Oh, but how they fought.* Only after her mother would disappear for days, though. He'd search for her in vain, then she'd finally show back up exhausted and withdrawn. That's when he'd go ballistic.

"My feller said the goal was to calm her down. People thought she was a bit of a wild child." His eyes widened. "I hope that doesn't upset you too much to hear that."

"No. I knew." Her head was still trying to wrap itself around her grandparents and father colluding in the kidnapping of her mother. Because an intervention was one thing. Bundling an adult off against her will was illegal. But could it be true? "All right. So, you've been fed a lead. How do we find this cult?"

"No clue yet. I just got off the call with Jethro half an hour ago. He didn't have any details."

Because it's probably a bunch of hogwash. But it was all that she had. "Well, we know when she disappeared. We're looking for a nomadic religious group coming through the area sometime shortly before then."

He tapped his temple with one finger. "I'm on it."

She nodded. "Thank you." She hadn't expected that she might lose something important about her father by looking for her mother. Gain one at the expense of the other. *Or gain nothing at the expense of both.*

Together she and Skeeter walked into the bar proper. Her girls waved at her. She waved back and smiled on autopilot, still dazed by Skeeter's news. Carrie was head-to-head with her pal Victoria. Kat and Dudley were playing chase with Juan Julio. This place was home to them, too. The people here, their family. *I was raised half feral in a bar by my father in front of my grandparents' noses, yet my mother was the wild one who needed to be forced into a religious cult?*

Mary shouted, "Boss lady, we're out of barbecue. You want a cheeseburger and fries? Your girls already ate."

Delaney said, "Hey. Sure. Thanks."

Mary waved at someone behind Delaney. "Hey, Shirleen. Someone told me you do hair now. Want to try to do something with this mop?"

A familiar voice said, "Sorry, but whoever said that was

wrong. And your hair is gorgeous. You okay, Delaney?" An arm slipped around Delaney's shoulder.

Delaney wasn't a hugger. At least not in public. But she leaned into Shirleen without hesitation. "Shirleen. It's been a day. How did the rest of the relief convoy go?"

"It went fine. But you're shaking. What's the matter?" Shirleen pulled her in tighter. "Come with me. Let's go sit where it's quieter."

She *was* shaking. Delaney let herself be led to the new front patio. She collapsed into one of the plastic chairs.

Mary appeared, a glass of rosy liquid in one hand. "Drink this. I'm sorry you had to hear it like that. Skeeter has no bedside manner."

Delaney took the glass and drained it. Cranberry with a kick. *Vodka*, she thought. She wasn't much of a drinker, but it was just right. Good bartenders always knew. "Did he announce it to the whole bar?"

"No. Just me. He tells me everything." Skeeter had harbored an unrequited crush on Mary for years. "I'll make sure it stays between us."

"Thank you."

Mary nodded. "I'd better get back in there. It's busy."

"I hope you have help starting soon."

Mary threw up her arms. "No one wants to work anymore. The pandemic payments ruined the labor market. I try and try. I'll keep trying."

And she was gone. Leo had said the same thing when it had taken him months to find a new deputy. Delaney thought it was more than that. A generational shift in what people valued. But who knew.

Shirleen had been carrying a beer mug in the hand that wasn't hugging Delaney. She set it on the table. "What was Mary talking about?"

On a vibrato sigh, Delaney said, "My mother. My long-lost

mother."

"Oh, I'm so sorry."

"It took me years to get over losing her and then my dad. Maybe I never have."

"You can't imagine how many of my clients have lost their parents. How they long for their mothers. And yet look at you. How great you turned out."

Heat flushed Delaney's cheeks. She didn't get compliments from women very often. *Ever.* "I wish the social workers had been like you back when I was a teenager being passed around like a hot potato. Thank you."

Shirleen smiled. "Now, tell me all about it."

And to her surprise, the words flowed out of Delaney. Shirleen was sitting with her hands clasped at her chest by the time Delaney finished explaining what Skeeter had told her.

Delaney shrugged. "The end, I guess. At least until we find her." She picked up a fry from the basket of food Kat had dropped off while Delaney had been talking. Somewhere along the way Delaney had polished off most of the burger and half the fries without realizing it.

"You will."

"I hope so. But job one is this homicide. Sorry we had to evict the relief operation."

Shirleen rolled her eyes. "Lucas moaned and complained about it."

"Of course. His MO."

"It wasn't just the upheaval. He's going to inherit the ranch when his grandfather passes. He was concerned about damage to the property or its reputation."

"Sounds like he plans to sell it. Cattle don't care about the reputation of the place where they eat their grass."

"I heard the victim was a woman?"

"Yes."

"With a sword through her belly?"

Delaney sighed. No use denying what was public knowledge. "Mm-hm."

"Do you know who she is?"

"Not yet. But we have some leads."

"Maybe someone reported her missing."

"I hope so. If she lives alone and didn't have plans or wasn't due to work, it could take a few days for the people in her life to realize she's gone, though."

Shirleen tapped short fingernails on her beer glass. It was inexpensive, but it was real glass. A step up from the old days when everything was served in disposable plastic. Score one for Mary and the installation of the commercial dishwasher. "You know, in my work I'm familiar with most of the young women living on the fringe of society around here. The vulnerable ones who are most likely to be crime victims. Or not reported missing. If I can help you, please let me know."

Delaney felt some of her tension release. It was true. Shirleen knew, or had contacts who knew, almost everyone in the at-risk community. "I really appreciate that. I may take you up on it."

"Call me whether you do or not. I want to know you're all right. I hate that you're going through this about your mother. Alone."

A dazzling yellow warmth spread through Delaney's chest. No one ever said things like that to her. Well, Leo, but not lately. She knew Mary and Skeeter cared, but they worked for her. "Thank you."

Shirleen pressed cold, dewy fingers into Delaney's arm, straight off her glass. "Is there anything else bothering you? Your eyes look a little wet."

The urge to confess her feelings for Leo came over Delaney. She'd never confessed them to anyone. Could she now? *No. He's running for sheriff. If Shirleen repeats it, even out of context, it could cost him the election.* She tamped her emotions down and deflected Shirleen's question. "You're the best mom! How many kids do you have, anyway?" She took her arm from Shirleen to wipe her eyes.

The light in Shirleen's eyes dimmed. "I had one child, when I was young. He passed away."

"Oh, my God. I had no idea. I am so, so sorry."

"It's okay. I actually like remembering him more than I mind the pain of it. I couldn't have any more babies after that since I had an emergency hysterectomy when he was born. I guess that's why I was drawn to social work. I get to take care of all the little lost sheep. Plus, I have spent most of my life dealing with a very troubled sibling, if that counts for anything."

Delaney was the one who reached over and squeezed Shirleen's arm this time. Pounding feet drew Delaney's attention away, though.

"AUNT DELANEY! MOM!" Kat threw herself into Delaney's lap, sobbing.

Delaney's heart nearly jumped out of her chest. "Kateena! What is it? Are you okay?"

EIGHT

Leo juggled a bakery bag as he took out his key card and swiped into the building. Inside it was quieter than normal. Early morning peaceful. He walked quickly to his office and pushed the door open. He flipped on the lights and gasped. Delaney was sitting in front of his desk, typing into her phone.

"You're in early. In the dark." Her hair was hanging loose and wet. Her eyes glowed like backlit emeralds.

"We had an emotional night at our house. Kat found out through the grapevine that Ashley and Freddy broke up. She couldn't believe he hadn't told her himself. After she calmed down, I stayed up late looking at similar cases and missing persons. I wanted to get in here and talk to you about all of that."

"And you knew I'd be here early." He took a seat and pushed the bag across to her.

"Of course. We have a homicide." She tapped her temple, smiling. "But I don't want to take your breakfast, even though it smells like manna from heaven."

"I got it for you."

"It appears you knew I'd be here, too." She dipped her chin

then lifted just her eyes, giving him a half smile. That move was achingly feminine and rare from her. She peeked in the bag. "Apple fritter. And it's warm. But aren't you going to have anything?"

He pointed at a spot of chocolate on his uniform shirt. "I already had mine."

She went after the apple fritter like a hungry lioness and moaned. "So good. And so bad for me."

"You're welcome. While you're chewing, let me update you."

She held up fingers coated in the apple fritter glaze and motioned for him to keep talking. She had sugar on her lips, too.

He looked away for a moment to wash the sight from his mind. "All right. Not only could I not find a Jenny, Jen, Jennifer, or any alternate spellings paired with Martin and any regional alternatives like Marton or other spellings in our area, I couldn't find a young black woman who looked anything like ours *anywhere* with a variation of that name." She widened her eyes. He grinned. "That was a mouthful. The 'too long didn't read' version is I couldn't find our victim anywhere under any variation of Jenny Martin."

She put her hand over her mouth. "So, it isn't your, um, friend? Or do you think she gave you a fake name online?"

"Dunno." He checked the time on his phone. "Drew should be at the meeting place by now, waiting for her. I messaged Jenny last night and this morning to confirm. She didn't answer."

Delaney nodded and stuffed the rest of the fritter in her mouth. Her cheeks bulged a little.

"Dr. Watson texted and asked if we'd come in later."

Delaney nodded, chewing.

"Sugar sent pictures of the crucifix." He airdropped them to his laptop from his phone, pulled them up, and turned the screen where both he and Delaney could see them.

Delaney was licking her lips and wiping her mouth with her hand. He found a napkin in his drawer and handed it to her.

"Thanks." She nodded at the blackened crucifix on the screen as she wiped her fingers. "I can't wait to see that engraving when they get it cleaned up. Maybe we'll get lucky, and it will be personalized in some way. Someone's name, a birthdate, the name of a church." She frowned. "A dry napkin is no match for an apple fritter."

He dug a bottle of water out of a side drawer. She uncapped it, wet the napkin, and went back to work on her hands.

He ticked on his fingers. "We've got a young black female victim anchored to the floor of a deserted farmhouse with a possibly medieval replica sword, maybe wearing a Halloween costume, and a fancy crucifix that may or may not be related."

Delaney balled her napkin and shot it at the garbage like a basketball. It went in. She swished two fingers down. "The judge turned me down on our search warrant for the dating site. It was worth a try. If Jenny doesn't show up today, I can call their company headquarters."

"Okay. What else do you have?"

"There are no missing persons named Jenny Martin. I combed the records searching for someone who looks like her. It's disturbing how many black women of about her age are missing, but I didn't get a strong feeling any was her. I pulled the possibles, and we can get Drew calling about them when he's back from dating your girlfriend."

"Delaney..."

"When Drew gets back from his wellness check on Jenny Martin."

"Thank you."

"We've got a few cases worth following up on, too. One involved a victim stabbed with a medieval sword. I don't hold out much hope as the victim was a man, and it was over a dispute at a gaming competition in Denver."

"That feels wrong, except for the replica sword not being a toy."

"In another case we've got burned-off fingerprints. No sword or medieval ties, but the victim is a young black woman. It was in Bismarck."

Leo pursed his lips. "Sounds like a longshot, too."

"Unless it's a killer who was working up to an MO he now uses. It was a year ago."

Leo turned to look out his window. The station wasn't in the prettiest part of town, but it didn't affect the beauty of the mountain view, which was phenomenal—except for today. The smoky haze hanging over most of north-central and eastern Wyoming washed out the color and obscured the peaks. The fires were pushing up into the foothills northwest of town. He hoped they didn't spread further into the national forest. The grassland would recover faster, as long as the firefighters could protect structures and lives. Trees took decades to grow back— grass usually came in stronger than before the fire. And trees were a scarce resource in the state.

"I can't believe we're breathing that air," Delaney said, following his gaze.

Leo said, "It's really been affecting my eyes and throat. The impact on the firefighters and property owners on the front lines —it has to be awful." He picked up his phone and glanced at the time. "I can't believe we haven't heard from Drew yet. When he gets in, I think we should have him run point on your cases. See if there's any further crossover."

"What about Joe?"

Deputy Joe Tarver was up against Leo for the party nomination. Mara Yellowtail, the chief of police, had been running for the other major party, but she'd dropped out. Whoever won between Joe and Leo would face the general election unopposed, as was often the case in Wyoming. Leo didn't claim membership in either party, but party alignment was his only chance of election. Even at that, him being from California was suspect to many voters. His incumbency helped—the county commissioners had considered him the best candidate available for the job, since Delaney had turned it down to focus on her daughters—but Joe was born and raised in the area with a long history of devoted affiliation to party principles.

It was going to be a close race.

Leo stood and began to pace. "Everything is political fodder, and the primary is only a week away. I feel like anything I give him he'll use to hurt me, which will hurt the operation of the department at a time it needs to run efficiently because of these fires and the homicide."

"His experience could be helpful on the homicide."

"True. But the community deserves our best support with this fire. He's great with that kind of thing."

She smiled. "The case for the criticality of his leadership on behalf of the community *is* strong."

"And it's true. He's better at that than homicide investigation."

"We may need to lean more heavily on other departments if this gets hot, then. Clint's already up to speed."

Clint was a good cop, but his interest in Delaney was a thorn in Leo's side. "The police chief will send us whoever we need. She's still scared we're going to get her fired." In their last big case, one of the victims had been kidnapped as a girl years before. Mara had worked the case and declared her a runaway. When it became clear after the girl's murder that Mara had been wrong, she covered up her earlier involvement, and Leo and Delaney knew it.

Leo's phone rang. He picked it up and read the screen. "Huh. I don't recognize the caller." He declined the call. Seconds later, it rang again. "Same number." He accepted it. "This is Sheriff Leo Palmer."

A familiar woman's voice said, "Holy shit balls, Sheriff. You better get over here quick."

It was Magda, the manager of the Cowpoke Café. In the last few months, he'd been a regular there for his one-and-done coffee dates—woman after woman failed to interest him, because none of them was Delaney. He'd given Magda his cell number when she was having trouble with a repeat customer who would occasionally get rowdy and drive away business.

"What's the matter, Magda?"

"Your new deputy is beating somebody to a bloody pulp in the middle of my restaurant."

NINE

One of the many things I loved about living in Wyoming was the prevalence of basements. Almost every house had one. From a topographical standpoint, they made good sense. The ground was rugged, and many times houses were built into the sides of hills, which allowed for convenient walk-out doors. Usually considered off-limits for guests. Basements were wonderful buffers against the weather, too. Cool in the summer. Warm in the winter. Great for storage and providing excellent natural sound insulation, made even better in my basement with the sound proofing I'd installed where it counted.

All of these attributes were important to me, because this is where I kept my treasures, in an antique armoire beside a full-length three-panel mirror. The mirror that was reflecting a glorious image of power now. A power that transcended centuries and a face full of a searing pain that could only be salved when the cause of it was eliminated. It had taken many years for the solution—the remedy—to reveal itself to me. During that time, I took many paths that led nowhere. False hopes had ended in despair.

I fasted, wept, sacrificed, and waited for a sign. Then I tried again. And again. And again. Until the truth was finally revealed. The Way. The only way. Then I built strength. Studied. Practiced. Perfected a craft. A set of skills. Began the initial steps of the Quest.

The metal of chain mail clinked as I lifted my sword, knees bent, arms raised as if ready for battle, sweat dripping down my neck, the odor of my own perspiration filling my nostrils. A beautiful, lethal longsword, smithed in the original style. The two-handed grip, the gold hand guard, and the head engraved with an intricate papal cross. Not a toy, not even a replica. A true Italian longsword, just as if it had been made in the eleventh century for a count or countess, a king or queen. Five swords I'd purchased—a year's salary spent.

It had been worth it.

Maybe there were no Italian nobles in Wyoming, but it had its royalty, nonetheless. Those beloved by family and public alike. That—that was the birthright stolen from me. The rend I had fallen through into a very different and lesser existence.

"Yah!"

I pointed the sword downward, still holding the grip high in the air, my legs staggered for stability. One deep breath. *Wait for it. Wait. Wait. Wait.*

I drove the point of the sword into the wood floor with all my strength, grunting with effort, my body absorbing the force of the impact. I pushed on the sword with a booted toe. It held firm.

A nod. A slight smile.

Things had turned out as I'd hoped with Genevieve. It was quite unfortunate that the house had not burned down with the girl in it. The vagary of wind and fire passing by was a timeline accelerant. But I had taken great care and left no unintended artifacts behind, I felt sure. At least, not with Genevieve. I had executed The Way with perfection.

It had not gone so smoothly with the other. With Anong.

Her body still lay undiscovered, to where I'd moved it. *Praise be to the most Holy.* If she was found, it could cause many problems. So many that I had almost disposed of her with more finality. That was outside The Way, though. It would transubstantiate the purity of the Quest. Turn it to something evil.

That could not happen. I must move quickly and with purpose instead.

Because this practice that had served the dual purposes of perfecting methodology and removing another of *them* from the world was near its end, now that I was the hunted *and* the hunter. I held up one hand where a fingernail had grown too long and was broken. It was time to cut the others short to match. I'd searched for the broken piece but never found it. I'd left evidence behind when I'd relocated Anong. There was no time to waste.

"One more. Only one more before *the* one."

I turned to look over my shoulder and deep into my own eyes. "I'm coming for you. Can you feel it?"

TEN

Delaney walked briskly through the door Leo held open for her. Their ride over had been tense. Not with each other, but with the unknown waiting for them at the Cowpoke Café. Neither of them had Drew getting in a fist fight on their bingo card for the day.

She peered toward the kitchen and saw Drew rising slowly to his feet. A substantial woman with long red hair going gray was helping him, her kaftan billowing as she stood. Drew turned toward the door. Blood speckled the front of his T-shirt. He had a package of frozen peas pressed into his face but raised his free hand in greeting. Muscles rippled under his shirt sleeves. The new deputy wasn't tall, but he was powerful.

"My God, Drew. Are you okay?" Delaney said.

"I've had better workdays but none this much fun." His smile was surprisingly cheerful.

The woman spoke directly to Leo. "I've been trying to get the numskull to go to the hospital."

Drew scoffed. "I used to make my beer money betting on myself in underground fighting rings. This is nothing."

Magda dabbed at Drew's face with a bulky wet rag. "He got cold-cocked."

"Sucker-punched. I never lost consciousness. Bounced right back up and gave him better than I got."

"So, someone attacked you?" Delaney said. "We thought you beat someone up."

Drew raised a fist like he was declaring himself a winner. "Both are true."

"Was it Timothy Gardner, Magda?" Leo asked.

"No. He hasn't given us any more trouble since you spoke to him," she said, her voice almost simpering. "You've been such a good friend, Sheriff. I tell everyone who comes in here to vote for Sheriff Leo. And you're so nice to the women you bring here, too. A true gentleman."

"Thank you, Magda."

Delaney lost in a battle not to roll her eyes. Magda was old enough to be his mother or maybe his grandmother, but not to be immune to the Leo Palmer charm. "What happened, Drew?"

"I was sitting at a table by myself, watching for this Jenny person. A big white guy comes in, acting tough. He looks around the place, walks up to me, and says, 'Leo?' I didn't want to bother explaining who I was, so I just said, 'Who are you?' And he punched me in the side of the head. Knocked me over backwards."

"He broke my chair." Magda widened her eyes at Leo. "It was new."

"We'll replace it." Leo patted her shoulder.

"Thank you, Sheriff." She batted her eyes at him.

Drew raised bloody knuckles. "Then he said, 'Where's Genevieve?' I said—and excuse my language—'Who the, um, eff is Genevieve?' and I got up swinging." He tapped his shirt. "Smashed his nose and sent him on his butt. He got up and busted through the door, hopped into the passenger seat of a car that was waiting out there, and they were outta here faster than I could run to the curb."

Delaney felt a quickening of excitement. "Genevieve. Leo, did you try Genevieve?"

Leo said a few blue words of his own. "No. And I didn't try Genny with a G either."

Drew pulled the bag of frozen veggies away from his face. His eye was puffy along his cheek bone. "Glad I could help."

"Now we just need you to come up with the identity of your attacker."

"Oh, no sweat. We traded digits and started a SnapChat group." He put the bag back on his face.

"Ha ha," Leo said.

Drew grinned. "I can give you a description, but I didn't get a name or a license plate number. But first I could use some painkillers."

"Will acetaminophen work?" Delaney asked.

"I hope."

She pulled a small tube from her purse and shook two out. He rolled his hand, and she added a third. He popped them in his mouth and chewed. She shuddered and nearly gagged.

He swallowed and took a second licking his lips and working his mouth. "I think I already said he was white. About five eleven. Strong but heavy through the middle."

"Wait!" Magda said. "I can just show you on our video."

"You installed cameras? I'm glad to hear it." Leo beamed like a proud son.

"Four of them." She held up one finger after another as she counted up. "The first facing the front door from outside. The second covering the dining area from behind the cash register. The third pointing at the bathroom doors. And the fourth facing the entrance from the alley door."

Delaney pictured them. "You should have good footage of the assailant then. But none of the vehicle in the street."

Magda nodded. "I think so."

"I'd put that outdoor camera above the front door. It would catch people going in and also whatever is closest on the street, which would be good since you have a front patio that could be vandalized or damaged."

"It has been. I'll do that."

Leo said, "Well, let's go take a look."

Five minutes later, the four of them were packed into a tiny office around a desktop monitor, just down the hall from an equally tiny bathroom with a community bulletin board by the door sporting a Renaissance Festival flier smack in the center of it. They'd walked past the revolving cold case of pies to get back there. She could still smell the peanut butter chocolate, and she hadn't ruled out taking a slice home.

Magda cued up the video outside the restaurant first. She scrolled to the approximate time of the assault, then moved slowly until the camera caught the assailant running out. It was a blink-and-you'll miss it black-and-white capture.

Delaney did a double take. "He was moving fast."

"I think it put the fear of God in him when I shouted 'Deputy Sheriff, freeze.'" Drew rotated his neck, popping it several times.

Leo smiled at Magda. "Let's try the dining room camera."

Again, Magda positioned it as close as she could to the precise time stamp. When she pressed play, they watched a white man stalk in, arms crossed over his chest—which wasn't as impressive as Drew's—and scan the tables. Then he advanced on Drew. Charged, almost. Drew was sitting in the middle of the restaurant facing the door. The man spoke, then he punched, and Drew's chair toppled sideways and backwards. Drew rolled back and used his hands to kip-up into a standing position, propelling himself toward the other man. His arm movement was perfectly timed to take advantage of his forward momentum. His fist moved like a snake, striking his attacker in the nose.

"Ow!" Leo grabbed his own nose as blood sprayed outward onscreen.

"I already cleaned that up. It's a health hazard," Magda said.

Drew went for the mid-section next, which drew the man's hands away from his face. Then Drew punched across the man's face and into his cheekbone. This was the punch that popped his attacker's head and neck back and sent him flying. He landed on his butt and skidded into the swinging door at the entrance. After only a split second of stillness, he was on his feet and sprinting toward a car.

The video played back the action perfectly. What it didn't catch was anything about the car waiting outside or a single defining characteristic of the man's face. The camera was simply too far away, although it would have been perfect placement if someone held up the cash register.

Delaney decided to keep any more constructive criticism about camera placement to herself for the time being. "Can you zoom in at all?"

Magda's face puckered. "I don't know how."

Leo gestured at the keyboard. "Do you mind if I drive?"

Magda looked relieved. "Please."

They traded places. In seconds, Leo had zoomed in on the attacker. The image pixelated. He worked it smaller until it regained enough granularity to be of use. "Anyone recognize him?"

Delaney and the others chorused "no" back at him.

"We agree he is Caucasian?"

Again, they chorused, this time a "yes."

Drew snorted. "His outfit couldn't be more generic. A plain black ball cap and gray hoodie with jeans and sunglasses."

"Is that a scar on his chin?" Delaney touched hers.

"Possible scar," Leo said. "Noted."

Drew said, "I think his hair was light colored. His arm hair and his eyebrows aren't dark."

"Good. I'd agree with you on height, by the way. Anything about his voice?"

"He didn't say much. But he had an accent. Maybe Cajun?"

Magda shook her head. "Didn't sound American to me."

Delaney said, "Play him walking in again."

Leo clicked a few times. The video restarted at approximately the same point.

"There!" Delaney pointed. "He's favoring his right leg."

"Hmm." Leo backed it up and restarted it again. "It's slight, but you're correct."

"Maybe it's the lingering effect of an earlier injury or medical issue. Or maybe it's only a recent injury."

"So, it could disappear on us. Tattoos or birthmarks?"

Delaney put her hands on her hips and leaned forward. "There might be something on his neck. Maybe that's why he wore the hoodie."

Leo was nodding. "Magda, can I have a copy of these videos?"

"Sure."

His fingers clicked keys. "I'm just emailing them to myself. When I get back to the station I'll screen capture the best shot of his neck and see if I can enhance it any." He lifted his hands. "I think we're done here."

Delaney started to walk out then turned back. "Anything about this guy that seemed medieval to either of you?"

Drew laughed. "Like the Dark Ages? That kind of medieval?"

Delaney slow nodded.

Magda bounced on her toes. "Like *Outlander*. Time traveling."

Leo smiled at Delaney. "For those of us who exist outside pop culture, *Outlander* is a book- and television-format fantasy series about a World War II nurse who meets a Scottish highlander when she travels back to the Renaissance time period."

Delaney wondered how people had time to watch fantasy TV series. She had so many other things she'd rather do. "Gotcha. Not a time traveler per se, Magda, but was there anything about him that made you think of the Middle Ages?"

Drew patted his hip. "He didn't carry a longsword. Or anything else oldern."

"Oldern?"

"From ancient times. I got it from this game I play."

"I don't think that's a word."

"You're being a stickler again," Leo said.

Delaney gave him her best glower.

Magda said, "Wait! I have something." She ran out of the room.

Leo shrugged. "I love her enthusiasm."

"And she loves your... yours." Delaney gave him a Cheshire cat grin.

Magda returned. She held out her hand. In it was a coin. A very old-looking coin.

Delaney took it and studied both sides. It was worn, but she could make out a cross and the side profile of a man. She handed it to Leo. "Where did you get this, Magda?"

"Someone left it with payment for their bill a few days ago. The server didn't notice it wasn't US money since it's about the size and color of a dime. I kept it in case they came back for it."

Drew leaned over for a better look. "Looks real to me."

"This is about that murder, isn't it?" Magda said, her voice rising in pitch. "The one with the sword!"

"Shh." Leo smiled at her, but his face was serious. "May we keep the coin, and you keep everything about this a secret?"

She looked crestfallen. "If I have to."

"You do." Delaney put her hand on the woman's elbow. "Now let's talk about you giving us more of that video."

"Why?"

"We have to find whoever left that coin at your restaurant."

ELEVEN

When Delaney pulled back into the station parking area after following Drew home, Leo let out a groan. "How many reporters are lined up outside the door?"

Delaney barely slowed down as she pulled into a parking space, then mashed the brakes so hard that his head whipped forward, then back. "I see that vulture from yesterday. The woman that was harassing you and Carrie." Delaney's phone rang. "Speaking of which, it's Carrie. Do you mind if I grab this?"

She always picked up for the girls, just in case they needed her. Nine times out of ten all they wanted was to tell her something funny about Dudley or ask for money. But Leo understood. He dropped everything for his sister and nephew. "No problem. I'll wait for you, and we'll run the gauntlet together."

"Hey, Carrie." Delaney put the call to audio through the truck's console. "I'm with Leo. You're on speaker."

"And you're all over the internet." The mirth in Carrie's voice spilled through the speakers. Someone was giggling in the background. "Play it again, Kat."

Leo heard Delaney's voice and another that was vaguely familiar.

"What are you talking about?" Delaney shook her head at Leo, smiling.

"When you clapped back at that reporter yesterday? It's getting shares all over social media. "You've got thousands of views. People are commenting like crazy."

Delaney let her forehead thunk on the steering wheel. "That's just great."

"You want me to send you a link?"

"No!"

"Send it to me," Leo said. Delaney had been ferocious. He'd love to play it again, over and over.

"Kay-kay."

"Anything else?" Delaney said.

"Nope. Oh! One thing. We're up at the Loading Shed."

"Loafing."

Leo laughed. Delaney hated the local nickname for the establishment. The Loading Shed, as in "where people go to get loaded," instead of the Loafing Shed, a place for livestock to take a break, out of the weather.

"Whatever. Mary needs help. Is it all right if I start working here part time?"

"What about Kat?"

"I'd just work when she's either with Clara and the nags or Skeeter or when she can come up here and do whatever. Mary likes her to bring Dudley and play with Juan Julio."

"We'll talk about it. It's fine for today."

"Please?"

"I said we'll talk about it. Love you."

"Love you, too."

Delaney ended the call and gestured at the crowd waiting for them on the sidewalk. "Too late to sneak in the back, I guess."

Leo opened his door. "Let's just get this over with. Don't make eye contact or say a word."

Delaney said, "Gladly."

Leo marched ahead of Delaney to give her cover. The reporters surged toward them, firing questions about the murder, their progress, the primaries, the fire, and Delaney's new-found internet stardom. He ushered Delaney in the door ahead of him, then turned to the throng. "I'll be answering questions later today. The time will be announced on the sheriff's department Facebook page. No comment until then."

The volume of their entreaties swelled. One female voice cut through the others.

"Is there any truth to the rumor that you are involved in a relationship with your deputy Delaney Pace?"

He faltered a step, but otherwise didn't react. *Where did that come from?* He shut the door firmly behind him.

Delaney was waiting just past the vestibule. "Did it go all right?"

He nodded, making a split-second decision to save news of the bombshell question about them for later. She'd had enough bad surprises in the last five minutes with her confrontation with the reporter going viral. Plus, he wanted to think about how to frame it. *Like, let's give them something real to talk about if they're going to talk anyway.* "I'll do a press conference later."

Behind them, the door opened. It was Drew.

Leo put his hands on his hips. "What are you doing here? We dropped you at home. You should be taking care of yourself."

Drew sauntered up to them. "Ain't no thang. It's a workday for me. Let me be useful."

Delaney waggled her eyebrows. "Coincidentally, while you were getting punched in the face, we were coming up with a worklist for you. On the homicide case. I'll take you and get you started if you're ready."

"Sounds great."

The two took off ahead of Leo, in step with each other and already talking about the case.

Leo called after them, "I'll see if I can find a Genevieve instead of a Jennifer."

Delaney held up an okay sign without turning back to him.

He hurried into his office. It had been a big miss not to consider Genevieve as the potential root of Jenny. He would get on it, as soon as he checked in with Sugar. From the flurry of messages on his phone during the ride back from the Cowpoke Café, she was still at work. His entire department was booking overtime, between the fire and the murder. The relatively quiet summer—despite the normal tourist mishaps he'd come to expect after his first year in Kearny—had allowed him to bank some budget, which was a godsend now. But if they had any more big incidents this year, he'd be in front of the county commissioners, hat in hand, asking for money.

He pressed the pre-set for Sugar's number.

A male voice answered. "Sugar's phone."

"Uh, this is Sheriff Palmer. Who's this?"

"Yo, Sheriff, this is Trey. As in everything is *trés bien*."

"From my one year of high school French, I understand that enough to know you mean you'll put Sugar on now."

"Um, yeah, here she is."

Sugar blew a horse laugh directly into the phone. "We've gotten a little punchy over in the lab. Long hours, bright lights, microscopes. Does funny things to the brain. Did you get my messages?"

"I haven't read them. We had something come up." He told her briefly about the attack on Drew.

"You still don't know if that woman was our victim, then?"

Sugar wasn't known for being overly sensitive, like worrying about Drew's wellbeing. But she caught the salient point, work-wise. "No. But in the course of our time there, the owner gave us a coin that looks medieval. She said someone left it with their payment."

"No BS?"

"None. I'd like you to take a look at it."

"You don't think it's fake and just related to the festival starting today?"

"Looks pretty real to me."

Something slapped over the phone's microphone. "Trey, run over to the sheriff's office. He has evidence for us." Then, to Leo, she said, "Has it been handled?"

"By many people. It's probably fruitless to test for prints, but if we can match some to a suspect later..."

"I know the drill. After we print it, I'll send it off for analysis."

"Good. Anything else for me?"

"We're testing the fibers we pulled from the victim's body. Some are consistent with the cheap polyester she was wearing. Trey browsed some Party City costumes, and he found a match for my hunch."

The pause invited him to humor her. "With?"

"A nun's habit."

"Then where was the white thing they wear on their necks or the thing for their heads? I didn't see them."

"You mean the wimple and the scapula."

"Those."

"We did not find them. But the dress was a gray nun's habit, and a little research yielded a nugget. You know which nuns wore gray?"

"Sugar, just tell me."

"Benedictine nuns from the Middle Ages. More medieval shit."

"You are one hundred percent positive that a young black murder victim at an abandoned old ranch house in Kearny County, Wyoming, died wearing a fake medieval nun's habit?"

"I'm rarely one hundred percent positive of anything. But I thought you should know."

"This case is getting weirder by the second."

"Tell me about it."

They ended the call. Leo took a minute to update his investigation plan then relaunched his name searches. Half an hour later he was ready to stab his eye out with his never-used letter opener. The new name had yielded nothing. Less than nothing. He gave his screen a rude one-finger salute with both hands for wasting his time.

Knuckles rapped on his door frame. "Sheriff Palmer. I'm here to pick up your evidence."

Leo looked at Trey and raised his brows. "You didn't see me do that, did you?"

"The sign language? Nah. I didn't."

Leo smiled. He wasn't sure how competent Trey was at his job yet, but he had a good sense of humor. Leo also knew Sugar would have given him an earful if the new crime scene tech wasn't any good. "Here you go." Leo pulled the baggie from his shirt pocket and held it across the desk.

"It's tiny." Trey held the bag up to look at the coin. "I expected it to be big and heavy."

"Thanks for coming to get it."

"No problem." The younger man saluted Leo and started whistling, holding eye contact.

"Am I supposed to recognize that tune?"

"Led Zeppelin. 'The Battle of Evermore.'"

"Which is significant why?"

"It's fantasy about the Middle Ages. You know, *Lord of the Rings*. Robert Plant is a Tolkien fan."

Leo smiled. "Clever."

Trey resumed whistling and walked out.

Leo turned to his window, mentally reviewing the evidence and the day. That brought the reporter back into his mind, the one who had asked about him and Delaney. He needed to find out who she was and a way to get on her good side, to cut off her attack on Delaney.

There had been a noticeable thawing between him and Delaney in the last twenty-four hours. More than a thawing. A re-electrification, if there was such a word. His hopes couldn't help but be up. It had never seemed like an issue for the two of them to date, not from a professional perspective. To him, anyway. It was just one in the litany of excuses Delaney had listed when she'd ended things. *But if it's an issue to her, it's an issue for me.*

But was it an issue for him in this *job?* To the voters? If so, what would *that* mean for Delaney? He didn't care what it meant for him. How much more intense would things get for her if she was called out as his girlfriend? The optics of her rebuttal to the reporter the day before played a lot differently if people believed they were involved. And sadly, the public and the media loved to blame the woman. He didn't understand it, but that didn't make it any less true.

There was another rap at his door. He heard a body land in the chair in front of his desk.

"Some of us are working this case and you're taking in the view again." Delaney's voice had a lilt to it that made him feel buoyant.

He turned to her. "It's how I think. I was reviewing how little progress I made in the last hour."

She sighed. "I take it you didn't find our victim under the name Genevieve."

"No. But I talked to Sugar and Trey." He filled her in briefly on Sugar's nun's habit theory.

"I keep going back to the Renaissance Festival. Maybe some of our clues are nothing more than a coincidence. The confluence of a murderer and victim with an event and all that goes with it."

"Or maybe they're completely related."

"The festival starts today. Suspects everywhere." She shook her head with her mouth open and tongue out a bit, like she was deranged. "I've had another idea on how to identify our victim, though."

"Hit me with it."

"You know Shirleen with Social Services?"

"Yes." He'd seen her at the crime scene with the other members of the relief convoy the day before. "She does good work."

"And she knows everyone living on the ragged edge of society in this part of Wyoming. She offered to look at pictures and see if she knows this woman. It feels like if we aren't finding her, she may fall into that category of people no one misses when they go missing."

"Sounds like a good idea to me."

"I'll contact her." Delaney typed rapidly on her phone, speaking aloud the words she was typing. "Per your offer, could I show you some pictures and see if you know the woman who was killed?" Then she looked up. "There, that's done." She stood.

"Do you have another second?" He tried to keep his tone light, but his words came out a little awkward.

She sat back down, a wary look in her eyes. "Ye-es?"

"The reporters earlier. One of them asked about you and me."

"You and me in what regard?"

"Whether we're in a relationship."

Her mouth opened, and her brows furrowed. Then she leaned forward, hands on her knees. "What did you say?"

"Nothing. I'd already told them I'd announce a press conference for later today and that I had no comments to make at that time."

They stared at each other. The silence tingled. Pulsed.

Crackled.

He spread his hands. "We're not, of course. Technically, we never have been."

"Did you tell anyone? About... our kiss?"

He swallowed. Hearing those words from her lips brought it all back. The pouring rain, the lightning flashes and thunder, her warm mouth. He remembered it all, down to the smell of sulfur and pine. "No. Did you?"

"No. No one."

"Okay, then. As far as the world knows, there's never been anything." *Except there was. And I think there still is.*

"Okay."

"Delaney..." He couldn't find the words.

"What?"

He drew in a deep breath, then released it. "I'd like there to be. Still. Very, very much."

"I'm not interrupting anything, am I?" Deputy Joe Tarver stood two feet inside the door to the office, arms crossed. "Seems a little intense in here."

Delaney made huge eyes at Leo.

What had Joe just overheard? Leo forced a laugh. "This case is intense. What can I do for you, Joe?"

Leo had always thought of Joe as an easy-going colleague before. A man who took the path of least resistance but was good to work with. Mild mannered. Then, per Joe, his wife had started pressuring him to work harder. Take the overtime. Earn more. It wasn't unwelcome to Leo, given that they were drowning in work and short-staffed after Deputy Tommy Miller had ended up in prison. Leo had taken it as a blessing when Joe got in shape, lost his paunch, and started pitching in.

Until Joe had filed the paperwork to run for sheriff. Now, they stomped around each other like bucks in rut, itching for an excuse to lock horns.

So, Leo had to assume Joe had heard the most damning

parts of the conversation and get in front of it. Delaney wasn't going to like it, but she'd agree once they talked. He just hoped that talk picked up right where they'd left off. With her staring into his eyes, getting ready to respond to what he'd said about wanting a relationship with her.

"Sheriff? Did you hear what I just said?"

Yes, Leo had heard Joe speaking. But it had been background noise to his panicked thoughts. He did a mental rewind and recalled the words. "Your update on fire duty. Yes. It all sounds good. I was thinking about staffing. Do you need more people? Drew, Delaney, and I will be tied up on this homicide full time. I can—"

"What do you mean 'Drew, Delaney, and I'? Where am I in that scenario?"

"I need you running community fire support."

"Am I being excluded here, Leo?"

"Excluded in what way?"

"From a high-profile homicide investigation. Sheriff hogs the glory for himself and his... his—"

Leo cut him off in a sharp tone. "Deputies. Deputies Pace and Knowles. And there's no hogging going on here." He stood. "There's two critical issues in front of our department right now." He held a hand up, palm out. "The support of our community and integration with law enforcement and emergency response in these unprecedented wildfires, and the investigation into a homicide. I'm assigning you to one of them. I'll take the other. I'll be giving you the bulk of the department manpower. I'll be working with Delaney and Drew."

"You take the homicide, the woman, and the black guy. The glory and the optics."

Delaney was on her feet now, too. "I resent the implication that my value to this department is because my gender makes us look woke."

Joe stepped forward. "I resent the fact that Leo favors you because he has the hots for you."

Leo's anger rose so fast he literally saw red. "That's out of line, Joe."

Delaney fisted her hands on her hips. "If you have a problem with my level of contribution and my role in this department, state your case with specifics, like an adult, instead of with smears."

Seconds ticked by as Joe looked between Leo and Delaney. Then he held up both hands. "You're a good deputy, Delaney. We're lucky to have you working here. But..."

"But what?"

He gave a one-sided smile. "No one is immune from how it looks if they're playing footsie with the boss."

Leo moved just fast enough to catch Delaney before she went at Joe with both hands extended for his throat.

Joe chuckled and shook his head. "Like I said." Then he was out the door.

TWELVE

Leo said, "You're not going after him if I let go, are you?"

He heard Delaney swallow—felt it—before she answered him. "I won't."

He released her, and she moved a few feet away. "Let's get out of here. We need a distraction." *And some privacy.* "Dr. Watson should be ready for us at the morgue."

She turned back toward him. Her voice was strained. "I dropped my phone."

He stepped aside, cheeks warm. For a moment, he'd thought she was going to slip into his arms. But her phone. Of course. *What an idiot I am.*

She snatched it up. "I'll get my truck and pick you up out back, okay? That way they don't get pictures of us together."

He nodded. "Good idea. But are you sure you want to face the reporters? We could switch roles."

"I don't want to hide from them. Especially now that Joe is going to feed his version of our story to them." Delaney walked out of his office, head high.

Leo was pretty sure Joe was doing exactly that down the

hall. He texted Dr. Watson to tell her they were on the way, then walked to Drew's desk.

Drew looked up, grinning when he saw Leo. "Man, I should have quit the railroad a long time ago. This is the best day I've ever had at a job."

"Then you're perfectly suited for it. Need anything from me? Delaney and I are heading to the morgue."

"I've never seen an autopsy."

Leo wished he hadn't himself. He feared he would never become immune to the smells. The sounds. The sight of the inside of a body that used to be a living person. "How about I bring you along next time, then?" It wouldn't be fair to Delaney to spring Drew on her. They had things to talk about on the drive.

"Thanks! Do you mind if I take an hour or two for the gym? It's legs day."

One thing Leo still made time for most days was working out. But not when he had a murder case pending. He didn't begrudge it for Drew. When the time came to ask more of him, the young deputy would be better off for the exercise now, mentally and physically. "No problem. Keep me posted on your results. And if you run out of work, I have a week of video to review and would be happy to share the load."

"Will do." Drew held out his knuckles.

Leo bumped them, feeling a little silly, but he certainly wasn't going to refuse the dap and make the moment uncomfortable. As he walked toward the back entrance, he checked Joe's desk. He wasn't there.

Outside, Delaney was pulling her truck to a stop. He climbed into his old, familiar spot—riding shotgun to Delaney's bad ass driver, inhaling the spicy scent of her mixed with leather and gasoline.

She had both hands on the steering wheel, index fingers drumming, and was staring straight ahead as she exited the parking area. "How are you going to handle the media? Joe looked rabid. He'll have them lying in wait for you at the press conference."

"We didn't do anything wrong. I could just tell them the truth."

"I kissed my boss. You let me kiss you."

He laughed. "I think I did more than let you."

A tiny smile curved her lips. "If he heard me mention the kiss, it's only our word against his. He has no proof."

"He could have recorded us."

"Oh, my God. I hadn't even thought of that."

"Delaney, can I be honest?"

"I hope you can't be anything but that."

"I can't, which is why if someone asks me point blank if we kissed, I have trouble saying no. But I can also say that we decided not to pursue the relationship. Those things are true."

She sighed. "I don't love that."

"And I'd like to pre-empt Joe by saying it in answer to the earlier question, before I'm accused of anything."

"Ugh. Leo!" Then she accelerated into a left turn.

"It's a lot better than answering defensively."

Her fingers drumming stopped. Her hands clenched the wheel so hard her knuckles went white. "That means I need to get on the phone with my girls. Carrie already told Kat about our interaction yesterday and Kat nearly had a... a cat. She thinks we could come between her and Freddy. I promised we had never and were not dating."

"You didn't lie."

"Yeah. Explain that to a tween girl."

"No thanks. You're the woman for that job."

She eased into a spot near the hospital and put the truck in park but left it running. "Say whatever you have to about us, as long as it includes that it's not happening and never did."

Leo unbuckled his seat belt and turned to face her. He was

going to do it. He was going to ask her to reconsider their relationship. "Thank you. And about us—"

"Now, Dr. Watson is waiting on us, I presume."

"Delaney..."

She bit her lip and held up a hand. "Leo, whatever you're going to say, don't. We've made it a year. Let's be what we're good at. Partners."

He felt like he'd been kicked in the gut. "We haven't been that lately."

"We'll be that again."

He finally looked up into her beautiful green eyes. Her sad, resolute green eyes. "Partners. Yes. Got it."

But he didn't have it. Wasn't giving up. What could he do to change her mind without driving her away again?

THIRTEEN

Anna Petrov had been pacing the tiny apartment for hours. She felt like she was wearing a trail in the carpet. How could she stay still, though? She didn't know what to do—her beautiful friend Gennie was missing. She wanted to report it, but she knew better than to call the cops.

She caught a glimpse of herself in the bathroom mirror. She shouldn't have looked. It was too depressing. She used to be told she was beautiful. "Anna, Anna," the boy next door would shout at her. "Give us a smile." Now, at twenty-three, she was an old woman. Skeletal, haggard, with big, dark circles around her eyes and thinning, dull hair. Gennie was still pretty, though. For now. She always told her so, because that's what friends are for. To encourage each other. Not that hers and Gennie's was a normal relationship. They shared the same *employer*, if that's what you could call their boss. To Anna he was the devil. But others would call him a *slaver*.

She stopped to stub out her cigarette. Slaves. That's what people like her and Gennie were to him. They'd done it to themselves. Sold themselves, trading one form of captivity for another. For Anna, it had been an escape from Russia, where she had no future. For Gennie, it had been from her abusive father in Haiti. Others, like their friend Anong, had been captured and sold from one slaver to another. The three of them had really bonded. They had more than being slaves in common. They each had something to live for. Secret lives.

But for now, they were just workers. Drones with a pulse. She shook another cigarette from the package and flicked her lighter, then touched the tip to the flame. It was big business. Female labor, child labor. Men, too, although not as many. Sometimes with their clothes off, but sometimes just as livestock —like oxen or mules—working free to make their masters rich.

At least they had an end date, her and Gennie. A debt to pay with years of their life, if they survived it. It wasn't easy. Their *employer* believed in punishment, up to and including the death penalty, which was reserved for those who betrayed him. Calling the cops would be the ultimate betrayal. She took a deep drag. The nicotine raced through her veins, and she started laps of her home again.

But she hadn't seen Gennie in days. Anong for even longer. Gennie wouldn't have just run off. She had a date she'd been excited about. Not that they were allowed to date men who didn't pay. But Gennie had a dream. She'd meet someone who would buy her out of her situation.

"You're not fucking *Cinderella*. Or even *Pretty Woman*," Anna had told her. "He's going to find out. He'll make you pay. You remember what he did to Alexis?" They didn't like to think about Alexis. He'd showed them pictures. He'd cut her face and her body before he'd killed her and dumped her body out in the badlands. Then he'd moved them all here.

Had he found out what Gennie was planning?

Anong was a different story. He was never going to let her go and didn't pretend he was. She'd work for him until she was of no more use, or she'd die first. Anna went to the window and pulled a slat in the blinds so she could see out. It was still hazy.

Her whole apartment smelled like smoke. Anong would run. Hopefully had run. *Godspeed, Anong.* She hoped the girl—the youngest of the three of them—was far, far away by now.

Who am I kidding?

She pulled her tiny phone from a hidden pocket in the waist of her jeans. The phone she'd bought just for this call. *He'd beat me if he knew I had it.* She dialed the number she'd memorized.

A woman's voice answered. "Kearny County Sheriff's Department. How can I help you?"

"My friend. Two of my friends." Her voice was barely a whisper. "They're... missing."

"May I ask who's calling, please?"

The doorbell rang.

She whimpered. *No. Already?*

She pulled the SIM card out. Ran into the kitchen. Took out a cast iron skillet that smelled of the cabbage she'd cooked last night and beat the SIM card until it was pulverized. The bell rang again. She opened the window. Threw the phone out.

The bell rang a third time.

"Sorry. I was sleeping. I'm coming." Her ears were ringing. Her breathing was shallow. But she walked to the door and peered through the peephole.

FOURTEEN

Standing on the sidewalk outside the morgue, Delaney already had her finger on the trigger, ready to dial Kat. "Give my apologies to Dr. Watson. I'll catch up as soon as I can. I need to make a phone call."

Leo looked up from his phone. "Clara said a young woman just called in two missing people to our main line then wouldn't give her name and hung up."

"Leo, my call?"

Leo lifted his face to the sun, such as it was, and rubbed mentholatum under his nose. The smoke from the fires blocked out most of the light but none of the suffocating heat. "That's okay. I can wait."

"Alone."

He gave her a surprised look. "Oh. All right, then. I'll see you inside." His pre-morgue prep cut short, he shoved the mentholatum into his pocket and walked away with his face down.

She knew she'd gutted him by cutting him off when he tried to talk about their relationship. She didn't feel so great herself. But she was doing the right thing. For the girls, herself, the department, and most of all, for him. There was *no way* she'd be the reason he flushed his career down the toilet. Maybe he didn't fully appreciate the rare opportunity he'd been given—or how much he might come to resent her for the loss of it later, especially if she was as awful with him as she'd been in every relationship in her life. Everyone knew outsiders didn't get *elected* sheriff in Kearny County. Sure, he'd been appointed to the job on an interim basis. That was not the same thing. He was a few months away from becoming the one exception. That was something he'd take with him forever, whether he stayed in Kearny or not.

She'd just chosen him and his future over her own possible happiness. *Maybe this really is love.*

When the door had closed behind him, she initiated the call. It was a conversation that would have been much better in person. Over milkshakes at Buns in the Barn or on a picnic at the top of the girls' favorite hill on the homestead. She hated that those options had been taken from her. The face of the reporter who had ambushed Leo yesterday and then released the video of Delaney loomed large in her mind, like Godzilla over Tokyo. It wasn't entirely the woman's fault. Delaney had kissed her boss, then she'd spoken about it in the office where others could—where Joe likely did—overhear. The tension between Joe and Leo was a catalyst.

But without click hunters giving gossip a platform, Delaney wouldn't be making this call.

"Guess where I am?" Kat said by way of greeting.

"Um, home, the Loafing Shed, or Clara's."

"You can only pick one."

"Clara's."

"Yes! Carrie is working at the Shed. Clara and I are taking care of all the horses that we rescued from the fire."

"I love that." *And I hate that what I'm about to tell her could ruin her great mood.* "Are you going to need a ride home?"

"I dunno. I'll text you."

"Okay. Well, listen, I have something I need to tell you."

"Wait a second. Clara's calling me." She put Delaney on hold without giving her a chance to object.

Delaney sighed. Sweat was accumulating at the base of her skull under her heavy braid. It was dripping down her sides, too. They didn't have summer weight sheriff's department uniforms. Summer in Kearny was too short to bother.

"I'm back. Clara said can it wait because we're in the middle of something."

"No. It cannot. Please don't put me on hold again. Leo and Dr. Watson are waiting for me."

"Are you in the morgue?"

"Outside it."

"Gross."

Delaney couldn't stand still in the suffocating heat any longer. She walked down the sidewalk. "Kat, listen to me. You know how with Leo running for sheriff people are always talking about him, good and bad?"

"Yeah."

"There are a bunch of reporters in town for the fires. They're interested in the murder yesterday and also in the sheriff's race."

"Uh-huh."

"A few months ago, um, one time and only one time, Leo and I, we uh, we kissed each other."

Delaney counted to three before Kat exploded.

"What? You said you never dated him!" Kat sounded surprised and betrayed. Not angry. Not sad. Not yet.

"We decided not to date each other. It was just a kiss."

Another long silence. "I don't get it. If you liked each other, why didn't you date?"

"It's complicated. Grown-up stuff. Work stuff."

"So, you're still not going to date him?"

"No." Delaney reached the end of the parking lot and turned back the way she'd come. Walked slower.

"Is it because I like Freddy?"

"No. That matters to me, but that's not the main reason."

"But do you like him? I mean, do you like him like a boyfriend?"

Delaney's mouth went dry. Was she supposed to lie to her daughter? "I don't know. It doesn't matter, though. Dating is the wrong thing for us now."

"Maybe someday?"

"The point is that a reporter asked Leo whether he was in a relationship with me. To them, that's the kind of gossip they like to turn into news. We think one of our co-workers knows. The one who is running against Leo for sheriff."

"That's bad."

Delaney stopped short of the entrance. "Yes, it is. Leo needs to tell the reporter the truth. That we have never dated but that we kissed once."

"Lying always gets you in trouble."

"Always."

"Because kissing someone is kind of a relationship. Even if it doesn't work out."

Delaney winced. Out of the mouth of babes. "Maybe so. But I wanted you to know about it before Leo talks to the reporters."

"I wish you would have told me before." Now there was a tinge of sadness.

Delaney smiled. "I don't tell you who I kiss, Kateena. That's not how this mom-daughter thing works."

"Does Carrie know?"

"I'm calling her next."

"I don't think she's going to be surprised."

Delaney turned and leaned against the wall in a small patch of shade. "Maybe not. Are we okay? You and me?"

"I'm not like mad at you, but this is weird. And it's going to be super embarrassing."

"Yes to all of that."

"I don't want it to ruin things with Freddy and me." Her voice was growing worried.

"It won't."

"I have to go. Clara's waiting on me."

"I love you."

But Kat had already hung up the phone. Delaney paused with her finger on Carrie's number. At first, the call with Kat had gone far better than she'd expected. The ending had her unsettled, though. She had a feeling she was going to get hit on the head by the other shoe when it dropped.

Get this over with.

She pressed the button to call Carrie.

Ten minutes later, Delaney joined Dr. Watson and Leo in the morgue, fresh off being teased mercilessly by Carrie. By the time they hung up, Kat had been texting her big sister, and Carrie had promised to keep Delaney informed if Kat started freaking out about the situation. "But I think you guys should just go for it. Leo is hot. And he's totally into you," she'd said.

How simple she makes it. Carrie didn't get it. Kat didn't either. Being a teenager was hard—Delaney didn't want to go through it again, that was for sure—but it came without adult responsibilities and perspective.

"Sorry I'm late," Delaney said, smiling at Dr. Watson.

The doctor was gowned, capped, masked, and gloved. She was also wrist deep in a cadaver. "Excuse me. I'm just putting her back together. Everything okay, dear?"

Delaney kept her eyes off Leo. "All good. What did I miss?"

"The usual boring recitation. A young woman of approximately twenty-one years of age. Well-nourished and in good health, and likely a mother."

Delaney's heart shot to her throat. Dr. Watson had explained to them the changes to a woman's body that signaled possible past pregnancies in a previous case. "Oh, no." There was a child out there whose mother had died? Where? With whom? Were they okay? All unanswerable questions at this point, but she couldn't keep her mind from spinning through them. "I hate making you repeat everything."

"That's okay. I'm putting time of death about forty-eight hours before her body was discovered."

"Right when the fire swept through. And cause?"

"She wasn't shot, stabbed, strangled, or any of the usual forms of violent death. And, as we discussed on the scene, she was already dead when the sword entered her abdomen. That makes me suspect poison or natural causes."

"Like a terror-induced heart attack?"

"It's possible."

"And if it's poison?"

"I can't find any needle marks or disturbance of the skin that makes me believe it would have entered her body that way, which leads me to ingestion. She had a dark fruit juice in her stomach. No food. I'll be sending the liquid off to test for toxicity."

"Any idea what type of poison?"

"Obviously one capable of causing death when ingested, but that doesn't limit it much. It would help if we knew the symptoms she experienced before she passed, but, again, we have nothing there. We're just going to have to wait for the test results."

"Are there any limits to the types of poisons the tests will look for?"

"Let me restate your question. Do we need to let the lab

know any poisons we suspect to ensure they test for those? And the answer is that it would definitely help."

Delaney cocked her head, thinking aloud. "Everything in this case points to someone fixated on the Middle Ages. I'm thinking if they're a purist, they'd use poisons consistent with that era."

Dr. Watson started nodding. "That's helpful. Things like hemlock, monkshood, foxglove, or deadly nightshade. All plants that would have been known poisons at the time and would have grown in Europe. I'll ask them to include those. And possibly a few others. Let me do a little research."

Leo smiled at Delaney. "Good call."

Delaney knew she had to act normal with him. She smiled back, as best she could. "Are all of those things that can be administered orally?"

"If my memory serves, yes. But I'll double-check."

Leo said, "Can any of them be grown around here?"

Dr. Watson started stitching the victim closed, tugging at the line when it became stuck on something. "I'm no botanist. I think you'll want to consult someone with expertise in that field."

Delaney said, "We can contact the local nursery."

"Or the agriculture department at the college." He took a few steps back, staring at the coolers and rubbing his cheek. "I'm trying to think about how I frame this in the press conference. I think all I can say is that cause of death is under examination pending further testing. And everyone will be thinking 'she had a sword through her gut, you moron,' but it is what it is."

Dr. Watson nodded. "I wish I had more for you. I wasn't able to salvage any of her fingerprints, but I have sent off for a DNA test. Maybe we'll get a match there."

Delaney's phone buzzed. She glanced at it, fearing it was

Kat, and that with time to think about it, the girl had gone from stunned to pissed off. But it was Shirleen.

I'd be happy to look at pictures. Would you like me to come to the station?

Delaney would have loved to say yes. But she'd been away from home for two days on the case. She'd dropped a bombshell on her girls. Involving a civilian in reviewing crime scene photos unrelated to her could wait until morning. There was still hope they'd identify the woman from Drew's research before then. And she sure wasn't going to transmit the pictures electronically to someone outside the department.

How about over breakfast at the Cowpoke Café?

Perfect.

They settled on a time. Early. Delaney appreciated that.

"Delaney?" Leo said.

"Sorry. I was answering Shirleen. We're meeting tomorrow to look at photos."

"Great. I was just asking if you had anything else for Dr. Watson?"

"Nope. Thank you, Louise. This was very helpful, as always."

Dr. Watson walked to the sink and began the process of removing a few layers of her protective clothing and washing up. "Glad to be of help. And nice to see the two of you have patched things up."

Delaney literally squirmed at her words.

Leo said, "Thank you, Dr. Watson."

"I hope you find out who she is soon. Someone out there is missing her."

Maybe a child. Delaney shuddered, thinking of her own girls. They had to ID this woman fast. A child's life could be at stake.

FIFTEEN

Leo stood in front of the station at a microphone, facing the assembled journalists and a haze of smoke that smelled like burned popcorn. He and Delaney had spent the last hour crafting his statement for the press and plotting strategy. Given that he was going to answer the question about his relationship with Delaney, they had decided she would not attend the press conference with him. But because there was strength in numbers, Drew would. The only thing more likely to upset Joe than Delaney on camera with Leo was Drew beside him. It was a small consolation to Leo. He would rather have faced this with his partner.

"Good afternoon, everyone. Thank you for coming." He paused, and the bombardment began. He held up a hand. "I'm going to read a prepared statement, then I'll answer a few questions. The statement should answer most of them, however."

The hand holding his notes was shaking, so he lowered it. He'd have to go by memory. He'd practiced. He was ready.

"First, let me introduce you to Drew Knowles. He's one of the key members of the team investigating the recent homicide, although he's fairly new to our department."

As planned, Drew stepped forward. They'd brought him in on the secret that would be revealed today, and he hadn't batted an eyelash. "Hello, everyone. I'm proud to be working on this case with Sheriff Palmer and the team." His voice was steady, his gaze like a laser. He nodded and stepped back, this time slightly behind and to the side of Leo.

He gives good camera.

Leo smiled. "I'm also pleased to tell you that Deputy Joe Tarver is leading our fire response in support of the community. It's critical work, and he's definitely the person for the job. I still remain involved with whatever the emergency response team needs, but he'll be the one to address the fire with the media.

"Now, on to the purpose we're gathered for." He cleared his throat. "Yesterday, a community member working on a fire relief delivery discovered the body of a young woman aged approximately twenty-one years on the Planter ranch northeast of Kearny. Deputy Delaney Pace was onsite to secure the scene. I joined her shortly thereafter. The scene has been thoroughly examined by crime scene techs led by Sugar Kuhk. Dr. Louise Watson is performing an autopsy. At this time, the identity of the victim is unknown and there are no suspects. The cause of death is under investigation pending results from testing done offsite."

His mind drifted for a moment back to the call that had come in earlier to their 911 operator about the two missing "friends" of the female caller. Gender of the friends not identified. Names not given. A return call to the number she'd called from had gone unanswered. Follow-up showed the number was linked to a burner-type phone. *Had that call been about our victim? If so, did that mean there would be more murders to come?*

"It is public knowledge in the community that the victim was discovered anchored to the ground with a large sword. The sword appears to be a replica of a type used centuries ago in

Europe." A buzz swept through the journalists. Everyone already knew this. But they now had him on film confirming it. He would go no further than that, however.

"Anyone with information on the victim's identity, the crime, or the perpetrator is asked to contact the Kearny County Sheriff's Department." He gave the number and an email address. "This young woman was someone's daughter. Maybe someone's partner. Friend. Sister. Mother. They may not realize she is missing. Her loved ones deserve to know what has happened to her. And she deserves justice, which I have every intention of securing for her, with my team.

"Now, if there are any questions?"

Twenty voices shouted at him.

One rose above the others. "Is it true you are reviewing security footage from the Cowpoke Café and think your suspect will be in those videos?"

Magda didn't keep the secret—no surprise. "We're reviewing a great deal of evidence and have yet to identify a subject at this time."

He next deliberately chose the reporter who'd ambushed him the day before. Drew had found her name from the video clips of Delaney currently burning up the internet. Melanie Pritchett. She was out of Denver and worked for an e-zine, the *Rocky Mountain Daily.* "Ms. Pritchett."

She made a funny face at his use of her name, like she was surprised. "Sheriff, earlier you mentioned Deputy Delaney Pace, who I'll assume unless you correct me is also on this homicide investigation team. My question is about whether it is appropriate for Ms. Pace—"

"Deputy Investigator Pace."

"Excuse me. Is it appropriate for Deputy Investigator Pace to participate in this team given the relationship between the two of you?"

From the buzz in the scrum, Leo felt sure Joe had fed the

information directly to Melanie and that she'd kept it to herself, like any journalist aiming for a scoop.

He held up a hand for the group to settle. "Deputy Investigator Delaney Pace is the best detective we have. Hell, she's probably one of if not *the* best in the state. She is absolutely essential to the success of our team. She and I have an outstanding partnership, which was first arranged by our mutual mentor, former Sheriff Fentworth Coltrane, may he rest in peace. Deputy Pace and I are not, nor have we ever been, involved in a romantic relationship. We are friends at work and outside work, which is not unusual in a department like ours. Our families are close as well. However, because I have nothing to hide and neither Deputy Pace nor I believe we did anything inappropriate, I want to fully disclose that we did share a kiss one time, a long time ago. And that was it. We laughed about it later and agreed it would go no further. Which it has not." He gave a wide grin. "If you think that I would keep my star detective off our most important cases just because she was unfortunate enough to fall against my face once, then you're crazy. It would be inappropriate *not* to include her. I'd have a revolt on my hands in the department."

He turned to Drew as follow-up questions bombarded them, one hand over the microphone, voice lowered. "I think it's time to wrap this up. Unless I missed anything? I didn't look at my notes."

Drew patted Leo's shoulder. "Pitch perfect, boss. And, for the record, I'd be one of the ones revolting if you hamstrung the team by keeping Delaney off it."

Leo chuckled, then faced the throng. "That's all for today. Further press conferences will be held when necessary and announced through the department's social media accounts."

Melanie Pritchett shouted over the din. "I have a recording, Sheriff. If you give me an exclusive interview, I won't release it."

Leo kept his face impassive, waved, and walked back into

the building. *A recording?* He'd return for the microphone later. Now, he had to talk to Delaney.

SIXTEEN

FIFTY YEARS BEFORE

The girl didn't understand what was happening to her. She'd already turned fourteen by the time she had her first period, long after her friends. A late bloomer, her mother had called her when she taught her how to use sanitary napkins. She didn't bleed every month, so it hadn't seemed weird to her when a few months went by without anything happening. That fall she'd gotten a stomach bug. It made her nauseous and tired, which made her dad angry with her.

"What is it with this one always coming up with excuses not to work?" he'd said to her mother. "We should have stopped after Jamie." Jamie was her brother, the fourth of five kids. She was the youngest.

By Christmas, she'd filled out so much that all she got under the tree was new underclothing. For clothes, she was finally able to wear her sister's hand-me-downs. Lil was ten years older than her and newly married. In the girl's bedroom, Lil handed over a garment and watched her undress to try it on. The girl hurried. The turkey smelled so good, and she was hungry.

"What's going on with your body?" Lil said.

"I've put on some weight."

Lil tilted her head, causing her shiny black hair to fall to the side. "No. Your chest has gotten a lot bigger. You stomach is round." She clapped a hand over her mouth. "You're pregnant!"

The girl shook her head. "No, I can't be." Married women got pregnant and had babies. Not teenage girls.

Lil jumped to her feet and poked her head out the door. "Mom? Mom!" she screamed.

"What are you doing?"

"You're pregnant. What are people going to say about us?" Lil was pacing now.

Their mother appeared in the doorway. "Have some decorum, Lil. You're a married woman now, not a hooligan."

The girl clutched the dress she'd been about to try on to her midsection, feeling her lack of clothing acutely. But if she raised the dress over her head now, she'd expose her body.

Lil pointed a shaking finger. "She's... she's... she's *with child.*"

Their mother shook her head. "No, she isn't. I would know."

"Look at her, mother. Just look at her." Lil snatched the dress away.

The girl gasped and folded in on herself, trying to become invisible.

Their mother pulled her arms from her stomach. "Stand up and let me see you."

The girl had no choice. She let her mother spread her arms. The expression that came over her mother's face was ugly to see.

"Oh, my God. Oh, my God in heaven. What boy have you been spreading your legs for? A daughter of mine! Having relations out of wedlock! Letting this happen!"

"There is no boy." The last thing the girl wanted was a boy in her life. If boys were like her Uncle Rick, she never wanted one near her. Luckily "something had come along" and Uncle

Rick had moved to Nevada a few months before. He had only cornered her a few times in the barn, and she'd been doing her best to forget it ever happened. If he moved back to their town, she'd run away.

"Liar!" Her mother slapped her across her face.

The girl gasped and pressed her own hand against the stinging skin.

"What—you're saying you're the Virgin Mary now?" Lil said. She was crying, her face splotchy.

The girl didn't understand. She hadn't done anything wrong. She hadn't hurt her sister or her mother.

"It's the truth," she said.

Her mother said, "This doesn't happen without a boy on top of you. Who was it?"

She blinked. She'd seen the bulls mount the cows, even though her father limited her work to the garden and the house most of the time. And then it hit her. They mounted them to make babies. Did that mean a woman could become pregnant before she was married, if a man did that to her? It went against everything she'd understood from Sunday school and her parents. "I'm not sure."

"Not sure who it was? Has there been more than one boy?"

The girl's hands moved to her belly. A baby was in there? Her head was reeling. She was dizzy with shock. "No. Only one. But he—he wasn't a boy."

"Dear God, don't tell me you've tempted a man away from his wife." Her mother shook her fist at the sky. "What did I do to deserve a daughter like this?"

The meekness left her body. The girl screamed, "I didn't do anything wrong. He held me down. I couldn't stop him. He told me not to scream or tell on him because no one would believe me."

Her mother charged at her and pushed her over backwards on the bed. "Who are you accusing with that filth?"

"You know. I told you."

"You most certainly did not."

"I told you that Uncle Rick was acting funny."

Her father appeared in the doorway. "What's going on in here?" His face was a storm cloud. "I carved the turkey half an hour ago. It's going to dry out." He seemed to notice the girl's nakedness for the first time. "For God's sake, put on some clothes or shut the door."

The girl's mother smiled at her husband. "Lil and her little sister were having a spat. Shoo now. I'll be right out."

"Fine. Just hurry. It's time for Christmas dinner."

She shut the door as he left. Then she turned to the girl. In a voice dripping in venom, she said, "Don't you ever let me hear you say that again."

"You're disgusting!" Lil said.

The girl put her hand over her mouth as tears spilled down her cheeks. Uncle Rick had been right. No one believed her.

SEVENTEEN

Kat sat astride Sunshine at the entrance to the arena. The golden horse danced from side to side. Kat had just earned the move up from Ghost—the pony she'd spent the last few months learning on—to the bigger horse a week ago. *A pony. Like a little kid.* She'd thought she was ready. She'd begged until Clara had broken down and agreed to give her a chance.

But that chance came in the form of a mare with a questionable attitude who jumped at shadows and plastic bags. A beautiful palomino with a white-blonde mane and tail, shiny black hooves, and a prance in her step even when she was just walking to her water trough. Clara had started Sunshine and rodeoed on her, then a Kearny High School girl had ridden her six years until moving to Laramie for college. At twenty, Sunshine was middle-aged in horse years, but she didn't act like it.

Kat patted the sweaty neck. Was it weird that she liked the smell of horse sweat? "Shh, girl. It's okay."

"Are you ready to take her through the pattern?" Clara shouted from the side of the arena where she was holding a stopwatch.

Kat bit the inside of her lip. They'd finished taking care of the displaced horses from ranches affected by the fires an hour earlier. She thought today's ride would just be more getting to know each other type of stuff. She'd barely ridden the horse before the fires, when all riding had come to a stop for a few days. Now Clara wanted Kat to take this firecracker through the barrels.

Kat had been running barrels—well, *loping* barrels—on Ghost for a month. He was solid. Nothing scared him. Getting him out of a walk took a lot of effort. Sunshine was the opposite. Kat had a hard time holding her to a walk. Any time she paid less than full attention or let the reins go slack or heaven forbid accidentally squeezed her legs, Sunshine would launch forward. The first time it happened, Kat had nearly been left behind in the dirt.

"Um, yeah, just a second." It didn't help Kat's frame of mind that she was super distracted by the call she'd gotten from Delaney. She couldn't believe it about her and Leo, but Kat couldn't let herself think about it right now. She stroked the horse again then whispered, "Let's just trot this nice and easy, Sunshine."

The horse's ears twitched. Not the thoughtful, slow movement Ghost's would make when he was listening to Kat. A jerk. A darting motion. Sunshine's head bobbed up and down. She pawed the ground.

"Please don't kill me." After a deep breath, Kat lifted the reins and clucked. She shifted forward in the saddle as gently as she could with no leg squeeze, braced for the propulsion.

Sunshine's ears flattened, her muscles bunched, and she shot forward.

Kat rocked back, putting her weight into the stirrups instead of into Sunshine's sides. She pulled on the reins. She didn't want to hurt the mare's mouth, but she didn't want to make the turn around the first barrel at a full gallop either.

Sunshine stretched her neck out, resisting the brakes.

The fence around the arena and the ranch buildings beyond it were a blur as Sunshine's stride levelled out. Wind cooled the sweat on Kat's face. Time slowed. She became hyper aware of her own breathing. The pounding of Sunshine's hooves in rhythm with her breaths sounded like muffled drumbeats.

They approached the first barrel. Kat nearly forgot what Clara had taught her. Just in time—about a stride length out— she sat deep in the saddle with her hands forward. She braced her outside hand on the saddle horn and extended her inside hand.

Sunshine barely eased her speed, then went nearly perpendicular to the ground as she dug in and rounded the barrel like she was attacking the ground with her hooves. *Shoulders up. Belly button forward.* It was easier said than done. The force pulling her inward toward the barrel was crazy. When Ghost had loped the barrels, he'd slowed down and made the turns upright. This was nothing like that. At the last second Kat remembered to make her inside leg soft and gently lift Sunshine's ribcage with it. Sort of. Mostly. It was super hard to do at speed.

As the horse finished the turn, Kat fully extended her inside arm, as if pointing at the next barrel. Again, Kat felt the powerful bunching of the mare's muscles, then, together they catapulted out of the turn.

Oh, my God, oh, my God, oh, my God.

On the way to the second barrel, Kat asked the mare to slow down with every trick she had. Again, Sunshine resisted her. Somehow, they finished the second turn with the barrel and horse upright and Kat still in the saddle.

A new sensation came over Kat. A lightness. An excitement. She could do this. It was like the craziest roller coaster ride ever, and she *liked* it. No, she *loved* it.

"Woo hoo!" she screamed.

Sunshine sped up even more. Kat remembered Clara's coaching. "You must believe you are the boss of Sunshine, or she'll be the boss of you."

I am the boss of you, horse! "Slow down!" Kat shouted, her words in sync with her attitude and actions.

This time, Sunshine slowed. Not a lot, but enough that they didn't do a somersault around the last barrel. Horse and rider only had the straightaway left, and Kat finally gave Sunshine her head, coaxing her for more speed as they raced toward the finish line, then through the gate and out of the arena.

Kat sat back hard and asked for a real stop, meaning it with everything inside her. Sunshine dropped her nose, tucked her large behind, and slid to a halt. Kat rocked forward onto the horse's neck but her hand on the saddle horn kept her from flying over Sunshine's head. The horn knocked the wind out of Kat, but she didn't even care.

She was breathing almost as hard as the horse. Her legs and arms were quivering.

"Oh, my gosh! That was the best!" She hugged Sunshine's neck.

If Freddy could see me now, would he be impressed? Maybe it didn't matter. Maybe nothing mattered but her pounding heart and the puffing breaths of the horse who had just pushed herself physically with no demands and not even much encouragement—purely for the fun of it. Like human athletes who did hard things but liked them.

A thought occurred to her. She had tickets to the Renaissance Festival. She'd already seen all the trailers pull into town a few days before, including horse trailers. She'd read about a jousting event. Riders wearing armor and carrying giant poles and shields ran their horses full speed at each other. Would Sunshine be able to learn to do something like that? She giggled. Like Kat would be strong enough to carry one of those jousting things. Unless hers was made of Styrofoam! She couldn't wait to see the event, though. Maybe Delaney-mom would let her go to the fairgrounds early to see the horses and talk to the jousters if Clara went with her.

She rode back into the arena and whooped. "How fast did we go?"

But Clara didn't look up. She had her phone out and was typing something.

"Clara? Did you see me?" She stopped Sunshine a few feet away from her instructor.

Finally, Clara raised her head. "What? No, sorry. I got an, um, I got a message."

She was on her phone that whole time? At first Kat was put out. She jumped down from Sunshine's back and held the reins in her hand. But then she noticed Clara had tears in her eyes. She looked like her dog had died. Literally, Clara loved her feisty Corgi—named Grendel—more than anything in the world except her grandkids.

"Are you okay?" *Please don't let it be Grendel.*

Clara wiped her face with her sleeve. "Someone is playing a really mean trick on me."

Kat couldn't believe it. Who would want to hurt someone as nice as Clara?

EIGHTEEN

Leo crept into his house at eleven that night, hungry and eager to get in bed. Tomorrow was going to come very early. Unfortunately, gone were the days of a quiet entry. Even when he didn't mess up the sequence, the alarm system announced him. He typed quickly in the keypad. Then, tiptoeing down the hall, he tried to avoid the creaky boards.

Who am I kidding? They all creak.

He slipped into his room and shut the door, eyeing his bed but realizing he was wired. His stomach growled. Freddy and Adriana had eaten hamburgers, if his nose didn't deceive him. But he wasn't going for a snack. He would use his awake time to progress the case. Good thing he always brought his laptop bag into his room so that no one else in the household could inadvertently pull up things they shouldn't see. He started it and left it to boot up while he locked his weapon in the gun safe, then got situated with the machine in his lap on his bed. A spartan bed. No fancy comforter or extra pillows to cushion his back while he worked.

Maybe reviewing the video footage from the Cowpoke Café would make him sleepy. Earlier that day, Magda had helped him narrow down the days the old coin might have been left at the restaurant. He played the video at maximum speed and fast forwarded through everything except sequences when people were leaving coins. Since most patrons paid with cards or large bills, this allowed him to skip seventy-five percent of the transactions. He sped through the first day and was well into the second, when there was a firm knock on his door.

Adriana's head poked into his bedroom. "Leo?" His petite sister had inherited their deceased mother's heart-shaped face, shiny dark hair, and even darker eyes. She and Leo only favored each other in their coloring.

He stopped, pasting on a smile. "Hey. Why are you up?"

"It's been a day."

He sensed work not getting done and sleepiness receding into the distance. "What happened?"

She retied her silk robe around her waist. "I got a final warning at work. They're such assholes."

"Oh, man. That sucks. I'm sorry."

"But that's not all. Freddy said some guy has been creeping him."

"A kid his age?"

"No. Freddy thinks a man in a car was following him today."

This was Leo's greatest fear. The cartel showing up, hunting his family. But if this was happening, the private security would have information on the vehicle and the driver. He was glad he'd hired them. "I'll look into it."

"I don't like it."

"I don't either."

"Maybe it's time to make a change."

"Are you going to start job hunting?"

She moved closer. "No, I mean maybe it's time to make a real change. We can get out of this backwater, Leo. Move to civilization."

He set his laptop aside. "You and Freddy?"

"Me, Freddy, you. All of us. Back to California. Or wherever. Just away."

He shut his laptop harder than he intended. "This is sudden."

"It's not."

"Unexpected."

"It's not. But you're not sounding much like you want to go. Like you want to take care of us. And you promised me you would. When I lost my husband and parents, or do you not remember?"

He'd said it more than once. He'd meant it. He still meant it. *Do I want to move away from Delaney, though? Or away from this place?* He'd miss the mountain views. The self-reliant people. The wildlife that was so commonplace he almost took it for granted now. Even the extremes in weather. The mudslides, the blizzards, the raging wildfires. But mostly he'd miss the woman. That confounding, beautiful creature who he had to convince to be his somehow.

He couldn't leave while there was still a chance. *Is there?*

"Adriana, I will always want to take care of you. Yours and Freddy's safety is very important to me."

"But?" Her tone was a challenge.

"But I didn't promise I'd follow wherever you go. You stayed in San Diego when I moved here."

"It was your job that put us at risk and forced us to move to Wyoming."

He shook his head. "And I'm very sorry about that."

Her words came out in a growl simmering with resentment. "Yeah. You'll think sorry if something happens to my son."

NINETEEN

Delaney smiled as Magda put the Spicy Elk Sausage Combo in front of her. She still mourned the removal of fried green tomatoes benedict from the Cowpoke Café's menu, but this smelled heavenly.

"And you had the French toast, Shirleen?" Magda said, sliding the plate to the other side of the table.

"Thank you, yes. It looks delicious."

"Did you not like the omelet?"

"I'm sorry?"

"Wasn't that what you had last week?"

Shirleen smiled. "Not me. Must have been my evil twin."

"My bad. You send that sheriff of yours back around to see me, okay?" Magda said to Delaney.

Delaney forced a smile. *Not my sheriff.* She'd eaten breakfast with him so many times before that damn kiss. Right now, he'd be grinning at her over his loaded avocado toast. Every one of her nerve endings would be on fire. She couldn't think about that now. "Will do."

"And about that thing…"

Delaney held a finger to her lips.

Magda's eyebrows elevated. "Ri-ight. Let me know if you need anything else. Enjoy." She made an abrupt retreat to the kitchen.

"What was that about?" Shirleen poured warm syrup from a metal pitcher onto thick slabs of battered and pan-fried toast.

"Oh, just something we're working on for her." Delaney stuffed a quick bite of sausage in. She wanted her friend to eat up and then look at pictures. Because Drew hadn't dug up any leads on the identity of their victim, Shirleen was their only hope of information at the moment.

"Got it. And how are *you*? Any news on your mother?"

Delaney couldn't believe her mother had fallen so far from her mind. "I'm fine. And Skeeter is working on tracking down my mom. This homicide will be my sole focus until we put it to rest. Well, except for my girls."

"If there's anything I can do?"

"You're doing it."

"I really don't mind looking at pictures while we eat, you know."

Delaney did. She swallowed a big bite of sausage on fried egg atop hash brown on toast. A sandwich stack. "After I finish. I've been dying to know how you got into social work."

"Well, I told you a little about my personal stuff the other day. My son."

Delaney wondered what the story behind that story was. She didn't get the impression Shirleen was married. Had she been? "Yes. I appreciated you sharing it with me."

"He was my motivation. I studied social work in school."

"Where'd you go?"

"St. Mary's College. In Indiana."

"Is that where you're from?"

"Sort of. But I've worked in many places."

"I remember—you were in Wisconsin most recently?"

She smiled and pushed her plate back, French toast only half eaten. "Yes."

Delaney finished up the last bite of her breakfast. Then she slid a file folder from a grocery bag and pulled out enlargements of photos taken in the morgue, keeping them face down. "I apologize in advance. People can look quite eerie after their life ends."

Shirleen waved her hand. "I've seen my share."

Delaney looked around the restaurant. No one else was close enough to see the pictures. She laid out a front and two side views, then held the folder fanned out and at the ready in case she needed to cover them.

Shirleen didn't hesitate. "Oh, yes. I'm very aware of who this is."

Delaney's pulse quickened. "Do you work with her?"

"Not directly. But I've tried to befriend some of the young women in her situation. It helps me help them later when they need it." She tapped a picture with a medium-length nail. "This is Genevieve Martine."

Delaney hadn't realized she was holding her breath until it came out in a rush. "Gennie Martin."

"What?"

"I believe she sometimes went by Gennie Martin. But spelled it J-E-N-N-Y."

"Hmm. I wasn't aware of that." She shook her head. "A sweet girl. Kind of new to town."

"Do you know her next of kin? We need to do a death notification."

"Sorry. I believe she said she is—was—from Haiti and that her parents are deceased. Maybe she'll have something in her personal effects about siblings."

"Do you know where she lived?"

"In an apartment complex on the southeast side of town. Riverside. It's pretty rough."

"I know the one. What about roommates, associates, friends?"

"I usually saw her with a young woman named Anna. A Russian girl."

Delaney scribbled notes. Two women from out of the state. Out of the *country*. "You said young women in her situation. What do you mean by that?"

"Young. Alone. Hand to mouth survivalism. Hanging out with the wrong people. Usually with an element of substance abuse. Ones I suspect of having sex for money."

Delaney frowned. That didn't sound like the girl she'd seen on Leo's app. The women Leo dated were nothing like Shirleen was describing. The ones he was attracted to—if Delaney was any indication—were... but then she stopped herself. Shirleen was describing the type of girl she'd been at eighteen, mostly. If Fentworth Coltrane hadn't helped her turn her life around and given her a job, where would she be now? Would she be as dead as Genevieve Martine? *Is that girl still in me? Maybe* that's *what Leo is drawn to in me?* "Wow. Okay."

Shirleen gathered the pictures and turned them face down. She put a hand on Delaney's. "How else can I help? Like I said, I know her world."

"Do you know if Genevieve was into cosplay?"

Shirleen tilted her head. "Whatever gave you that idea?"

Delaney pushed ahead. "Or had any interest in the Middle Ages or medieval things?"

"Not to my knowledge." Then she nodded. "But you know everyone in town is excited about this Renaissance Festival."

Delaney considered asking about the nun's habit costume. But going more granular didn't seem likely to yield more information, plus she needed to take care not to reveal too much. That nixed asking about the coin, specifics about the sword, or the crucifix. Besides, Shirleen had already said she didn't know Genevieve to have an interest in cosplay or the Middle Ages.

There was something she could ask, though. The man who had attacked Drew had been looking for Genevieve. She pulled a video up on her phone and pushed play. "The resolution isn't great. Do you recognize this guy?"

Shirleen took the phone and moved it closer. She put a hand over her mouth.

"I take that as a yes?"

Shirleen's eyes were wide. "Listen, I don't know any of this for sure but..."

"But, what?"

"I suspect he was trafficking the girls."

"A pimp?"

"Think bigger than that. Think more like a... a... a slaver."

Delaney's mouth hung open. She couldn't have felt more foolish if she were drooling with crossed eyes. A slaver trafficking humans in her little town? How had she not heard of this? Of him?

"His name is Albert Tuttle. He's just moved to Kearny from North Dakota. All the girls are scared of him. I'm scared of him. You should be, too."

Anong Leela smoothed her black hair. It felt silky under her fingers. She liked the new cut. Layers around her face. Curtain bangs.

She turned to the driver. "Turn here, please." Her Thai accent was still very thick. Maybe it always would be, no matter how hard she tried with her free English classes on YouTube videos. At least she was allowed access to the internet for them. They were helping her communicate better with customers. But the chat she'd struck up in the comments with a man was the most important thing she'd gotten from them.

"I know a shorter way," the driver said.

Anong wasn't sure she understood correctly. That happened a lot. And she was really tired. She yawned, then said. "Uh, okay."

She thought about the man. They'd started talking in a private chat room when she was supposed to be doing her lessons. In the chat, he told her how to delete her comments and her internet browser history so they wouldn't get caught. He asked for pictures of her. He liked them and asked for more. He sent her one, too. His looked nice, and he said he wanted a wife to spoil and make happy. That he liked kids and wanted many, many of them.

It sounded wonderful to Anong. Anything would be better than her life. So, she'd agreed to meet him. Here, in Kearny, Wyoming. Today. And if he asked, she would leave with him. He knew it was dangerous for him to even come here. He said he didn't care. He said he was falling in love with her. She'd explained she would have to change her name and her looks and hide if she ever left, and he still didn't care.

Anong realized she'd been daydreaming—or maybe she'd fallen asleep?—when she saw the Kearny city limit sign. The driver had passed by all the turns and was heading out of town. Maybe she hadn't understood after all.

"'Scuse me. My apartment. Back there."

The driver didn't look at her. Didn't speak.

"Not a shorter way. Wrong way."

When the driver ignored her again, she started to get scared.

"Take home. Now. Not ha ha."

Finally, the driver turned to her. "Are you feeling sleepy, Anong?"

She was. She really was. And she shouldn't be. She thought about the drink she'd accepted earlier when she first got in the car. What might have been in it. How nothing good came after being drugged, like being kidnapped and forced to work for no money. That she was not safe. She felt terror—bright, sharp, shiny—but like she was watching it happen to someone else in a movie while bundled under a big fluffy comforter with a fire in the wood-burning stove back home with her sisters giggling beside her at the scariest parts.

No! Don't sleep! You will die! Bad things will happen!!

Her instincts told her to run. To get out of the car and run. That if she didn't do it soon, it would be too late. For her, her future, for the little one. That it was probably already too late.

She unbuckled her seatbelt.

"What do you think you're doing, Anong?" The driver laughed.

She threw the door to the vehicle open and dived out head-first, aiming for the brown grass and weeds on the edge of the road. Wondering why they smelled like the tea her mother used to make. Wondering if anyone would even realize she was gone or question what had happened to her, until she hit the pavement. Then she didn't wonder anything anymore.

TWENTY-ONE

Delaney rushed into the station, dying to tell Leo the news since he hadn't answered her excited texts. *We have a name for our victim! And a person of interest/potential suspect!*

Clara didn't look up, even though Delaney was pounding like an elephant past her desk.

Delaney stopped. "Clara? Are you all right?"

The older woman raised her face. It was pale and drawn with hollowed eye sockets. "Yes. Of course."

"Are you sure?"

Clara shuddered a sigh. "I didn't sleep well. It happens when you get to be my age."

Delaney wondered how old she was, exactly. Older than she looked, probably, with her great posture and athletic gait. Past retirement age for sure but showing no signs of slowing down, thank goodness. "Should I keep Kat at bay this week?"

"Oh, no. Kat is one of my greatest joys. She's invited me to the festival. I'm taking off a half day to go with her tomorrow."

Guilt swept through Delaney, along with a little bit of jealousy. She should be going with the girl. *Just be grateful—you can't take off during a murder case.* She swallowed her feelings and walked away backwards, pointing at Clara. "Let me know if you change your mind."

Clara shooed her away with both hands. "It's all good. Go catch a killer."

Delaney fast-walked down the hall, texting Kat as she went. *Is Clara okay?* She wanted to add, *I heard you're going to the festival with her.* But she didn't. Then she burst into Leo's office.

He looked up from a call and pointed at his chair. He seemed intense, in a personal way. She dropped into the seat and pretended to be doing something on her phone instead of eavesdropping and watching him.

"You're sure there was no one?" A short pause. "Can I see your log for the last week and any photos you've taken?" A longer pause. Leo's face turned red. "We agreed when I hired you that you would keep those and provide them upon request." An even longer pause. "Well, see that you do going forward. I need to know whether someone is following him." He ended the call and set the phone down on his desk a little too hard.

"Sorry about that," he said.

She met his gaze. Everything he was feeling, everything in his troubled gaze, jolted into her like she'd grabbed an electric fence wire. "Leo?"

He swallowed, then looked away. When he caught her eyes again, his were more placid. "How did it go with Shirleen?"

She frowned. He was changing the subject after he was that upset. Giving her the stiff arm. "You didn't get my texts?"

He pointed at his phone and shook his head. "That thing has been glued to my ear since I got in. My first call was from our esteemed mayor who was in a snit. He desires more face time with me so he can be the source of truth to the community. Joe apparently is not of lofty enough stature to fit the bill."

"Sorry." Their mayor was a prima donna who loved the sound of his own voice. But that hadn't been who he was talking to when she came in. She waited for him to go on. What was he keeping from her? She didn't like secrets between them in their renewed partnership. *He doesn't know about the search for my mom, though. So, how can I be resentful when I haven't filled him in on all my personal stuff either?* The answer to that was "not rationally" but rationality was a choice, and she didn't want to make it right now. She settled on not getting bent out of shape yet. He'd fill her in when the right time came. Like she would him. Unless that wasn't fast enough for her, in which case she reserved the right to shake it out of him. Besides, she was too pumped about the information from Shirleen to let anything derail her from sharing it.

After a few seconds of silence, she said, "Good news, bad news. Shirleen confirmed Genevieve and your Jenny are the same person. And that she is our victim."

"Not my Jenny."

Delaney winced internally. She didn't like hearing him say it, even if to correct her. "I made a critical point that seems to have flown right past your pretty head."

He gave a weak smile. He was off. Clara was off. Something was in the air besides smoke. "That's great."

"She had a decent amount of surprising info about her. But there's more. She ID'ed the guy who assaulted Drew."

"Whoa. Unexpected."

Delaney filled him in quickly on all the other details. "I want to get out to Genevieve's place five minutes ago. Do you want to go with me?"

"Want to? Very much. But my face is required with the mayor. How about I meet you back here and we can spend the afternoon wrapping up this murder?"

She guffawed. "I wish."

"I have news, too. Sugar called. They found a large quantity of blood soaked into the dirt in the closet at the farmhouse on the Planter place."

Delaney chewed the inside of her lip, thinking. "But

Genevieve wasn't injured. Dr. Watson thinks she was poisoned."

"Bingo. And it's human blood."

"Oh, my God."

"Drew is going out to search a larger area."

"Would it be too much to hope it's the killer's blood?"

"Sugar says the quantity doesn't point toward a live person."

"On that cheerful note..." She got to her feet. "See you later. And whatever is eating you—"

"Nothing is eating me."

"—I hope it works out okay."

The manager of the Riverside Apartments—which were not by the side of a river, unless you counted the drainage ditch behind the dumpsters—escorted Delaney to an eight-unit structure with a sagging staircase, the least well-maintained building in the complex and furthest from the street view. Trash swirled around the parking lot in the wind. Some distance to the northeast, she saw an orange glow. The fire. It didn't seem to be getting any further away or any smaller. The opposite, in fact.

The manager twirled the keys on tattooed fingers. Joaquim Smith hadn't been still long enough for Delaney to identify the tattoos. He was prematurely bald if she was guessing his age right at mid-thirties. "Gennie has been here a few months. Her girlfriend you asked about, Anna, about the same. From what I see, they don't spend much time at home."

"Did Gennie have many visitors?"

He trotted ahead of her up the sketchy staircase. "It's against the rules."

"Why?"

"That's not the kind of place I run. My other tenants don't like the girls in this building as it is. I told Albert from the beginning—"

Now they were getting somewhere. "Albert? Who's that?"

"Their, um, broker."

Delaney would have laughed, but nothing about trafficking was funny. "You told him what?"

"That I'd be happy taking his money, but not at the expense of my business. I have ten buildings here. I have to keep the people in the other nine happy or I got no business." He knocked on the door to 1-F. "Gennie. It's Joaquim with management. Cops here for you. Open up."

"Albert brokers all the women in this building?"

"That is my impression."

They waited in silence for the woman Delaney knew would never come.

"Gennie, open up. I'm not standing out here for my health in this smoke."

"How about you just let me take a quick look inside to see if she's all right?" Getting inside immediately without a warrant had been her goal all along.

"One of those what-do-you-call-'em checks?"

"Welfare checks." She had Shirleen identifying her, but without more they couldn't confirm who Genevieve was, so a welfare check made sense. However, in her gut she knew Shirleen was right and Genevieve Martine was no longer alive.

"Yeah. Can I come, too?"

"It would be better if you wait in the doorway. In case of any evidence."

He looked crestfallen, but he unlocked the door. "I warned you, Gennie. The cop is coming in for an, um, welfare check." He waved Delaney in.

"Thanks." She slipped on a pair of gloves. Keeping a hand on her gun, she scanned the room quickly, taking a mental inventory of impressions, cognizant that the apartment might be tampered with before she could get a warrant and be back to execute it. "Gennie, this is Deputy Investigator Delaney Pace.

We're worried about you. You didn't show up where you were expected to be yesterday." Nothing hung on the walls. The furniture was boxy and cheap, like the kind that was rented by the room. It was tidy, though, and the place smelled like a plug-in room deodorizer. She passed into the kitchen, which was really part of the same room. Every surface shone.

An old-school day timer lay on the two-top kitchen table. It was open to the previous Monday. At eight a.m. in a careful printed hand, it read, HAIR. She flipped backwards and saw nothing else written in it for weeks prior. Moving forward, she discovered the same thing.

Whatever Gennie had going on last Monday morning, it was important enough to write down. Delaney didn't attach the same gravity to her own twice-yearly trims, but her daughters did, so she understood, sort of. She took a picture then checked for contacts in the address book section. There was a list of numbers in that same tight print. Anna. Anong. Mika. Albert. Again, she captured it in a photo.

"You okay in there, Deputy?"

"All good. Moving on to the back of the place." She walked out of the kitchen, feeling like a bad actor reading stilted dialogue. "Gennie, I'm coming into the bathroom."

She poked her head in. The top was clear of toiletries and wiped clean. *She is—was—a neat freak.* Opening a cabinet, she saw a makeup bag, a teeth cleaning caddy, a basket of hair products, tools, and accessories, and a skin care bag. Beside them were extra rolls of toilet paper and cleaning supplies. She closed the cabinet. Two threadbare but dry towels hung on the rack.

"No one in the bathroom," she called. "Gennie, I'm coming into your bedroom, okay?"

Of course, there was no answer.

"Man, this is taking forever, deputy. I gotta get back to my office."

"One minute." She hurried into the only bedroom, looking

for evidence of the last place Gennie had gone, and with whom. Was it willingly or not?

The room was as tidy as the others. Bed made. Clothes put away. Almost like no one lived there. Except for one thing. A paper on the bedside table, ticket shaped. Delaney leaned over to read it.

RENAISSANCE FESTIVAL.

The date was tomorrow. The hair on her arms rose and her Spidey-senses tingled on high alert.

Picture of the ticket taken and saved on her phone, Delaney rushed out. "She's definitely not in there. Which unit is Anna's?"

"Anna Petrov?"

Is there more than one Anna in this building who we've been talking about? "Yes. I'd like to talk to her."

"Listen, deputy. Albert's not gonna like the thought of me introducing you to his girls."

"Does he live here?"

"No."

"Where does he live?"

"Somewhere on the edge of town. I'm not sure."

This is the edge of town. His eyes were darting at the eaves.

Delaney looked in the same direction. A camera. "Are those your security cameras or his?"

"They're, uh, they're mine."

Lie. She crossed her arms. "I have all day."

The look he gave her was sheer terror. The kind Shirleen had mentioned. "Please," he whispered.

"Go back up front and pretend this never happened."

"You'll leave?"

"Soon."

His eyes went to the camera again. Then he took off at a fast jog for the blissful ignorance of his office.

Delaney went door to door on the second floor, knocking and calling for Anna. The third door opened before her fist struck it. The blonde had a black eye.

"Anna's not home."

Delaney smiled at her. "And you are?"

"Mika."

"When did you last see her?"

The girl shrugged. "Yesterday, maybe."

"Is this her place?" Delaney pointed at 1E on the door.

"No. She's in H." Mika also glanced at the camera. "I've gotta go."

"Wait." Delaney held out a card. Her hands were still in gloves. Mika's eyes widened. "Call me if you see her."

The girl shook her head and shut the door.

"All right, then." Delaney went to H and tried the doorknob. It opened. *Why is it unlocked?* She paused. "Ms. Petrov? Deputy Investigator Delaney Pace. May I have a word?"

When there was no answer, she remembered the call to the station. A woman reporting two friends missing, no names. Could it have been Mika calling about Anna and Gennie? It was a good working theory. One that gave enough justification to enter and check on Anna's welfare. She pushed the door open.

"Anna?" She slipped inside.

The place gave her the creeps immediately. For starters, it was far too messy to tell if Anna had left voluntarily or with a struggle. Secondly, it stunk, like a rotten chicken carcass, the mother of all stink. And lastly, it wasn't silent. Music was blaring from the back of the apartment. She drew her gun and pointed it down. "Anna Petrov, are you in here?"

Nothing about the living room or kitchen caught her attention, so she went straight to the source of the music. It was a tablet in the bedroom. A screensaver with a password blocked Delaney from turning off the music or snooping further. But the picture on the screen gave her pause. It was a photo of a toddler. She was no good at baby ages, but she guessed the towhead was between one and two. Old enough that he was walking with his arms overhead, like he wanted to be picked up.

Did Anna have a child? Or a little brother? Which reminded her that she hadn't seen any evidence of a child at Gennie's apartment.

She made a slow lap of the room, examining but not touching piles of dirty clothes sized for a very tiny woman, wilted wildflowers slowly rotting in a water glass, fast food receipts, and loose change. Nothing useful. The bathroom was even worse. An unsanitary jumble of the best goops and potions Walmart had to offer.

She'd try for a warrant on this place, too, although unless someone confirmed she'd missed work or appointments, Delaney didn't hold out much hope for one.

As she exited and turned to shut the door, she remembered she hadn't searched the kitchen. But when she started to re-enter, she heard pounding steps coming up the rickety stairs outside.

A man's voice shouted, "Whoa, whoa, whoa. You can't be in there."

Delaney put her hand on her weapon and turned to face Albert Tuttle, sans his hoodie from the Cowpoke Café but still wearing his Ray Bans. Drew had been right—his hair was light-colored. But what she'd thought was a tattoo was a scar. No. It was a *brand*. Neck brands were not a thing in Kearny. "Says who?"

"Says me, bitch. Show a warrant or beat feet."

"You're too late." She smiled. "I performed a welfare check based on reasonable suspicion that Anna Petrov has come to harm."

"Quit shoveling bullshit. Why are you in here?"

She didn't want to raise his suspicion of Mika. She didn't even know if Mika had been the one to call the department. "Based on the fact that her friend Genevieve Martine was murdered a few days ago and now we can't find Anna."

He rushed at her, puffed up like cobra. She'd been right about the limp. "The fuck you say."

He hadn't drawn a weapon, but that didn't mean he didn't have one. She made a split-second decision and drew her pepper spray instead of her gun, pointing it straight at his face. "Are you going to assault me like you did Deputy Drew Knowles at the Cowpoke Café, Mr. Tuttle?"

He stopped, his face a glowering mask of rage.

"What—you didn't think their security video would show you? The picture was very clear. As will be the one on my body camera. Please take two giant steps back, sir."

He stared at her. Into her.

"I don't lose pissing contests, Albert. Back up, now."

He muttered a few words. She didn't have to hear them to understand exactly what he meant. She needed to place him under arrest. Wondered what her chances of success were. Decided to see if she could get him talking first.

"Thank you. When was the last time you saw Anna?"

"I don't remember."

"Genevieve?"

He took a toothpick out of a pocket in his jeans and began to work on his incisors.

When he hadn't answered after fifteen seconds, she said, "How do you know Anna and Genevieve?"

The work continued, now with disgusting sucking noises.

"Can you tell me where either of them work?"

He flicked the toothpick to the ground between them. *And I'll be putting that in a baggie for DNA testing.*

"Aren't you going to ask me how Genevieve died?"

His only answer was the middle finger of his right hand.

She decided not to tip him off that she knew about the camera before she got a warrant. If he stored images to the Cloud, they could be very useful. "Where were you Monday morning of last week between nine and noon?"

"Am I under arrest, lady cop?"

"Your cooperation into our homicide investigation would be greatly appreciated."

He let out a howling laugh. "Yeah, right. Later."

"Then I'm going to have place you under arrest for the assault of Deputy Drew Knowles."

"You and what army?"

"Put your hands over your head and turn around."

He snorted, whirled, and ran down the steps.

She sprinted after him. Shooting him in the back wasn't an option. Tackling him on the decrepit stairs was a good way to break her neck. When he reached the bottom, he turned, looking surprised to see her giving chase. It was just enough time for her to catch up with him. She drew out a pair of flexi-cuffs, holding the open loop like a snare. As he took off again, she leapt on his back. They went down together, and she grabbed a wrist, putting all her effort into snagging it with the cuffs. He jumped up like her weight was insubstantial and shook her off. She held onto the wrist for a few seconds. He dragged her two steps then pivoted and kicked her in the solar plexus. All the air went out of her lungs and her grip loosened. He pried his wrist loose and loped across the parking lot then disappeared around a corner. As she rolled and clutched her diaphragm, she heard a motorcycle engine rev and then race away.

She'd be adding resisting arrest to his warrant.

She sighed and climbed to her hands and knees and then her feet. *That was embarrassing. And painful.* Her phone rang. It was Leo. Would her heart do an undignified hop and a skip every time she saw his name on caller ID for the rest of her life? "Hello, Sheriff."

"Are you still at Genevieve's apartment?"

"Yes. Lots to tell you. But what's up?"

"We've got another body. How fast can you get out to the Planter ranch?"

TWENTY-TWO

I knew her routines. I knew when she broke them. I had her memorized. The ponytail that didn't let hair blow in her eyes. The way she dressed like an ad for *Western World* magazine, and how when it grew colder she added a fleece vest or a flannel shacket but never wore short sleeves no matter how warm. I knew who she spent time with and how often she texted or talked on her phone. What she liked to eat and how much, although I didn't understand how she kept fat off her slender frame. I knew she never stopped, never, ever, ever stopped—was always busy.

I would have admired her if I didn't hate her.

She emerged from the building where she worked now, cheerfully waving at every person she passed. It was her habit to walk to lunch. Fifteen minutes each way into downtown. There was far less foot traffic on the sidewalks since the fires started. Air quality had gone to hell. With the festival starting that evening, people were walking the streets in costume, which was very odd to see in Kearny, Wyoming, especially with the gloom and smoke.

If the smoke bothered her, she didn't show it. For that

matter, if the messages I'd been sending her from different burner phones had her rattled, she was hiding that well, too. Ranch raised kids grew up tough.

I paced her, keeping a block separation. Close enough not to lose her, but too far away to hear her breezy exchanges with passersby, what with the wind and sounds of cars. It was a Friday. On Fridays she ordered ahead at Buns in the Barn and walked an extra ten minutes each direction, eating her burger and fries and drinking her milkshake on her walk back. I wondered if she spritzed perfume when she returned to her work to cover up the sweaty outdoor scent of a brisk walk in the heat, but I doubted it. She wasn't the kind of woman who worried about things like that.

I caught a glimpse of myself in the plate glass window of a boutique and lifted my shoulders, having been raised to maintain good posture. If I disobeyed too often, I faced a lashing.

My father would say, "Don't slump. It's disrespectful to God. He made you tall so you'd be closer to heaven." I doubted that, but I didn't argue. I needed God on my side.

There had been lashes for other things as well, all of it subjective. Bad attitude. Backtalk. Disobedience. A lack of manners. Talking about what went on in our house outside it. That was the worst offense of all. My father had long since passed, but still when I put on the chain mail, I yearned to scream in his face. "Hit me now, you coward! Take your best shot!"

My brother had taken his place, and our mother had let it happen, like she always let it happen.

I felt exposed without the chain mail and imagined it on my body now. Heavy. Thick. Creaky. Wearing it was the best I ever felt. I imagined it made me invisible, which was silly, since it made me more visible. Today it might stick out less, though.

Ahead, the woman entered the fast-food restaurant. Her food would be ready. Mine would, too, since I'd started ordering ahead for pick-up. Exactly the same order as her. I timed it so I entered as she left, almost exactly. I was too close, so I slowed.

This would be the last time for this dance. It had to be just right. I approached the door and opened it. Held it and made eye contact with her.

She smiled broadly. Her food bag was in her purse and her shake in one hand. "You again. Thanks!"

"You're welcome."

"I feel like we know each other. But you haven't lived here very long, have you?"

"Not all that long."

"Let me buy you a cup of coffee. I love sharing our history with newcomers."

"If you're sure." I wanted to pump a fist. Was this the opening I'd been hoping for?

"Absolutely." She named a place and time for the next day.

"I'll see you then."

And the woman waved and walked back toward her job.

I moved to the counter as if in a dream. Everything was coming together even better than planned. The last practice round was complete. It had been hard, which was perfect—the best training for what was to come. I couldn't follow her anymore, but that was okay. I had a reason to be seen with her now.

It wouldn't be much longer until I could settle old scores. Fulfill my quest in The One Way.

Quiet the noise in my head.

TWENTY-THREE

Leo, Delaney, and Drew stomped over the blackened ground at the Planter ranch toward the body. Leo was holding a bandana to his face. The smoke was even worse today. He and Joe had been part of the discussion to switch to an offensive mode that morning, based on increased fire activity in the foothills overnight threatening the city's water supply. The fire crews were taking advantage of better weather to burn brush and grass—controlled burns to exhaust fuel the wildfire might otherwise use for expansion.

His phone chimed. He pulled it out of his pocket and read a text from Clara. *Phone ringing off the hook about new fire and smoke.*

He sent a quick reply. *Public information officer has a statement ready to go up on social media. Hopefully soon.*

That won't slow the talk down.

He tripped over a rock as he put the phone back in his pocket. She was right. A large part of their community was in deep resistance to obtaining information via Facebook. But it was the most efficient way to disseminate it. The holdouts had to come on board eventually.

Drew said, "Watch your step there, Sheriff. Emergency responders are stretched pretty thin."

Delaney said, "How in the world did you find this body, Drew?"

"Boss man said search the property. It's massive and rough as hell, so I started with structures. Got unlucky on my first one." He pointed at the charred remains of a loafing shed. "We're almost there."

"Forgive me if I'm retreading ground, but Leo and I didn't have a chance to talk. Do you know who it is?"

"Not yet. It's a woman. She's pretty burned up. I didn't recognize her, but I'm not sure I would have. I couldn't find any ID or... anything."

"Does it appear to be connected to the other homicide?"

"If you mean does she have an old sword through her guts, then yes."

Ahead, the silhouette of a body and sword came into view. Leo's stomach churned.

Behind them, he heard shouting. He turned and saw Sugar, Trey, Dr. Watson, and the coroner. Sugar was in a heated discussion with what looked like a reporter and a camera operator. She was pointing emphatically back at the paved road. The reporter—his new buddy Melanie Pritchett—was not following instructions.

Leo was about to go help when Trey stepped between Sugar and the woman. He put his arm around the woman's shoulders and started walking her back to her car.

And she didn't resist.

"I'll catch up with you guys in a second," he said to Delaney and Drew.

Delaney waved him off, seemingly distracted already by the work before them.

Back at the road, Melanie and her cameraman were moving their vehicle out to the paved road. Trey was putting the yellow crime scene tape back in place—it had been lowered for the county personnel to enter. Then he rejoined the others, and the group made their way toward Leo.

"Hello, everyone. Thanks for getting out here so quickly again," he said.

"Anything to help you stop this guy as soon as possible," Dr. Watson said.

Tom Ellis, the coroner, said, "Louise told me how horrific the first murder was. I trust this to her, but I did need to make an appearance." He was a small man, fine-boned, with wire-rimmed glasses and curly gray hair. He looked out of place on the ranch. And in Wyoming. But he was earnest and hardworking, and Leo liked Tom a lot.

"It won't be something you'll ever get out of your brain once you see it," Dr. Watson replied.

Leo put a hand on Trey's shoulder. "Nice work getting rid of the reporter."

"Just call me *trés* persuasive," Trey said.

"She's pretty dogged. How'd you do it?"

"I have a certain *je ne sais quoi* charm."

Leo had honed his one year of high school French backpacking in France for a summer. If he hadn't been familiar with the language, he would never have understood Trey's pronunciation. "Huh. You know French??"

Trey grinned. "Nah. I just learned a few phrases because people used to give me crap about my name. It means *very* in French."

"I know," Sugar said at the same time as Leo. The two of them shared a raised eyebrow look.

They reached the death scene. Delaney and Drew were standing side by side just beyond the ruins of the loafing shed, staring at a small body and a large sword. Everything was blackened. The whole area smelled putrid.

Tom gasped and turned away.

Drew looked up. "I would have planted evidence flags, but, honestly, I couldn't find anything out here but her."

"And you should have worn gloves," Sugar said, pointing at his bare hands. "Your prints are going to be all over anything you touched out here. If you touched anything. Tell me you didn't."

"Uh, yeah, I touched the sword. Sorry. First time at a murder scene. I was a little freaked out and for a second there I thought I should pull it out."

"You owe me a doughnut for every second of time I waste on your prints, rookie."

Leo barely heard their words. His eyes were fixed on the fire-ravaged body of their victim. He'd been expecting worse, but it was bad enough. Most of her clothes had burned off, and the rest had melted into what was left of her. And what was left was unforgettable. Skin split open and mostly blackened. Hair gone. But her body itself was largely intact. Enough so that he felt sure he'd never seen her before. He exhaled, ragged, and fought a sense of lightheadedness. He hadn't realized until that moment how scared he was to see whether this victim was also someone he knew. Someone he'd dated or talked to through an app.

Delaney was shaking her head. "I wish I had a picture of the woman I think is missing to know if this is her."

Trey said, "Is her name Anong? Because that's who this is, and man, do I hate seeing her like this."

"Are you sure her name is Anong?" Delaney said. "I thought this might be Anna Petrov."

Dr. Watson knelt at the woman's side, put a hand on what was left of her wrist, and closed her eyes, lips moving.

Trey was nodding. "This is definitely Anong. She cleans my place. I think her last name is Layla or Layella or something like that. She was really nice. Pretty. Did a damn good job, too."

Delaney muttered, "Then where is Anna?"

"Good job at what?" Sugar said, sounding a little put out.

"House cleaning." Trey gave Sugar a little tone.

Leo raised his brows. He would have expected Trey to be living like a frat boy with beer cans and pizza boxes. "Did she work for you directly or a company?"

"A company. A1 Cleaning or House Cleaners, I think."

Dr. Watson finished her moment of silence with the dead. She leaned over Anong's throat. "It's likely that Anong's cause of death is different from Genevieve's." She shook her head. "Although I shouldn't jump to conclusions."

"What do you see?" Leo said.

"I can't rule out poison, of course, and the fire did too much damage to the torso for me to be definitive about blood splatter, but I can tell you that someone cut this girl's throat with enough force to sever the larynx and—" she tilted the young woman's chin, "to leave marks on the vertebrae in her neck."

"What does that mean?"

"That she was very nearly decapitated. I think the killer was very, very angry with her."

TWENTY-FOUR

After dropping his truck at the station, Delaney drove Leo toward A1 House Cleaners, where they hoped to get information about Anong from her employer. An address and phone number. Known associates. Last time seen. The usual stuff. Sugar, Trey, and Drew stayed at the scene, but the coroner had left when they did.

"What kind of name is A1 anyway?" Delaney took off her sunglasses. They were headed east, and the sun had nearly finished setting behind the mountains anyway.

"I don't love it, but it's making me hungry."

It took her a second, but she laughed. "You got the fancy A1 Sauce growing up in Cali?"

"Boasting the distinctive flavor of every preservative and chemical allowed by the Food and Drug Administration and available on your neighborhood grocery shelf. Didn't you have it here?"

"My grandmother didn't believe in store bought. Salt, pepper, and butter. That was all she used."

"I suspect it was not only healthier but tasted better."

She smiled. To her thinking, there was no better beef in the world than in Wyoming, and she'd never eaten any tastier than the cattle raised and butchered by hand on their own place in Kearny. It almost made her want to graze a few steers, except that the last thing she needed was more work and stress. "I didn't realize it then, but yes, it was the best." She still shopped direct from ranchers at the weekly farmers' market when she could.

Leo had his tablet in his lap and was typing as he talked. "I've updated Genevieve's investigation plan and started one for Anong. Did you see anything in Genevieve's apartment that suggested how she made money?"

"No. But Shirleen believed she was being trafficked along with her friend Anna. And Joaquim the apartment manager thought all the girls in the building worked for Albert Tuttle." She told him about the cameras, the scared apartment manager and neighbor, and the angry, threatening appearance of said Albert Tuttle. "I tried to arrest him, but he declined the opportunity." She gave a few details, downplaying the danger to herself in the incident.

"That escalates things. Let me get the word out to bring him in ASAP." Leo's face was ashen as he typed on his tablet. "He could have killed you. We should have gone together."

"You're going to bang that old drum again?"

"I'm serious."

"So am I. I'm a law enforcement officer. It's a high-risk job. But I don't want to die. I won't try again without backup."

Leo reached for her hand and squeezed it. Sparks shot up her arm. "You are showing some growth."

She tried to force herself to remove her hand, but it seemed to have a mind of its own and stayed tucked into Leo's on the seat. "Thank you." Her voice sounded funny. She cleared her throat. "I think we're here." She needed the hand to turn the steering wheel and tugged it gently.

He gave it one last squeeze. She looked at him. He smiled. She shook her head and smiled back, then claimed her hand and turned into the driveway of a newish home sided with gray hardi-plank. *What did I just let happen there?*

She parked and turned off the engine. "Leo, this can't..."

He was still smiling. "Let's just go inside and do our job, partner."

She didn't have a comeback for that. His touch and her response had her flummoxed. She took a deep breath. *You're on the job. One that is inherently dangerous. Bring all of you to it at all times so you can bring all of you home.*

They met at the front of the truck. Delaney avoided eye contact and walked three feet away from him. Her body was hyperaware of his, his simple presence tickling her skin.

At the door, he knocked and rang the bell. "A1 appears to operate from a private home."

She licked her lips. "Cheaper than a store front. Besides who needs to shop at their local house cleaning company?"

"Still, I would have expected a little sign in the window. Or something on the mailbox." He nodded at the metal container to the side of the door.

The door swung open, but no one was standing in front of it. The smell of cleaning supplies wafted out, lemon fresh.

"Hello?" Leo said. "Is anyone here? We've come to talk to someone with A1 House Cleaning."

Suddenly, Delaney's instincts kicked in. "Down," she screamed, and flung herself at Leo, knocking him to the side, just as a shotgun blast reverberated from inside the house, peppering the ground behind where they'd been standing.

Delaney rolled to the side of the door and came up on her knees with her Staccato raised. Something was stinging her arm. Leo was on his belly beside her, also in a firing position.

"Come out with your hands up," Leo shouted. "Sheriff's department."

A man laughed. "Scared of a little rock salt?"

The stinging. She'd been hit with rock salt. White hot rage blurred her vision, mixed with embarrassment and frustration. Who shot at people who came to their door? She should have been more focused. If it had been real ammunition, they could have been killed.

Leo was very calm. "You just assaulted two law enforcement officers. You can come out the easy way or the hard way."

Delaney muttered. "And it would be his third assault of an officer in as many days."

"What?" Leo whispered back.

"I know that voice. That's Albert Tuttle in there."

"The guy who attacked Drew?"

"And threatened me. The one Shirleen says traffics women. Humans of other varieties for all I know."

"You're sure?"

"One hundred percent."

Several more shots were fired in rapid succession. "That's not a shotgun."

"Then it's not rock salt."

"Cover me while I call it in."

"Got it."

He pulled out his phone and pushed a number. "Clara, this is Leo. Delaney and I are outside a business called A1 Home Cleaners. It's located in a home. A suspect inside fired on us. His name is Albert Tuttle. We need backup immediately." He gave the address. "Thanks."

Delaney heard a noise in the back of the house. "That sounds like a door slamming."

Leo cocked his head, listening or a few seconds. "A vehicle engine?"

"Yes."

"The son of a bitch made a run for it."

"Let's go!"

They ran for the truck. But it wasn't going anywhere with two flat tires.

The girl woke in a strange bed in a strange place, confused and groggy. She'd been staying with extended family so that no one who knew her or her parents would find out about her condition. An aunt and uncle, much older than her mother. Strangers to her with a ranch east of Sheridan, to the west of her own family's place. It was rugged and remote—they didn't leave it often, and visitors were even more rare.

Every time one pulled up the drive, though, her heart would slam wildly in her throat. *Please don't be Daddy or Uncle Rick.* Her father had given her the worst whupping of her life after her mother had told him she was pregnant and how it had happened. They'd locked her in her room for days, refusing to give her anything to eat until she told them what boy she'd "ruined herself" for. When she'd remained steadfast to the truth, they'd loaded her in the car with a ham sandwich and small bag of her things and brought her to this desolate, dusty ranch.

She missed her mother, although she wasn't sure why.

The useful land wasn't that big by Wyoming ranch standards. Enough for fifty head in a cow-calf operation with space for her aunt's huge garden and chickens. The rest they left wild to the mule deer and coyotes, the occasional herd of elk, the rare sightings of bear and mountain lion. They ran it alone.

"The kids used to help," Aunt Sissy had explained without a hint of emotion in her voice. Cousins the girl had never met. "The truth is, they caused more work than they did. Life is easier without them to take care of." She was a hard woman. Bone, muscle, and grit. Tall as a man, too. "We don't want no more of that with you here. You'll pull your own weight until you leave."

"Yes, ma'am," she'd said.

"Honest labor is good for you, no matter your condition."

Her Uncle Dean had grunted. She could count on one hand the number of times she'd heard him speak in her presence, none of them to her.

So, the girl had carried on doing the things she'd done back home. Laundry by hand, scrubbing floors with pine cleaner and a brush, and cooking meals. Changing linens and carrying out the first spring cleaning the house had seen in years. Pulling weeds, hoeing, picking vegetables, feeding chickens and gathering eggs past when her belly allowed her to lean over, when she'd started squatting. Each time she did, the pressure was intense. Something was going to pop.

Surely the baby was coming soon? She was enormous. She'd heard her aunt tell her uncle that she suspected a whole litter of babies was crammed into that belly.

When she'd been there several months—it was hard to keep track of the days, but the weather had grown sharp—she picked up the newspaper on the kitchen table. Reading it once a week was her only connection to the outside world. She opened and folded it to display an article. KEARNY MAN DIES IN UTAH HOUSE FIRE. She gasped when she saw the picture. Him. Uncle Rick. "There are no suspects, although the evidence clearly showed gasoline and a pile of rags had been used to start a fire on the porch near where he was sleeping."

She slept soundly that night for the first time since the day he'd cornered her in Bip's stall. God had answered her prayers, as awful as they were.

One morning awful cramps woke her. She was cold and wet. She called for her aunt.

Sissy had taken one look at the sheets and pointed at the door. "First babies come slow. Wash the sheet and mattress you soiled first."

Somehow, despite blinding bouts of pain, the girl had managed, including propping the mattress on the sun porch to dry, and hanging the sheets on the line, before she'd collapsed in the yard.

The next thing she remembered, she was waking in her bed with light shining through the tied-back chintz curtains.

"You're awake," a woman said.

"Where am I? What happened?" She put her hand on her stomach. It was smaller. Softer. "Where's my baby?"

"You're safe. I'm the midwife. Your family will come for you soon."

"My family?"

"Your mother and father."

"Is my baby okay?"

"Everything was fine."

"When can I see my baby? Is it a boy or a girl?"

"The new family has already come and gone. It's for the best."

"New family? No!" The only thing that had kept her going all these months was the thought of holding her baby in her arms. Loving it. Protecting it. Being a better mother than hers had been to her. She'd dreamed of how the baby would love her back. It would be the two of them against the world. "I don't want to give up my baby."

"The papers were in order. It's too late."

"No!" She jerked her arm, intent on getting out of bed. Something tugged at her wrist. She gasped when she saw the restraints. "Why am I tied up?"

"It's for the best. New mothers can get emotional." The midwife moved closer. "Do I need to give you something to make you sleep or will you calm down?"

The girl was sobbing now. She'd never seen the child. Never held it. Hadn't had the chance to tell the baby how much she loved it, no matter what had been done to her to bring about its birth.

The midwife clucked and shook her head. "You'd best pull yourself together before your parents arrive. I'll leave you to it."

But the girl barely heard her, lost in a world with nothing but the sound of her own keening voice and the cries of a red-faced infant flailing tiny fists in the air.

After putting out an all-points bulletin on Tuttle, Delaney and Leo and their backup checked and secured the A1 house. So far, Tuttle was nowhere to be found. Back at the station, Leo left without saying where he was going. Delaney ate a Taco Bell burrito at her desk while she worked. And it was productive time. So productive that after an hour had passed without Leo's return, she called him.

"What's taking you so long?" she said by way of greeting. She sniffed. Did the entire department smell like taco meat now or just her area from the bag in her trash.

His pause let her know he didn't want to talk about it.

"Forget I asked."

"No. You should know." He sighed. "My former handler at the Drug Enforcement Agency thinks the cartel figured out I was undercover. She doesn't think they have my real identity, but I've been taking precautions, like hiring someone to keep an eye on Freddy and Adriana. Freddy thinks he's being followed. My security guy couldn't produce the pictures and log he'd been promising to keep. So, I followed Freddy some today. Just to see if I could spot a tail."

"Leo! I'm so sorry."

"It's all good. He was clean. But I have to replace the security."

"What about Skeeter?"

"He's hard to book. And I was doing this on the down low. Freddy would recognize Skeeter."

"Do you think that's wise—keeping it a secret?"

"I didn't want to freak Adriana out."

"This may be a lesser-of-two-evils situation."

"Yeah. I'll think about it. But that's not why you called."

For a moment her mind went blank. Then she rallied. "Just an update. I had a hunch on where Anong lived. And what Genevieve's real job was."

"Yeah?"

"Anong lived at the Riverside apartments, too. A team went into her place and secured it pending a warrant. Also, you'll be shocked to learn A1 is owned by Alfred Q. Tuttle."

"Floored."

"So, if Anong worked for A1 which was owned by Tuttle and lived in Riverside..."

"Then Genevieve was probably doing the same thing as Anong."

"Exactly."

"Anything else?"

"The warrant came in on Genevieve's house, I put more heat into the arrest warrant for Tuttle, and I sent a request in for a search warrant on A1."

"All good."

"I'm no slacker. And I want to hit interviews hard this afternoon. Lucas Planter. Jake Hemmler. Mika, another of the women who lived in the building with Genevieve and Anong. And I've had a thought. Or maybe just the sight of half our town wandering the streets dressed like knights and tavern wenches for the Renaissance Festival has pushed me to it."

"What's that?"

"I want to go out to the festival grounds and poke around. Flash some pictures. Maybe we can find someone who knows about replica swords."

"It's not a terrible idea."

"Stop with the overwhelming praise. It's going to my head. A few more things. Clara said that Joe asked her to tell you that the containment didn't hold on the fire because the winds picked up. Meeting this afternoon with—and I quote—everyone."

"Shit."

"Yeah. She said check your email for the time."

"Okay. I'm on my way back. Don't go on these interviews without me."

"I won't."

"I'm serious."

"Last but not least, Carrie has informed me that none of her friends believe we're not having a torrid affair. My words. You don't want to hear what she said. Apparently, we're the talk of the town. Watch your back. You're going to get more questions."

"I'm ready. Which reminds me. I really liked holding your hand yesterday."

Heat rushed Delaney's face. Her pulse shot up. Clara approached. *I can't have a conversation about that in front of her.* Delaney made static noises into the phone. "Call's breaking up."

"That trick doesn't work with me."

"Gotta run." She ended the call. "Hey, Clara."

Clara said, "You've been quite sought after. Someone named Shirleen called for you."

Delaney smiled. "She's that new social worker."

Clara shrugged. "Haven't met her. Also, your friend Skeeter came by. I told him you were on the phone with the sheriff. He wants you to call him."

Delaney looked at her cell phone call log. She had three missed calls from him, but none from Shirleen. She checked texts. Two *Call me* messages from Skeeter. "Did he say what it was about?" If it was about the girls, he would have told Clara, or he would have said so in his texts.

"No."

"If you had to guess?"

"He was excited. Happy."

"Huh. Okay, well, that's good. Thanks."

Clara didn't leave. "Also, I wanted to see if you're okay with me entering Kat in a few end-of-season barrel races. It will all be young people, learning and having fun."

"She's ready?"

"She had a real breakthrough this week. I think she is."

"She's in love with that horse Sunshine."

Clara smiled. "Ornery old girl but fast as the dickens and can run the pattern in her sleep."

"Ornery. Sounds like Kat has found a soulmate."

"She has. Well, I'm off for the afternoon, then."

"Have fun." Delaney felt a flicker of envy. Clara and Kat would be together at the festival. But she gave herself a mental finger wag. Kat would be with a responsible adult while Delaney worked on catching a dangerous killer during her normal work hours. There would be other festivals.

Skeeter picked up on the first ring when she called a minute later. "Good news for ya."

"Thank goodness. You've never dropped by before. I was worried."

"I found a group of wackos that had a religious road show in the area right before your mother went missing."

Delaney's leg tingled where the chain of her mother's anklet was touching it. She didn't often wear it with her tactical boots —not because it clashed but because she'd lost it once in a battle with a suspect and didn't ever want to risk that again—but something had made her slip it on today. That, and paint her toenails fire engine red. "Okay. Do they have a name?"

"They did. They're out of business now. Kaput. Dead. De-funked."

Delaney smiled at his malapropism. She almost told him the word he was looking for was defunct. "Name, please."

"The Rocky Rollers. Their tagline was 'holy rolling through the Rockies.'"

"Wow. Where does that leave you?"

"Tracking down people that were in the cult, I guess. After I finish my Calamity Jane."

Skeeter's favorite breakfast was the cinnamon roll French toast at the Golden Spur, an always packed greasy diner open only for breakfast and lunch, beloved by locals, but recently discovered by hipsters who were hyping it up on social media, much to the chagrin of the owner and wait staff. "Thanks for the update."

"I'm taking food back to the girls. Then we'll meet Clara at the festival."

A second adult at the festival. It just kept getting better. "Sounds fun. Thanks, Skeeter."

She heard Leo's voice down the hall, loud talking on his cell phone, and her cheeks warmed. He had liked holding her hand the day before. She'd liked it, too.

He came straight to her cubicle, ending his call at the last moment. "Big Horn County law enforcement called. They have Tuttle in their sights and are in hot pursuit."

TWENTY-SEVEN

Jake Hemmler eyed Delaney and Leo warily. "What would I have to tell you that you couldn't see for yourself?" The trucker was hunched over a 40-gallon water tank on the back of an off-road vehicle, filling it. His eyes were hollowed and cheeks gaunt from lack of rest.

Delaney worried about him and the others. Mistakes happened when exhaustion set in. Mistakes around fire could be deadly. Not only had he been helping with relief deliveries, but he was also fire fighting alongside volunteers as part of a crew gaining a reputation as the Hillbilly Hot Shots. They weren't trained fire fighters. They were land and homeowners concerned for themselves and their neighbors. They knew their terrain, the water sources, and the roads better than the out-of-town help. The federal emergency response organizations didn't love them, but they'd been credited as key to saving several structures so far.

"What made you go in the house at all?" she asked. She and Leo had agreed she'd lead the interviews because of her relationship with Jake and Lucas, unless it seemed to be going poorly. Leo deferred to her most of the time when they interviewed together. On rare occasions he led, but only when it was obvious that Delaney had put a witness's back up. Leo said she was better at interviews than him. Who was she to argue with the truth?

"What do you mean?"

"We were there to offload supplies onto smaller delivery vehicles. You were transporting the heavy equipment we were using. Something must have made you go into the house instead of unloading your trailer."

"Oh. Yeah. Well, I'd never seen the inside of it. It's been around in one form or another as long as I've been alive. It was a split-second decision."

Leo had been standing a few steps away next to a weathered red barn. He moved closer. "How did you see the body? Did you have a flashlight?"

"Just my phone. I nearly stepped on her."

Delaney had marked footprints at the scene. "Could we make a cast of the shoes you were wearing? We need to establish which footprints were yours."

"Yeah. I had on the boots I wear any time I drive my rig. My wife is up at the house. She knows which ones and can get them for you."

"Thanks. Did you touch anything?"

"I don't think so."

"Could you share fingerprints with us if it becomes necessary?"

Water shot out of the mouth of the tank. Jake stalked to the spigot and turned off the faucet. "Sure. But it's got to wait. People are counting on me." He walked to the end of a hose and began rolling it.

"Understood. What about things you were carrying—did you drop anything inside or outside?"

"I'm not sure. I don't think so."

"You're not missing anything?"

Jake dropped his rolled hose on the ground beside the faucet. "Is this going somewhere? If so, give me a clue so we can shortcut this."

Delaney decided to take that as a no about the crucifix. She handed him a card. Leo did, too.

Leo said, "Thanks for talking to us. And for letting us take your shoes. Someone will get them back to you in a few days. Please contact us if anything else happens or you think of something helpful. And thank you for everything you're doing for our community."

"Be safe out there," Delaney added.

Jake's shoulders dropped a visible inch. "It was awful, you know. Worst thing I ever seen or imagined. And you found another one out there, I heard."

"Yes."

"Jesus." He pulled gloves from his rear pocket and slapped them against his thigh. "Maybe the fire will get 'im. Seems like sending him to hell in an inferno on earth would be the right end for a sick bastard like him."

Delaney wouldn't argue with that.

Leo resettled his ball cap. "One more question. Has anyone approached you to tell your story of discovering the body in a way that you found odd or unusual?"

"Everybody wants to hear about it. I mean, come on."

"Sure. But there's wanting to know, and then there's creepy. Sometimes a killer revisits their own scene or goes to funerals of their victims or tries to get thrills by other close access to the people impacted by their crimes. Like you."

Jake made a face, but then it turned thoughtful. "The reporters are pushy and ask questions that are offensive, even to a crusty fart like me. But the one that was a little weird, frankly, was Lucas Planter."

Delaney said, "Weird in what way?"

"To know how much blood there was. What it smelled like. Whether it looked like she'd been tortured. How it made me *feel*." He stared into the distance, shaking his head. "Not the kind of things a normal person thinks about, if you ask me."

TWENTY-EIGHT

Lucas Planter was scowling at Delaney and Leo, standing outside the home improvement store where he was a manager in the construction supplies area. The yellow rig he'd been driving for the relief efforts belonged to the store, who had also made a generous donation. "I've only got ten minutes until a staff meeting. And this will use up all my break time."

But he didn't refuse to talk to them. With Jake's words still lingering in her mind, Delaney thought about Lucas. She hadn't loved working with him. His overt misogyny was something she was used to. It wasn't that. It was more that every interaction with him was awkward. His comments, odd. His eye contact, off putting. He liked to pose non sequitur questions, inappropriate for the situation. But if she'd been asked a week ago whether he was a serial killer, she would have said he was most likely not. Detectives never rule anything out, but he wouldn't have been high on her watch list.

Maybe he should be.

Leo settled his weight against a short concrete post and nodded at her.

"We'll make it fast then. Tell me the last time you'd visited your grandfather's ranch before the relief convoy."

"The day before, to make sure there were no more hot spots." He pulled a pack of Marlboros from his pocket. Delaney felt like she saw fewer people smoking in Kearny than when she'd lived there a decade ago, and of those that did, a higher percentage were sucking on e-cigs. But for men who lit up, it was Marlboros two to one. She couldn't stand the smell.

"Did you see anything out of the ordinary?"

He shook out a cigarette. "Like what?"

"People. Vehicles. Dead bodies. Things that shouldn't have been there."

He snorted. The red and white pack made crinkle noises as he stuffed it into his breast pocket. "Nothing like that. But then I didn't go in the house."

"Where on the property did you go?"

He put the cigarette between his lips, where it bounced as he talked. "Just the area where we all parked. I used binoculars to look for smoke." He retrieved a lighter from his pants pocket and flicked it several times before he got a flame. Then he cupped his hand and lit his cigarette.

"You didn't go to the shed?"

His eyes glimmered. He made a pull on his cigarette and held it in his lungs. "Where you found the second one," he said through his exhalation. The lighter went back in his pocket.

"Yes."

"No, I didn't."

"Had you visited the property recently before it burned?"

"Yes. I was the caretaker." He blew smoke in her direction. She hated the smell, but she didn't flinch. "I was out there about once a week."

"Do you ever find anyone trespassing out there?"

"Oh, I run off poachers a coupla times a year. Kids drinking beer or making out."

The smoke was making her nauseous. She moved upwind of him in the guise of stretching her legs. "Does your grandfather ever go out there anymore?"

"Nope. He doesn't leave the nursing home."

"Does anyone else work out there?"

"Not a soul."

Delaney didn't like the glint in his eye, like he was amused to be giving as little information as possible, trying to wear her down by making her ask a lot of questions. *He won't.* "Do people visit with your permission? Or your grandfather's?"

"My grandfather was pretty disagreeable. But I let my brother use it for hunting. And I hunt out there, too."

"And you haven't seen anything unusual or odd when you're hunting?"

"How many ways you gonna ask me that question? No. If I had, I would have done something about it. It's a big ranch with a lot of game. Nothing odd about that."

"How often is your brother out there?"

"Once or twice a year in hunting season."

"Had he been out there yet this year?"

"Not so far as I know."

Delaney made a mental note to follow up on the brother before they finished talking to Lucas, but she didn't see any tie between hunting for animals and poisoning people and skewering them to the ground with medieval swords. Hunting was a normal Wyoming activity. "Leo, any questions?"

He stood from the post and nodded at Planter. "Sure am sorry the place lost all its grazing land."

"For now. It'll come back stronger," Lucas said around his cigarette.

"Who will own it when your grandfather passes?"

"His will says me. My parents don't want it. He's leaving them his house and my brother some other junk."

It wasn't much as far as new information went, but Delaney

filed it away. "You planning on running cattle or building out here?"

"No. I'm planning on selling it to the first person who coughs up enough cash."

She nodded, pausing to let the last question and answer fade, then changing up her approach. "It's been crazy in town. Are you heading out to the Renaissance Festival?"

He scowled then spit some tobacco residue on the ground. "And watch a bunch of fag—um, fairies parade around in costumes? I couldn't think of much worse." *Maybe Lucas is an equal opportunity bigot and not just a misogynist.* "My brother will be there, though. That's for sure."

She remained quiet. Lucas had volunteered the last comment, and she didn't want to startle him off it if he had more to say.

When he didn't fill the silence after nearly ten seconds, she kept her voice nonchalant. "Is he into that kind of thing?"

"Yeah. Gaming. Fantasy." Lucas turned to watch a young woman push a metal sled to her truck loaded with cement bags. His beady eyes seemed to be focused on her tush. "And he wonders why our grandfather liked me better."

"He's the younger brother, I'll bet," Leo said.

Lucas made a gun of his finger and thumb and shot it at Leo. "Bullseye. My mother babied him."

"Planter," a woman yelled from the door to the store. "Are you going to come run your own damn meeting or stay out here jawing all day?" Then she seemed to notice Delaney and Leo. "Oh, sorry. I didn't—um. What do you want me to tell people?"

Lucas glowered. "Don't tell 'em shit. I'll be inside in one minute."

Delaney smiled. "Anything else you can think of that might help us in the investigation?"

"Nah." He walked a few feet to a concrete ashtray beside a

trash can. He stubbed out his smoke and threw it on the ground beside the receptacle.

"Hey, do you mind giving us your brother's name and number?"

His glower turned to a murderous glare. "Yeah, I sure as hell do."

She held out her card. Leo offered his, too.

He took hers and tore it into bits, did the same thing with Leo's, then walked into the store, whistling.

TWENTY-NINE

The drive to the Riverside apartments was short but gave Leo just enough time to pull up information on Larry Planter, younger brother of Lucas and a resident of Sheridan, while Delaney drove. A few email notifications caught his attention, too. Their warrants had been granted to search Genevieve's and Anong's apartments. He forwarded them to the apartment manager.

Five minutes later, an unhappy Joaquim Smith threw open Gennie's and Anong's doors for Delaney and Leo.

"Have you seen Anna?" Delaney asked as she put on a pair of gloves.

Joaquim was casting furtive glances at the cameras again and easing away. "Why would I have?"

"Mr. Tuttle is not in town." Delaney pointed at the camera. "Last seen across the mountains to the west." Unfortunately, Tuttle had eluded the cops in Big Horn County and was still at large.

He licked his lips. "That don't mean nothing."

"What do you mean?"

"You think he ain't got people?" He turned his back on the cameras.

"Who are they?" Leo asked.

"Different guys. One woman. I don't have names. They don't talk to me, and I don't even look at them."

"If you're so scared of them, why do you rent to them?" Leo asked.

"He showed up here and rented this whole building six months ago. The crappiest, smallest, cheapest units. He said he had work crews. How was I to know he was bad news?"

"Have you seen Anna?"

He sighed. "I hope she got somewhere far, far away. She was a nice girl. Now, I have to go. Rents are due today. I have to be in the office." He hurried down the steps.

Leo jerked his finger at Genevieve's door. "How about I take this one since you've already been through it?"

"Fine by me."

He went inside then popped right back out. "Didn't you say she was a neat freak?"

"Yes."

"Take a look."

Delaney poked her head in, then sucked in a sharp breath. It was like a bomb had gone off in the apartment. The couch and chairs were slit, and stuffing was strewn all over the room. She walked in. A quick check revealed every item from the cabinets and drawers on the floor. And of those, most were destroyed.

"Someone was very thorough," she said.

"And very angry?" Leo asked.

"Maybe. Except that *everything* is trashed. Don't angry people usually target things that remind them specifically of a person or what they did? But bending silverware? Dumping out salt? Ripping towels? It's more like a person *pretending* to be angry."

"Sending a message?"

"That's what I'm thinking."

"But what's the message?"

She narrowed her eyes. "Maybe it's a message of terror. Like taking credit for what happened to Gennie and saying this could happen to the other girls."

"You're thinking Tuttle."

"I'm thinking I want a warrant on his video. Although, if it was him that did this—or had it done—he would have turned the camera off first."

"I hear you. But, alternate theory. What if this is the killer trying to erase connections between the victims?"

"Again, I want that camera footage."

"I'll get Drew working on a warrant for them." He stopped to type on his phone.

"Have him look for Anong on the dating sites, too. And Anna Petrov."

Leo nodded and kept typing.

"I think I should search here with you after all, since the scene is so different."

He pocketed his phone. "Agreed."

The two of them spent half an hour combing through what was left of Gennie's life. It was depressing. It was tedious. It yielded nothing new.

"If she had secrets, she kept them well." Leo was putting trash back in a garbage can after sifting through it.

"I'm bothered there was no laptop or phone."

"Not when you were here the first time either?"

"Nope."

"But you said Anna had a tablet?"

"Yes."

They shut Genevieve's place and entered Anong's apartment. Delaney catalogued quick impressions. Spartan. Not overly clean but sanitary. Most notably, it was still intact.

Leo turned in a circle, hands on his hips, surveying the living room. "Why didn't whoever tossed Genevieve's do hers, too? Either of our theories would anticipate that. Tuttle sending a message if he thought they'd run off, or the killer erasing something about the victims that might identify him."

Delaney opened the refrigerator. "She cooked." She pulled out bok choy and bean sprouts. "Asian food."

Leo said, "Her name sounds Thai to me. And she definitely looks Asian in her pictures."

"I wonder why Tuttle wasn't afraid women from around the world would stand out in a small Wyoming town? We're not renowned as a melting pot." She replaced the vegetables and started a search of the cabinets. She shook a coffee can. It didn't feel like coffee. She peeled off the lid and tilted it. Coffee shifted off a plastic baggie of money. "I think she was planning to run away."

Leo said, "Do you mind if I look?"

"Be my guest."

He pulled the baggie out of the can and turned it over a few times. "There's a card in here." After separating the zip-lock sides of the bag, he eased the cash onto the cabinet and plucked the card from the stack.

STANLEY ARNOLD, LICENSED REAL ESTATE BROKER, it read. Below the name was a phone number and address in Bismarck.

"Was she buying a house?" Delaney pointed at the card.

"Maybe an old boyfriend?" Leo took a photo with his phone. "Someone she met on a dating app who she believed would save her?"

"It seems like I heard Tuttle came here from North Dakota."

"I'm sending a picture of it to Drew." After emailing the photo, Leo put the card and money away then bagged and tagged them. "I don't know how Albert and these women weren't on our radar."

"It would have been more likely they'd be on Chief Yellowtail's." While Wyoming statute allowed for overlap and required cooperation between the different branches of law enforcement in the state, the sheriff's department normally handled cases that arose outside city limits within the county, and the municipal cops handled the cases arising inside them. Anong and Gennie had been found dead outside any town proper, but the apartments fell inside Kearny. "And they hadn't been here long, according to Joaquim Smith."

"True."

Since the kitchen had been Anong's hiding place once, Delaney slowed down for a more thorough search. She hit pay dirt in a cannister of rice. "I've got another baggie."

Leo returned from his search of the bathroom. "What's in it?"

She dangled it. Inside was a tiny pair of socks with pink ruffles. "Baby booties."

"I haven't seen anything to suggest there'd been a child here, have you?"

"Nope. But Genevieve most likely had borne a child. Maybe Anong did, too."

"Feels important."

"Yep." She photographed, bagged, and tagged it.

Fifteen minutes more of careful searching was fruitless.

Delaney shut the cabinet doors in the kitchen. "One thing that jumps out at me about all three of the apartments I've been in is that there's really nothing personal in them."

"You said Anna had a photo on her tablet."

"Yeah. Of a little boy. But it could have been a stock photo. Something that came with the screensaver app."

"That's depressing. Anything else you want to do here?"

"Let's try to talk to the girl across the hall."

He shut the door behind them. "I'll follow your lead."

Delaney knocked on the door across the mezzanine. When there was no answer, she raised her voice and said, "Mika—are you in there?"

"It doesn't seem like she's home."

She frowned, then pounded on the door. "I don't like it. She'd be the fourth girl on this floor of a single apartment building to go missing. I've got to get inside."

"I'm going back to the truck. I need to be able to plead ignorance of whatever you do next. But if it's going to take long, I need a ride back to the station first. I have a command performance meeting about the fires."

A whisper interrupted them. "Follow me." Joaquim had appeared out of nowhere. He motioned for them to follow and led them down the stairs and to a patch of grass beside the buildings. "Mika's gone."

"How do you know?" Delaney said.

Joaquim was twisting his hands one inside the other, over and over. "Two of them are dead. Anna hasn't come home. Mika is just a kid. I had to do something. So, I delivered a flier about a power outage. I wrote a note to come to the office for a package. She showed up, and I handed her a box with two hundred bucks and another note in it telling her if she wanted to leave I could help her."

Delaney's eyes felt prickly. It was a surprisingly kind and generous thing for him to do. "And then what?"

"She started crying. Said she couldn't go back to her apartment. I took her to the bus station. She left with nothing."

"Where did she go?" Leo asked.

"She said she was going back home."

"Do you know where that is?"

Joaquim shook his head.

"Did she have a phone with her?"

"Yeah, I gave her mine. I got a new one." He recited a number.

"Thank you. Was she, um, a special friend of yours?"

"I barely knew her. Or any of them. It wasn't in my best interest, ya know? But she reminded me of my little sister." A solitary tear made its unsteady way down his cheekbone. His voice grew hoarse. "Becca died of an overdose the year after she graduated from high school."

"I'm so sorry," Delaney said. She gave him a few seconds, then added. "You know about the swords, from the news?"

He rolled his lips inward and nodded. "It's horrible."

"Were any of these women or anyone you saw in their lives into fantasy, costumes, gaming, or the Middle Ages?"

He lifted up his hands and dropped them. "I don't know. The only thing I can think of is that festival in town."

"Did they have any trouble with people in the complex?" Leo asked.

Joaquim shook his head. "If they did, they never told me."

"I'll need to send someone around to talk to residents."

"I wish you wouldn't, but I understand. These girls. They matter." Another tear rolled down his cheek. This one he brushed away brusquely. "I have to get back to the office."

"We'll be in touch."

Joaquim hurried away. Delaney took a step back toward the staircase, feeling a crunching underfoot that was unlike grass. She stopped. Lifted her boot to reveal something black. Broken. Small. She picked it up, then looked above them at a window. She thought about the layout of the units. It had to be Anna's. Leo was watching her, head cocked.

She held out her hand. A phone. No SIM card. By the looks of it, it had been crushed deliberately.

THIRTY

Leo just had enough time before the fire briefing to stop in his office with Delaney for a few calls. The first was a return to Dr. Watson.

"Hello, Sheriff. Would you like to come in to go over my findings on Anong Leela?" she said.

Leo sat on his credenza and held the phone flat in his hand facing up. "I wish I could. Can you give it to Delaney and me over the phone for now? I've got you on speaker."

"Sure. Hello, Delaney, dear."

Delaney smiled. She was standing close to the microphone, which made her close to Leo. It was creating a current in the air that he liked. "Hi, Louise. What did you find out for us?"

"As you know, Anong's body was damaged severely by the fire."

Leo had seen that, of course. "Could you tell whether her fingerprints had been burned off deliberately?"

"Yes. I believe they were."

Someone tried to hide her identity, like with Genevieve. Luckily, Trey had known who she was. "Did she die before the fire?"

"Yes. Like Genevieve, she died before the staging. She'd been dead longer, though."

"How much?"

"Another twenty-four hours. But unlike Gennie, she died of blood loss. The wound to her throat. Someone slashed it."

Delaney and Leo shared a pained look. He'd known it, but hearing about someone's suffering was still hard.

"She also had a significant closed head wound. It didn't kill her, but it might have given enough time."

Leo pulled at his bottom lip. "Could you tell what caused it?"

"My best guess is a fall. The fire destroyed a lot of clues, though."

"Was there poison in her system?"

"I've sent off for lab tests."

Delaney frowned at Leo. "You're thinking they tried to kill her with the poison but she resisted and things got messy?"

"Yeah. Maybe she tried to get away." He touched his head. "And he caught her." He touched his throat.

She nodded. "It's a reasonable theory."

"We really need that video from outside their apartments."

"Tell me about it."

A voice from the door said, "I promise I wasn't eavesdropping, but I'm here about the warrant for the video and I just heard you mention it."

Leo looked up to see Drew. "We're on with Dr. Watson."

"Sorry to interrupt."

"What is it?"

"The judge granted the warrant on the video."

"That's great. They're tricky to enforce. Can you go straight to the county attorney's office with this? They'll want to help."

"I'm on it." Drew saluted and walked away quickly.

Leo said, "Sorry, Dr. Watson. Anything else we should know?"

Dr. Watson said. "No problem. There is another thing. I wouldn't be surprised if Anong had borne a child, too."

"We found baby booties hidden in her apartment," Delaney said. "These women were trafficked."

"Then I'd guess it wouldn't be hard for them to become pregnant."

Delaney shook her head. "Wouldn't the trafficker make them take precautions against pregnancy? I would think pregnancy would be bad for business." Then she sighed. "But what do I know. Maybe it's not."

Leo had a hollow feeling in his stomach along with an idea he didn't like. "What if he could make more money by selling the babies than he did by running the women?"

"That's a sick thought."

"I don't envy you two working this case. I'll let you know what I get back on the tests," Dr. Watson said.

"Thank you so much." Leo ended the call.

"Ugh." Delaney sat down heavily in the chair in front of his desk.

Leo moved to his chair and slumped into it, too. The more information they uncovered on the murders, the less coherent his thoughts were on the cases. Two dead women, staged in hideous manners that made no sense in the wild west of Kearny, Wyoming. Maybe not anywhere. Causes of death different, but modus operandi similar. Poison, burned fingerprints. Two more women missing—although one was potentially fine and on her way out of town, if Joaquim's story checked out. All neighbors. All being trafficked.

He opened the investigation plans and began typing. "Let's talk about our links. Genevieve was from Haiti. Anong from Thailand. Where was Anna Petrov from?"

Delaney tapped her nose twice with her pointer finger. "I didn't meet her. I can find out from Joaquim. I'll ask him about whether Genevieve and Anong had out-of-country accents, too."

"It may be nothing."

"No, this is good. More links—they worked together. They lived next door to each other."

"Two of them had borne children."

"They were young. Attractive."

"I would assume all of them were poor. Now and growing up."

"I'm going to check with Shirleen and see if she knew anything about a history of abuse. It's likely, given their circumstances. I owe Shirleen a call anyway."

He chewed the inside of his lip. "I'm opening a plan for Anna as a missing person. Even though no one has reported her as one yet."

"Good idea. Don't forget the busted phone outside her window."

Leo's fingers flew rat-a-tat-tat on the keys. "Got it. Who are the people they knew in common?"

"Albert and his henchmen. Each other. Joaquim, the apartment manager. I'll find out if Shirleen knew Anong."

"We should find out if Trey knew the others, too."

Delaney's face registered surprise, then she nodded. "You're right. We can't be wearing blinders when it comes to our own people."

A lesson they'd learned the hard way with Deputy Tommy Miller earlier that year. "How about things that differentiated them?"

"Skin color. Country of origin. Genevieve had two tickets to the festival. Maybe she was going with Anong or Anna. Oh! And we only found one crucifix."

"Good." He caught up with her ideas, then said, "Let's brainstorm more directly on possible suspects." He opened the suspects part of his investigation plan for Genevieve and sat with fingers poised.

"Tuttle, in some form or fashion. Someone they met through work."

"Cleaning?"

"Sure. Á la Trey. Or... I'd assume he had them working in other ways."

"Johns. Yes. Or a jealous partner of a john."

Delaney was ticking ideas on fingers now, talking fast. "Someone one of them met through a dating site. A jealous boyfriend. Through competitors of Tuttle's trying to hurt his business. Someone where they lived."

"Yeah. Joaquim's not out of the question."

"If they both had kids who didn't live with them—revisiting that baby-selling theory—what if it was someone they met through that or that wanted a baby and didn't get one?"

Leo closed his eyes, a cold dread seeping over him. *A baby-selling ring in Kearny?* Just when he thought things couldn't get any worse.

THIRTY-ONE

Leo enjoyed visiting the county's small lab. It wasn't up to the standards of crime scene units on television, but it had everything they could afford, carefully selected from Sugar's "Santa list" each year to meet their needs. Microscopes, fume hoods, chromatographs and spectrometers, a cyanoacrylate fuming chamber for lifting latent fingerprints, cameras and video recording equipment with alternative light sources, plus the invisible software and analysis tools. What they couldn't do inhouse, they sent offsite.

He stopped to peek through a microscope after handing Sugar the phone and other evidence collected at Riverside. "Any progress on the sword?"

"Nothing definitive. Trey had been making calls, but with the evidence coming in so fast and furious," she waved her hand at the new pile, distributing the scent of antibacterial soap, "and us such a small team, it's been hard."

"Understood. Where is Trey?"

"Lunch break. He's started working out with Drew. Kind of a personal training situation."

Leo smiled. Trey could definitely stand to build some

muscle mass. "Say, did he mention whether he knew the other victim—Genevieve Martine?"

She tossed her rainbow hair and narrowed her eyes. "Why would he?"

"They both worked at the cleaning service he used. We're trying to talk to anyone who knew Genevieve at all."

"He didn't say. Want me to have him call you?"

Leo wished he hadn't asked Sugar. She was going to tell Trey, unless he reached him first. "No, that's okay. I'll catch up with him later."

"I've got some great news."

"And why have you waited this long to tell me?"

She laughed. "We found something under Anong's body after you left. A fingernail."

"Real or fake?"

"Real. Just a piece that broke off, not the nail bed. Anong's body protected it from the fire. And it's not from her. I've sent it off for DNA analysis."

Leo whooped. They had DNA. "That's great news."

"Also, I'm pretty sure the fabric left on her body was identical to what Genevieve was wearing."

"So, she was in a costume?"

"Who knows? I'm just about the evidence." Sugar shrugged. "Pay me more, and I'll do your job, too."

They parted ways and Leo headed to the mayor's office. He called Trey on the drive over, but he didn't pick up. His voicemail was brief. "Call me."

He glanced at the clock on his dashboard panel. He was going to just barely make it on time. He got lucky and found a close parking spot and started walking briskly toward the building. His phone rang, and he answered it without looking, expecting Trey or Gus. "Sheriff Palmer."

A woman spoke, sounding hesitant. "Um, hi, Sheriff, my name is Sherlynn Burde. My brother and I own a lease on a cabin up in the Bighorn National Forest. You and Deputy Delaney Pace visited it a few months ago."

He had fallen in love with the cabin when he and Delaney searched it for a case. "Hello, Sherlynn. I only have a minute before I duck into a meeting. What can I do for you?" Leo opened the door to the lobby and waved to the woman behind the front desk.

She pointed down the hall and smiled. He gave her a thumbs-up in return.

"You wrote to me that you'd be interested if we ever decided to sell the lease on the cabin. Well, my brother and I decided we want to. We're just not using it anymore. Would you like to make us an offer? And it's okay if you don't. I'm sure we won't have trouble selling it. We just liked the idea that someone can enjoy it who is working so hard on behalf of the community."

Leo stopped in his tracks. He still had dreams about the place. In them, he was sitting on a porch rocker with a beautiful green-eyed woman beside him, their fingers intertwined. There were other parts to the dream, but they involved adult content. "Yes. Very. Can I call you back to talk about it?"

"That makes me so happy! Yes, please call me back. Does your caller ID show my number?"

He glanced at the screen. "It does. Give me a few days, okay? We have a few big cases and an angry wildfire."

"I saw them on the news. Of course. I'll talk to you soon."

"Thank you for thinking of me." Leo put his phone in his pocket and walked into the conference room, grinning.

The room was filled to capacity. All the city and county leaders were there in addition to the Bighorn National Forest and Rocky Mountain region personnel. Fire and police. Emergency management. People with public utilities. And more. The only thing missing was media.

Mayor Jesse Marshall broke away from Joe Tarver, angling

himself so his voice would carry to everyone in the room. "Nice of you to join us, Sheriff. Since I never see you at these meetings."

Leo gritted his teeth. "I have every confidence in Joe to represent our office on the fire so other staff, including me, can handle the homicide investigations at the same time."

"The former sheriff met with me twice daily to brief me during our last major fire."

"During which time there were not two homicides."

"That's right. During his tenure there were no double homicides of young women."

Leo sighed and turned to face the screen and lectern. He was used to fires from his years in southern California. But not in his current role. And not in areas so resistant to firefighting. It had been one thing when it was mostly a prairie fire east of town, largely in badlands. With the spread, now it was threatening the national forest and their town. Besides, southern California had just been where he lived. Sometime over the last year, Kearny and these mountains had become his home, with people he cared about.

The operations chief cleared his throat and began, briefing them on the status of the fire and resources deployed to fight it. "Our biggest challenge has been the weather."

A droll meteorologist moved to the lectern, adjusting the loose, boxy shoulders of a button-front shirt with short sleeves. "Heat, strong and erratic winds, and low humidity have combined to make this fire unpredictable. There's not a hint of precipitation in any of my forecasting models for the next few days. In forty-eight hours, we're expecting powerful southwest winds of fifty to seventy miles per hour, especially in the foothills where the fire has spread. With the topography there, wind can be funneled into a myriad of directions, which is highly undesirable. If we can hold on that long, we should finally get significant rain in four days."

The room grew deathly quiet. Tension was thick in the air.

"So, you're saying we should expect rain in four days," the mayor said.

The meteorologist shook his head. "No. What I'm saying is that things are about to get a whole lot worse."

THIRTY-TWO

Back at her desk, Delaney opened up the Cowpoke Café video. She'd been blisteringly productive that afternoon. She'd looked for—and not found—Anong Leela and Anna Petrov on dating sites. Learned from Shirleen that she'd only known Anong in passing. The social worker had misplaced her phone temporarily, so she'd called Delaney at the station earlier to reiterate her offer to help. It was a nice gesture. Delaney had also left messages for Trey to call her and for Drew to get himself or someone else out searching A1 ASAP since the judge had granted their warrant. Talked to Joaquim who said Anong, Anna, and Genevieve all had foreign accents—Anna's Russian.

With Drew's notes as a guide and Leo's work to compare to on the restaurant's video, she quickly deduced she would have to duplicate everything Drew said he had done. How could she speed it up? Leo had focused on only cash transactions. That was a good plan, but not enough. She decided to zero in on a tighter time frame. He'd been moving forward from the beginning of the provided footage. She skipped ahead two days, theorizing that she should start on the day the festival personnel arrived in town. In her mind, it was highly unlikely the coin was relevant. It was probably just a replica passed on by a festival worker.

But on the off chance it wasn't, they had to complete this exercise.

She registered the familiar faces of friends and neighbors as she sped through the transactions. Skeeter. Shirleen. Marge, the owner of Buns in the Barn. Lucas Planter. None of them seemed to be leaving change. Then she came to a customer waiting on the return of the check folder. He took cash out of it then he fished something from his wallet and dropped it on the table. A handful of coins. *This could be it!*

She backed the video up and zoomed in. The man had his back to the camera. He was wearing a baseball cap and long sleeve shirt. It immediately struck her as odd. Long sleeves in August was unusual, as everyone in northern Wyoming was enjoying the brief warm months. With less surprise than she would have felt a year ago, she saw that his skin was dark. Possibly African American? Some Native Americans and people of Latino descent had skin that color, though. She realized she wasn't going to get a face shot, so she switched to the camera by the door and quickly accessed the correct day and time.

As the face enlarged it pixelated, and she eased back. Then gasped.

It was Drew. Deputy Drew Knowles.

THIRTY-THREE

Delaney snuck a look at Leo. Walking beside him at the fairgrounds was almost like a date, albeit one in sheriff's department uniforms, while working two homicides. If she was ever going to date Leo—which she'd promised herself she wouldn't do because it would ruin his career—this would be just about perfect.

Having principles sucked sometimes.

Leo, however, seemed stressed and was quiet. She figured the fire meeting had gone badly. So, she filled him in on her progress and lack thereof. She left out the discovery of Drew on the video. It just seemed like the wrong time to upset him further, not until she'd had a chance to ask Drew about it.

After she finished her recitation, Leo said, "Thank you."

To the point. She refocused on the goal of finding someone to talk to about the swords. They passed a stand selling roasted turkey legs. They smelled great, but the workers there wouldn't be the right people.

"Over there." Delaney pointed. "The woman with the tablet in her hand shouting orders. She looks official. Let's talk to her."

Leo grunted. It sounded like agreement to Delaney.

She strode up to the woman. "Excuse me."

The woman held up a hand and kept shouting instructions to a group of men. After a minute or two waiting, Delaney repeated herself, but this time ignored the hand and said, "I'm Deputy Investigator Delaney Pace with the Kearny County Sheriff's Office." She hiked a thumb at Leo. "This is the sheriff. We're here about two homicides. We need five minutes or less of your time."

Icy blue eyes stared at her in irritation. "Why me?"

"Because you seem like someone in charge who can connect us with the right people."

The woman turned to the workers and shouted, "What are you guys standing around for? Was I not clear? Have you not done this a million times before? GO!" Then she issued a put upon sigh and turned back to Delaney and Leo. "Walk. And talk quickly."

Leo nodded at Delaney. *Yeah, because this woman and I have such great rapport.* "Your name and role with the festival, first, please."

"Talia Swift. I'm the road manager."

"Thanks. Since your crew came into town, two women in their early twenties have been murdered—one wearing a nun's costume—and anchored to the ground by what looked to be medieval swords."

"We're a Renaissance Festival. What does this have to do with us?"

"Two things. The first being that almost no one in Wyoming knows the difference—old and European is all the same around here. The second is that we're trying to find someone who might be able to help us track down the maker of the swords." She held up a hand when Talia was about to speak. "Sorry. And a third thing. We're going to need to talk to your employees."

Talia screeched a laugh. "I have thirty overworked, under-paid people with this shit show. We're bleeding money because of the horrible weather and fires. I need my workers working."

"And we need to stop a killer from killing. We'll have a deputy out here within the hour to begin the conversations. Five to ten minutes apiece. One at a time. I'll leave it to you to decide in what order to have them interviewed, but our deputy will need a list so he can ensure that he doesn't miss anyone." Delaney smiled. "Be sure you're on that list, too, please, as well as any contractors who aren't actually your employees but are here working with the festival."

Talia's expletive would have earned her time on her knees in the gravel praying and reciting scripture if she'd grown up with Delaney's grandparents.

"So that I can let you get started on the list, please direct us to the right person to talk to about old swords."

"Our blacksmith. His name is Bull Hood. He's got a bellows going at his wagon and is likely shoeing horses. About halfway down the line of attractions."

Delaney gave her a toothy smile. "Thank you."

Leo tipped his ball cap. "Welcome to Kearny. We're glad to have you."

Talia rolled her eyes, unmollified. "Are we done here?"

Delaney said, "Your contact information, please, and then we will be."

Talia gave it to Delaney who texted it to Drew. She felt a twinge of misgiving. But surely he'd be able to explain why he was on that video in a way that made sense. Why he hadn't told her and Leo they'd find him on it.

"Deputy Drew Knowles will be here soon," she said.

"Peachy." Talia was yelling instructions at her crew before they'd taken two steps away from her.

"Want me to call Drew with the assignment?" Delaney said to Leo.

But he was staring at something and didn't answer. She followed his gaze. The smoke columns, more north than east from town now. Maybe even a little bit to the west. She decided that no answer from him meant she should run with it, so she sent Drew instructions for the rest of his day.

When she was finished, she snapped her fingers in Leo's line of vision. "Ready to talk to Bull?"

His phone rang. He held it up. "I'll follow you. This is Trey."

She began walking and blatantly eavesdropping, because they were partners after all.

"Thanks for calling me back, Trey. Listen, I don't know if you knew this, but our other homicide victim worked for the same cleaning service as Anong. I was wondering if you'd ever met Genevieve Martine? She sometimes went by Gennie Martin." He grew silent, listening, then started asking more questions, with Delaney hanging on his side of the conversation. "Okay. Okay. Well, did you meet any other employees with the cleaning service? Mmm-hmm. And how did you find them to hire Anong? Right. Got it. Did you ever see anyone with Anong? Okay. Did she ever talk about being scared of anyone or someone bothering her? No, okay. How about any interest in anything medieval? A desire to run away? Last question: did she talk about a child or baby at all? I see. Well, that's all I have. I appreciate your help. Uh-huh, see you later."

Delaney whirled. "Well?"

"That was not a particularly helpful conversation."

"See nothing, hear nothing, say nothing?"

"Pretty much."

"Not even how he came to hire a human trafficker to send an enslaved woman to clean his house?"

"He said someone slid a flier under his door."

Delaney experienced a moment of gut-to-brain connection.

She just didn't believe Trey was telling the truth. At least not all of it.

But she tabled the thought. They'd arrived at a tent where a man was hammering a translucent red horseshoe on an anvil in front of an admiring throng, gripping the metal with a pair of giant tongs. A tall person, he had long, bulging arms, big shoulders, and narrow hips under a thick leather apron. His tools looked old and authentic enough to be ripped from the 1500s. A black horse with half-closed eyes and a thick, wavy mane stood tied to a hitching post a few feet away.

Leo again nodded her to the forefront.

She moved within range of flying bits of metal, unclipping and holding out her badge. The roar of the bellows was too much to compete with.

The blacksmith looked up at her through thick-lensed glasses. His expression was curious, nothing more. He nodded and set down his hammer, then held up a finger. He dropped the horseshoe in a pile of metal, hung his tongs, and shut down the bellows. Lastly, he took a bandana off his head, revealing a smooth shaved scalp. He wiped his brow and neck then used it on his hands, too, before depositing it on a stack of discards.

His voice was high-pitched. "I'm Bull."

"I'm Deputy Investigator Delaney Pace. This is Sheriff Leo Palmer. Can we have a word?" she said.

He nodded. "It's a little warm in here. How about we step out into the breeze?"

"Sure." Delaney wasn't sure it was any cooler outside the tent. She nudged Leo. He was standing by the coals in the bellows, his eyes roving the ground, like he was looking for burning embers. "Outside?"

"Um, yeah," Leo said.

The three of them stepped out of the tent together.

Delaney said, "We're trying to find potential manufacturers

for longsword replicas. Middle Ages most likely. Talia said you might be able to help us."

He grinned. "She knows me too well. I have a passion for all things metal, swords included, the older the better. I don't just work on horseshoes here, in fact. I keep all the metal in the show in tiptop shape. Armor. Weapons. Even dinnerware."

"Excellent. Can I show you some pictures?"

He rubbed his hands together. "Please."

"I should warn you ahead of time, these swords were used in two homicides."

His mouth set in a grim line. "So, they weren't toys."

"Nope. Sharp enough to anchor a human through the torso to the ground."

He shook his head. "That's horrible. Not just for the people who died. It's bad for the sword manufacturer and other sword enthusiasts."

"Swords don't kill people, people kill people?"

He shrugged. "It's true, even though you're paraphrasing gun advocates. But I will say that swords don't have the capacity —even misused—for mass violence that semi-autos and autos do. I'm not opposed to guns, but they aren't my thing."

"Same." She opened her photos app. "I'll be showing you photos of the swords after they were removed from the scene. However, they can't be cleaned up as they're evidence in a homicide. What you see on them will be exactly what you think it is."

"Understood."

She pulled up the first sword, the one used on Genevieve.

"May I?" He reached for the phone.

"Be my guest."

He enlarged the photo and moved the image around to study different aspects of the sword, nodding. "Can I see the other?"

"Swipe right."

He did. "Oh, wow."

"What?"

"They're not identical. But they are made by the same metalsmith."

"How do you know?"

"Some things only a metal geek like me would see, like the lines and the timbre of the steel. But there's a dead giveaway. The company logo."

"Aha." Delaney hadn't seen a logo. "What is significant, if anything, about the differences?"

"Can I pull up a website on your phone?"

She loved his manners. "Yes, please do."

A few swipes and keystrokes later, he showed her a site. "I'm almost positive this is who made your swords. They have standard models that they sell through their website, but they also do custom work." Keeping the screen where they could both see it, Bull clicked the stock swords menu option, opened the longswords category, and scrolled down the page. Leo was looking over her shoulder, his warm breath tickling her ear. She didn't want to be noticing it at a time like this, but it was impossible not to.

"Here," Bull said. "And here. These are your swords."

Leo leaned closer. To her and the phone. "Are you sure?"

Delaney stared at the screen. To her untrained eye, the one pictured looked identical to the one used on Anong. It also seemed expensive, with a note below its description that said Prices Provided Upon Request. Serious Inquiries Only. *If you have to ask, you can't afford it*, she thought.

"Very close to one hundred percent. There are other great metalsmiths who could do this work but look at this etching." He showed them a curled infinity symbol with an eye in the middle. "That's the logo. And it's on both your swords, worked into the design. See it?"

Delaney hadn't noticed an infinity symbol before. It was

integrated so seamlessly that it was hard to see unless you knew what you were looking for. "Wow. Yes."

He switched to the other picture and zoomed in on the hilt design on the other sword. Delaney nodded. There it was. An identical infinity symbol.

"It aligns with their catchphrase. *From antiquity to infinity, a sword's beauty is in the eye of the beholder.* They call themselves Infiniquity."

Delaney had seen the name Infiniquity at the top of the page, but now she understood what it meant. "That's amazing. We've been trying to figure this out for days, and here you were in Kearny this whole time."

"This helped?"

"Infinitely."

He smiled, then his face went slack. "Do you have any idea who did it?"

"No. But this might help us track them down."

He shook his head. "Good luck with that. People in our world are pretty cutesy and cagey about identities."

Leo said, "Have you ever run across anyone in your world who talked about fantasies of harming young women with longswords or anything that made you think they were a danger to others?"

"I meet a lot of weirdos, Sheriff."

"Understood. And I know it was a broad question. But you're the kind of person they might brag to. Want to impress."

"First off, it wouldn't impress me. But secondly, no one comes to mind."

Delaney handed him a card. "If you think of anything, please reach out?"

Leo followed up with one of his.

Bull tucked them in the pocket of his trousers. "Of course. Would you mind me asking how they did it? Methodology is a signature in the fantasy world."

Delaney knew the media had run with the story of the bodies skewered, but they hadn't released how they were killed. She turned to Leo. He shook his head.

"The swords were largely about staging and were used to anchor them to the ground."

She watched him very closely for his reaction. His nod was somber, his eyes intent, not stimulated. "Okay. I'll keep my ears open."

"Thanks."

They shook hands all around. Bull returned to his tent. Delaney and Leo strolled away.

Leo said, "That was a jackpot."

She smiled. "The best lead we've had so far."

Running footsteps sounded behind them.

"Delaney! Mom!"

Delaney turned toward Carrie, a smile on her face that quickly fell. Carrie was panting, her eyes wide. Skeeter was running up behind her, carrying Juan Julio on one hip. "What's the matter?"

"Kat and Clara were supposed to meet us at jousting. They didn't show up."

Delaney held up a hand as Skeeter caught up to them. "They're probably just running late."

"We've looked everywhere for them. And jousting is *over!*"

Juan Julio was squirming and shouting, "Put me down!"

Skeeter didn't pay him any attention. "We've called and texted both their numbers. A lot of times. For an hour."

Leo said, "Delaney—do you want to go look for her?"

Skeeter's and Carrie's alarm was rubbing off on her. "Yes."

"I'll come with you."

"You have a press conference, don't you?"

"This is more important."

Delaney shook her head. "I'll call Drew to help me. We'll find her. I'm sure it's just a misunderstanding. Kat probably convinced Clara her time was better spent practicing for the rodeo Clara signed her up for." She'd have to put her disquietude about Drew aside for now. If he'd just told her and Leo he would be on that video. That would have been the right thing to do. Why hadn't he done the right thing? But Kat was all that mattered now.

"I feel crummy about this."

"The community needs you. Go. I promise it's okay."

He started to leave then shook his head. "We're in your truck."

She tossed him the keys. "I'll get a ride with Skeeter or Drew."

He still looked conflicted.

"Leo, go."

He sighed and walked quickly away.

Delaney called Drew.

"I got your message. I'm on my way to the fairgrounds," he said.

She filled him in about Kat and Clara. "Can you drive out to the Eckhardt ranch before you come? See if they're out there?"

"Sure."

"Thanks. Call me as soon as you know one way or the other."

She ended the call and then turned to Skeeter and Carrie, fighting rising panic. "Now, take me to the last place you saw her. Them." *They were missing, here, at the Renaissance Festival, with a serial killer on the loose. One obsessed with swords.*

I'd planned everything to a T. Nothing I'd done at coffee with Clara had raised her suspicions. She'd chosen the spot. The Golden Spur, a claustrophobic diner that smelled like bacon grease. The walls were crowded with kitschy Western posters, half of them homilies, the other half bad humor. It wouldn't have been the place I would have chosen, but it was perfect.

"I've taken the whole afternoon off," she'd said as she stirred two plastic capsules of creamer into her coffee.

"Oh? What's the occasion?" I'd asked.

"I'm going to the Renaissance Festival."

Now the site of their coffee made sense. This place was close to the fairgrounds. "By yourself?"

Clara had smiled. "Would you like to come with me?"

"Maybe. If I can clear my calendar."

"I haven't even asked—what do you do?"

"Hair."

"Oh, goodness. I'm so glad to meet a hairdresser! Mine moved away." She touched her limp locks. "I'm overdue."

My heart rate sped up. "Ever since I first saw you, I've been dying to do your hair."

"Really?"

"A pixie cut."

Clara laughed. "I've never had hair that short before."

"You should try it."

Her brow furrowed but then she said, "Can I make an appointment?"

"Of course." I pretended to check my phone. "I had a cancellation. Could you do it now?"

Clara had checked the time. "How long do you think it would take?"

"If we leave now, I can have you done in half an hour."

She'd leaned forward. "This is so much fun. Why not!"

I put a ten on the table. "That will cover it."

As we were leaving I saw Clara add another five. I didn't mention it.

In the parking lot, I said, "Do you mind driving since you're in a hurry? I walked."

"No problem."

Clara had chattered amiably on the way to my house.

When we arrived, Clara parked on the driveway nearest the path to the lowest floor. "I work out of the basement."

"Makes sense not to spend extra money for a salon. I love your house."

I didn't think much about it one way or another except for its location, its orientation to the neighborhood, and its price. While it was in-town, it was on a long driveway such that the entrance to the basement—and the house proper starting one story above—was obscured by trees and didn't face any other road or houses directly.

I led Clara down to the basement and in the walk-out door.

"Have a seat here." I'd patted the back of a stylist chair. "I'll just get my things."

"It's so dark in here!" The chair squeaked as Clara sat.

"The light switch is down the hall. Hang on."

"Okay. No problem."

I hurried to the armoire on the other side of the room. Under cover of darkness, I removed my suit from a special, heavy-duty hook and slipped it on over my clothes.

"My phone doesn't have signal," Clara said.

By design. Later, someone might look for that phone's last location. By then, I would have had time to move it someplace else. "Sorry. Would you like something to drink?"

"Do you have a Coke?"

"Diet."

"That's fine."

I pulled a regular Coca-Cola from the refrigerator then scooped ice from a machine into a tumbler. I tapped in a small amount of my bitter magic powder from a glass vial as I slowly poured the soft drink. The sugar in the soda would mask the taste and make it seem like a diet drink. Re-capping the vial securely, I put it up before stirring the Coke. On the way back, I wheeled over a cart that held canisters of combs and scissors, brushes, conditioners, and styling supplies. A blow drier and a curling iron hung from the side. I grabbed a black smock and draped it over Clara with one hand then gave her the drink before securing the smock.

"The lights?" Clara asked.

"Right." I switched them on and returned.

Clara's mouth made an O. "Wow. This place is like a museum."

Except that museums were for displays and gawkers. My items were for using. The old pharmacy bottles. The costumes. The coins and tools. "Thank you."

She looked up into a mirror and caught a glimpse of my outfit. "You're coming with me to the Renaissance Festival!"

"My calendar is all yours. How about I dry cut your hair? That way we're working with it in the shape you'll wear it in."

"You're the professional."

I had turned Clara away from the mirror, brushed her wiry hair, then switched to a comb and pair of scissors.

"How long have you been doing hair?"

"As long as I can remember." I snipped length off Clara's hair quickly.

"Did you always want to be a hairdresser?"

"It's a means to an end."

"Is there somewhere I can set my drink?"

I wanted it in her hands. "I'm sorry. Not close enough. Can I take it from you in a minute?"

"Oh, sure." Clara set it in her lap and cradled both hands around it. "Great costume. It looks so real. Now I feel like I should have dressed up. Have you been to one of these before?"

"Hold still." Without hesitation, I chopped bangs across Clara's forehead. A gleeful thrill seized me, and I laughed.

"What is it?"

"Are you not going to drink that?"

Clara held it up.

I had set it aside. *Switching to plan B.* "I need to adjust the chair."

"Okay."

Standing behind the chair and reaching under the sides of the seat, I lifted old school metal handcuffs, one on each side attached just below the chair's arms. "Put your arms on the rests for a moment, please."

Clara did as she was asked without hesitation. She had no reason to fear me. Not yet.

I snapped both cuffs tightly shut simultaneously, a move I'd practiced many times on the mannikin hidden out of sight in a closet.

"What... um... hey..." Clara said, stumbling over her words. "Why did you attach me to the chair?"

I turned the chair around again to face the mirror.

Clara gasped. The cut I'd given her was short, lopsided, and choppy. Deliberately unattractive. "My hair. Why did you..."

I moved in front of her and finally smiled. "Why did I *what*? Make you look as ugly as I see you?"

Then I took Clara's phone from her lap, turned it off, and left the basement, ignoring her shouted questions and protests.

And it felt so, so good.

THIRTY-FIVE

Leo waited his turn to speak at the press conference in the largest conference room in the mayor's building. If it wasn't for the critical nature of the information being conveyed, he'd be convinced it was solely political grandstanding by the mayor. As it was, the location spoke volumes, as did the way the mayor yammered on about everything "he" had done. It was in stark contrast to the other team-oriented presenters.

Cameras recorded and livestreamed their every word. The space was packed and smelled like sweat and burned coffee. The by-invitation-only reporters were lapping the content up like thirsty dogs. They'd been very courteous so far, holding questions for the end. Unfortunately, Leo was the last speaker, delivering the "what does this mean for all of you in practical terms" portion of the presentation. He'd been trying his best to focus on the messages being conveyed, but his mind kept returning to Delaney. To Kat and Clara. He didn't dare check his phone until this was over, and he prayed there was already a text or voicemail telling him they'd been found and were safe.

"Sheriff Leo Palmer will speak to you now on evacuations and road closures," their public information officer said.

Leo took his place at the front of the room, notes in hand. "First, thank you to all the brave and skilled men and women who are working to stop this fire. I'm convinced we have the right people in place. Secondly, I know that the news we are sharing today isn't what any of you wanted to hear. But our community is strong, and we'll get through this together. The sheriff's department's role in the fire response is being led very capably by Deputy Joe Tarver." Leo gestured at the colleague he'd grown to hate. Joe was out of the sight line of the camera, but he waved to everyone in the room. "Earlier today on social media, we released an update on the road closures and evacuations." He explained what that meant in terms of communities that needed to be ready for a change in status, set to evacuate upon notice, or in the process of evacuating currently. "In addition, we are asking everyone to be more cautious and vigilant than ever to prevent introducing new fires into the landscape. We are under a burn ban. Please, if you can do it safely, extinguish any fires you encounter, and always report them. At this time, we are open for questions for any of the presenters."

He started to return to his seat, until the reporter Melanie barked out her first question.

"Sheriff, do you have any suspects for the two homicides yet? And isn't your failure to close those cases creating a distraction from the needs of the community during this unprecedented fire?" she said.

He went back to the podium and microphone. "No and no." He smiled, then walked away again.

"Just a follow-up on that, if you don't mind. What do you have to say to the report that your sister was just rescued by state cops from a broken-down vehicle on a closed road in a 'Go' evacuation zone?"

A buzz went through the room. There was no better news than bad news, especially the gossipy kind.

Leo took a deep breath. *My sister what?!*

THIRTY-SIX

Delaney and Carrie ran to the concession area beneath the rodeo arena, passing Wyoming neighbors decked out in Renaissance costumes. Delaney saw more than one gray nun habit as well as some white and black ones. It gave her the creeps. They'd already searched by the entry gate where Carrie and Skeeter had left Kat as well as in the crowds along the sidewalk.

Carrie was talking breathlessly on the way. "Clara was late. She was getting a haircut. She texted Kat where they'd meet so they could still make it to the arena in time for the jousting. Kat was all about the jousting. Juan Julio had to go to the bathroom, so we left her there to wait for Clara. And then we haven't been able to find either of them since!"

Anything to do with horses, Kat was all about. Delaney pulled up Kat's picture and held her phone out open to vendor after vendor—yeasty beer, funnel cakes dusted with powdered sugar, and cheap souvenirs all being sold by falsely enthusiastic proprietors. She asked each one if they'd seen her. The responses were *nos* across the board.

"I could try the bathroom." Carrie was already walking away.

"No. We stay together. I'll come with you." It already bothered Delaney that they'd separated from Skeeter and Juan Julio.

Her phone buzzed. Carrie pushed through the bathroom door ahead of Delaney, shouting for her sister. Delaney did a quick scan inside for blood or signs of a disturbance, although differentiating between a disturbance and normal usage on a heavy attendance day wasn't an exact science. Still, she saw nothing to set off alarm bells, so she checked her messages.

A new one from Drew. *Kat and Clara not here. OMW.*

She knew what he meant. They weren't at the Eckhardt ranch. He was now on his way to the fairgrounds. So, if Kat hadn't opted for Sunshine and barrel racing or the jousting, what would she have wanted to do, if she had the choice?

"Where are they keeping the horses here?" she asked.

"Out in the livestock barns. You know, where the big animals are during the county fair."

"Let's go."

They ran again, this time a long way. Both of them were out of breath after they'd made it across the complex and over to the long rows of outdoor stalls, where the odor of horse was strong. The run had given Delaney time to think. She texted Drew asking for a BOLO on Clara's truck. Then she texted Clara and Kat in a group string.

Getting worried. Can't find the two of you. Please call or text if you can.

Carrie started peering in stalls and calling Kat's name.

Delaney called dispatch.

"How can I help you, Deputy?" the man who answered asked.

"I need to reach Mark Eckhardt. Clara's husband. Can you text me a number?"

"Let's see... Yes, I have one here in her records. Do you want me to just try him myself and put you through?"

"Sure. But text me the number, too. I may need to call him again."

"Got it. And it's already ringing. I'm sending you through now, then watch for a text."

"Thank you."

"Of course."

The phone began ringing in her ear. After four rings, it went to voicemail.

"Mr. Eckhardt—Mark. This is Deputy Investigator Delaney Pace. Clara was supposed to meet my daughter Kat at the Renaissance Festival today. We can't find either of them or raise them on their phones. I'm hoping you know where she is or can see her phone's location. Please call me as soon as you can." She recited her number and ended the call.

Carrie had circled back to her and been listening. "Find My Phone!"

"Yes."

Delaney was pulling it up on her phone. "I don't see her. Why don't I see her?"

"Um, it's not going to show Kat. But maybe Mr. Eckhardt can use it to find Clara."

"Why isn't it going to show Kat?"

"She removed herself from it."

"She didn't have my permission for that. Or my password." She bored a hole in Carrie's face with her glare. "How did this happen?"

"She's a little more bothered about you and Leo than she let on."

"So?"

"I may have found out your password and given it to her."

Delaney took a step closer. "Carrie!"

Carrie threw up her hands. "I thought it would make her

feel better. I didn't know this would be the day we needed to find her."

"It's not about feelings. It's about safety. That is my job, and Find My Phone is one of my tools. You guys know this. You've lived this."

Carrie—normally the hardened one in their household—burst into tears. "I know I messed up. You don't have to rub it in."

Delaney pulled her in for a hug. "You're right. I'm sorry. I'm just scared."

Carrie's voice was muffled against Delaney's shoulder. "I'm scared, too."

"Does this mean she's off your Find My Phone, too?"

"The whole account. Yes."

"Does she do location sharing with you?"

"She used to. But it's not showing on my phone today."

Delaney released Carrie and checked her text string with Kat, pulling her up to check the map. "She isn't showing on my phone either."

"Maybe she was mad at both of us."

"Why would she be mad at you?"

"Because I took your side."

Tears pricked Delaney's eyes. "So, we're blind. But we can show her picture to everyone in these stalls. All over the festival for that matter."

Her phone buzzed. Drew. *I'm here.*

She texted him the picture. *Please start searching. Kat Pace. 13 yo. Last seen at entrance gate two hours ago.*

"Delaney Pace?"

Delaney looked up to see a tiny woman with very white hair leaning on a four-footed metal cane. "Yes?"

"You don't remember me?"

"I'm sorry, I don't. Refresh my memory."

"I was friends with your grandmother. I used to come over

and do my canning with her. I made the best sauerkraut in the county. Still would if it wasn't for my arthritis. I'm Gilda Frank."

"Oh, Mrs. Frank. So, sorry. Yes, I remember you. And your sauerkraut. But right now, I'm in the middle of an emergency. I'm sorry, but I need to go."

The woman reached out and grabbed her wrist. Her grip was fierce. "What would your grandmother think about how you and that sheriff have been carrying on?"

Delaney recoiled like she'd been bitten. Which she had, in a way. She didn't have the time or energy to fight back. "Excuse me. Take care of yourself."

"We're praying for you in my women's group. You need to get yourself back to church!"

Delaney took a few big strides away. *How dare she!* Was this what everyone in town was thinking about Delaney?

A warm presence pushed up against her. She looked down. Carrie. The girl gave her a sad smile. Delaney pulled her in close to her side.

"Hey, guys. What are you doing here?"

Delaney whirled.

Kat was shoving her phone in her pocket, a snarly look on her face.

She didn't know whether to hug her or yell at her. She did neither. "Where's Clara?"

"Isn't she with you?" Kat asked.

After that bad news sunk in, Delaney threw her arms around her daughter. "Where have you been?"

"I was waiting for Clara, then Freddy called me—you're never going to believe what's happened to him today—and I just started talking to him. Clara was late, so I walked around and talked to Freddy until my phone went dead." She held it up. "I figured I'd find everybody later."

"Yeah, well, you should have texted us." Carrie was yelling

at the top of her lungs. "You could have been dead. You scared me!"

Delaney wanted to cheer.

Kat's jaw dropped. "Jeez, Carrie, calm down."

"I will *not* calm down. I told Delaney what you did. Turning off Find My Phone. Stopping sharing your location with us. And you know what? I totally get it now. It's not cool. It's not cool at all."

Kat now matched her sister's raised voice. "Yeah, and you know why. Freddy is not okay with what they're doing either."

"I don't care. We still have to know you're safe."

"You sound like a mother." Kat said the last word with complete scorn.

Carrie screamed so loudly that everyone in earshot turned in their direction. "You sound like a spoiled brat. Delaney can kiss who she wants. Clara is missing, you idiot, and all you care about is Freddy."

"What do you mean, missing?"

"Like no one can find her. And she's not just a bratty kid hiding out like you. She is a grown-up who was responsible for you today and didn't show up. After all she's done for you, I'd think you'd give a shit."

THIRTY-SEVEN

Delaney stood at the mouth of the parking lot to the fairgrounds, watching for Leo. Questioning Kat had been next to useless. Delaney had given up in frustration and sent the girl home with Skeeter, Carrie, and Juan Julio. Once Kat had gotten over the surprise of Clara being gone, she'd reverted to acting like the injured party. She insisted she knew nothing. Hadn't seen Clara. Hadn't talked to her since earlier in the day when they'd agreed to meet. Didn't know where she might have gone. Had no idea where Mark Eckhardt was.

Her voice had been full-on bratty. "She's like, a grown-up. Maybe she had somewhere to be."

"You really think she'd stand you up without letting you know?" Delaney had asked.

"Maybe she thought she texted me, but it didn't send. It happens."

It did, and it was possible. But Delaney's gut was screaming at the top of its lungs that something was wrong. Clara worked in law enforcement, whether she wore the uniform or not. She knew not to create a crisis. Not to scare the people who cared about her and burden law enforcement resources without a good reason. And not only was Clara one of their own, but she was also Kat's mentor. Had been coming to meet her. That made Delaney involved on both a professional and very, very personal level.

Drew walked up. "I checked every car in the lot and walked the adjacent streets. Her car's not here. Not wearing its own plates, and not in disguise with different plates."

"Thank you." Delaney shook her head. "I don't like this, Drew. You haven't known her long, but this is not a woman who doesn't show up."

"I'm just glad you found your daughter."

"Me, too." Again, she fought her worry about Drew and the Cowpoke Café video. She decided to get it over with—to ask him outright why he hadn't told her and Leo he would be on that video. *A team is nothing without trust.* "Listen, I have something else I need to talk to you about."

Leo pulled up beside her. "Hey, guys. Thank God about Kat. Anything on Clara?"

Delaney swallowed. The conversation with Drew would have to wait. "I think we've exhausted what we can do looking for her here for now."

"Okay. What do you think about Drew getting on with the personnel interviews out here on the homicides, and you and I can strategize back at the station?"

Drew was nodding. "I met the lady in charge. She's got a redwood-sized stick up her butt, but she had the list of people and was kind of annoyed I wasn't ready to start."

"Okay, then." Delaney hopped into the passenger side of the truck. She hated it when Leo drove.

Drew waved goodbye as Leo backed out and accelerated away.

"All right," he said. "Where do we stand?"

Delaney re-upped her decision to talk to Drew before she mentioned the video to Leo. "BOLO out on her car. I've left a message with her husband. We found no evidence she ever arrived at the fairgrounds. I talked to her a few hours ago at work, and she confirmed the plan, as she did with Kat as well. Drew went by her place, and she wasn't there, nor was her husband. She's not answering her phone."

"Damn. Do you think she's somewhere with Mark?"

"Not without telling Kat, at the least, even it was an emergency. Speaking of which, Kat's moved from sort of okay with our news to really pissed, and she swears Freddy is, too." Delaney cocked her head, frowning. "She said something cryptic about the unbelievable thing that happened to him today, and I didn't follow up on that. Sorry."

"I'll bet I already know. I got blindsided at the press conference about Adriana requiring rescue because of car problems on a closed road in an evacuated area."

"Oh, crap."

"Yeah. She got fired today and decided to take Freddy to go see the fire."

"Just what they don't want people doing."

"Yeah. Well, she ran off the road into a ditch—"

"I guess the same person must have taught you both to drive?" Leo had infamously driven onto a rock and stump amongst other mishaps with department vehicles.

"You're hilarious." His voice was dry, but his eyes twinkled when he looked at her. "Listen, you probably didn't see the fire update, but it's not good. It's spreading. People are going to be tense at best."

"Freaking out at worst. It's not coming south, is it?"

"No guarantees. The wind can't make up its mind which way to blow. Your place is still looking pretty good, unless it gains traction up in the lower elevations of the mountains and slingshots south with all the trees as great fuel."

"That's what I'm worried about."

He parked and the two of them walked in.

"Was the press conference okay otherwise?"

"Is that code for 'did my name come up?'"

"Sort of."

"It did not."

Her phone rang. Her screen read MARK ECKHARDT. "Clara's husband."

"Put it on speaker and we'll take it in my office?"

They hustled down the hall. Delaney hit ACCEPT and SPEAKER as they approached the door. "Detective Delaney Pace and Sheriff Leo Palmer. Mark?"

"Hello. Yes. I got your message. I just heard from Clara. A text." Delaney stopped dead, her forehead wrinkled. That had not been what she was expecting to hear.

"Well, thank God."

"That depends on your perspective. She left town without any warning."

"That sounds so unlike her."

"Extremely."

"Where did she go?"

"She said she went to Boston and will be back Sunday."

"Boston?" She put the phone in the center of Leo's desk and sat in front of it.

"Yes."

"And this is a complete surprise?"

"A total surprise. I'm in Billings at a livestock auction overnight. But I was home earlier today. She was going to take Kat to the Renaissance Festival for the afternoon. She never mentioned travel."

"Does she have friends or family or a special interest in Boston?"

"No."

"Where you, um, fighting or anything?"

"Everything was normal."

Delaney didn't think that was really an answer.

Leo walked behind his desk to his own chair. "I agree this sounds strange, Mark. Has she ever done anything like this before?"

Mark snorted. "Uh, no. Clara is a creature of habit."

"I've got to tell you, she didn't ask for time off work, either."

"Or warn Kat that lessons were suspended," Delaney added. "Or that she wasn't coming to the festival."

Leo was scrolling through his phone. "Hold it. I got a text message about ten minutes ago. While I was driving."

"From Clara?"

"Yes."

"Can you read it aloud?"

Leo read, "*Sorry for last minute notice. I'm taking paid time off the rest of the week.*"

"What else does it say?"

"That's it."

Mark said, "She doesn't send long texts."

Delaney was nodding. "She uses all the abbreviations and acronyms, though. Did she really spell out 'paid time off'?"

"Yes."

Mark said, "I'm taking a screen shot of the message to me. Can I text it to this number?"

"Please," Delaney said. Then, a few seconds later, "Got it." She read aloud. "*Taking a few mental health days in Boston. Home Sunday night. Sorry.*"

"Does that sound like her?" Leo asked.

"Mostly. Her message would be short. She wouldn't be lovey dovey. But it doesn't sound right to me. Mental health days? She's never seen a counselor in her life. I've never heard her use that phrase. Of course, she's never taken a trip for plea-sure without me either."

"Does she share her location with you?" Delaney said.

"No. But she showed me how to do Find My Phone. I'm pulling it up now." There were a few seconds of silence. "Huh."

"What is it?"

"She's at the airport."

"Here in Kearny?" Delaney shook her head at Leo, confused.

"Yes."

"There are no more flights out today. Not commercial, anyway."

"Right. If she really needed to get out of town and missed the scheduled flights, I would have thought she would drive to Billings or Denver and fly out of one of those airports."

"Could she be flying private? Maybe charter?"

Mark snorted. "Jeez. I wouldn't think she'd spend that kind of money."

Delaney frowned. "Does she know anyone who'd give her a ride?"

"Until right now I would have said no. But apparently I don't know my own wife." He sounded sad.

Delaney hurt for him. "I'm troubled that she hasn't answered Kat or me. We've been trying to find her."

Mark sighed. "I'm sorry, Delaney. But it's sounding to me like whatever she's doing, she's embarrassed about it and doesn't want to talk about it."

"Okay, Mark," Leo said, making a sad face at Delaney. "Thanks for calling us. If you hear from her again let us know. And would you mind keeping us updated on that location on her phone if something weird happens?"

"I will. I don't mind telling you this is all really unsettling. Troubling."

"Hang in there. We'll see if we can reach her, and, of course, we'll let you know if something changes, too."

Delaney nodded and ended the call. She put a hand on either side of her head. "What the hell is this?"

Leo swung around toward his window and the invisible

mountains. "Could Clara be having some kind of breakdown? Midlife crisis? Affair?"

"I just don't see it."

He spun back around. "Why don't you try to raise her—I'm going to the airport and see if I can find her."

Delaney was already typing a message—*I'm worried about you! Please let me know you're okay.* Then she sent one to her daughter. *Important: Did Clara mention going to Boston?*

She leapt to her feet. Leo was already out the door and down the hall. "Wait. I'm coming with you!"

THIRTY-EIGHT

Kat gently tapped Juan Julio on the shoulder. She shouted, "Tag. You're it!"

The little boy giggled. Dudley yapped and chased his nub of a tail in a circle. Kat wheeled and trotted away from Juan Julio. His laughter escalated as he ran after her. Then she bumped into something solid.

"Whoa, watch where you're going, young lady." Skeeter was carrying a tray of hamburger patties from the grill to the kitchen.

Juan Julio smacked her on the behind with both palms. "You it, Katty Kat."

"Who wants a burger?" Skeeter said, grinning.

Carrie was bussing tables. "Does that mean I get a break?"

From behind the bar, Mary said, "Eat them while they're hot." She smiled. "But don't take forever doing it."

Carrie's friend Victoria came in carrying a load of clean glasses to the bar. She'd started working there, too. They were always together. "One for me, please!"

Kat's stomach growled. The burgers smelled *so* good. But she didn't want to eat with Carrie.

She was still pissed her sister had sided with Delaney earlier. Kat hadn't made her phone invisible all by herself. And honestly, Carrie hadn't liked any boys since her boyfriend Noah had died. And Noah's dad, who Kat wasn't supposed to know details about but did. Carrie had been with him before Noah. *Gross—he was like so old.* So, she didn't understand how Kat felt. It wasn't a secret that she'd been crushing on Freddy for a while. I mean, DUH-laney. And the two people closest in the world to her didn't seem to get it that Delaney embarrassing Freddy put Kat in a bad position with him. And he totally said he was embarrassed that his uncle might lose the election because of it. *Because of Delaney.*

She read his text again. *I kinda always hoped if a Palmer and a Pace would hook up it would be you and me someday.* His words were a lightning bolt of happiness every time she saw them. He didn't *not* like her, even if he didn't like her. There was hope.

She'd replied, *I know, right?*

And then he'd started talking about how their car accident was on the news and his mom was freaking out over losing her job and that they might move back to California or somewhere, especially now that this thing had come out about Leo and Delaney and Leo might not be the sheriff anymore.

In other words, if he has to move, it will all be Delaney's fault. And if he moved, Kat's life would be ruined. R-U-I-N-E-D.

Was it any wonder she'd forgotten about Clara?

"That's a burger for my little man, for Carrie and Victoria, for me, for Mary, for Dudley, and earth to Kat," Skeeter said. "Burger or not?"

"I'll eat at home," she mumbled.

Carrie muttered, "Good."

"I hear you," Kat said.

"Good." Carrie took off her apron and held her hand out to Juan Julio. "Let's go eat some yummy dinner."

The little traitor took her hand. Victoria took his other one. He skipped between the girls out to the front patio.

Skeeter retreated into the kitchen. The bar was mostly empty because everyone in town was at the festival. It was totes unfair that she had to be here. She had tickets and everything. Freddy had asked her if she was going tonight. Not *to* go, but it was almost the same thing. But Delaney had sent her back to the bar to babymind like she was a baby herself.

She checked her phone to see if she'd heard from Freddy again. There was nothing new. But Delaney had texted. She rolled her eyes and almost didn't read it but then wondered if Clara had come home.

Important: Did Clara mention going to Boston?

She couldn't not answer. She loved Clara. *No.*

Before she could put her phone away another message came in. *Has she contacted you?*

No. Then she sent another. *Did she text somebody?*

We don't know. Maybe.

That didn't make sense. You either knew if someone sent you a message or if they didn't. An image filled her mind. Clara, upset and anxious, putting away her phone in the arena the first day Kat had ridden Sunshine around the barrels. She'd said something weird that day about it, too. Like she was getting messages, and someone was playing a sick joke on her.

Is this about the person sending her mean messages?

Someone was sending her mean messages?

I guess. That's what she said.

When?

A few days ago

Who?

She didn't say. She was upset tho.

She stared at the screen, waiting for another text to come through, but there weren't even three little dots. *Whatever.*

THIRTY-NINE

I pulled in the garage at my house and listened in the darkness, senses acute. There were no sounds coming from the basement. All was as it should be. Bringing Clara here today had been impulsive. Law enforcement was still crawling all over the Planter ranch. There was no choice but to keep her here, for now.

Alive. Because to end the Quest here was not The One Way. *It isn't going to be easy. None of this has been easy.*

Beside me was Clara's truck, which I'd moved inside earlier before leaving with her phone. I shut the garage then walked around to the exterior basement entrance, unlocking two dead-bolts in the steel reinforced security door identical to one at the top of the basement stairs leading into the main house. Again, I listened and heard nothing. I pulled the door open.

The handcuffs rattled and clanked. I'd left the lights on in case Clara got loose. She wouldn't be able to escape the basement—the glass windows had been replaced with miniature keyed steel doors as well. Apparently, it wasn't unheard of for security-obsessed folks to swap them out, especially in the cities.

"You can't keep me here. People will miss me. My husband.

My daughter." Clara's voice was raspy, probably from screaming. And she smelled like a dog left inside too long. All of the women had wet themselves eventually.

"You should have drunk your drink." I hadn't given her anything that would kill her. Just a little ancient sleeping potion, a mixture medieval monks used. Mandrake, deadly nightshade, and datura. I'd been looking forward to it, as it could cause hallucinations. What would Clara see and what would she do if that happened? It would be most enlightening.

"Did you hear me?"

"Clara, you already told me your husband is away overnight. Your kid only contacts you when she needs a babysitter. No one will miss you until work in the morning. But you solved that for us."

"What? How?"

"Before I shipped your phone via FedEx to Boston, I sent a few messages. You've run away on a little mental health break trip. Claiming a few days of paid time off and checking out of your life, but you should be home Sunday."

"No." Clara's voice sounded closer to defeat, but I wasn't fooled. I'd watched her long enough to know how tough she was. How rarely she gave up. She looked at me. "You'll let me go home Sunday?"

I ignored her and instead brought over a bag of zip ties. I fastened one around Clara's ankles. Then I released one wrist, moved it beside the other still cuffed one, zip tied them together, and removed the second handcuff. "Stand up."

She stood. "Where are you taking me?"

"Sit on the ground."

She sat.

I grabbed her by the feet and began pulling her across the tiled floor.

"Hey! Stop it!"

I didn't. And I was once again impressed as Clara remained

upright and kicking in what could only be called a moving boat posture, like in the yoga classes I took online for strength and mental clarity. She wasn't just strong for her age—she was strong for any age.

But I was stronger.

I dragged her down a short hall and into a special room. I'd been told that the previous owners had called it a safe room, storing supplies and weapons in it. It had exhaust, an air source, and a drain in the floor. Preppers, people would have called them. Ready for a nuclear blast, an electromagnetic pulse event, anarchy, or the zombie apocalypse. I had moved all the shelves out but otherwise left it the same.

Well, that wasn't true. I'd added one feature. A concrete stanchion with an iron ring. I put handcuffs back on Clara and fastened her to it then cut away the flexicuffs.

I pointed at the drain. "Waste." To a wicker basket. "Water bottles. Food." If you could call the disgusting energy bars actual food products. I wouldn't have eaten them, but they'd do for the survival of my guest.

Clara looked around the room then directly into my eyes. "Your costume earlier. Is it for the festival?"

"No."

"Did you kill those girls? Genevieve Martine and Anong Leela?"

I smiled. I liked that Clara was smart and uncowed.

"Okay." Clara swallowed. "But why me?"

I might like her brain, but that didn't mean I was letting down my guard around her. I shut the door and locked it behind me.

I would be patient and follow The One Way. It had brought me this far. There was no shortcutting it now.

FORTY

Leo led the way from the airport parking lot to the main terminal, his stride at full-length. Since he'd taken over as sheriff, he'd begun to feel responsible for the staff. Not just their work life and careers, but their physical and mental well-being outside the station, too. He hadn't expected this change. Sometimes it was a heavy load. With Clara missing, it was like a bomb had gone off in his central nervous system. He was crackling with motivation and energy, the kind that couldn't be contained by dialing phones, leaving voicemails, and waiting for replies that wouldn't come. The station was less than ten minutes from the airport. It would just be better to show up and shake trees, since he'd already exhausted the information he could get from his Federal Aviation Administration contact out of Salt Lake City via phone. That's how he had learned there had been no plans filed for passenger flights that evening out of Sheridan headed east.

His FAA contact had said, "Looks like all that's registered is a regular parcel delivery flight. A little plane that hops back and forth to Billings for expedited shipments."

It wasn't what they were looking for. Kearny was an uncontrolled airport that didn't have a tower. That meant that anyone could take off from it at any time without filing a flight plan. Unfortunately, from Kearny and throughout the west, a pilot could hopscotch around to uncontrolled airports and leave no trace with the FAA. Things didn't become tricky until further east, and even then flying under the radar—so to speak—was still possible. Difficult and out of the way, but possible. It made policing more challenging.

Leo marched up to the counter through tarps and dust. The place was a construction zone, inside and out, but the terminal was small, with only one airline servicing the community and only two flights in and two out per day. No one was behind the counter.

Delaney was keeping up, just barely. "They only staff the counter when flights are leaving or coming in."

"There has to be someone here."

"You can see, but my experience is often that there is not."

Leo smacked the old-fashioned bell on the counter. The chime it emitted was unsatisfactorily soft. "Hello, back there! This is Sheriff Leo Palmer." When no one appeared, he hopped over the luggage scale.

"Leo!"

"I'm badged. This is an emergency."

"Maybe."

He looked back at her. "Clara being missing isn't an emergency?"

"Yes. It is. But her running off to Boston isn't."

"Until I get confirmation she's there and wants to be, she's missing to me."

He heard her sigh, then the sound of her feet landing on the other side of the luggage scale, too.

"You're not going anywhere without backup."

He grunted and tried the door handle. It was locked. "I'm finally rubbing off on you."

Then the door burst open. "Hey! You can't be..." The woman stopped speaking. "I've seen you on TV. Are you the sheriff?"

Leo took her hand and pumped it before she could object. "Sheriff Leo Palmer. This is Deputy Investigator Delaney Pace. We have reason to believe a missing person—a sheriff's department employee—is up at the airport intending to fly to Boston tonight. We need your help."

She looked bewildered. "We don't have any flights leaving tonight."

Delaney smiled at her. "I didn't catch your name."

"Rhonda Chatterly."

"Ms. Chatterly, if we want to find out whether anyone is leaving on a private plane tonight without filing a flight plan, where would we do that?"

"I don't understand."

"Who would know what planes are leaving and when?"

"Oh. Well, um, I don't know a lot about that. I mostly handle bags and check-in. But you can talk to the airport manager."

"How?"

"I guess, uh, I could put you through?"

Leo said, "As quickly as possible, thank you."

He removed himself to the customer side of the counter, then drummed his fingers until Rhonda handed him her phone. Delaney came to stand beside him.

In his ear, a man said, "Chuck Saenz."

"This is Sheriff Leo Palmer up at the main terminal. I've got a bit of an emergency."

The man's voice was wary but friendly enough. "Hello, Sheriff. How can I help?"

He told Chuck he was putting him on speaker and what they were looking for. "Who would be the person in the best position to know if a plane without a flight plan might be leaving and where it would be going?"

Chuck's answer was immediate. "Ronnie. He works for Bighorn Airways. He fuels up planes. Most pilots don't fuel up until they make final decisions about load and destination, and he normally has a really good idea of who's about to leave. Pilots are a chatty bunch, so he usually hears where they're headed and who's riding with them."

"Thanks, Mr. Saenz. Can you let Bighorn Airways know we're on our way over—if there's anyone there this time of night?" Leo said.

"Oh, they're there. No problem."

Chuck ended the call. Rhonda took her phone.

"Thank you," Leo said. "You helped a lot."

She giggled nervously. "You're welcome. Good luck."

Leo shot Delaney a look. "Feel like racing?"

She made a muscle. "And me without my running shoes." Then she shot ahead of him, immediately out of sight around a corner.

He flashed Rhonda a smile before taking off after his partner. "Have a good night, Ms. Chatterly."

He caught up with Delaney just as they reached the door to Bighorn Airways, which she held open for him.

"You can walk faster than me, but I don't think you have an edge on me running," she said.

"I let you win."

She snorted and entered behind him.

A woman was already moving in their direction. "Chuck just called and said to send you out to talk to Ronnie."

"If you don't mind, that would be great," Leo said.

She waved at a door out to the tarmac, beside a picture window facing the runways and mountains. Like the one from his office windows a few miles away, the view here was thick and brown. One difference—from this vantage point, he could see fire in the distance. *God, I hope the containment operations do some good tonight.*

"Thanks." Delaney was already holding the door again.

"People are going to start to talk about us if you keep doing that for me."

She rolled her eyes. "Fuel truck is over there." She pointed at the truck and the man—tall, skinny, and wearing a drooping wool cap over dreadlocks. "I assume you'll continue taking the lead."

He usually deferred to Delaney on witness questioning. Not only because she was good but because his position sometimes felt threatening to witnesses. But this wasn't the same. It was unrelated to a homicide. "Yes. I'll keep it."

Ronnie had seen them and beckoned them over. He was holding a fuel nozzle inserted into a plane's tank.

They moved closer, walking against the wind. It was eerie to smell smoke at an airport, especially when mixed with the odor of fuel.

Ronnie's voice had a sleepy, dreamy quality. "I heard you're looking to see who's flying out tonight."

"We are. I'm Sheriff Palmer. This is Deputy Investigator Pace."

They all nodded at each other.

"It's been real busy with the fire, but I'm guessing you don't care about the planes in and out on fire response."

"Not really."

"Or about the ones the FAA coulda already told you about. Like this one here."

Maybe, maybe not. "Where's it going?"

"Billings. It goes regular, though. Carries the packages people pay extra for when it absolutely positively has to be there overnight."

"Yeah, I knew about that one."

"The only one that's a little interesting is that twin over

yonder. With the white-on-white paint job. The pilot had me fuel 'er up an hour ago. See his head in there?"

The plane started rolling forward. "Yes."

"Now you see him, now you don't. He's a new face and that's a new plane to me. He took on a pretty heavy fuel load. So, he ain't carrying much. Weird thing was he paid cash for it. Over five grand. Nobody does that anymore. I tried chatting him up, but he wasn't interested in conversating. At first I thought maybe he didn't know much English, but it turned out his accent is pure New England. You know. Chowdah. Buttah."

Leo felt himself bounce once on his toes, excited. An involuntary reaction. "Did he say where he was going?"

"Nope. He didn't say nothing interesting."

"Who's with him?" Outside, the sound of the plane's engines grew louder. Leo looked toward the noise. It was on the runway now and moving fast. Then it lifted and disappeared into the smoky air.

"I didn't get a look at her. An older lady."

"Big, small?"

"Small."

"Short hair or long?"

"Medium."

"Did she seem to be there of her own free will?"

"As opposed to forced?"

"Right."

"She looked fine to me. Jeez, I sound lame. Sorry I can't be more help. I was working on one of the fire service planes when he brought the woman through."

It was consistent with Clara. Not a positive ID, but, coupled with the Find My Phone information, it painted a picture. But what in the world could have happened that Clara wanted out of town so fast? "Anything else you can think of?"

"Sorry, no. I hope it helped."

"It did. Have a good night."

Again, they traded nods. Delaney was looking at her feet as they walked through the little terminal and back to the truck. When they reached it, she stopped and pounded her fist into her other palm. "It doesn't feel right, Leo."

"It's definitely out of character. But the circumstances are accumulating. That description sounded like her."

"It's more than out of character. I'm not convinced she's gone to Boston."

"What are you suggesting?"

"That I want to see her phone records."

"Not a chance in hell on getting a warrant. Her husband doesn't think she's missing."

"Could this be related to our homicides?"

Leo blew a long, slow raspberry. "I don't see any links."

"So, we just have to accept our friend and co-worker ran off without telling any of us?"

He held up his phone. "I got a text."

She winced. "Yeah, but she didn't tell Kat. Or me."

"Until we have any evidence to think otherwise, yes, I think you have to assume that something caused her to act out of character. We prioritize the homicides. Justice for two young women. Prevention of another murder."

Delaney's green eyes seemed to glow, but she didn't argue.

"Sheriff? Deputy?" The woman who had let them into Bighorn Airways appeared.

"Yes?" Leo said.

"Ronnie told you about the plane taking off now?"

"Yes."

"He said he told you about a woman. I didn't see the woman he did, but I did see the other passenger."

"Oh! I didn't know there were two," Leo said.

"I don't think Ronnie did either. He's been chasing his tail in a circle. This damn fire."

Leo nodded. She seemed lost in thought for a moment, so he said, "And the person you saw?"

"It was a young man. I found him a little comical, so I remembered him. One of those types who look like he needs to work outside more. He had on Wranglers with cowboy boots and had a big droopy moustache."

Delaney said to Leo, "Doesn't sound like anyone I've seen Clara with."

"Did you catch a name?" Leo said.

"Oh, no. I didn't meet him. Just had a giggle. I don't imagine he grew up here. But who knows these days. Even in Wyoming lifestyles are changing. I worry that kids aren't as tough as they used to be."

Leo thought of his nephew. An athletic kid, but city raised in California. He rarely lifted a finger to help unless he was forced to, and then it was more like housework than the kind of work that raised callouses. But Leo's upbringing hadn't been a whole lot different and he'd toughened up. Maybe there was hope for the younger generation. "Thank you. This has been very helpful."

Delaney took the woman's contact information, then they made their way back to the station, both of them pensive and flat on the drive. They barely spoke until they reached the entrance, where Sugar was waiting, a smile on her face.

"Tell us something good," Leo said.

"Basilica of the Sacred Heart."

Leo glanced at Delaney. She threw up her hands in a who-knows gesture.

"The cathedral on the University of Notre Dame campus."

"I'm still stumped," Leo said.

"It's the engraving on the crucifix we found out at the Planter ranch!"

"Oh! That's great." Notre Dame. Did he know someone who'd gone to school there?

"You're welcome." She seemed put out by their lack of enthusiasm.

"Thank you. Thank you very much for doing your job so well."

She harrumphed. "By the way, I'm working solo. Trey had a death in the family and had to fly home."

Bells started ringing in Leo's head, but he was interrupted by Brawny—that was his actual, given name—who was covering for Clara while she was out. It had only been planned for today but was about to get extended through the week. Leo would break it to him later.

"Sheriff, Chief Yellowtail asked me to tell you that someone named Albert Tuttle was just pulled over for a busted taillight here in Kearny. They arrested him, and they're on the way to the jail with him now."

For half a second, there was silence. Then Delaney let out an excited, "Whoop!"

Sugar turned back from her retreat to the lab. "Now you show some enthusiasm."

Leo pumped his fist. Just the guy he most wanted to talk to.

FORTY-ONE

Drew caught up with Delaney and Leo just as they headed into his office to plan the Tuttle interview.

"Did you find Clara?" he said.

"Maybe. We think so," Delaney responded.

"That's cryptic."

"Just inconclusive."

"Ah. She's solid. I'll be praying for her. But, hey, I have something else. On the homicides. I talked to the owner at that fancy sword company the festival guy turned us onto. Infiniquity."

"That's great," Leo said, taking a seat behind his desk.

Delaney remained standing since there was only one more chair.

"Mostly great. He won't give us a customer list without a warrant."

"Did you get him one?"

"I wanted to see if you wanted me to get one."

Delaney saw Leo's jaw tighten.

"I would have thought you had one ready to go, anticipating

this happening, so we wouldn't lose time. Those swords are our most critical pieces of evidence. A possible link to the killer."

Drew's Adam's apple bulged. "Sorry. I, uh—"

Leo said, "I should have been more direct with my instructions."

But it was Delaney who had given him guidance, and she'd asked him to get the warrant going before he even contacted Infiniquity. Had he substituted his judgment for hers or just messed up?

Drew shifted back and forth on his feet. "Thank you."

Leo said, "But you shouldn't still be standing here. We need that warrant *yesterday*."

"Got it. I have a conflict, though. I was going to go to dinner—"

"Cancel or reschedule. Get that warrant going. And when you're done with that, huddle with Sugar, put a team together, and go search A1 House Cleaners. With everything that happened today, it slipped off our radar, and now we're about to interview Tuttle."

"Yes, sir." Drew's expression was a little annoyed behind his surprise. He walked away with heavy feet.

Again, Delaney wondered if she could trust him. Her loyalty was to the department and to Leo, but still she felt like she needed to give Drew a chance. She would talk to him about why he'd withheld information about the Cowpoke Café video. Soon.

Ten minutes later, Delaney and Leo were set up in an interview room with Albert Tuttle, his booking having been held off until after their conversation. She eyed Leo appraisingly. He looked as tired as she felt. Her body tingled in a strange way. After a second she recognized it. She wanted to give Leo a hug.

She was not going to. But she wanted to oh-so-badly.

Focus, Delaney, focus. She couldn't believe their luck that he'd been arrested. The two Kearny cops who'd seen the broken taillight—Caitlin Porter and Devon Peele—had no idea who they'd netted since he'd switched out license plates. They'd pulled up behind him in an unmarked vehicle after he parked and walked up on either side of him. When he resisted, they were in the perfect position to catch him and did, only to learn once they ran his ID what a big fish they'd landed.

Delaney gave him a sunbeam smile while holding her breath. The man needed a shower or to be dunked in disinfectant. "Great to see you home safe and sound, Mr. Tuttle. Even more, without you pointing any kind of weapon at me."

"Or me," Leo said.

"Lawyer," Tuttle said.

Leo sipped from a cup of coffee. "A Legal Aid attorney is on her way. In the meantime, you are free not to answer any questions. We are also free to sit with you and chat with each other. So, that's what Delaney and I are going to do. Just chat with the cameras running because that's how we like it."

Delaney said, "I'm going to Mirandize him on camera, Leo. Devon and Caitlin already did, but I'd like one for our keepsake memories album, too."

Tuttle said, "Fuck you, lady cop."

"Oops, got that on there. I hope no one in posterity is easily offended." Delaney recited the Miranda warnings and dragged Tuttle through the acknowledgments. Then she said, "On to the good stuff! Hey, Sheriff, did I hear that you're going to charge Mr. Tuttle with two counts of attempted first degree murder and another two of aggravated assault?"

Leo responded in a cheerful voice. "You heard right. Not only that, all four charges involve police officers. Guess what that means?"

Delaney gave a happy gasp. "Longer sentences!"

"Damn straight. Unless the defendant cuts a deal."

"But how can a defendant make himself attractive for a deal when he's a low-life human trafficking pimp with a long list of convictions and outstanding warrants all across the US?"

Leo pointed at her. "That's the million-dollar question. To which the answer is that he provides information that aids in the apprehension and conviction of the scum sucker who murdered two young women in Kearny last week."

"I don't know shit about that," Tuttle spat out.

"Didn't ask you if you did," Delaney said. "Let the video record reflect that neither Leo nor I asked Mr. Tuttle any questions."

"So reflected," Leo said.

"You know what I want to know, Leo?"

"What, Delaney?"

"I want to know where Anna Petrov is."

"You and me both, bitch," Tuttle said. "And Mika."

"Language, Mr. Tuttle," Leo said.

"Like I give two shits. Or one."

Delaney lifted her shoulders and dropped them. "Sticks and guns may break my buns, but words will never hurt me. Back to the topic at hand. The other thing that is keeping me up at night is what happened to Anong's and Genevieve's babies."

Tuttle crossed his arms and looked down.

Leo nodded. "I could forgive a lot if I just knew how all that went down, where they are, how they got there, you know? The details of an illegal adoption ring would go a long way toward a great plea deal on these pesky first-degree cop killer charges."

"I didn't kill no cop!" Tuttle's handcuffs rattled as he jerked at them.

Delaney leaned toward Tuttle, looking directly into his eyes. "A smart guy would tell us."

"You ain't got the stroke to make no deals."

Leo laughed. "I've got the stroke to request them. Or oppose them."

Tuttle was shaking his head. "I didn't hurt no babies."

Delaney said, "Leo, did you think he hurt babies?"

"Nope. I think he sold babies that made some parents very happy."

"Damn straight," Tuttle said. "I make people happy. I'm in the 'make people happy' business."

"Albert," Delaney purred. "I don't want you to talk about this. Your attorney isn't here yet."

"Well, get the jerk here so I can."

She snapped her fingers. "You know what, Leo? You could ask the County Attorney what kind of deal he'd be willing to cut if Albert were to tell us who had the babies and how he connected with the parents? Anything else?"

"I'd think he'd want to tell us the fathers or any boyfriends of the mothers, if he knew who they were."

"Only if he wanted to."

"True."

"Call him," Tuttle said. "I want to. I want my attorney, and I want a deal, and I want it all now."

FORTY-TWO

Leo poured himself coffee and cereal from his secret stash in the breakroom and took them to his office. Milk sloshed over the side of the bowl onto his desk. He blotted it with a Kleenex, too tired to go for a rag to clean up the mess. Did he even sleep at all the night before? Some days he wondered why he was running for the sheriff job. He shoveled in a mouthful of cereal then opened his email, hoping for a miracle. Several would be good. The fire at bay. Clara, home. And a killer behind bars, having turned himself in.

He went zero for three.

He decided to call Skeeter. It was early, but the private detective picked up on the first ring and agreed to start shadowing Freddy several hours a week immediately. The arrangement couldn't go on forever. Leo was dipping hard into the money he'd inherited from his parents. He couldn't think of a better way to use it, but the supply wasn't infinite.

He turned his attention to the backlog accumulating on his desk. As he was reading an operations update on the fire—work had been difficult and slow while the spread was steady and heartbreaking—there was a knock on his door frame. He smiled, expecting Delaney, but he smelled a strong, flowery perfume. A familiar one.

"Good morning, brother."

Leo turned to face his sister. *How in the world did she get in the building, and what is she doing here so early?* "Good morning, sister."

She flopped into the seat in front of his desk. "I can't believe I have to get up at the crack of dawn and chase you to work if I want an audience with you."

He nearly laughed, but not with good humor. "A lot going on at the moment, Adriana."

"Like the world revolves around you."

"More like I'm revolving around it."

"This bombshell about you and Delaney is causing a lot of embarrassment for Freddy. And for me, too, frankly."

Leo clenched his teeth. "Speaking of embarrassment, I heard you had some car trouble yesterday."

"Yet you didn't call to check on me."

"I didn't need to. Since you were violating road closure and evacuation orders, you got plenty of attention from people that had other, more important jobs to be doing. Like I did. In addition to the fire and the murders, Clara is—"

"I got fired yesterday, Leo."

This was no shock to him and should not have surprised her either, since she was on final warning. "I'm sorry to hear that. What was the reason?"

"They said I was late, and that a final warning meant 'any further infractions of the rules would result in immediate termination.'" She made air quotes with her fingers. "If I'd known that, I wouldn't have been late, would I?"

Leo took another big bite of cereal. Adriana would have to look for sympathy for not respecting rules other people had to follow someplace else. This is exactly what had gotten her in trouble with the road closures the day before, too.

"As soon as I find a job and a place to live, I'm out of here, whether you're coming or not. I was up sending emails to old contacts in San Diego all night."

"I'm not leaving Kearny." He hated telling her this while she was upset about her job, but he had to. "And I think you should reconsider. The cartel has figured out I was working undercover when I was with them. They don't know my real identity, but they're trying to figure it out. Skeeter Rawlins is going to start keeping an eye on Freddy and you. For security reasons."

Her eyes narrowed to slits and vertical lines appeared between her eyebrows. "You're kidding me. Please tell me you're kidding me."

Even if his sister was a pain in the butt and planning to move away, he loved her and Freddy, and he would do anything necessary to keep them safe. "I wish I was."

She shook her head and flicked her hair. "Like I said, I'm out of here. You're a danger to us." She got up and walked toward the door.

"Where are you headed at seven a.m.?" *Without Freddy.*

"To the Loafing Shed. Not that you'd care, but Mary asked if I could help her out. So, I'm starting with the breakfast shift, until I figure out where Freddy and I are going. It's not like I can leave town today even if I wanted to. Freddy has tickets to the Renaissance Festival. Again."

She couldn't make it to her job at ten a.m., but the day after she was fired, she could be out the door at dawn? *She's her own worst enemy.* "That's nice of you. Delaney said Carrie's working up there, too. And Kat's helping watch Juan Julio some."

She turned back to him, hands on hips. "By the way, there's something going on there. Just so you and Delaney know there's more at stake in your little will-they-won't-they than just yourselves."

Adriana was so angry lately. So unhappy. A few months

before she'd encouraged him to pursue Delaney. Maybe moving *would* help her. Or being with Mary. Mary was a hardworking and super positive single mother whose baby daddy was dead. "What's going on?"

"Something between Freddy and Kat. Their texts. Very flirty."

Leo couldn't keep up. Last he'd known, Freddy was inconsolable over Ashley dumping him. "Did he show them to you?"

"I'm his *mother*. I have the password to his phone."

Suddenly, two shapes filled his doorway. Drew and Delaney. Drew's eyes popped when they landed on Adriana. She did a double take as well, then smiled at him. Drew smiled back at her, sappy and decidedly unlike his normally cool self.

"Goodbye, Leo. If you need me, remember I'll be at the Loafing Shed all day." She never broke eye contact with Drew as she made the announcement.

"Talk to you later, Adriana."

She threw Drew one more smoldering glance before she disappeared into the hall.

Drew looked dazed. He walked backwards into the office, watching the doorway as if Adriana would magically return through it. "Who was that?"

Leo shook his head. "My sister. I love her but consider this a warning. She's a challenge."

"She's gorgeous. Is she married?"

Delaney put a hand on his shoulder. "Slow your roll, Romeo. We need your update before you dive off the deep end."

Drew sucked in a deep breath, then grinned. "Sorry."

Delaney dropped into her usual chair in front of Leo's desk. She looked tired. Beautiful as always, but tired. "Junior is in early today to give us an update."

Drew nodded. "Genevieve's place was empty. Like professionally-cleaned-after-someone-moved-out empty. Sugar is there trying to raise something."

"May the force be with her," Leo said. "She has a neighbor. Mika, who is also now missing, but believed to be heading home. Can you try to track her down?"

"Sure, boss. My list is getting long, but I like it. Backing up a little bit, though, yesterday when I was getting nowhere on similar cases, I called the Casper office of the FBI."

"Why?" Delaney rolled her eyes at Leo.

"I dated the special agent in charge a few times. She's good people. She's searching their databases nationwide for better matches to our cases."

"They have more information than we do, Delaney," Leo said. "And free manpower. You know it's unlikely this is the first time our killer has done bad things."

She made grumbly noises.

Drew flicked lint off his shirt then adjusted it. It was a little snug around his upper arms and none too loose anywhere else. In Drew's shoes—or shirt—Leo would have gone up a size or two for comfort. "When I got to work this morning, she'd sent me a profile for our killer."

Delaney threw her hands up in the air. "Oh, let me guess. White male, mid to late thirties, a history of abuse, mommy issues, and he was mean to kitty cats as a child."

Drew actually laughed. "It's like you read it."

"Our job is about finding and following actual evidence, not looking for evidence to match a bedtime story."

"How do you really feel about it, Delaney?" Leo raised his eyebrows at her.

She shrugged, then she smiled, too. Their eye contact seemed like only a moment, but it must have been more because Drew cleared his throat.

He said, "On to other items—I finished the interviews at the festival. It was a long day. And night."

"Anything useful?" Leo said. Were his cheeks red? They felt warm.

Drew rocked his hand, palm down. "I don't really think so. But we'll see how things develop."

"What are you up to now?" Leo asked.

"I'm grabbing some chow. Maybe at the Loafing Shed." He grinned sheepishly. "It's going to be another long day. Want anything?"

"Nothing for me," Delaney said. "But come find me when you're back, okay? I'd like to go over something."

Drew gave her a thumbs-up.

Leo shrugged, then remembered his cereal. "Thanks, but I already ate. And seriously—my sister? Think twice."

Drew was laughing as he left.

Delaney said, "I'm going to set up a meeting ASAP with Planter's brother, Larry. The one who might be jealous of Lucas's good fortune and loves all things fantasy and dress-up."

"I want to be there."

"Also, uh, I'm taking over the video work from Drew."

"I thought he was done with it and didn't find anything."

She looked at her feet for a moment, then back up at him. "Oh—good news. I'm serving Drew's warrant on Infiniquity."

"I'm still upset about how he handled that one. We lost twenty-four hours."

"Let me keep a closer eye on him and report back. Hopefully it's just learning pains."

Leo hoped so, too. Kearny County couldn't handle another bad cop, and he sure didn't want someone he had hired to turn out dirty.

FORTY-THREE

Later that morning, Delaney stood waiting for Larry Planter at the department's entrance desk. The man who sashayed in the door in a cape and feathered cap had Lucas Planter's height, but not his muscular build or broad girth. This man was slim and elegant, graying at the temples with crepey skin around his eyes. She could picture him wielding a rapier, sword-fighting at Versailles, Three Musketeers-style. Here, in twenty-first-century Wyoming, it was hard to sell the look, but he was doing a decent job of it.

"Mr. Planter?" she said.

He led with his gloved hand extended. "Larry."

She took it and shook. "Larry."

"Ms. Pace."

She didn't offer her given name or correct him, even though her title was Deputy Investigator. Usually, she assumed people of a certain age made the mistake out of a misguided attempt at good manners and let it go until they proved her wrong. She considered herself a feminist—and a helluva lot stronger than many modern feminists who talked big but couldn't back it up with old-fashioned self-sufficiency—but a traditional one. She didn't give a good goldurn how the rest of the world classified her. Every year, though, she felt the weight of change creeping up on her. She'd held it at bay on the ice roads of Canada and even in the wilds of Wyoming. But the old ways were changing. The face of Wyoming was changing. It wasn't just people from California moving in. It was people from all over the world—with their current cases as a prime example. Objectively, she knew this was inevitable and even good. Still, a part of her wanted to hang on to the cherished past forever.

"Thanks for coming in so quickly after I called."

"Of course. I'm here for the festival today. I hope you don't mind?" He flourished a sleeve with an immaculate lace ruffle at the wrist. "I was already dressed and on my way here."

"Not at all. You liven up the place." She gestured ahead of her. "Take your first right. Third door on your left."

Leo was working his phone at the conference table, but he looked up as they entered, then stood. Delaney introduced the two men, then took the seat next to Leo.

Larry sat across from them and spoke before she or Leo had a chance to. "I've been waiting for my phone to ring. Lucas told me my name came up in his interview the other day. I was beginning to feel slighted." His smile seemed genuine. Like coming here today was entertainment.

"No, it's just been crazy busy. The homicides and the fire. Our small department." Leo didn't smile back at him.

Something's eating at Leo. Had he taken a dislike to Larry? She slipped into her usual lead questioning role. "Tell us about you, Larry. What you do for a living, your relationship with your brother, your connection to your grandfather's ranch. Just your story, however you'd like it to unfold."

"I teach art at Sheridan College. Sculpture. Not drawing or painting, although clearly all the visual arts are intertwined. What I create and teach is very physical."

"Like clay?"

"Yes, but also wood working and metalsmithing. An artist has to be able to work with many different mediums."

Delaney nodded. "What kinds of things do you metalsmith?"

He waved a hand through the air. "We start with welding. We let our imaginations guide us."

"Have you ever made blades?"

"I've tried my hand, but I wouldn't say they're my specialty. I'm more interested in metal without sharp edges. Violence doesn't express who I am."

"What about your students? Any with a particular interest in swords?"

"Who doesn't love a good sword, Ms. Pace?"

Leo shook his head. "Deputy Investigator Pace."

"My apologies, Deputy Investigator."

She dipped her head, feeling heat in her neck. Leo always stuck up for her, but he stuck up for everyone in the department. It was one of the things she loved about him. *Like—that I like about him.* "Any particular students come to mind when I ask this question?"

"I had one a few years ago who loved metalsmithing and swords. I'll get his name for you when I get home. Right now, it escapes me."

"All right. Let's move on to your relationship with Lucas. Tell me about it."

"My big brother is a bit of an Ist."

"What do you mean by that?"

"Rac-ist. Misogyn-ist. He's anti anything but straight white Christian males and their women. We aren't in contact unless he has something to say that may hurt me, in which case he can't make that call fast enough."

"Okay. Then I can assume you don't have much of a relationship?"

Larry snorted. "He doesn't like any of my boyfriends, for starters."

Aha. She hadn't wanted to assume he was gay, but if pressed, that would have been her guess.

"Or my girlfriends."

And a good thing she hadn't assumed.

"He was always the favorite. The football player. The steer wrestler. The one who got married and had two point five kids before his wife wised up and left him."

"The favorite?"

"The one who got invited to dinner on Sundays and inherits the family ranch."

There it is. "And you?"

"I'm the one they wished stayed in Albuquerque after I graduated from New Mexico State. The real irony? I'm the blood relation. Lucas isn't."

"What do you mean?"

"Lucas is adopted. My parents thought they couldn't have kids. Then when Lucas was a baby, I came along. But blood isn't thicker than water in this case."

Delaney nodded. "I'm sorry. That must hurt."

"Not nearly as much as you'd think, anymore." He winked at her.

"Why is that?"

"Maturity. Apathy. Perspective. My family is a bunch of miserable jerks. I'm creatively and emotionally fulfilled and happy."

"Are you going to inherit anything or does everything go to your brother?"

"Everything to him. The funny thing is that as a child, it was me who was close to my grandparents. I spent time out at the ranch. I know every inch of it by heart. I tended garden with Nana. I rode fence with Papa. I still hunt out there but mostly shooting with a lens and not a rifle. But in the end they didn't know how to reconcile loving me with loving the words written long ago by people they never knew who claimed to be speaking for God." A lump rose in his throat. "I was right there in front of them. Living, breathing, loving. But the dead guys who wrote the Bible won that round."

Delaney could relate. But this wasn't the time for her story. "If you've found creative and emotional fulfillment and happiness, I think you win."

He smiled, eyes bright.

"When was the last time you were out at the ranch?"

"Oh, my. Maybe a month ago? A little less?"

More recently than Lucas knew. "Did you notice anything that gave you pause?"

He frowned and then pulled at his upper lip. "I couldn't say anything for sure. I don't control who comes and goes, obviously. But I did notice the back gate was a little loose."

Leo raised his hand. "California upbringing. Can you explain what you mean, please?"

"It's a wire loop gate. Quite hard to open, usually. Last time I visited, it felt like it had been stretched out. I didn't have to strain to open it."

"Gotcha."

Delaney said, "Did you tell your brother?"

"No. I never thought about it again until you asked. But it wouldn't have made a difference if I did. To him, nothing I say matters, nothing I do matters, nothing I am matters."

Delaney couldn't think of an adequate reply. She let the emotional resonance of his words hang in the air until the edges melted to expose an anger so deep and seething that it raised her eyebrows and the hair on her arms.

After a debrief with Leo on Larry Planter, Delaney felt a niggling sense of something she needed to do. She went back to her work area, hoping she'd jog her memory there somehow. The first thing she did was check for messages, hoping she'd heard from Drew. A text. A call. A note on her desk. She couldn't wait much longer to talk to Leo about the video.

There was nothing from him, nor did she see him at his desk. But she had other messages.

A text from Carrie. *Kat is going to the festival today WITH FREDDY.*

None from Kat, who was still freezing her out. She prayed Freddy wasn't leading Kat on. Or using her to try to make Ashley jealous.

One from Skeeter. *Progress. When can you talk?*

In her email, she found one she was hoping for, from Infiniquity. She'd arranged for an old buddy of Leo's to be waiting at their offices in Sacramento to serve the warrant. She read eagerly.

Detective: We have been expecting your warrant since our conversation with Deputy Knowles and prepared the attached document in advance. We have no problem providing it—we just needed that warrant to protect our company. I hope this information is helpful. It's horrible for everyone that something like this happened, including us and our customers. Dawn Andrine, Owner

Delaney opened the attachment, holding her breath. Everything Kearny County had asked for in the warrant was there. Lists of customers who had purchased either of the swords used in the homicides, broken down by type. One list a hundred long, the other seventy-nine. And a third list: customers who bought both of them. Only ten people on that one. But there was more. A fourth list—people who also bought *additional* swords. It was three people long.

She felt sharp tingles of anticipation, forcing air into her lungs. What had the metalsmith at the festival told them? How people in their world were cagey and cutesy about names? She took the list of ten, none of whom she recognized—but why would she?—and starred the three who had purchased even more. Her intuition told her to start with those three, even though it sickened her to consider what that meant. That the killer either had already used additional swords or planned to. The most enthusiastic purchasers had bought *five* different longswords.

God forbid they used them all. A worse thought seized her. *Or were getting additional swords from different suppliers, too.*

The first one of the three was Questway, out of Wisconsin. The order had been placed by Matilda Tuscany. That sounded like a gaming company, which might make some sense in the context of sword collecting.

Next was a Robbin Hood, out of Missouri. She rolled her eyes. Not original, Robbin. But definitely medieval.

The third one made her clutch her stomach. Not because of the name—Numero Unobae. It meant nothing to her. But because of the place. An address in Kearny, Wyoming. One she knew. She'd been there very recently.

"Leo," she shouted. "You've got to see this."

Footsteps came at her from three directions. She looked up to see Joe first. "You're about to get a call from a reporter about the sexual discrimination in our department."

She shook her head to clear her thoughts, taken aback. "What?"

"Your assignment to these homicides instead of me. I'm more senior than you. I believe it's because of sexual favoritism by Leo. I wanted you to hear it from me first."

Behind her, a second voice. Drew. "What do you have, Delaney? Because I've got something for you and Leo."

And then a third. Leo. "This is between you and me, Joe. Leave Delaney out of it."

Joe's voice was sneering. "How can I, when she's right in the middle?"

"She doesn't make the decisions. I do."

She stood. "If I was Leo I'd choose me, too, because I have my priorities straight. I don't pull stunts that distract us from our jobs to the detriment of public safety, unlike you. And, if I were you, I'd see the fire assignment as a compliment. He knows how terrible I'd be at what you're doing and how great you *should* have been at it if it weren't for your obsession with this. Or with the primary voting, rather. It's not my job to talk to reporters, so your friend won't be speaking with me. Right now, you won't be either. We're at a critical point in our investigation." She made a shooing motion with her hand.

Joe's face went beet red. "How dare you speak to me like that!"

She turned to Leo, catching sight of Drew's face as she did. He was grinning and nodding.

"Go," Leo said. "You and I will talk later."

"We most certainly will." Joe's face receded from Delaney's line of sight.

"What have you guys got?" Leo said.

Delaney shook her head. "Mine is for one-on-one. Your office."

Drew frowned. "Before you go, then. I talked to Mika's mother. She wasn't warm and fuzzy. She hadn't known Mika was in Kearny, and she hasn't seen or heard from her in a year."

"That's disappointing," Leo said. "I thought the manager at her apartments was telling us the truth."

Drew turned to go. As he did, he said, "Maybe he was. Maybe Mika lied to him. Or hasn't told her mother she's on the way home and isn't there yet. Or changed her mind."

"Or someone changed it for her." Delaney was halfway to Leo's office. She sped up and went in before Leo then walked all the way to the window. She pressed her fingers into the frame, unseeing.

Leo shut the door behind him. "What is it?"

"So many things." She closed her eyes.

"I'm sorry about Joe."

She turned around, waving the Joe issue off. "Infiniquity responded to the warrant. They went above and beyond."

"And?"

"There's someone on their lists who's purchased swords like the ones used on Anong and Genevieve as well as three other longswords. They have a Kearny, Wyoming, address. There are a few others in that category as well who live elsewhere, but this one I needed to tell you about ASAP."

"Wow, okay. Kearny—that sounds like a great lead. But you seem upset. Why?"

"Because the address belongs to the same person I saw on video at the Cowpoke Café potentially passing a medieval coin."

"Potentially?"

"You can't tell for sure with the video. Definitely leaving change, and now with the sword purchase, my antennae are up."

"This is great. Who is it? We can go pick him up now."

She held up a palm. "It's sticky situation, Leo."

"Why?"

"Because the address belongs to Drew Knowles."

FORTY-FOUR

FORTY-EIGHT YEARS BEFORE

The girl became reckless. Not about boys. Never about boys. About *horses*. The horses her father barely used to let her touch. She still did what he called the women's work, but now he stood at the fence and watched her when she saddled up at dusk, skipping dinner to work the three-year-old who was so quick none of the men wanted to train him. When they did, often as not they ended up on their hind ends on packed dirt.

But she never lost her seat.

She set up the three-barrel pattern and took the horse through them like she didn't care if she lived or died, because she didn't. The horse frothed at the mouth and pawed the ground, desperate to run. Her father shouted instructions to her sometimes. She never looked at him and didn't seem to hear him.

One day he showed up with a cowboy. "He's going to teach you a few things."

She shrugged and kept riding.

Now the cowboy shouted the instructions. She listened to him, sometimes. She learned. The horse improved. So did she.

The cowboy said, "Your father's paying me, you know. He wants you to enter a race."

She'd looked him in the eye for the first time. Racing was something she'd like to do. "Okay."

"There's decent prize money in it. If you win, he said he'd split it with me."

"What part is mine?"

When the cowboy didn't have an answer, she asked her father.

"When you pay me back," he said.

"For what?"

"The cowboy. The horse. Anything else it costs to get you entered and to the rodeos."

She asked him to write it down and sign it. He did. She surprised everyone by winning at her first rodeo. The cowboy was standing with her father when she brought over the prize money. Every weekend that summer, they took her to a different town. By the end of the summer, her father signed the horse over to her.

The next summer after she graduated high school and between rodeos, the cowboy asked her to marry him. She was surprised. He'd never shown any sign of wanting to make her do the things her uncle had. When she told him no, he didn't act upset. Just told her he'd see her the next day.

Her mother asked her that night what answer she'd given him.

"How did you know about it?"

"He had to ask your father for your hand."

"I don't want to marry anyone. I told him that."

Her mother shook her head. "It's time for you to get married. You can't stay here anymore. He has a family ranch. He'll be a good provider."

"I can provide for myself." The girl had plans. If things

went well then by the end of this summer, she'd have enough saved to move out.

"Barrel racing? There's no security in that. You could get injured and never ride again. We worked hard not to let your past cost you a future, with a husband and other children and a home. But we won't be supporting you the rest of your life. Your father told him yes."

The girl was upset. She woke up the next morning having decided that the cowboy was a better option than her parents, though. She told him she'd changed her mind.

He nodded, rubbing his chin. "How about this Thursday? Before we leave for the next rodeo. Then your father doesn't have to come with us."

The girl had one friend from school. She grew up at the next ranch down the road. She'd married her boyfriend the weekend after graduation and moved to town. The girl told the cowboy, "I will if you take me to see Lisa today."

"Your dad won't like it if you don't practice the barrels."

"By Thursday it won't matter anymore what he likes."

The cowboy drove her to see Lisa. When Lisa opened the door, the smell of cookies baking enveloped the girl. It was how she'd wished her own home had smelled like and never known it until that second. Welcoming. She would make her own home like that.

Lisa squealed and hugged her. "Come in! I'm so glad to see you."

The girl didn't waste time. The cowboy was waiting in the truck outside. "I'm getting married in two days."

"That's wonderful." Lisa hugged her. "I'm so happy for you."

The girl blurted out what she'd come to say. "Does your husband hurt you?"

Lisa laughed. "Goodness no."

"In the way between men and women?"

"No. He's very gentle. Sweet. It hurt a little at first, but I like it now. Which is a good thing, because he wants to before work, at lunch, when he comes home, and after dinner." She waggled her eyebrows. "Are you scared?"

"I had someone who forced me when I was younger. It was very bad."

"Oh, my God! I'm so sorry. You poor thing! Forcing you is a crime. Was he punished?"

The girl believed he had been, by God. "Yes."

"Marriage is different. You'll be okay. And it can lead to babies."

Without warning a big, fat tear ran down the girl's face. "It already did."

Lisa grabbed her by both wrists. "You have a child?" she whispered.

The girl shook her head. "They took it away."

"That's where you were—when you left school that spring!"

"Yes. At my aunt and uncle's ranch."

Lisa pulled her into a tight hug. "Does your fiancé know?"

"No. And you can't tell anyone. Ever."

"Your secret is safe with me."

FORTY-FIVE

Leo and Delaney left his office together and headed straight for Drew's workstation, which was empty.

"Have you seen Drew?" Leo asked Joe.

Joe kept typing at his computer. "He left five minutes ago."

"Left? What do you mean?"

Joe raised his fingers and his voice. He spoke slowly. "That he is no longer here."

Leo didn't take the bait. "I mean, was he headed to the break room or out of the building?"

"I'm not the hall monitor." Joe put his hands back on his keyboard.

Leo gritted his teeth. Delaney shook her head. They walked back by her desk.

She pointed at the papers on it. "I left the lists there. Maybe he saw them."

Leo took out his phone. "I'm calling him." After a few seconds, he said, "This is the sheriff. Call me immediately."

"Should we put out an all-points bulletin?"

Leo motioned for her to follow him back into his office.

Once they were in it with the door shut, he said, "I'd really like to keep this quiet. Not go through monitored channels."

"Why don't I see if Clint is close? He'd go find him on the down-low."

A pained expression crossed Leo's face.

"We need someone we can trust, Leo."

He hesitated, then nodded.

Eyes locked on his, she made the call. Clint picked up on the first ring.

She explained their situation on speaker. "We want to talk to him, but without scaring people. Sending someone out to pick up a cop would cause a panic. But lollygagging on this would be even worse." She turned to Leo. "What do the trackers say about his location?"

Leo was already pulling them up on his screen. He'd installed locators on department vehicles and phones for the safety and security of his deputies. "His vehicle is in the parking lot here. But his phone shows him at..." He looked up, frowning. "What the hell?"

"What is it?"

"He's at my house."

"Oh, my God," Delaney said.

Leo recited his address. "Clint, please hurry. Are you by yourself?"

"No. I have another state cop with me. All good. I'll be in touch as soon as I know something."

"Thank you," Delaney said.

"Anything to help."

She ended the call and stared at Leo, shaking her head. "I don't get it."

"I don't like it."

"At least Freddy should be at the festival, from what I hear. Him and Kat."

The way Leo cut his eyes away told her that he knew something was brewing between his nephew and her daughter.

"You knew?"

"I'm not surprised. Adriana said it's getting pretty flirty."

"Well, hopefully that means he's safe, anyway."

"And Adriana is working at the Loafing Shed."

Delaney started pacing the office. "I just can't figure out why he'd be going there."

"Maybe he's not. Maybe he's just out taking a walk." Leo refreshed his results. He grimaced and shook his head. "Still there."

"You want me to drive you over?"

He turned to look out at the view. Over his shoulder, she saw nothing but smoke.

"I don't want to draw any attention to this until we have to."

"It could just be you going home to pick up something you forgot, to anyone that saw you."

"Or you and me heading to my house mid-day looking cozy."

He had a point. Delaney's phone rang. Expecting Clint, she picked up.

Before she said a word, a woman's voice rolled over her. "Detective Pace, this is Melanie Pritchett. I'm calling to see if you'd like to comment—"

Her face grew so hot so fast it felt like needle pricks under her skin. "No comment."

"—on the story about Joe Tarver facing sex discrimination at the Kearny County Sheriff's Department?"

"No comment."

"Or on the audiotape in my possession of you and Sheriff Palmer discussing your relationship?"

"No comment."

"Or on whether it is appropriate for Leo Palmer to be running for sheriff when he is dating you?"

"We aren't dating. No further comment."

"Fine. Swapping spit."

Delaney hung up the phone.

Leo stood and walked over to her. "Was that the horrible reporter?"

She sighed, feeling deflated. "Yes. It's going to be hard to prove nothing is happening. It's like showing the absence of evidence. No one will believe us."

He stepped closer. "I don't care."

"I do. Kat has her nose out of joint. And this could cost you the election."

He put his hands on her upper arms. "It's okay."

Every nerve ending in her body caught fire. "It's not."

He pulled her into the hug she'd yearned to give him not long before. She wanted to tell him it was a bad idea. The worst. But right at that moment, being encircled by his arms felt like the best idea in the world. The heat of his body was soothing but exhilarating at the same time. Her cheek pressed into his shoulder. His heart thumped against her ear. His chest rose and fell under her neck. And the way he smelled, like sunshine and pheromones and bad decisions.

She lifted her hands. Touched his shoulder blades with her fingertips. Using every bit of her will power, she swallowed hard, then disengaged. Gently. Regretfully. Sadly.

Her phone rang again. She took a step back and this time read her caller ID. "It's Clint." She answered him on speaker. "You've got Leo and me."

"The suspect has been apprehended." Something about Clint's voice suggested mirth. "In flagrante delicto."

"Caught in the act of what?" she said.

"Fornicating." Now there was a definite smile in Clint's tone.

"He's naked?" Leo's voice was incredulous.

"As the day he was born. Apparently, he received a lift from the department and an invitation to enter and remove his clothing from one of the residents at your address."

Leo groaned and put a hand on his head. "Adriana."

"Yes, sir."

Delaney burst out laughing. "They work fast. They just met this morning."

"Jesus," Leo said. "Well, bring him in. We need to talk to him."

"With his clothes on," Delaney added.

FORTY-SIX

Leo and Delaney parked next to a row of travel trailers at the fairgrounds. He was going to let Drew stew in his own juices for an hour before going back to talk to him. It would give Leo time to calm down, too. Around them, people in their idea of Renaissance garb laughed and jostled as they headed for the entrance to the festival. The juxtaposition of evacuees from the fire setting up temporary housing amidst the ongoing revelry was surreal, with the sounds of raucous laughter and the smell of roasted corn mixing with smoke in the air. What other choice did the county have to offer the evacuees, though? The parking lot here had water, electrical and sewer hook-ups, and room for everyone, even with the Renaissance Festival staff using a fair number of the spots. It decreased the available parking spaces for festival goers, but parking wasn't a scarce commodity in Kearny. People would have to walk a little further. No one was complaining—or not many were—because of the reason.

The fire.

Leo looked toward the mountains. For the first time, he could see the orange glow of fire in that direction from town. It was sobering. Scary, even.

A man stood on the steps to a trailer. His teeth were pegged, but his face was healthy and his weight good. *A former meth addict?* He raised a hand, then gestured for Delaney and Leo to enter.

"You're Mr. Kestrel?" Leo said. He had gone to the county attorney about a deal for Tuttle that morning, and the county attorney had immediately taken an offer to Tuttle's public defender. They hadn't agreed to terms yet, but, as a sign of good faith with more information promised when things were official, Tuttle had given them two names: Mitch and Laurel Kestrel. Leo had tracked them down only to discover that they'd been evacuated from their home because of the fire. Luckily, they hadn't gone far. Just to the fairgrounds.

"I am. The missus is inside. Please come in," he said.

On their way over, Delaney had tried calling Shirleen to see if she could give them any context, but the social worker hadn't picked up. Leo didn't like going into this meeting with so little information, but so be it.

They entered the trailer. Leo had expected it to be cramped and dismal, but it was actually cheerful. The trailer had sliders extended on both sides. The floor plan was a series of sections broken up by different elevations. A bedroom high in the back, through which he could see clothes piled. A cluttered kitchen and dining area low in the middle. A living room high again in the front. There were numerous windows, all with the blinds up and curtains drawn back. Leo stepped on something and looked down. A tiny plastic dump truck. Luckily, he hadn't broken it.

A woman was standing in the living area holding a blond-haired little boy. He wasn't an infant, but not really yet a toddler. Her face looked drawn and her eyes like she'd been crying. The tension in the air crackled.

"Mrs. Kestrel?" Leo said. "I'm Sheriff Palmer. This is Deputy Pace." He deliberately shorthanded their introductions.

This family was under a lot of strain. He waited for Mitch to join them.

"Call me Laurel. My husband is Mitch. He said you're here about our son?"

"Yes, we are."

"Please, have a seat. Sorry, there's not much room," Mitch said.

"When did you relocate here?" Delaney said.

"Last night. Some of your folks came door to door telling everyone it was time to go."

Leo nodded. "It gives the fire personnel room to do their jobs. Hopefully you'll be back home in no time."

"Why are you here?"

Delaney took over. "We were given your name because you adopted your son a year ago."

The Kestrels looked at each other.

"Yes," Mitch said. "We did."

"Can you tell us about the adoption process?"

"What do you mean?"

"How did you come to adopt your son?"

"We were referred to an agency in North Dakota who found him for us."

"What was the name of the agency?"

"Loving Hands."

"And who did you work with?"

"A woman. Do you remember her name, honey?"

Laurel set her son on the floor. He immediately crawled over to a water dish on the floor and dumped it. Cat-sized, but no sign of the cat. His parents didn't seem to notice, and he splashed happily. "Not off the top of my head. She was really sweet. Tall with long gray hair. She reminded me of your mother, Mitch."

"And your son—did you meet his birth parents?"

"No. We were told she didn't want to meet us and that he'd

never been in the picture. She just wanted him to go to a good home and then to leave the whole thing behind her."

"So, it's a closed adoption."

"Yes. We don't know who she is. And we are told she knew everything about us except our names."

"And how much did you pay Loving Hands?"

Again, they shared a look.

Laurel said, "Is that really relevant?"

Leo hadn't been sure before, but he was after her question. He said, "I'm afraid so."

"You have to understand, we'd been trying to have a baby for years. Then adopt, for years. We were desperate. I know we overpaid, but this agency guaranteed results. And we had the cash from an insurance settlement."

"I understand. How much was it?" Delaney said, her voice gentle.

"One hundred thousand. And they were great. From beginning to end. The best."

Leo kept his face impassive. He hadn't been involved in any adoptions, but he had expected forty or fifty grand. One hundred thousand was a heck of a lot of money.

"He's a beautiful little boy." Delaney gave the child a big smile. He had crawled back to his mother and was peeking around her knee. "I have a few names for you. Tell me if they sound familiar."

"Okay," Laurel said as Mitch nodded.

"Albert Tuttle."

"No."

"Drew Knowles."

Leo looked at her with wide eyes.

"No."

"Mika Alberty."

"No."

"Anna Petrov."

"No."

"Gennie or Genevieve Martine."

Laurel frowned. "I don't think so." She picked her son up and bounced him on her knee as he giggled.

"Anong Leela."

"Wait. I think I heard that name on the news. Is she... was she... oh, my God—is she one of the girls that was murdered?"

"Yes."

"Is she the mother of our son?"

Leo thought of Anong's Thai heritage and compared it to the boy. "I don't know. I don't think so."

"But one of them might be?"

"It's possible. But, again, I don't know. I was hoping you might have a picture or a name, but it doesn't sound like you do."

"Oh, we have a picture," Mitch said. "Just not a name."

Leo felt a quickening of excitement.

"Can we see it?"

"Of course. I have it on my phone." He started scrolling. "Here it is. This is our son's birth mother. She looked nice to us."

He turned the phone toward them and Leo took it. Disappointment surged through him. He'd never seen the young woman before. He handed it to Delaney. She looked up at him with a terse nod and mouthed, "Mika." *We're on to something.* Delaney gave the phone back to Mitch.

"Will you send me this photo and the contact information for Loving Hands?" Leo offered Mitch a card.

"Of course."

He stood. "We really appreciate your help."

"And we'll be praying for you and everyone else with this fire," Delaney said.

Laurel's face softened. Her voice came out a whisper. "Thank you. I painted a mural in the nursery. I even drew it

myself by hand. It's all based on 'Jesus loves me.' The song."
Tears overflowed her lashes. "Grass grows back. Houses can be
rebuilt. That room means something to me."

Leo watched in amazement as Delaney took a step toward
Laurel and put her arms around the woman and her son. She
hugged them both, patting Laurel's back. Whatever she said,
Leo couldn't hear, but Laurel was nodding and smiling through
her tears.

He shook hands with Mitch, then he and Delaney walked
away from the trailer.

Leo exhaled a shuddering breath. "Well, there's confirmation the women were having babies who were being sold for top
dollar."

"But nothing that would tie the adoptions to the murders.
Mika is still alive and well." Delaney stopped short.

Leo looked up to see what had gotten her attention. Kat and
Freddy were twenty feet away. Kat was leaning back against the
fence around the parking area. Freddy had grasped the chain
link fence in each hand on either side of her head. Their faces
were inches apart.

"What in God's name does she have on?" Delaney spat the
words out like they were burning her mouth.

Leo squinted, trying to figure out the costume. It looked like
some of the tavern wench outfits he'd seen the day before, but
different. Shorter. His eyes bugged. Really short. Like he hoped
she was wearing shorts under it.

"And that makeup! I'm going to kill her."

"Maybe wait—"

"Kateena Pace!" Delaney shouted.

Kat jumped, bumping into Freddy, who moved away from
the fence, giving Leo an even clearer view of the girl. Delaney
had been right. Her makeup was too much for a girl her age.
Hell, it was just too much. Heavy eyeliner. Lots of mascara and

green eye shadow. Bright lipstick on a mouth that suddenly turned into a full scowl.

"What?" Kat said, arms crossed, then uncrossed.

"Home. Change. Wash face. Now."

Hand to hip. Arms crossed again. "Are you kidding me? I just got here."

"Do I look like I'm kidding?" Delaney had advanced and was a foot away from her daughter now.

"I don't have a ride."

"You're looking at her."

Kat's voice lowered to a hiss. "I can't believe you're embarrassing me like this."

"You did this all on your own."

"And of course you're with Leo. Can't you give it a rest for a day until people quit talking about you?"

Freddy had moved a few yards away. Leo jerked his head from Freddy to Delaney, trying to demand manners from the boy with his eyes. He wondered where Skeeter was. He probably hadn't had time to find Freddy yet.

"Uh, hey, Delaney. Good to see ya," Freddy said.

Delaney glared at him and started herding Kat ahead of her.

Skeeter materialized from between two nearby trailers. "I've got the boy," he said.

Leo relaxed a little. "Thanks, Skeeter." He pointed at Freddy. "You're with Skeeter. And headed home, too."

"Not cool." Freddy shot him a scathing look. "You're not my mom."

"But you're my nephew who lives in my house. You heard me."

Delaney looked back at Leo. "Are you coming?"

"Right behind you." Although he couldn't think of many places he less wanted to be than trapped in a vehicle with Delaney and Kat right now.

FORTY-SEVEN

Half an hour later, Clint escorted Drew into the interview room. The young deputy was glowering. Delaney was surprised. She'd expected embarrassment. Maybe fear. For her part, she was still coming down off the anger she'd felt at the fairgrounds. Kat was set up in a conference room closer to Brawny, who was working the front desk and had been instructed not to let the miscreant pre-teen past him.

"Please remove your duty belt and all weapons," Leo said to Drew.

Drew stopped and handed two guns and his duty belt to Clint.

"Sheriff, where would you like these?" Clint said.

"I'll take them."

Clint made the handoff. Leo put the items in the credenza behind him.

"Anything else you need before I take off?" Clint said. He still sounded—and looked—amused.

"Your continued discretion. Thank you for everything."

"No problem." Clint nodded at him, winked at Delaney, and shut the door as he left.

"Do you know why you're in here?" Leo asked Drew.

"It better not be because I was in bed with your sister. Brother targets black man for sleeping with white sister doesn't give good copy."

Leo stood. "I would've had to know about it for that even to be a possibility, but that's still insulting. On second thoughts, I'm going to take your weapons to the gun safe. Delaney, the interview is yours. To avoid any appearance of… what he said." Without waiting for a reply, he retrieved the weapons and gun belt and stalked out.

Delaney had the video of Drew leaving coins at the Cowboy Café cued on her laptop. She turned the screen toward him and pressed play, watching him watch himself. When it was over, she switched to the one that showed his face as he was leaving.

Then she crossed her arms and waited.

Drew threw up his hands. "What do you want me to say? It's me. On video."

"I want to know why you didn't tell Leo and me about this."

"Because I didn't leave the weird coin, and I knew it."

It wasn't a good enough answer. She pushed the short list from Infiniquity across the table to him.

He frowned at it. "What's this?"

"A list of people who purchased multiple swords from Infiniquity, including the two models used in our homicides." Again, she remained silent and waited.

He stared at the list, then his mouth dropped open. "This is bullshit."

"Is this your address?"

He sneered. "You know it is."

"Is that your name?"

Now he crossed his arms. "You know that it's not."

She sat up straighter. "Do you know whose it is?"

"It *was* mine. A nickname from my girlfriend. My ex-girlfriend."

She slitted her eyes at him. "Start talking, Deputy."

"She was really into cosplay. It grew on me, too. She got swords for me for my costumes."

That was a lot of costumes, if it was true. "Who has them now?"

"I do. But they're all in a case in my bedroom. You can check it out and see."

"Oh, I will. What I want to know is why you didn't tell us about this earlier? You prepared the warrant for Infiniquity."

"Honestly, I didn't know where she got them. They were a gift. A crazy, extravagant Christmas gift."

"You know how bad this looks? With your fingerprints at the scene on the sword?"

"You know that was an accident."

"Do I?"

Drew's lips moved but he didn't speak. He stared at the wall. Then he slumped and put his head in his hands. "Yes. I understand now how bad this looks."

"Obviously, we're going to need you to give us an account of your time on the days these women likely went missing and were killed."

"I understand." All of the fight had gone out of his voice.

"But before we do that, let's talk about who left that coin at the restaurant."

For the first time, she saw the fear she'd expected. He grasped the edge of the table and rocked front to back a few times. "Delaney, I've got no clue. I swear."

"Then approach this like a member of the team. Let's analyze it together. Is someone trying to frame you? You go first."

He wobbled his head side to side for a few moments, then

locked eyes on her. "If they are, it's someone who knew me or knew of me at least as long as three months ago."

"Yes."

"And also knew about Infiniquity and the swords. When I didn't even know myself."

She nodded.

"Who wanted to create a smokescreen and knew this would be a good way to do it. That's a lot." He bobbed his head like he was thinking hard. "I think they just got lucky on the coin at Cowpoke Café."

"Unless they'd been following you."

"Shit. Yeah."

An idea hit her. "The crucifix."

"What about it?"

"Is it yours?"

"Hell, no. I'm not Catholic."

"Do you have any ties to Notre Dame?"

"Other than giving Trey shit about them, no."

"Why Trey?"

"That's where he went to college. Pretty fancy pants for a Wyoming boy."

"I'll say." She made a note to tell Leo about Trey's ties to Notre Dame. Then she circled it. Then she drew two asterisks beside it. "Does Trey know about your swords?"

"He's been to my place. He could have seen them, but I don't know."

Delaney drew an arrow by her circles and asterisks. "Is there anything about you that would make you attractive as a fall guy?"

"You mean things that might make me a suspect?"

"Yes."

He shook his head slowly. "I don't fit the profile. I'm younger. Not white. Have a wonderful mom and never suffered abuse, unless you count my older brothers thumping me on a regular basis."

"Gaming? History? The Middle Ages?"

"I was a history major at the University of Wyoming. World history. World War II was my thing. And the Civil War here in the US."

"No wonder you had to go work for the railroad."

He laughed but without any joy to it. "I know. Luckily, I was on a scholarship. And then my old girlfriend got pregnant. I saw my future flash before my eyes. Literally had no idea how I was going to pay for that. But it turned out she didn't really like me all that much, and she didn't want to raise a baby with me, so she gave it up for adoption."

Alarm bells went off in Delaney's head. "You have a child out there somewhere?"

"Someone else has a child. I was a sperm donor."

"Boy or girl?"

"Boy."

"Do you know his name?"

"Why is this relevant?"

"Why wouldn't it be? We can't come up with anything that would link you to a killer who has taken the lives of two young women. Both bore children but show no sign that they are raising them. You seem connected now too and had a child but are not raising him."

Drew's eyes widened. His pupils dilated open. "You think?"

Delaney snapped her laptop shut. "I think the first thing I need from you is those alibis we talked about, then I need you to find out who Robbin Hood and Matilda Tuscany are, because they're the other two suspects on this list from Infiniquity. Do not leave this building without checking with me first. Keep your phone on and only move about with it on your person and in your department vehicle. If you go anywhere without permission, we will consider that flight and send Clint after you again."

"I won't. I swear. This is personal now."

She took a notebook from a stack on the credenza and tossed it in front of him. "Get to writing."

FORTY-EIGHT

A clap startled Leo. Delaney was standing in front of his desk. "Penny for your thoughts."

He jumped. "They're not worth half that."

"Snap to it." She updated him quickly on her conversation with Drew. "I can tell you more on our way."

"Our way where?"

"Trust me."

Leo shoved his baseball cap on his head and beat Delaney out the door. Once they were in his truck with Delaney driving, he said, "You believe Drew about the swords?"

"I will once we verify his story."

"Which will be when?"

She turned down a residential street and parked at a tiny, rundown house. "Right now. He told me where to find them. And where he hides a key." At the front door, she rotated a welcome sign. A Ziplock bag was taped to it, a key inside.

"Not high on stealth."

"Oh, the kids these days." She let them in. No alarm sounded. "He said they're in a case in his bedroom."

They walked slowly through a square, sparse living room.

Behind it was a kitchen and eating nook and behind those were two bedrooms and a bathroom. Drew clearly did not hire anyone to help keep his house clean, and Leo wondered if there was penicillin growing in any of the dishes he saw piled in the sink.

Delaney poked her head in one of the bedrooms. "Boxes. No furniture. Nothing on the walls. I can see why he didn't bring Adriana here."

Leo groaned. "Too soon."

They went into the primary bedroom together. The unmade bed was musty or maybe the smell came from the mountain of workout clothes in the mouth of the closet. The two things in the room that looked organized were a gun safe, which was dustless, free of clutter, and shut tight. The other was an absolutely stupendous sword case in which five longswords were displayed. A cord was hanging from it. Leo found a switch and the case lit up. A plaque at the top of the case read FOR MY NUMERO UNO BAE I LOVE YOU.

"How many did she buy?" Leo asked.

"Five."

"Unless these are fakes, I'd say they're all here. And that she has a really good job."

"How do you propose we determine if they're authentic?"

"The infinity logo is supposed to be worked into the hilt design."

Delaney opened the cabinet and inspected each sword. "They all have the logo."

Leo pulled one out of the case and held it in front of him, closing one eye and sighting down it. "It's perfect, isn't it? The weight feels right to me. Not like it was a replica made with cheap stuff. I feel good about their authenticity. As good as I can without an Infiniquity rep here vouching for them."

"Me, too. You all right with me texting him and turning him loose to start hunting down the other buyers?"

"Yes. But he and I are going to have a serious talk about trust." Even if Drew was guilty of nothing, this was a setback for Leo.

She turned to him. "Oh! I almost forgot to tell you. Did you know Trey went to Notre Dame?"

Leo threw his head back. He'd had a brain ping on the engraving on the crucifix but hadn't been able to figure out what it was about. Now he knew. He'd seen Trey's alma mater on his résumé and application. "I completely forgot. We've got to talk to him."

Delaney stopped and voice texted a message to Drew while Leo wandered back to the front of the house. A van had pulled up behind his truck. Delaney joined him just as the intrepid reporter Melanie Pritchett and her trusty videographer alit.

"No," she said.

"Oh, yes," Leo said. "Let's ignore them and move quickly."

They started down the front walk, beelining for Leo's truck, faces averted from the video camera.

Melanie said, "Did we interrupt something, Sheriff?"

He looked up with a smile. "A murder investigation. Make that two, rather."

"Oh? Does a suspect live here?"

"If one did, I would not be giving out that information publicly."

"How are we to know you aren't covering up a tryst with your lover?"

Leo stopped, turned, and laughed at the camera. "Because I don't have a lover." *I only wish I did.*

FORTY-NINE

Delaney's head spun as she dropped Leo back at the station and picked up Kat. The girl huffed, slammed her door, and flopped against the seat. An hour and a half without her phone in the station hadn't given the girl enough time to calm down. It probably hadn't been enough for Delaney, either, and she hoped she could keep her cool.

She drove her angry, sullen daughter home, neither of them speaking the whole way. As she turned in through the gate and wound up the long driveway to the old white homestead, she realized school would be starting that next week. Kat would be an eighth grader. Carrie a senior. Even though they'd only been a family a short time, the thought of this being the last year that Carrie lived with them at home brought a hitch to her breath. She'd just started cracking the Carrie code. The hours they'd spent in Gabrielle—just the two of them—sharing their love of the road and mechanics had been healing for them both. It had forged a personal bond that Delaney hadn't even realized was missing.

Would it survive the girl growing up and leaving? Delaney

didn't have a frame of reference since she'd lost her own mother so young.

She parked the truck and automatically looked over to see if Dudley was in the run. He wasn't. He went everywhere with the girls during the summer. Lately that had mostly been to the Loafing Shed. He was possibly the luckiest dog on the planet.

"Where's Duds?"

"With Carrie." Kat slammed the truck door again and ran into the house.

Delaney walked after slowly and stuck her head inside. The quiet house—she didn't like it. Someday, it would just be her here. A return to the way it had been before, only it would never be the same again for her. Love had changed everything. Even the worst days with her daughters were better than the best of the lonely days.

That thought brought a searing flash of Leo's face along with it.

She said, "I'll talk to you later, Kat. You are to stay put with no visitors. Text me when Carrie gets home."

She heard a muffled answer that sounded like Kat had her face buried in a fuzzy pillow. To be sure, she peeked into the girl's room. *Yep.* She was on her stomach in her black and purple cave of a bedroom, knees bent and legs kicking. Delaney let her be.

She went to the barn, where she found her beautiful Shotgun Shelly, the 1969 Chevelle SS her dad had raced and then left to her when he died. She'd restored it to its original beauty with great love, care, and expense, and she thanked the good Lord above her—He who normally didn't show her much compassion and to whom she gave very little consideration in return—for His grace in allowing this car to still exist and be in her life for times like these.

Between the homicides, the revelations about baby brokering,

Clara's continued absence and silence, and Kat's behavior, everything was too much. She needed to drive through wide open spaces. She needed wind in her face. She considered texting Leo that she was going for a drive but changed her mind. This was a thinking and unthinking mission. It wasn't chasing down a suspect. Besides, one of the things she was sure her brain would turn to was Leo. She didn't need him insisting he be with her.

She uncovered Shelly and gave the engine time to warm up, then drove the car slowly from the barn, popping a .38 Special tape into the eight-track player and cranking it all the way up. She kept it slow as she didn't love the gravel pinging the paint job. But when she reached pavement, she set the horses free. Her head slammed back against the seat, and it was as if her dad was there whooping and shouting instructions. Downshift. Tighten up your turns. Feel the road. Give her more! Give her more! Which was ironic since she'd been too young to drive Shelly while he was alive. All of this was her imaginings. And oh, what wonderful imaginings they were. She turned away from town and ignored the speed limit of seventy-five miles an hour, pushing Shelly over one hundred on the straightaways.

When she'd outrun her thinking brain, she slowed and rolled the windows down. The wind would work the rest of her demons out of her. When she sped back up, her cheeks quivered and stretched.

It was heaven.

Twenty minutes later, she turned around. Refreshed. A new woman, one whose brain had recovered from its stressors. Her road therapy. Yoga on four tires. A true moving meditation.

She took the return more slowly than the way out, allowing conscious thought to creep back in. By the time she got to the first red light in town, she was almost herself again. No problems had been solved, but they felt more manageable.

From the car next to her, a voice said, "Are you Delaney Pace?"

She turned. It was an older woman in a Cadillac Seville, also riding with her windows down. Really, she wasn't too old. Maybe around Clara's age or a bit more. "Yes, I am. Hello."

"Fate or God or whatever you believe in is strong today. I was just wrestling with whether or not to come to the sheriff's department and ask to see you."

The light turned green. The woman looked distressed.

Delaney said, "Let's finish this in a safer place. Follow me to Buns in the Barn?"

The woman nodded, smiling. "Meet you there."

Delaney waited at the door as the pretty gray-haired woman parked and walked over to her. Although she moved a little stiffly, she was fit, although not as fit as Clara. It was Delaney's opinion that women in Wyoming tended to be tougher and stay that way by the necessity of their lifestyles and livelihood. Not from workouts in the gym or fitness classes.

"I'm Lisa Nelson," she said. "Clara Eckhardt has been my best friend since we were teens. I need to talk to you about her."

Delaney opened the door and swept a hand at the entrance. She didn't try to hide her surprise or eagerness. "If you're friends with Clara then I'm dying to talk to you, too."

Over cheeseburgers, fries, and milkshakes, Lisa shared her background living in Kearny and being friends with Clara all her life. "It's how I knew about you. And about your talented daughter who Clara is teaching to follow in her footsteps. I've seen you in the paper and on TV with that cute sheriff, too!"

Delaney squirmed a little at the last part. "What do you need to tell me?"

"Mark told me Clara went to Boston. I don't believe it for a second."

"Why is that?"

"Because she tells me everything, and she's never said a thing about Boston."

Delaney felt resistance start in her core. *Is she of those women who show up during tragedy to talk about how well they know the subject?* But she just said, "Oh?"

"Yes. It's something she told me and no one else that I think I should tell you, even though I've kept the secret for a lifetime, at her request."

"What's that?"

"First, I guess to make me feel better, I want to tell you that the only reason I'm going to betray her trust is because if she really left of her own free will, there can be only one reason why."

"Okay, if you'd like to start there, why is that?"

"To find the child who was taken from her."

Delaney's forehead bunched. "She and Mark lost a child?"

"No. Clara had a baby in high school and her family gave it up for adoption. It's haunted her ever since."

Now she had Delaney's undivided attention.

FIFTY

Drew Knowles was so shook he could barely see the screen in front of him as he typed in a Google search for Matilda Tuscany in Wisconsin. Just a few hours ago, he'd been loving his new job and enjoying the trust of his boss and Delaney. He was signing up personal training clients right and left—as many as he could fit into his schedule. Soon he'd have enough money to book a trip to the New York Comic Con. Yes, he was a nerd, but he'd gotten hooked on the things with his ex. Then this morning, he'd met the woman of his dreams, and a few hours later was knocking boots with her, so to speak.

All of that had come to a crashing halt when some state cops had busted in on him and Adriana, while they were going at it. They hadn't handcuffed him, but they might as well have. When they'd dragged him out, Adriana had been screaming at the cop named Clint, while barely wrapped in a silk robe. She'd looked fine as hell but so incredibly pissed. Now three new men had seen her naked today. And two hadn't been invited.

She'll probably never speak to me again.

He hadn't even imagined how bad it could get, though. Back at the station, Delaney sat him down and treated him like a suspect. At first he was thinking it was blame-the-black-guy shit. But the swords. The damn swords. Gabby, his ex, had bought them for him the year before. He'd never even used them except to carry around in a scabbard and look cool with. She'd tried to take them back, too, when they split up. He'd called bullshit on that. Yes, she'd spent money like a damn fool on him—but that was her bad.

Men like him went to jail for shit like this. Those women were *impaled*. It was messed up, and his stupid ass hadn't thought to tell Delaney and the sheriff he owned fancy swords. Because this is what he'd been afraid of! But it was way worse that they found out this way. Way worse.

Thank you, Jesus, that they believe me.

He had to clear his name by finding the person who really did this, and it had white homie written all over it. All over it. Wisconsin was filled with them, so he had to find this Matilda Tuscany there. He rubbed his eyes and studied the screen. There were no numbers for her in Wisconsin, at the address he'd typed in or any address. He entered the company name instead. Questway. He didn't get any with that either. He looked up the address and found it was one of those rent-a-box stores and was able to get a phone number for it. He tapped a pen on his teeth as he waited for someone to answer.

"Sack and Pack, Boxes and Gifts." The person who answered sounded bored. But it wasn't a kid. The voice sounded a lot like his Aunt Gloria, to be honest. Aunt Gloria liked good manners. He hoped this woman did, too.

"Hello, ma'am. I'm Deputy Drew Knowles from Kearny, Wyoming—"

"Where?"

"Kearny. We're a little town in north-central Wyoming."

"Do you need to mail something?"

"No, actually, we have a double homicide case here—"

"I'm sorry to hear that."

"Yes, well, one of our suspects ordered five big swords from a company called Infiniquity and had them shipped to your address about seven months ago. I was wondering if you know—"

"Oh, I remember that delivery. It's not often we get such big items. And the packaging was awfully sturdy. They had a fancy return address label. The font they used looked like something out of a fairy tale. I didn't know they were swords, but I'll never forget that logo and label."

Drew wanted to reach through the phone and hug her. "Do you remember if it was a man or a woman who picked them up?"

"Oh, a woman."

"Matilda Tuscany of Questway?"

"Sounds right. You don't encounter a great many Matildas in today's world."

"No, you don't. What did this one look like?"

"Should I be answering these questions without my attorney? Or a warrant?"

"Well, I'm not asking you for private information. I already have the address and the name. I just wanted to see if you could describe her for me. Which is public. Anyone who sees her knows what she looks like."

"If you say so. Well, she's about my age." She laughed. "But in a lot better shape than me. I guess you'd call her sporty. Maybe it's from lifting heavy swords."

"And how old would that make her, ma'am?"

"Sorry, you don't know how old I am, of course not. I'd say she'd be around fifty, but only because of her hair. It had turned, you know. I imagine she had dark hair when she was younger. And less wrinkles. I've been blessed not to have the wrinkles, myself, but I never had a figure like hers. And her tall like that? She could've played in the WNBA if we'd had it back when we were young."

"Is there anything else you can remember about her?"

"She was friendly and courteous, and she paid on time."

"You said *paid*. Not *pay*. Is she not a customer anymore?"

"No, young man. She told me she was moving out west. That was the last time I saw her."

Drew wanted to weep with joy over the lead, except that he had no way to find this Matilda. He took the woman's name. "Oh, and one more thing. Do you recall if she paid with cash or a credit card?"

"Always cash."

He'd been afraid of that. He thanked her and ended the call. Matilda didn't fit the profile. His FBI contact/former girl-friend Jillian had bet him a steak dinner that their killer would be a white guy in his thirties. That was after she hadn't had any good matches on prior similar cases on her first pass. She was persistent, though, and said she wasn't giving up.

He went to the second name on the list. Robbin Hood. At first he snickered, then he frowned. He'd seen that name before, and not just in Disney movies. He'd interviewed him at the Renaissance Festival. The guy went by a nickname, but the site manager, Talia, had sworn Robbin Hood was his legal name. Then she'd slipped him her phone number and told him she'd only be in town for three more days. He would have called, but now there was Adriana.

Adriana. Good thing they'd traded numbers before the rude interruption. He sent her a quick text.

Man, that was whack. So sorry. I told you how I work for your brother? Well, somebody was trying to frame me for something. It's all cool now. I hated them barging in on us. On you. And just when things were going so good. I need to make it up to you. Let me take you out to dinner. You pick anywhere you want.

He would have asked her out anyway. It was sick how into her he was after just meeting her.

He turned his attention back to Robbin Hood. He'd head back out to the festival and talk to the guy again. He was easy to find. He was the blacksmith. A guy who went by the handle of Bull.

FIFTY-ONE

Delaney and Leo didn't bother stopping at the house at the Eckhardt ranch. Mark was a rancher. It was the middle of the morning. He wouldn't be drinking coffee in his kitchen. They saw a vehicle and man in the distance, so Delaney drove Leo's truck straight through the series of open gates over the two-track marks and open pasture to reach him.

Leo's phone rang. "It's Drew." He answered. "Hello? Hello?" He growled. "Call dropped." Then his phone chimed. "He just sent a text. Told me to call him back. That he has sensitive information."

Delaney absorbed a jarring bump with her arms on the steering wheel. "Then hurry. We're almost there."

"Hopefully we'll have signal this time." Leo put his phone on speaker. It rang and Drew answered. "Talk to us."

"We just got a call from a police officer in Oshkosh, Wisconsin. They brought Trey in for driving over a hundred in a residential area there. They were calling to verify his identity with us before they let him go."

"Oshkosh? I thought Trey was from southeast Wyoming?"

"He's with a young woman. He told them she's a witness and that he was following a suspect."

"I'll repeat, in Oshkosh?"

Delaney said, "I hope someone told him it was bullshit. He's not even a cop."

There was some static, then Drew's voice came back through. "I did. But it's more than that. The young woman's name is Mika Alberty."

"What?!" Delaney said.

"Since he lied, they're arresting him for reckless driving. They said they'll hold him until we can get someone to talk to him."

"What about her?" Delaney locked down the brakes to stop five yards from Mark's Can-Am off-road vehicle.

"She refused assistance. They didn't have any reason to detain her. She left the station."

"Dammit!" Leo said. "We can't leave in the middle of everything we have going on. We can't be back in an hour or two. Can you ask them to set up a video interview for us later?"

"I'm on it."

"Let me know when you know."

"Sheriff?"

"Yes?"

"I have more updates."

"Text me." Leo ended the call.

"Why does God keep taunting us with the possibility of someone dirty in the department?" Delaney said.

Leo was snarling mad. "He's either going to jail or I'm going to fire him."

She shared Leo's sentiment, although she tried to remind herself there were always two sides or more to every story. "Good plan for later. Let's go."

Dual doors slammed, four feet were running seconds later.

Delaney's eyes started watering immediately. The smoke was terrible. Wind tore at her braid and impeded her forward motion. Mark was walking toward them, a look of fear on his face.

Leo reached him first. "We need to talk to you about Clara."

Mark was pulling off work gloves and nodding. "What's happened? Is she okay?"

Delaney stopped beside her partner. "You know Lisa Nelson?"

"Yes. Clara's best friend. What's going on?"

Delaney dialed it back. "Where does your Find My Phone show her phone to be right now?"

Mark slid his phone from his pocket and checked it. "The Excelsior Hotel in Boston."

Delaney didn't understand this. Not any of it. But, as she'd explained to Leo on the way, they could try to make sense of it later. Since she'd spoken to Lisa Nelson, every instinct in Delaney's body was screaming that Clara's time was running out. That she had to find her friend before it was too late. And beg her forgiveness for invading her privacy later, if she was wrong.

"Could she be looking for the baby she gave up for adoption?"

Mark's face went slack. He looked from her to Leo and back. "Is that a joke?"

"You didn't know?"

"I have no idea what you're talking about!"

"Lisa said Clara had a baby in her teens that her parents adopted out."

Mark's knees buckled. Leo caught him and held him upright. After a few seconds, Mark shook him off. "I'm okay now. Thank you."

"Let's back this up. When did you meet your wife?"

"She was eighteen. Her father brought me in to coach her. She had the makings of a rodeo cowgirl. Honestly, I think he just wanted to make money off her. But he was right. She was fearless and gifted on her crazy horse. They became champions. I convinced her to marry me. That's all. Do you know, um, do you know who the father was?"

"Lisa said it was a relative who raped her and later died."

"Poor Clara. Why didn't she tell me?" He was shaking his head. "Our entire life makes more sense now."

"How so?"

"She didn't want to get married. She was scared of me, physically, no matter how gentle I was. I loved my wife. Love her. Over time she came to trust me more, and we are good partners. But she's never let me close to her. Not really. I thought she just didn't love me. Hell, maybe she doesn't. Or maybe she can't. But I've always loved her enough for both of us."

Delaney thought that she'd never seen a man react so quickly and rationally to an emotional issue. Was this really all a surprise? "Lisa said they sent her away to have the baby."

"Where?"

"Her father's sister's place."

He gripped his head by the temples. "No. Oh, my God, I didn't know. I never would have, I just... I didn't know!"

Leo took him by the arm, but Mark brushed him off. "What the matter?"

"She hated that family and abhorred the ranch. Her aunt and uncle died in a car wreck a few years into our marriage. I wanted to buy the place. You know—have a ranch of our own instead of live here with my parents. She refused. She really never put her foot down about much, but about this, she was adamant. I pushed her. I got really upset with her. I stayed mad at her for a long time about it. What a jerk I was." He leaned over on his knees and began to sob. Big, wracking, back-heaving sobs.

Delaney was beginning to believe him. "I'm sorry."

Suddenly he stood, his face red and wet. "It's been hard on her, you know. These murders."

The abrupt change of topic made Delaney look over at Leo. He shrugged, eyebrows rising and falling.

She said, "Yes. They're very disturbing. Is there anything in particular that bothered her about them?"

Mark was nodding. "Of course."

"And that would be...?"

"You really don't know?"

"Know what?"

"The location. They were at her aunt and uncle's old ranch. The one she wouldn't let me buy."

FIFTY-TWO

Leo pounded his fist on the dashboard.

"Stop! You're going to set off my airbag." Delaney was mashing her foot to the floor, and the truck was responding with all it had. Luckily they were on a rural straightaway heading back to the station. Leo had a text from Drew telling him the police chief in Oshkosh wanted to be in on their video interview with Trey and confirmed a time.

"I don't understand. What are we missing? Two young immigrant women—victims of trafficking—are murdered in a grotesque and very odd way calling back to medieval Europe at a Wyoming ranch. Babies are being sold for top dollar. And Clara is missing. Is it connected to her somehow? It just doesn't make sense!"

"It doesn't make sense to me either. Clara was banished to that same ranch for a teen pregnancy. That had to be fifty years ago, though. I'm so afraid that focusing on the homicide location could be some kind of crazy red herring that distracts us from looking for Clara."

"Except this isn't a Sherlock Holmes novel."

"I know. I'm wracking my brain. The stuff it's spitting back out at me is ludicrous."

"Don't hold back. Ludicrous may be all we've got."

"Okay. Okay." She was nodding. "We now know the Planter family has only owned the ranch for about forty years. Since Clara talked Mark out of buying it after her aunt and uncle died."

"Right."

Delaney said, "One theory we've had is whether the homicides were related to the *Planter* family. Someone in it or someone out to harm someone in it."

"Right. And it hasn't gotten us anywhere."

"Let's extend that to the previous owners."

Leo turned to her. "Meaning something to do with Clara's aunt and uncle. Someone out to harm them."

"Something like that."

"We don't know anything about them."

Delaney held up a finger. "We know Clara hated them. We know she lived there during a pregnancy. We know they died in a car wreck."

"Sounds like Clara is the one who would want to hurt them."

"Agreed. But I don't see her murdering these women to do it. If we were talking about the cause of the car wreck forty years ago, I'd look a little harder, but she's never struck me as the type, even for that."

Leo was drumming on his leg. "Lisa said the baby's father is dead. The guy who raped her."

"Maybe I'm rethinking Clara as vengeful."

"But not as murdering young women."

Delaney shuddered, thinking of how casually she'd welcomed Clara into Kat's life. And how when the investigations into the murders heated up, that was when Clara had disappeared. "No. Please, no. I just can't go down this road. I have to believe no."

"You've said it yourself before. We can't let anything but evidence rule out a suspect. And the murders did stop when she left town."

Delaney felt traitorous even having the conversation. "Okay, then. Search warrant for the Eckhardt place?"

"I think we have to."

Delaney's voice rose—high, quavering. "Leo, I don't see how she'd even know those girls!"

"Let's hope she didn't but pursue finding out if she did." Leo was typing on his phone. "I'll get Drew on it."

"Okay." She turned onto the main street of Kearny, the one leading back to the station. "But the point of brainstorming is to generate a lot of ideas. Not just one. Can we get back to that?"

"Yes. We have all kinds of threads. Tuttle. The baby brokering. Trey running off after his 'cleaner' is killed. His tie to Notre Dame which may link him to the crucifix. Him getting arrested for acting shady with Mika, whose baby was brokered. Planter the older being a weird unit and wishing ill on his brother. Planter the younger being a metalsmith. Every last person involved with the festival—the staff and the people who dressed up and went. I'm not overjoyed with Drew's tie to medieval swords and his fingerprints on the sword used on Anong."

"When you put it all out there like that, I want to vomit."

"Does any of this seem related to Clara?"

"My radar says no. Other than the homicide victims losing babies—if they did—and her losing a baby. And Drew giving one up." Delaney pondered that. "Fifty years apart."

"Yeah. But we're brainstorming."

"Okay. What else related to Clara or the Planter ranch or her hunting for a baby in Boston comes to mind?"

"Say that again."

"Which part."

"The last part.

"Her hunting for a baby in Boston?"

Leo punched the air with a pointer finger. "Bingo. You're making an assumption. We don't know why she's in Boston, right?"

"Right. I guess I was just connecting it to what we've learned."

"But her husband gave the name of a hotel."

"The Excelsior."

"In the excitement that kind of slipped past us. We have another way to try to get in touch with her."

"Crap! You're right."

"I'm calling now." He typed on his phone for a few moments, then put it to his ear. After an introduction, he asked to be transferred to Clara's room. He frowned. "Are you sure? How about any guests with that last name? Okay, what about with that first name?" Again, a pause. Then he put the phone on speaker and said, "This woman is a missing person in Wyoming, and we are showing her phone as located in your hotel." He described Clara. "Anyone like that come to mind?"

"Sheriff, you've just described half our guests. But we've had a bit of a scare today related to a phone. It was mailed to us here. Not to a guest. After the Boston marathon bomb, no one takes anything for granted anymore, so we called the police. Their bomb squad came out. They're still here. They said it was a Wyoming phone. And the return address was Clara Planter."

"Clara *Planter*?" Delaney stomped on the brakes at their last red light, which she'd almost driven through. The seatbelt dug into her chest.

Leo said, "Oomph."

The phone flew out of his hand, hit the dashboard, and landed on the floor. "Sheriff, are you there? Is anyone there?"

"She's not in Boston," Delaney said.

"And the cases are one hundred percent linked. What did she stumble into?" Leo picked up the phone. Into it he said, "May I speak to someone with the bomb squad, please?"

FIFTY-THREE

Drew stood in front of the blacksmith trailer at the fairgrounds, but the bellows was cold, and the shop was closed. Festival goers were walking by in both directions, brandishing beers and big-ass turkey legs, but he didn't see Bull anywhere.

The last thing he wanted to do was talk to Talia again, but he didn't have another good option. This was the job. He texted her he was coming, then walked quickly to the office trailer she'd met with him in yesterday, stretching his triceps on the way. He'd gone up in weight and he could feel it.

She opened the door before he knocked, one hip cocked, one arm over her head against the side of the door frame. She flipped her red hair over one shoulder. "I'm working." She pouted shiny lips.

"Me, too. I need to talk to Robbin Hood. Bull. His shop is closed."

A dark look crossed her face, and she stood up straight, moving back a step. "If you see him, tell him he's fired for me. He no showed on me today, and his rig is gone."

"Isn't the blacksmith trailer his rig?"

"That's *my* rig. He just gets to use it. Or did." She moved to shut the door.

He caught it in his hand, flashing her the add-on teeth-whitening special smile from his last dental cleaning. "What does he drive? In case I can find him."

"A piece of shit Chevy Tahoe with a spoiler on the back. White. Pulling an old R-pod trailer."

"Do you have a phone number? Or know where he lives when he's not working?"

"I assumed you would have asked for that kind of stuff when you had the chance."

He had. But witnesses lied all the time. It was one of the first things he'd learned on the job. They lied about everything. Usually little bitty things that didn't matter. Sometimes great big whoppers. "It would be a huge help."

"Well, I am pretty hungry. I could slip away for dinner tonight."

"That sounds like something no sane man would pass up."

"Good." She pulled him inside and slammed the door.

Drew knew better than to let a witness put him in a compromising position. He was really into Adriana, too. But he wasn't going anywhere without what he came for.

She leaned close, her lips inches from his, warm, sugary breath in his face. "Let me get that for you." Then she released him with a slight push backward into the fold down table.

He gave a half grin. "You know where to find me."

She sashayed to her computer, typed some keys, made a duck face at him, then did a slinky walk to her printer. She folded the paper into a little square, tucked it down the front of her top, and shimmied over to him. "All yours, Drew."

"Whoa. Well, Talia, seeing as how I'm in uniform, that's not something I can retrieve."

"Take it off then, deputy. The uniform."

"I'm on the clock. But I won't be tonight."

Again, the pout. She fished out the paper and put in his palm, closing her fingers around his. "I can't wait."

He hightailed it out of her trailer. *The woman is a piranha!* There was no way he was going to dinner with her, but she'd figure that out later when he ghosted her. He opened the paper. The address matched the one that Infiniquity had sent the swords to in Missouri. He called the phone number. It went straight to voicemail. "Mr. Hood, this is Deputy Knowles. A few follow-up questions from our talk the other day. Call me at your earliest opportunity. Thank you." He added his number.

Then he texted Delaney with an update. *Robbin Hood aka Bull is MIA and not answering his phone.* Five minutes later, he hadn't heard back from her, so he forwarded the message to Leo with the same result.

Standing at the exit to the fairgrounds he decided it was important enough for a BOLO. If only he knew how to do one.

FIFTY-FOUR

After a long wait and a lot of explaining and re-explaining of who he was and what was going on, Leo was finally connected to a Boston Police Department detective from the bomb squad. Jeff Ricardo. By that time, he and Delaney were parked in the lot at the station and Leo had the phone on speaker and had introduced Delaney.

"We can confirm the phone is not armed with explosives," Jeff said, in a voice more Puerto Rico than Boston. Leo had roomed with a guy from north Boston in college and was very familiar with the accent.

"I'm glad to hear that," Leo replied. "We think whoever mailed it is holding Clara Eckhardt hostage."

"Your Eckhardt—does she have any relation to the name Stiles?"

Delaney shrugged and started typing. "I'll find out."

"Why do you ask?" Leo said.

"The name on the return address is Clara Stiles Planter."

"We were told Clara Planter earlier. That's the first I heard of the Stiles middle name."

"Yeah. And here's the address." He read it to them. "You familiar with that place?"

"Delaney, is that the Eckhardt ranch?"

Delaney said, "Yes. Clara and Mark's place. But I happen to know that none of the ranches out that direction get rural delivery. So, it's their *physical* address, not their *mailing* address. Which probably isn't relevant but popped into my head."

Leo said, "I think it might point to a kidnapping. Like if someone took Clara and knew where she lived but hadn't ever mailed anything to her."

"Good thinking. What else you got, Ricardo?"

"We dusted for prints. Does your Eckhardt have any on file?"

"Yes. She works at the sheriff's department."

"I'll send these over, then. There were others on there, but they were smudged. I'll be floored if our perp didn't wear gloves, though."

"Anything else that jumped out at you?"

"Looks like it was mailed from Kearny, Wyoming. That's you guys, right?"

"Right."

"It was shipped FedEx First Overnight. Somebody forked out some dough on it."

Leo was nodding. A lead to follow-up on with FedEx in Kearny. A great one. Maybe their cameras caught the shipper. Or an employee could give a description. "Clara's husband originally saw her phone at the airport using his Find My Phone app. We thought she was at the airport herself. But in retrospect, the phone was probably catching a ride on a little plane that carries expedited packages to the nearest shipping hub in Billings."

"Any idea where she is now?"

"I wish we knew. Is there anything we can do to help you?"

"It doesn't sound like a crime was committed on our end.

It's not illegal to mail a cell phone. This was an incredible scare and waste of resources, though. Let us know when you nail the guy."

"Will do. Thanks for your help."

"Anything else you need, don't hesitate."

The call ended.

"We need to get hold of FedEx," Leo said.

"Agreed." Delaney put her head on the steering wheel. "Whoever killed those women has Clara. You know it. I know it."

"We just don't know why."

"Or who's doing it, and how to stop him."

Leo looked down at his phone. "Damn. I have way too many messages coming in."

"No more bad news, please."

Leo said, "Huh. That's weird."

"What is it?"

"Drew said that Matilda Tuscany of Wisconsin—from the Infiniquity list—is a late middle-aged woman."

"That's descriptive."

"Actually, he said she was described as tall and athletic in her fifties with long gray hair."

"Okay. That's better."

"Here's where it gets weird. He said Robbin Hood is the real name of the metalsmith at the Renaissance Festival."

"Bull? He didn't mention having Infiniquity swords, but he knew how to find them immediately."

"Maybe he's just a collector and has a lot of them from more than one maker."

"Or maybe he skewered Genevieve and Anong to the ground with two of them."

Leo winced. "Here's where the bad news starts. Drew said Bull is missing from the festival. He wants to know whether to put out a BOLO. And how to do one."

"Uh, yes."

Leo raised his brows at her. He typed a message to Drew: *BOLO now please. Anyone at the station can help you do one. Call Brawny.* His lips moved as he read another message. Then he looked up. "You have to hear this one. It's from Larry Planter about the student he had that was into swords."

"Okay."

"*The student I had who was both talented and very interested in swords was Robbin Hood. Yes, that's really his name. He was from Missouri, but that's all I remember about him.*"

"What?!"

"We either have a hell of a coincidence or a new top suspect."

FIFTY-FIVE

"Drew!" Leo shouted from his desk. "I need you in here." He heard the edge in his own voice. The call to FedEx had been a bust. Their security system, including the cameras, was down. The sole employee working at the time of the—naturally—cash transaction to ship Clara's phone was on a fishing trip in Alaska with his parents and hadn't answered calls to his cell phone. It was frustrating, but there was no reason to take that out on Drew. He took a deep, cleansing breath.

He heard running footsteps. Drew's face appeared in the office door.

"Yes, Sheriff?"

"Sorry about that. This call with the Oshkosh Police Chief and Trey is about to start and my head is exploding. We need you."

"No problem."

"Pull up a chair. Please."

Delaney was seated in her usual spot in front of his desk. Drew dragged one from the side of the office and positioned it beside her before he sat.

Leo updated Drew on Clara's child and her phone having

been mailed to the hotel in Boston. Then he said, "Matilda. Where in Wisconsin is she?"

"No longer there as of about six months ago, but she was in Appleton. The person I talked to said Matilda was moving west, but she didn't know where."

"We'll track her down after this call." Leo already had Google Maps open, and he typed quickly. "Appleton is only half an hour away from Oshkosh. Do we know what ties Trey has to Oshkosh? Or any Mika has?"

Drew shook his head. His eyes were a little wide. "No, sir."

Leo groaned. "This is moving so fast I haven't even updated my investigation plans."

Delaney twisted her hair up into a fresher messy bun. "Trey's on our radar because he went to Notre Dame and is connected to Anong and Mika."

Drew was nodding. "He didn't have access to swords."

Leo said, "All of yours are accounted for, otherwise I'd point out he had access as your friend."

"Not really my friend. I was his personal trainer. Trey needed to add some bulk."

Can't argue with that. "We need his alibis, if he knows where Clara is, and any ties to Matilda Tuscany and her swords."

Drew shook his head. "Yeah. But I just don't see it in him."

Delaney shrugged. "I don't want to see it, but I will if we can't find evidence that eliminates him."

Leo started typing. "I'm updating the plans as we go. Anything else on Trey?"

No one spoke.

"I'm taking that as a no. On to Robbin Hood. Did he have means and opportunity? Maybe and maybe. But I haven't seen connections to the victims. It's especially hard to imagine one to Clara. And what would be his motive?"

Drew said, "His alibis were weak and not directly corroborated. He denied knowing Genevieve or Anong. And I didn't talk to him about Clara."

Delaney held up a finger. "A message just came in. We have a hit on the Tahoe."

Leo leaned forward, hands off keys. "What? Where?"

"Looks like it's in Bozeman."

"What the heck? He's from Missouri. He doesn't have a link we know of to Montana."

"Could he be running to Canada?" Drew asked.

Leo looked at Delaney. "Ask them to pull him in. He's wanted for questioning in two homicides."

"Will do." Delaney's fingers flew.

"Time for our call." Leo turned the laptop to face Delaney and Drew and moved his chair around to the other side of the desk. "It will be a tight squeeze. Drew, you'll be off camera, I'm afraid."

"I'll feel better that way."

Leo connected to the video call. A glowering face filled the screen, crew cut hair standing up straight except for a cowlick in the middle of his forehead. "Hello, I'm Sheriff Leo Palmer in Kearny County, Wyoming. This is Deputy Investigator Delaney Pace with me. Off screen we have Deputy Drew Knowles."

"Chief Billy Eustiss. Oshkosh, Wisconsin. Is it true our reckless driver is wanted for killing two girls?"

He cuts right to the chase. "For questioning in relation to their deaths. The woman he was with worked with the two who were killed. We're desperately trying to get a lead on a real suspect."

"But he could be it?"

"He's our longshot. But he might be. He's actually an employee of the county. Works in crime scene investigation."

"So, the sumbuck had access to the scenes and knows all about covering his tracks."

"Yes."

"I don't like it."

"Like I said, he may have information. Let's talk to him and see."

Eustiss grumbled, nodded, and appeared to press buttons off screen. "Bring him in."

A minute later, Trey slumped and clanked into a chair beside the police chief. "Sheriff. Delaney."

Leo frowned. Trey looked like he'd had a bloody nose that hadn't been cleaned up. "Trey. We've got some questions for you."

"Yes, sir."

"Starting with why you flew out of Kearny on a private flight the other night."

"I was in a hurry. It was the only seat I could get."

"For a family emergency?"

He squirmed. "Sort of."

"Don't waste my time."

"Mika called me. She was in trouble. She asked for my help."

"Okay. How do you know Mika?"

"She filled in one time for Anong and we, uh, hit it off."

"So, she's your girlfriend."

"I guess you could say that. I like her a lot."

"Did you like Anong?"

"Not in that way."

"What about Genevieve?"

His forehead creased. "I didn't know Genevieve."

"What are your ties to Clara Eckhardt?"

"She works for the department. She gives me butternut toffee candy. She's good at her job."

"Outside of work."

He did a double take. "None. Why are you asking about her?"

"Where'd you go to college, Trey?"

His eyes rounded. "Notre Dame. What's this about, Sheriff? What's going on?"

"You know what the engraving on that crucifix said? The one Sugar found between where Genevieve and Anong were killed?"

"No."

"Basilica of the Sacred Heart. The cathedral at Notre Dame."

He was shaking his head almost violently. "I've never been there."

"Is it yours?"

"What? No! Sheriff, I had nothing to do with what happened to those girls."

Leo didn't let up. "You understand that Anong and Mika were being trafficked."

He looked down. His voice was a whisper. "I didn't. I do now."

"Look up at me, son."

Trey's head flew up. He had tears in his eyes. "Yes, sir?"

"Mika is a material witness in a human trafficking case. More than that, she's a potential victim. She knew both our murder victims well and likely their closest associates, too. Has she told you anything that would lead us to who killed her friends?"

"No, sir. She's terrified because she doesn't know who to be scared of."

"Where were you headed when you got pulled over?"

"Mika's family is in Green Bay. I was taking her there."

"Not to Matilda Tuscany's?"

"Who?"

"Oh, come on. You know her."

"I don't. I've never heard the name."

Leo tapped his foot against Delaney's, letting her know it

was her turn to ask questions if she had any. She tapped his back and kept her eyes on the screen. A few seconds of silence passed. He took it as the highest praise from her—she had no further questions.

"Here's the deal. You work for Kearny County. You need to get back to Kearny County. And you somehow need to convince Mika to come with you. Tell her that Albert Tuttle is in jail and won't be getting out. You come straight to us, and we'll protect her."

"Sheriff, she's not going to like it."

"Would you like us to arrest her?"

"Don't do that."

"Then bring her back here."

Delaney held up her phone. "Leo, sorry to interrupt, but Bozeman law enforcement just lost Robbin Hood."

After the video call, Delaney took Shelly out to pick up food. Her stomach had started growling back when they were at the Eckhardt ranch talking to Mark. Now it was mid-afternoon. With Mika and Trey on their way back to Kearny courtesy of cross-country sheriff's department escorts, the baby brokering issue and its possible connection to Clara was really gnawing at Delaney. She decided to drop by Shirleen's house and talk to her about it. Maybe it was a little bit pushy since Shirleen hadn't answered a text earlier, but then again, there could have been a technology glitch. More than once Delaney had sent texts that people never received. It would be easier to talk to her in person, anyway, given how many uncertainties and contingencies there were to explore. Maybe Shirleen would want something to eat, too.

She pulled into the driveway, admiring the location of the house. It was near the river without being so close that mosquitos were an issue, and the natural landscaping was amazing. Last time she'd been here, three deer had walked out of the brush and trees, invisible one moment and five yards away the next. That was one thing about the Pace homestead—there really wasn't permanently running water on the property, so they didn't get the thick, low plant life or the towering cottonwoods like those along the big creeks or the Cheyenne River.

Delaney went to the door and rang the bell. There were no cars out front, but Shirleen had a garage, so Delaney didn't take the absence of a car as definitive. When Shirleen didn't come to the door, Delaney knocked. She hadn't actually *heard* the doorbell. Maybe it wasn't working.

To her surprise, the door swung open, but no one was standing on the other side. Unlocked, unlatched. As a friend, she was concerned that her friend's door latching mechanism might be broken. But as a deputy, she immediately went on high alert. They had two dead young women and one missing older woman. A connection to Shirleen wasn't apparent, but it hadn't been for Clara either. Had someone broken in and taken Shirleen? If so, how long had she been missing? Did she have anyone in her life to notice when she wasn't where she was supposed to be? Or was she like the community she served— unnoticed to the outside world?

Delaney brushed the thoughts away. There was probably nothing wrong in this house, but in case there was, she didn't want to become part of the problem for some other cop because she wasn't paying attention and was bested by a perp.

She shouted, "Shirleen, it's Delaney. Are you here?"

There was no answer.

She was going to have to search the house. Her stomach growled again, but she ignored it and put her gun at low ready. For a split second, she thought about calling for backup. It would have been what Leo wanted her to do. But there was no vibe of danger here. No odd smells or sounds. Something was off, but she didn't sense the presence of menace.

The first room she came to was Shirleen's office. She did a quick walk-through and verified no one was behind or under the desk. There was no closet, so she moved on quickly, not taking the time to rummage through the desk or read the diplomas, other than to note there were several—go, Shirleen!—but no personal photos. She didn't see a phone either.

She moved on through the kitchen, an eating area, the living room, several hall closets, a laundry room, and a half bath. All were clear, neat, and moderately clean. The sterility of the place bothered her, though, especially for someone as warm as Shirleen. No family photos, no graduation photos. Nothing reminiscent of the child she'd lost. Despite that, Delaney had to admit the decorating was top notch. Not Wyoming, not Western, but beautiful. Feminine, with a floral scent coming from somewhere. Warm tones that felt ancient, timeless. The wood dark and rough-hewn. The fixtures and cabinet knobs made of thick metal with heavy latches.

Delaney would have enjoyed living in a place decorated like this.

She decided to do the wing of bedrooms next, where she discovered two guest bedrooms, a full bathroom accessible from the hallway, and a main bedroom with a big ensuite bathroom. She moved methodically but quickly, frequently calling out for Shirleen and re-announcing herself.

In the hallway, she found a locked door. It required a key. "Not going to be anyone hiding behind that."

And then suddenly she stopped, goosebumps cascading from her hairline down to the tips of her fingers. Not about danger. A foreboding. Connected to... the office. Something in the office was calling her back. What had she missed?

She hurried in and started with the desk, running her fingers over everything on the surface. Work documents on State of Wyoming letterhead. An envelope labeled MT with nothing in it. She shook her head. Whatever had struck her wasn't on the desk. She turned to the wall of certificates and diplomas. She immediately saw the St. Mary's diploma for a degree in social work. Then she stopped to read a larger one.

Doctor of Philosophy in Medieval Studies. Shirleen Hancock. The school conferring the degree was Notre Dame.

She frowned. Had Shirleen ever mentioned going to Notre Dame? Having a Ph.D. in Medieval Studies? Being a freaking *expert* on the Middle Ages?

No. No she did not.

Alarm sirens reverberated in her head. *It could be a coincidence. Like with Drew and the swords.* She spun in a circle. Swords—she hadn't seen any. Or a crucifix. Or old coins. She was blowing this all out of proportion. Trey had a connection to Notre Dame, too. Larry Planter had an interest in medieval fantasy. It didn't mean either of them were murderers. This was just one data point about Shirleen.

She went back to the door in the hallway. The locked door. A closet? She thought about the topography and the shape of the house. Built into the side of a hill like many in the area. Was this door the interior entrance to the basement? Most people didn't keep theirs deadbolted, in her experience, but Shirleen might have security concerns about windows or doors in the below-ground walkout.

She headed toward the front door, then stopped. From where she stood, she had a clear view through the house and out into the back yard. There was no patio furniture. No grill. No nothing. Nothing to search there, except maybe the woods themselves. But she had forgotten to search one thing on the ground floor.

The garage.

The door had been closed from the outside, so she went back to the kitchen where there was a hallway between it and the laundry room. She walked through a mudroom and to another door. The sirens in her head were screeching now. Her goosebumps had turned into chills so intense she felt sick. She opened the door. Turned on the light. Stepped into the garage.

And found Clara's truck.

FIFTY-SEVEN

I navigated a turn carefully in my truck, turning the steering wheel hand over hand. I'd been driving one mile per hour over the speed limit, using my signal, and coming to full stops along the way. Attracting law enforcement attention when I had an unconscious woman cuffed in the truck bed would be very bad. I didn't like drugging Clara. If I had my way, she'd be awake for every second of this, so that I could see her reaction when she realized where I was taking her. But I couldn't afford screams or escape attempts in transit. Nor could I let her die from too much of the sleeping potion. Dosing with medieval herbal concoctions was a cultivated art, definitely not all science. And I'd had to increase the amount, as Clara had shown herself to be somewhat resistant to it thus far.

It was risky, returning here so soon after Genevieve and Anong had been found. I didn't have a choice, though. It was The One Way. So, I'd scouted it that morning. The crime scene tape was still up. That would keep people out. There'd been no sign of police activity, nor was there any talk of them returning to the scene, and I'd been careful to stay abreast of that. Just to be sure, I'd set up cameras, one mile away in each direction. It wasn't the first time I'd hacked into the internet of the houses near each site to access my Google Home account. I'd receive a notification any time a vehicle headed for the ranch entrance. Traffic was still discouraged because of the fires, so the false positives were low.

Besides, I wouldn't be driving and parking anywhere near the investigation sites. I knew my way in across the property from its opposite side, through a wire gate accessed by a gravel road. I'd invested many days exploring the place on foot and in an off-road vehicle over the unpaved roads and open terrain months before. Preparation was key to success, because I'd only get one chance to finish the Quest.

This alternate route was a longer drive, but it was more private. As private as the ranch would allow, given that there was not a single tree except along the creek bottoms for the short stretch where the waterway crossed the property. The best cover was the rise and fall of the landscape, but I'd be visible at times to the very few people that could be watching from a long distance. That meant subterfuge, which was one of the reasons I drove a cheap, nondescript white truck. Keeping my speed down so I wouldn't generate a dust trail. Transporting a quiet victim. If I'd thought I'd be less detectable bringing her in on a horse or carrying her on my back for ten miles, I would have done it.

Whatever it took. As long as it was consistent with The One Way.

I opened the gate, proud of how easily I handled the tight wire loop, city raising be damned. It was surprising how much of the fence was still standing after the fire had swept through, but very few of the posts were wooden. Most were green metal now singed black.

I followed an old two-track, the truck jolting as it rolled slowly over dirt ruts. In the bed, Clara's body thumped as it bounced. She'd be bruised, if she lived long enough. I didn't care. She deserved everything she had coming to her. I wondered if she'd been awake whether she would have recognized where we were yet. As far as the eye could see was black, at least in the distance. But up close, there were patches that hadn't burned. A jackrabbit popped up out of singed sagebrush and darted in front of me. I'd seen video that morning of a herd of elk racing out of the path of the fire. The path and its destruction—its selectiveness—didn't make sense, but the evidence was undeniable.

After half an hour, I angled down a ravine at a place where the side was less steep and the dirt firmer. From a distance, the ravine was hidden. It just looked like an expanse of flat prairie. The truck would be well concealed down there.

I pulled a camouflage tarp off the Polaris RZR off-road vehicle I'd used for reconnaissance. I took a moment to thank God in the highest for saving it from the fire, for saving it for this moment, then fastened the folded tarp and a bag of supplies to the RZR with the bungees already on it. Then, most importantly, I secured the longsword in its scabbard, checking it three times to be sure it wouldn't come loose.

Returning to the truck, I found Clara stirring. *How much can one small body take?* There was no denying she was tough. Strong in a way that belied her years. I would have to hurry. I cut the zip tie from the D-ring securing her to the bed and hoisted her into my arms. She mumbled unintelligibly as I marched back to the RZR, where I belted her into the passenger seat and zip tied her to another D-ring. I drove as fast as I dared across the blackened pasture to the house, stopping twice to use binoculars.

All was clear.

I'd thought I'd be excited at this moment, but a deadly calm had settled over me by the time I parked behind the house. Running now, I took the sword and bag into the house then returned for Clara.

But she wasn't in the RZR.

I screamed. This was not supposed to happen. There was no time to figure out how she'd gotten out of the restraints. I simply had to find her. I turned in a slow circle, snarling, panting. Movement caught my eye—*there!* A small figure was stumbling toward the road.

FIFTY-EIGHT

As Delaney stood beside Clara's truck in Shirleen's garage, her mind raced, sputtered, and raced again. Clara had been here. At Shirleen's house. Shirleen who had a Medieval Studies graduate degree from Notre Dame. She clutched her stomach. She'd spotted Shirleen on the video from the Cowpoke Café, and she hadn't given a second thought to the possibility that it was her who'd passed the medieval coin. Magda had even said she'd seen Shirleen the week before when Delaney had taken her to breakfast, although Shirleen had denied it. But Delaney had watched the video with her own eyes. And a Basilica of the Sacred Heart crucifix had been found at the Planter ranch near where the bodies of Genevieve Martine and Anong Leela had been staged, anchored to the ground by medieval longswords.

The ranch! The Planter ranch, tied to Clara by her hatred of the place and the name on the return address of the package shipped to Boston containing her phone. Where she'd been sent as a girl to have a baby. A baby that was taken from her.

Whatever was going to happen to Clara now was going to happen at the Planter ranch.

I have to get out there!

She pulled out her phone as she ran to Shelly. Leo answered on the first ring. She spilled the story, words bursting from her like automatic weapon fire as she jumped into her muscle car and pulled out of the driveway with tires spitting up gravel.

"I'm heading to the Planter ranch. Everything in me says she's out there and we don't have much time. But there's another story to Shirleen's house. A walk-out basement. It was locked from above. I didn't search it. If I'm wrong about the ranch, there's a chance Clara's down there."

Leo's voice took on the urgency she felt. "I'll get someone out to search the basement. I'm coming to you." She heard clattering in the background, like he was already up and moving.

Delaney was speeding down Main Street on the outskirts of town now, very aware that she was in a vintage sports car and not her truck. Better yet her truck with an off-road vehicle chained in the bed. "You'd better hurry. I'm in Shelly. Also, bring a department ORV. Oh, and a map of the ranch. I'm not familiar with it."

"I will. But listen to me. Please, Delaney. Please. Don't make this even worse by getting yourself hurt or killed. Just wait for me. Or do you want me to find someone else who can get to you faster?"

How long would it take for Leo to find officers to respond to her alternate theory about Shirleen's basement? And then more of them to come to the ranch? He was stretched too thin. But he was her partner. He was the one she trusted.

"I'd prefer to work with you."

"I'll come as fast as I can, then. I just need your commitment to do what we've been asking the public to do. Don't put yourself in danger that pulls manpower off where it's needed."

She knew he had good reason for pressing the point, even if it stung. "Message received and processed. See you there."

She reached the area blackened by fire a few days before

and shivered. It was like the Chevelle was gliding through a post-apocalyptic hellscape. Flames flickered on the horizon. Smoke hung heavy, and visibility was low. There were fewer cars on the road than usual here as people were heeding the public warnings about the fire. She accelerated on a straight-away. The speedometer read one hundred and ten, then one hundred and twenty. The farmhouse came into view ahead on the right, and she began a rapid deceleration. The crime scene tape had come loose or been torn down, and one end was fluttering like a windsock.

She turned in the gate, eyes scanning for Shirleen's vehicle. For signs of humans. For anything out of the ordinary. There was nothing. The farmhouse had a cold, deserted aura. She had to look inside anyway, which she dreaded. If Clara was there—if her friend was already dead with a sword through her like the other women—she didn't know what she'd do. How she'd forgive herself for failing to prevent it. But she couldn't think like that. She had to believe Clara was alive. That she could still save her.

She parked near the house. Took a deep breath. Checked that her gun and extra cartridges of ammo were ready and accessible. That her lapel radio was on. She went through a mental checklist. *Use all your senses. Don't mess up evidence. Don't put yourself in the line of fire.* Then she got out and began a slow, careful walk to the house, using Shelly as cover until she was near the door. The dirt on the far side of the frame looked disturbed. *Footprints. New ones that hadn't blown away.* Her stomach tightened.

Was it better to use the element of surprise—bust the door open and barge in—or announce herself first? Did she even have the element of surprise after driving a car with a loud engine up to the house? Probably not.

She turned the handle and kicked the door in. "Sheriff's Department. Freeze!"

She waited for gunshots. Scurrying feet. Heavy breathing. A scream.

They never came.

She ducked inside, checking the interior quickly, including the closet where Sugar had found the pool of blood. There was no one. She shone a flashlight at the ground. Again, she found disturbances in the dirt. She couldn't be sure, but she thought they were fresh. That didn't mean they were nefarious. They could be from teenagers here on a dare or a traveler looking for shelter.

Or a killer returning to the scene of a crime.

Outside, she followed the footprints. There was a set coming and going. They led around the side of the house facing away from the road and ended at knubby tire tracks set closer together than those of a full-sized vehicle. The tracks circled and took off toward the highway. She frowned. Was that a second set of footprints heading toward the road as well? She followed the footprints, walking, then running. They were footprints, and they weren't large. She'd bet Shelly that they belonged to someone smaller than herself. Between Clara and Shirleen, that would be Clara. Then the ORV tracks reversed course in a loop and drove a slightly different track toward the house.

There were no more footprints after it turned around.

She tried to flesh out the story the evidence was telling her. It was all just supposition but inside her, it had the ring of truth. Someone jumped off the ORV and made a break for the road. Clara, in all likelihood. The ORV had followed and caught up to the person, who had then returned to the ORV before it headed in the opposite direction.

Her heart sank. If her hypothesis was right, Clara hadn't made it very far before the person recaptured her.

She heard engine noise approaching and trotted back to the house, this time crossing between it and the highway. Leo's truck was pulling up. As requested, he'd brought an ORV, and he'd come quickly. So quickly that she could only imagine how hard it was for him to drive that fast.

He jumped out. "You didn't wait."

"There's no one inside. But there's a set of ORV tracks to follow out back."

He sighed and ran his hand through his hair. "You're impossible. And I'm glad you're all right."

But she was already climbing into Leo's truck and barely heard him as she shut the door to the driver's side. She'd come back for Shelly later. He hopped in, and she floored the gas.

Ten minutes later, Delaney and Leo were pulling a tarp off an ORV parked in a ravine.

She put her hand on the hood. "The engine is still warm."

Leo's phone chimed. He glanced at it. "It's Drew. He's on his way to Shirleen's with an emergency warrant. Thank God for our Wyoming judges. Devon is meeting him at Shirleen's."

"Devon with the police?"

"Yes."

"Good." Delaney was taking photographs and examining the ground again. "I wish I was a better tracker, but you see these?" She pointed at faint tracks leading out of the ravine.

They walked up the side together. The tire tracks became clearer in the black of the scorched earth.

"A full-sized vehicle."

Delaney nodded. "Heading to the opposite boundary of the property, it looks like."

"Someone's been accessing it and keeps their own ORV here? This is feeling like one of the Planter boys." He held up a hand to stop her. "Hear me out on this. What if Shirleen's been taken hostage, too? Maybe she was in the wrong place at the wrong time. Or maybe there's a connection we don't know yet."

"I'm listening."

"There could have been more than two people in that RZR. The only people we know it can't be are Tuttle, Trey, and Drew."

"So, you're saying Larry or Lucas Planter."

"Or anyone. Hell, it could be the metalsmith from the festival. We don't know it was him in his car in Montana. It could be anyone."

"I don't know."

"And that's the point. We don't *know* anything yet. We have to stay open."

Delaney pushed her hair off her face. The wind was ripping it from her braid. "I'm trying. Let's see if we can find where they went."

They ran back to the truck and Delaney took off after the tracks, taking care to stay wide of them, with her window down so that she could occasionally lean out for a better look. The ground was rough, but the fire had taken down the flora, so she was able to see rocks, depressions, and other obstacles and avoid them. Before long, the only thing ahead of them was a fence line. They stopped at the wire gate. Delaney opened it easily. Almost effortlessly. The tracks continued on the other side but disappeared in the rocks of the gravel road.

"This is that wire gate Larry Planter said was loosened, I'll bet," Delaney said, standing with her hands on her hips. "And I can't see him telling us that if it was his ORV hidden back in the ravine."

Leo pointed toward the mountains. "We know they turned left here."

Delaney paced the fence line, part of her looking for clues from the multiple trips their suspect would have made through the gate, part of her letting her mind process the background information they had so far. Where would the killer have taken Clara? And had it even been the two of them here? Her gut told her yes. If so, something had motivated the killer to come out to this ranch, and something had motivated him to leave it. Was there anything that might have replacement value as a kill site? Assuming this ranch was chosen because of Clara, which was a leap, but she went with it—assuming it was because she'd lived here while she was pregnant—would the ranch where she lived when she became pregnant mean anything? The ranch where she was *raped?*

"Leo, I have an idea."

"Thank God, because I've got nothing."

"What if they went to the ranch where Clara grew up? I don't know where that is, but if this is about her pregnancy all those years ago, that ranch might be part of the—I don't know, trip down memory lane? It's a stretch, and it will require some research to find it but—"

"Stiles."

"What?" she cocked her head.

"The package in Boston. It was addressed to Clara *Stiles* Planter. Could Stiles be her maiden name?"

"I don't know. Maybe so. We could ask Mark."

Leo nodded and initiated a call. There was no answer. He followed up with a text. Then he said, "I don't know of a Stiles family property around here."

Delaney frowned, thinking. "There isn't one. But when I was a kid my dad raced with a guy named Jamie Stiles. I went with my dad out to his place a few times. I don't remember anything that would have linked Clara to him, but I guess Jamie would have been close to the age she was then."

"Like she could have been his sister?"

"It would fit. If she is a Stiles."

Leo sent another text. Then his phone chimed. He pumped his fist. "That was from Mark. Stiles is her maiden name. Jamie is her brother. He lived on their old family place for years, but he sold it."

Delaney thumped her hand on the steering wheel. "This is a good lead. The place Jamie Stiles lived is called Cottonwood Falls now."

"What?"

"I know. It's a crazy name. But it had amazing creek access. It's been turned it into a summer campground." She pointed at the mountains. "It's closer to the foothills."

They faced the orange band across the base of the mountains together. From this vantage point, it seemed as tall as the mountains themselves, a gradient of color from almost red to yellow at the tips that would have been beautiful if it wasn't testament to the extreme heat in the flames.

"Up there? Near the fire?"

She nodded. "Unfortunately, that's exactly where it is."

Clara's breaths were so heavy as she ran from the RZR to the highway that she was seeing stars in daylight. She'd thought she was in good shape for her age. Maybe her breathing was in part the bad air that tasted like burnt toast. Maybe it was the drugs in her system. Her fear. Her absolute terror, down to the tiniest bits of matter in her cells.

Behind her she heard the RZR's engine roar to life. She pumped her legs harder. She had to reach the road. She had to flag down a vehicle. She had to get away. Had to.

None of this made sense. Her new friend turning out to be batshit crazy. Handcuffing her to a chair in a basement. Throwing her into a room and locking her up. Drugging her. Bringing her out to the Planter ranch. Who did things like that?

A killer, that's who. If she hadn't been sure before, she was after she saw the big sword strapped onto the side of the RZR. Just like the ones that had been used on those two poor women who had been murdered.

Murdered *here*. One of them found in the little house they'd parked beside. Not the house from Clara's teen years. She'd torched it years ago, right after her aunt and uncle died, and people had chalked it up to lightning. But she knew this old farmhouse well, too. It had been abandoned even fifty years ago and spooky to her then. So, there was no way she wasn't going to make a run for it when she got a chance.

That had started with getting out of the restraints. When she'd been unable to slip her wrists through the zip tie, she'd fallen back on the training from the sheriff's department. She'd tightened the ties and raised her hands over her head, then smashed them down on the dashboard while she jerked her elbows back. It had taken her four tries before she had put enough force into it—her hands were going to be sore for a long time to come—but she'd done it. And then she'd run like mad.

The sound of the RZR grew closer. She screamed with effort, but as hard as she pumped her short legs, she knew she wasn't going to make it across the fence.

I don't want to die!

Suddenly and surprisingly, she wanted to stay alive more than anything. There had been long stretches in her life where she wasn't sure she did. She'd stayed bright on the outside and hid the sadness in her core. The guilt she'd carried. Her husband—a good man who deserved someone who could love him instead of the woman who treated him like a roommate most of the time. Her daughter—a wonderful girl, better than Clara in every way. And her grandkids—the first people in her life she'd truly been able to let loose in front of and be happy around. Before that, horses and work had been her only real escapes.

She wanted to stay alive for all of it. All of them. To say she was sorry and would do better. She'd unburden herself of the secret that had kept her frozen off for so long. She'd enjoy them. Hug her dog. Join a seniors' rodeo circuit. She'd book the vacation to the Grand Canyon Mark had asked her to take for years.

Mark. Did he miss her? Was he worried about her? Where did he think she was? How she wished she'd told him the truth about everything, from the very beginning. Let him be close to her. Trusted him. How different their life would have been. Maybe it could still be that way. So, if she was so damn sure life was worth living, the question was how to stay alive?

What did she know about her attacker? Basically nothing. Except the choice of this place, this one horribly significant place. But was that related to her or the other two women or was it just the bad luck of access and opportunity?

I don't believe it's random.

The RZR cut in front of her. She fell to her hands and knees, clawed her way to her feet, then launched herself toward the fence only five yards away. But her attacker tackled her, flattening her body to the ground. Charred vegetation was jammed up her nose and into her mouth. She coughed and gagged.

"Stop fighting and this will go much better for you," the voice behind her said.

Clara wanted to cry but instead she raised her head. "Who are you, really? Why are you doing this to me?"

Knees dug painfully into her back. A zip tie closed around her wrists, this time behind her. The weight left her back. "Get up."

Clara rolled over and onto her side, levering herself to a seat, then put her face to the ground as she got her knees under her. She pushed off and climbed to her feet. "Why?" she repeated. "*Why?*"

The only answer was a finger pointed at the RZR passenger seat. Clara had no other choice. She sat and let herself be strapped into the seat. The RZR accelerated across the rough ground.

"I'll give you one guess."

"What do I get if I'm right?"

"The answer to your question."

"And if I'm wrong?"

"I'll laugh in your face before I finish the Quest."

"What's the quest?"

"Guess or don't. I don't care."

Clara stared at the person. They were tall and big boned. Completely unlike her own tiny frame. So much like her father's side of her family. But did she see blue eyes the color of her own? A slight uptilt at the end of the nose like her mother?

She swallowed. "Because I'm your mother."

"Which makes you the worst kind of human garbage."

Because of the answer or because it was right? "I don't understand."

"Mothers who abandon their babies are despicable."

Because I am right. Her heart shattered like a glass jar on cold ceramic tile. "I didn't, I couldn't have, I wouldn't have. No —that's not what happened."

"Of course it is. And do you know what happened to me, Mommy Dearest? I was adopted by more human garbage. A father who treated me like a servant. A mother who wouldn't lift a finger to help me. And then, when I finally rid the world of my so-called father—you'll get a laugh out of this—I married my stepsibling. What I wouldn't have done back then for someone who was kind to me after a lifetime of abuse. And as soon as we were wed, history repeated itself. The abuse started. Mother did nothing for me. Nine months later we had a son. A beautiful son. I vowed that I would fight for my child. I would never let anyone hurt him. Never let him go. And then. And then." A fist pounded a knee. "He died. He was taken from me, a parent who deserved him. Meanwhile, mothers like you give away their children to be mistreated."

"I'm so, so sorry."

"I ran away. I worked. I saved money. I took a job keeping babies away from people like you."

"You have it wrong. You have it so wrong."

"Don't gaslight me. I live this life. I own my truth. I do the work."

Clara decided her best bet was to keep quiet. She had waited her whole life to meet her child. She had imagined it going so differently. In her mind, there had been anger and sadness but there had been forgiveness and there had most definitely been no madness. Still, she would give her child the chance to tell their story. She could try to talk the craziness away. She would keep talking as long as necessary if it meant her life would be spared. "I apologize. That wasn't my intention. I want to hear what you have to say."

The voice was a sneer. "I began to see. It was all because of you. And if I ever wanted to free myself of my horrible feelings and escape my horrible life, I had to free myself of you. I had to find you. I had to send you to the Hell you deserved. It became my Quest. I just had no idea how I was to fulfill it."

It was so much worse than Clara had ever dreamed it could be.

"It was in a feminist class on the Middle Ages, where we explored the heroines of that period—that's when I knew. Researching the women of that era showed me the way. I spent years immersed in the most magical, transformative experience of my life. Researching, writing, learning. Because I found her. I found it, you see. The One Way. The One Way to my Quest."

"I don't understand. I wish I did, but I don't."

The longer the two of them talked, the more formal the language became. It was like watching someone change into a different person. "She was Matilda of Tuscany."

Clara stared at them. She felt something was expected of her, but she had never heard of a Matilda of Tuscany. "I'm sorry. Tell me about her."

"Matilda of Tuscany was an Italian countess. A devout woman of faith who fought for the Pope. A warrior for God. A woman who married her stepbrother and lost her only child. Who didn't brook women of low morals even amongst nuns. It couldn't have been more clear. She was the way for us!"

Us? Clara licked her lips. "I... I see."

"Do you know how many years it took for me to figure out The One Way?"

She didn't even know what "the one way" was. "No?"

"Seven. And many more perfecting it. Practicing it as I got closer to my Quest."

"Practicing?"

"On women who had abandoned their children. Like you did me."

The zeal in those eyes was the most frightening thing Clara had ever beheld. A religious zeal. She had always believed that some of the most cruel and atrocious things in the history of mankind had been done in the name of God. And this person, inspired by a devout woman of faith, had killed other women to... practice... for killing Clara? Those poor girls. Genevieve Martine and Anong Meela. Were there others, too? *Please, God. No!*

"The ones before—they were mothers?"

"If you can call them that. Having babies they didn't want and selling them to the highest bidder."

To think she'd given birth to this person who was anchoring young women to the ground with swords. How? How had that baby turned out like this? She thought of the daughter she'd raised. She was sweet, good. This one had turned out so different. Was it all because of a horrible upbringing? Or was it the rapist father? A combination? Or was this person even her child? She had no way of verifying it. And God forgive her, she felt a flicker of hope.

She turned to look straight into the crazy, zealous eyes. "Please believe me. You were taken from me and given away without my permission. I woke up and you were gone. I never even saw you." Tears overflowed the rims of her eyes and slid down her face. She hadn't cried about her lost child in years. And now to discover a monster worse than the father—it was a stiletto through her soul. The most intense pain Clara had ever felt.

"Lies to save yourself."

"It's all true. I was a teenage girl. My parents sent me away, sent me *here* after my uncle raped me. I was a prisoner at home. I was a prisoner here. I'm so sorry."

"I expected the devil to speak through you with denials."

It wasn't my fault. Why did it still feel so humiliating, when she'd been the victim of a violent sexual assault by a predator? And now, she was here, literally begging for her life from someone who didn't see she had been a victim, too. "Please. Please believe me. I wanted the chance to love you. I did love you. I've loved you all your life."

The monster child stared into the distance, then smashed fists into the steering wheel. "Where? Where did these things supposedly happen?"

"In the barn on my family's ranch."

SIXTY

Delaney slowed to a stop on the last paved road up toward Cottonwood Falls. Joe Tarver was standing at a sawhorse road-block. She rolled down her window. Leo lowered his, too.

He approached the truck on Leo's side, strutting. "What are you doing out here, Leo? Taking a Sunday drive with your lady?" Joe said.

Leo shook his head. *Don't take the bait.* "Heading out to— what's it called again, Delaney?"

"Cottonwood Falls," she said.

"That's in the Go zone," Joe said, referring to the final evac- uation level.

"Yes. It's also where we have reason to believe our suspect has taken Clara Eckhardt."

Joe frowned. "Clara?"

"Yes."

Joe stepped back and shouted, "Has anyone let any vehicles through to Cottonwood Falls?"

Leo rolled his eyes at Delaney. "Because a killer would drive up to a road closure with a kidnapping victim and announce where he was taking her."

"The good people of Kearny County had better vote for you. That's all I'm saying." She made a zipping motion over her lips.

Leo leaned out the passenger side window. "Joe, move the sawhorse."

Joe turned back. "They haven't been through. Nobody's up there."

"Great. Now let us through."

Joe leaned on the window. "I know I shouldn't have to tell you this, *Sheriff*, but please don't cause a situation that draws down on the resources being used to protect your neighbors from the monster on the hill. You wouldn't want that on your record right when people are heading to the polls."

"I wouldn't want that for my community at any time, any more than I'd want to leave a killer running loose or one of my co-workers at their mercy."

Tires squealed and the smell of burning rubber filled the cab. Delaney had the truck through the road as the sawhorse was being moved aside. She was certain Joe hadn't heard a word of the last thing Leo said.

"You nearly ran over my foot!" she heard Joe scream, just before Leo rolled up the window.

"I used to like him," Leo said.

Delaney snorted. They drove for about a minute, gathering speed, with Leo clinging to the panic strap above the window.

Her phone dinged. "Can you check that for me?"

"Gladly." Leo knew her passcode. She knew his, too. It saved a lot of time.

It was a text from Clint. He gritted his teeth and read aloud. "Clint says, *Joe just sent out a very public message that you're on the way to Cottonwood Falls in pursuit of a suspect with Leo. I'm nearby and heading there to back you up.*"

"That's good."

"Great," Leo said. *Of course it is, you jealous dummy. Get over it.*

Delaney rocketed through the curves in the road. The smoke thickened. Ash was accumulating on the windshield, although she kept most of it off with the wipers. In the low visibility and at this speed, Leo wouldn't have recognized the road if he hadn't known he'd driven it before.

The truck dipped like a rollercoaster as the road fell and ran along the creek. Cottonwood trees suddenly loomed above them.

Delaney slowed. "The entrance is around here somewhere."

"You've been out here since it became a campground?"

"Once for a disturbing the peace call. Drunk camper doing doughnuts in the parking lot while blasting Whitesnake tunes. It's a lot different than when I was a kid. They built a few kit cabins by the creek—itty bitty ones—and put in hook-ups for RVs and travel trailers. As I recall, there is also a modular house now just inside the entrance. It's for registration and has a little store in it. The family house is about a hundred yards further in, if I remember right."

"That's a whole lot of places to search."

"But if my theory is right, none of those new places will matter. The killer will be taking Clara back to the old places. I vote we start with them." She turned on a blinker. "There's the entrance."

She drove through a gate with a COTTONWOOD FALLS CAMPGROUND sign suspended overhead, the letters painted on water distressed logs. They looked like they weighed a ton, so how they didn't tumble down in the wild local winds defied logic.

"We need a plan."

"We don't know what's out there yet."

"A plan with contingencies."

"All right."

They drove by a white modular building with OFFICE above the door. Leo saw picnic tables and grills over low stone fire pits. Behind them were a few tiny cabins. But what was most notable about the space was how barren it was. He'd learned in the fire meetings that Hot Shot crews had come through this area over the last few days to prep for fire resistance. The grass had been weed whacked down to the dirt. The lower branches of the trees had been removed. All the vegetation had been cut back around the structures. In the distance, he saw a big pile of the cleared debris, far enough away that if it ignited, it wasn't a threat to anything else. And in the middle of the picnic area, a bright red temporary water tank had been erected. Two thousand gallons of water lapped at the sides in the strong wind. The tank was critical, as the creek beside the campgrounds was nearly dry.

The place was ready for the monster on the hill, if it came this way. But had another monster gotten here first?

"Describe what you remember about the old buildings," he prompted.

"A modest house. Two-story. Normal ranch outbuildings for that era. A silo. A barn bigger than the house. A root cellar. A well. A few other little shed-type structures. It was a cool place. I liked playing out there when Dad would visit."

"Assuming we want to remain unseen as long as possible, where do we park?"

"I've been thinking about that. Here on the edge of the campground, I think. In the trees. We can walk along the creek bed to the house. It's not far."

"Sounds good."

"I can't imagine our perp would park outside. That means the barn, most likely, as houses built as long ago as this one didn't usually have garages. So, my vote is we clear the barn first."

Leo was nodding. "I'm a little concerned that we'll have fire crews in and out of here. The danger they're expecting comes from sparks and embers, not being caught in the crossfire of gun battle. I'm going to ask them to stand down with respect to this property, for the time being." He turned over his phone. "No signal." He picked up the radio instead.

"Good thinking." Delaney turned and pulled into the trees lining the dry creek bed.

As he finished passing along the message, Delaney put the truck in park and shut it down. The two of them got out and spent a minute checking and readying their gear. Leo drew his weapon and pointed to down ready. Delaney did the same.

Leo said, "I thought it was dark out here but now I feel way too exposed. At least the wind gives us good sound cover."

"And it's blowing from the west. That's optimal for us."

They trotted through the trees, along the uneven ground, making quick progress to the barn.

"Let's make a circuit, see what we hear, and then you can cover me entering through the front? Unless we find a better entrance?"

Delaney nodded. "Or you can cover me."

"I'm pulling rank this time."

She shrugged. "Try to keep up, then."

Her pace increased. At the barn, they stopped, listening.

"Voices."

Leo winced. "That's Clara. Do you recognize the other one?"

"I don't."

"Me either."

They took off again and had just reached the far side of the barn and were coming back around to the front when Leo heard a vehicle approaching. Saw its headlights. Watched it pull up between the barn and the house.

Joe Tarver got out with a bullhorn in his hand.

SIXTY-ONE
HALF AN HOUR EARLIER

They drove cross country, over ranches, through gates, traversing gravel roads, and past a wall of fire and smoke so vast it was like the mountain itself. Clara had never been more terrified, but she kept her wits about her the best she could as she gave directions into the barn of the old Stiles ranch of her childhood. They parked and she was jerked out of the passenger seat. The pain in her shoulder was like a stab wound, but it was nowhere near as bad as the pain in her heart. She'd come full circle. To the place where she'd been assaulted and raped, here with the person whose life started in those horrible moments. She walked over to the stall, empty now, that had been filled with fresh straw that day.

Suddenly, she was back in that moment. The straw scratching her exposed skin. Stabbing her eyes, choking her. His hot breath on her face, how it smelled like liverwurst. The awful weight of him, the terrible force, the pain, the degradation. The filthy things he'd said. The crushing things. That no one would believe her. That she was his, and he would do this to her again, whenever he wanted, as often as he wanted, for as long as he'd wanted.

How he'd been right about all of it.

"Here," she said, nodding at the stall.

The smell of the smoke was overpowering. The fire was so close. She shivered. Which was worse—this person or the approach of the inferno? It was like the man or the bear question. She couldn't pick.

"What was his name?"

"Rick Stiles."

"Where is he now?"

"Dead."

"Did you love him?"

Clara's mouth fell open. "He *raped me*. I hated him."

Her attacker paced in a circle, whispering and muttering. "You can't get out of this by trying to elicit my pity. It changes nothing."

"How can it change nothing?"

"A truly good parent, a truly worthy mother fights for her child. You didn't fight for me. No one ever did."

"I was fifteen years old!"

"I was a baby." A hand shot out and grabbed Clara's wrists and pulled her over backwards.

Clara's body was inverted past the ways in which she stretched in her normal exercise. She screamed in agony. She lay in a contorted heap on the ground.

"Don't move."

She heard rummaging noises in the bed of the truck.

Like hell she wouldn't move. She'd done everything she could. She'd told the truth. Maybe she'd lied all her life, thinking she was doing the right thing. But here, now, she'd told the horrible truth.

She was not going to die for it. For a person who might or might not be the baby she'd borne but was definitely a crazed killer. She'd seen the pictures of those other women. The swords impaling them to the ground. That would not be her.

She struggled to her feet, chest heaving.

Her attacker came back with a thermos, unscrewed the lid, and poured liquid into it, not remarking on her disobedience. "Drink this."

Clara shook her head. She'd already been drugged. Hadn't she heard Leo say one of the murder victims had died from poison? "No."

"You can't subvert The One Way."

Clara's chest rose and fell but she stood resolute. "Fine."

A hand clasped Clara's hair, jerked her head back, her chin up. Clara whimpered, but she kept her mouth clamped shut.

"You won't defeat the Quest."

Clara was shoved back to the ground. This time the knees were in her chest. One hand pinched her nostrils shut. Clara whipped her head back and forth but the grip on her nose was so tight that it felt like it was going to rip off her face. She kicked and bucked her way across the floor. She finally opened her mouth to gasp for air. The cup emptied into it. She gagged and sputtered. She choked and spit. But as hard as she tried to prevent it, some of the liquid made its way down her throat. What had been a splash became a deluge into her eyes, down her cheeks and neck, and again into her mouth. She recovered enough to open her eyes after a few moments, and she was just barely able to make out the image of the thermos flung to the floor without its lid.

"Please," Clara choked out. "Please."

Footsteps crunched back toward the truck. Clara knew she'd just ingested poison, maybe enough to kill her. She had no weapon. Her vision was compromised. Her arms were bound so tightly behind her that she had lost feeling in her hands.

All the advantages were against her, except one. The attacker believed Clara was their mother.

Maybe, just maybe, she could talk her way out of this. Make

an emotional appeal and play on the need for a mother's love. And who knew—maybe they could be her child. Someone who might love her. Who she might love. It wasn't impossible. She had to try.

She swallowed and licked her lips, tasting the bitter concoction again. "I'm sorry about everything that happened to you. I wish I could change it, but all I can do is promise you that I can let this go. We can get past this. I'll protect you and never tell a soul. Because that's what a good mother would do. Fight for their child. Fight to protect them. I didn't have the chance before, but I do now, and I want that for you. For us. I want to... to... to be your mother."

Metal rattled and clinked. Clara opened her eyes to see a long, lethal sword above her.

"I prepared for this moment, for the words you might say, and they mean nothing to me, as I know they mean nothing to you." The sword rose with the blade pointed down. Two hands grasped the hilt high in the air.

"Please. Give us a chance."

"It's too late."

A man's voice crackled and squelched, as loud as if he were shouting in Clara's ear from an inch away. "This is the Kearny County Sheriff's Department. Send Clara Eckhardt out unharmed and you won't be hurt."

SIXTY-TWO

"No!" Delaney hissed in the silence after Joe's command through the bullhorn. "You don't negotiate with a psychopath!"

"We have to go in." Leo spat the words, sounding angrier than Delaney had ever heard him. "Now."

"I've got you," she said, running into position and crouching by the door.

Leo grabbed the door handle. "Ready?"

"Ready."

He slid it back.

Delaney dashed across the opening, gun up, peeking inside. Leo was right behind her.

"Dead center of the room. I'm not sure if the killer is armed, but they have Clara." She angled herself into a ready position for firing if necessary.

She left out the rest. That the figure was large and dressed in chain mail and a helmet with a giant feather on top, like some kind of medieval knight. And the worst part—he was holding a longsword in the air over Clara's body. Clara who was awfully, awfully still.

One wrong move, and that sword would cleave through her.

Leo didn't hesitate. Delaney knew he would dash around the door in a buttonhook fashion, staying close to the outer perimeter and then moving outside the fatal funnel of the doorway as fast as he could, leaving her room to fire across the opening if needed.

That is what he would have done if he got a chance, anyway, which he did not.

As he stepped into the funnel and Delaney went low with her weapon pointed inside, a gunshot cracked. Leo went down.

"Leo!" Delaney threw her body after him, landing in the dirt short of his feet.

There was no time to assess his condition. No time to worry about whether she could live without him. To process the fact that someone had just shot the most important person in her life. The man she loved. All that mattered was getting him out of the line of fire. She holstered her gun. Staying low to the ground, she grabbed his ankles and jerked him toward her, slithered herself back, then jerked him again.

"I thought you said I'd be unharmed if I let Clara go!" a voice shouted.

Delaney almost had Leo where she needed him to be. She was barely listening, but she knew the words didn't make sense. She hadn't shot at Clara's captor. The only shot had been the one that hit Leo. She gave one last heave, and Leo's body cleared the door. As an officer, Delaney knew that Leo would tell her Clara was the priority. That she should leave him now that he was out of the line of fire and focus on the hostage.

But this was Leo.

He groaned and tried to sit up. The adrenaline had to be kicking in. He was way too spry for someone who'd just been shot.

"Stay down. You were shot." She held him by his shoulders.

A large person suddenly dropped to the ground by Delaney.

She went for her gun and almost had it up and pointed at the figure when it said, "Delaney, it's Clint. Don't shoot."

"Oh, my God, Clint. I nearly blew your face off!"

"Who's out there? Who's shooting at me?" the voice from inside the barn called again.

Clint said, "Sorry. When I saw Joe shoot Leo in the back, I knew I had to get over here as fast as I could."

"What?! Joe?" Delaney craned to see the area where his truck had been parked earlier, but it wasn't there. She looked back down at Leo. No headwounds. No blood on his torso or arms.

"That son of a buck," Leo said.

He sounded like he was in pain, but not as much as Delaney would have expected. His voice was almost clear.

Clint snorted. "He took off out of here like a bat out of hell, too."

The voice in the barn shouted again. "This is The One Way. The only Way. I will complete my Quest."

That sounded nutso bad. She had to hurry.

She shouted back, "You're surrounded. Send Clara out unharmed. Then we can talk."

"No talking." The voice was a shriek now.

A sound in the barn chilled her—a thud so loud it had to have been something heavy dropping —but Clara didn't scream. *She's okay. She's got to be okay.* Delaney continued her visual and tactile scan down Leo's lower body. Still no sign of wounds. But if Joe had shot him, it would have been in the back. "I need to roll you over."

"You need to get Clara. I'm fine."

"Roll over, now, if you're so fine."

And he did, protesting and grunting. That's when she saw it. Leo's vest had stopped the bullet, which was caught in the fabric. She put her palm over it. It was still warm. A flood of emotion swept through her. She couldn't form the words that were crashing through her brain. *I love you, Leo, and you're going to be okay.*

Finally, she managed, "Thank God for that vest."

"I'm better by the second. Now there's three of us. Let's do this."

Clint put a hand out, palm down. "You cover, Palmer. You may be better, but you're not one hundred percent yet."

Leo shook his head violently. But he said, "Fine."

Delaney still had her hand on Leo's back, although he had rolled to his side and was starting to sit up. "Clara's in the middle of the barn, Clint. I'm going in after you to get the angle on the perp. There's a truck in there. I'll take cover behind it."

He nodded. "Got it."

"Swell," Leo muttered.

Seconds later, the three of them were executing the entry, with Delaney moving fast to the right where she stationed herself on the far side of the truck bed without a shot being fired. She took quick notice of the fact that she didn't recognize the truck. Did that mean it wasn't Shirleen? She didn't know what Larry drove. She didn't think it was anything she'd seen Lucas drive when they'd been organizing the relief efforts.

Clint sprinted in behind her, joining her at the truck. He was about to dash across at a diagonal behind an old tractor to get closer to the center of the space, when Delaney grabbed his arm. The barn had gone quiet except for the wind outside. Was she imagining it, or did she hear the roar of a fire in the distance? What she did not see or hear was the chainmail-clad figure.

"Wait, Clint. I think they're gone."

Moving cautiously, Delaney came around the truck into the area where she'd seen and heard the voice of their perpetrator.

Clara lay face up, her chest and shoulders at an odd angle, and her eyes wide open. Her lower body was pinned to the ground by a round bale of hay. Delaney gasped. Those things weighed up to nine hundred pounds. It could be crushing her legs, her pelvis, her hips. She had to get it off her, but with its flat side down, it couldn't be rolled and was too heavy to drag. She looked up for a hay hook and a wench. Found nothing but saw a few more round bales along the side of the space, balanced on their rounded sides.

Clint recognized the problem at the same time as Delaney. "There's a tractor." He was already running over to it. He climbed up and cranked the engine. "Battery's dead."

Leo had approached Clara. Delaney glanced over at him. He was moving normally and looked like he had shaken off the worst of the bullet's impact. Delaney couldn't hear him, but it seemed like he was checking on Clara and soothing her.

She turned her attention to the tractor. She recognized the model with its clutch and stick shift. They weren't easy to drive. Her grandfather had kept one just like it. His had a weak battery, and she'd seen him jump start it many times.

She said, "I need a screwdriver. Or something metal."

Most old tractors broke down a lot. There had to be a box of tools nearby. She turned slowly, searching, and saw a toolbox against the opposite wall from the hay storage. She ran to it and found just what she needed. A good plastic-handled long screwdriver.

She opened the hood on the tractor. "Turn the key."

Clint didn't question her, just did as she asked.

She slipped the screwdriver in and held it against the posts connecting the battery to the starter and the starter to the engine, both at the same time. A few sparks flew. The engine turned over then sputtered to a stop. She removed the screwdriver and tried again with the same result.

"Come on, come on!" she shouted at it.

"Don't electrocute yourself, please," Clint said.

She made a third try and the engine roared to life. She

pulled the screwdriver out quickly. "Do you know how to drive that thing?"

Clint put it in neutral and threw the brake. "I feel sure you'll be better at this than me."

"You and Leo be ready to keep it off her upper body in case something goes wrong." She jumped into the seat he vacated. It was a better division of labor, not just because she'd made her living driving for a decade. Both of them were stronger than her.

She positioned the tractor near her friend, at an angle. Leo stood on one side of Clara and Clint on the other. She lowered the bucket a foot off the ground then moved it forward, jamming the corner into the bale. When she felt like it had a good grip on the bale, she lifted the bucket and eased the tractor forward, then turned the tractor and flipped the bale away from her friend.

Delaney turned off the tractor after she put it in park and set the brake. Then she leapt from the seat.

"Clara!" She knelt beside her.

Clara groaned.

The odd tilt of her shoulders was because her arms were restrained behind her back. Delaney removed a multitool from her duty belt. She rolled Clara on her side and cut the zip tie binding her wrists, then lowered her gently. The woman's eyes were filmy, and her pupils were so dilated that the normally light blue iris was almost consumed by the black.

In a thin, high-pitched voice, she said, "Leave me be. I won't let you touch me again."

"Clara, it's Delaney. I won't let anyone hurt you."

"Get away from me! Don't touch me!" Clara shrieked.

Clint touched Delaney's shoulder. "She must be hallucinating."

Delaney was stricken. "I think she's been poisoned. We've got to get her to a hospital."

"I just tried to call out but couldn't get a signal."

Leo said, "Rock-Below, resources are stretched thin. Would you drive her and keep calling for an ambulance until you get one? You could meet them wherever they can get to."

Clint was taking Clara's pulse. "I'll drive her all the way to the ER if necessary. Her heart is beating like a hummingbird's wings. Any reason I shouldn't pick her up and get her to my truck?"

Delaney inspected Clara's neck. "I don't see any signs of a back or neck injury. But I'm not a doctor."

Clint nodded. "I think the risk to her life outweighs other considerations." He scooped her up. He took a few steps then turned. "You guys be careful out there. I'll ask for more backup for you."

"Thanks," Delaney said.

Leo was nodding and called after him. "We'll need a statement about Joe."

"Of course."

The partners were alone in the barn.

Delaney began pacing, looking for a sign of where the killer had gone. "It wasn't the front door."

"The back entrance was locked when we went around."

Delaney was shaking her head as she looked at the dirt floor. "There are too many footprints all over each other for me to see what's what." She waved her hand around. "There's a hay loft, and I'm sure there's a cellar. But we would have already been shot if they were still here."

Leo walked to the back side of the barn, where they'd seen the door earlier. He turned, smiling. "Good for us then—it's unlocked and was left open."

She sprinted after him. "Hell, yeah."

"I want this bastard alive, Delaney. They've killed at least two women and tried to kill Clara."

If Clara survives the poison that killed Genevieve.

She stopped. "Leo, the door being open could be an attempt to throw us off."

"We'll know soon enough. Stay together."

"They didn't have a gun."

"You don't know that. Plus, they had a sword. And chain mail."

"And they're getting away," Delaney said, and then she was out of the barn and pulling out her flashlight.

She studied the ground. Whoever it was hadn't tried for stealth. Heavy footprints led out of the barn and into the trees along the creek, away from the campground. Upstream, toward the foothills. Toward the fire. Were they running to something, like a stashed vehicle—a trick they'd used once before—or a friend they'd called for a ride? Delaney couldn't fathom it otherwise.

"Leo, this way. I have a trail! Hurry!" Then she took off after the prints.

The first thing Delaney found was the helmet, about half a mile from the barn. The only surprise was that the chain mail wasn't with it. Their perp must be in great aerobic shape and strong to boot to run uphill bearing that load. The sword alone was several pounds. She picked up the helmet. Another couple. And the suit? She'd read somewhere they weighed upwards of forty pounds.

It would take an Olympic-caliber athlete to pull this feat off much longer. *Or a killer hyped up on adrenaline, running for their life.* So, what would she do if she were the perp? Her stop to look at the helmet gave Leo time to catch up with her.

She pointed at it. "Shedding gear. I think they're going to be ditching the suit soon. That, or turning on us to fight."

"A sword against two armed cops?"

"The fire isn't much further ahead."

He nodded, concern etched on his face. "It's closer than I thought."

Delaney wiped sweat from her brow. "And getting closer by the second."

"I don't like this, Delaney. We could be barging into an ambush. I want eyes on this perp, or I want us to come back with dogs and trackers."

Delaney didn't disagree, but she trusted her instincts. "Five more minutes. This psychopath has been hiding in plain sight in our little town. If we don't catch them, who knows what they'll do next or if anyone will ever find them. Their trail may be consumed by the fire."

"Five more minutes. But don't get ahead of me."

She set her phone timer for five minutes and kept it in her hand, not trusting herself to keep track without it. "I'm pretty happy we're together right now. And that you're not dead with friendly fire in your back." Before her sentiments could overwhelm her, she took off again, keeping the flashlight in constant motion to search out broken branches and crushed underbrush.

"The fire is on both sides of the creek," Leo said. "Just ahead of us."

The wall of orange extended north and south as far as Delaney could see in each direction. She understood his point. The water wasn't a fire break. It would provide no protective barrier. She knew that in the right conditions a wildfire could move far faster than she and Leo could run. She'd never been this close to one before. Were they already too close for escape if conditions changed?

She checked her phone. Four more minutes. Everything was starting to hurt, from cramps in her side to searing pain in her lungs from breathing smoke. She ran harder. Genevieve. Anong. Clara. They deserved justice. They wouldn't get it if she didn't stay tough. She stumbled on a root, going down hard on one hand.

"Are you okay?" Leo's arm was reaching for her.

"I'm okay." Her hand stung and it was probably bleeding, but it didn't seem broken. "My vision is messed up."

"Mine, too. The smoke." He pulled her to her feet. "You ready to call it?"

Her eyes went to her phone. "We have three more minutes."

Leo was shaking his head. "The wind is picking up. I think the fire is moving toward us faster now. This is one evil monster."

"You just wasted thirty seconds but that still leaves two and a half minutes."

She forced herself into a run, knowing Leo would have her back, hating herself for pushing him past his comfort zone, hating the fire, hating their perp worst of all. A fire was nature's demon, but it didn't choose to be evil. It was a force beyond will or control. But this person they were chasing had poisoned and deliberately driven swords into the soft bodies of healthy young women. Slit one's delicate throat. Trapped Clara under the crushing weight of a round bale. And if Delaney and Leo weren't careful, that human demon would take their lives as well. That was true evil. The kind she was far more scared of than fire.

She dodged to avoid an obstacle directly in front of her. A heap of something.

She stopped, assessing it quickly. "The chain mail."

Leo was beside her. "The fire."

Delaney could feel the heat. Hear the pops, groans, and roars. But when she looked up, what she saw was a woman with an orange aura all around her. Their perp. And she was devastatingly familiar.

"Shirleen!" Delaney screamed. "Let us get you out of here."

Loose hair whipped around broad shoulders and a lined

face. By her side hung the sword, which she still clutched in one hand. She didn't answer. Didn't move.

Delaney held a hand toward her. "We need to get away from the fire, Shirleen. Come on."

The older woman stayed rooted to the earth.

Leo said, "I'm radioing our position in."

Delaney moved a few steps closer, eyes on the sword.

"Stop!" the woman screamed. "I thought you were one of the good guys."

Delaney saw Leo trying and retrying on his radio. "I am. Let me help you."

"Radio won't work," he said.

The woman shouted, "No. You're a liar. Everyone lies. Lies. Lies. Lies."

"I'm not lying. Take my hand. Let's go."

"My mother. Genevieve and Anong and those other women pretending they didn't have children. I see you on TV lying about your relationship with the sheriff. God, the biggest liar of all, promising me if I would follow The One Way, he'd lead me through my Quest."

Delaney was hyper conscious of Leo's eyes on her. Shirleen wasn't completely wrong. She owed her daughters a truth—that they might have a grandmother alive out there somewhere. She owed Leo the truth about how she really felt.

She needed to build trust with Shirleen and decided to take a chance. "I'll tell you the truth. I do love Leo." She shot a glance at him and nodded to emphasize it. His face was streaked with dirt and sweat, and he had never looked better to her. She directed her gaze back to Shirleen. "And you are in terrible danger from the fire. You have done some very bad things, but we don't have to talk about them right now. We just have to all three get away from here."

They were going to have to take Shirleen by force soon. It was going to be dangerous at close quarters with that longsword. They should have done it already. But Delaney held still, giving Shirleen a little more time for voluntary compliance.

Leo switched from his radio to his phone. "One bar." He pressed a number. "It's ringing!" Then, "Drew, this is Leo. I've got you on speaker. Sorry, it's loud where I am."

"Sheriff, I've been trying to call! Where are you?"

Leo read off their coordinates. "We've got Shirleen, who is armed and very dangerous, but the fire is almost on us. If help is near, send it. We're going to do our best to get out of here."

Drew started shouting instructions at someone to call in help for Leo and Delaney, then he returned to the conversation. "But, Sheriff, listen—that can't be Shirleen. We found Shirleen chained up in her basement. She was unconscious and has been taken to the hospital."

Delaney stared at the woman in front of her. Whoever she was, she didn't react to Drew's words. She had to be Shirleen. Didn't she?

"Come again?" Leo said.

"We finished the search at her house. There definitely had been people held captive in that basement before Shirleen. We found Clara's purse. It also looked like someone has been living down there. But not Shirleen. She was definitely living upstairs."

"This makes no sense. But we've got to go. We're marching east along the creek. Send help. And wish us luck." He ended the call. "Come on, ladies."

Delaney reached for the woman's hand, tense and ready to leap back if the sword arm went up. "What's your name?"

The woman took Delaney's hand. "I go by Matilda. Matilda of Tuscany."

"Follow me, Matilda."

Leo snapped a handcuff around Matilda's other wrist, the arm holding the sword. She screamed and wheeled on him, pointing the tip of the sword in his face. She was close enough to drive it through his eye.

He didn't let go of the handcuff.

Delaney acted by pure instinct, cuffing the wrist of the hand she still had hold of. She pulled the arm as hard as she could and straightened hers. On the other side, Leo did the same. They had Matilda's arms spread wide now, so the sword didn't reach either of them.

Matilda howled at the sky, writhing her shoulders. The sword pointed at the ground, but she hung on to it.

Delaney and Leo held firm, their eyes locked on each other.

"Are you good?" Leo said.

"I am. You?"

"I've never been better. You just said you love me. And this time you can't tell me it's like a brother or friend or whatever you said last time."

"Leo, you've been shot. You almost got skewered. You still might. You sound delirious. Are you okay?"

He grinned. "Figure out a way to get her to drop that sword and sprout some wings to fly us out of here, and I'll be perfect. Otherwise, I'm going to die happy."

Delaney couldn't help smiling back, despite the heat of the fire on her back and a growing sense of sadness that she might have gotten them into a situation with no escape. That she might be leaving Kat and Carrie without a parent again, but at least with each other. That she did love Leo and wasn't taking it back this time.

"Come on," Leo said. "Let's move. This feels like a south wind. Our eastern path back may be safe for a little while longer."

They started moving across the uneven terrain by the creek, dragging Matilda along, her arms spread like a raptor's wings, the sword a very lethal talon. It was slow going in the dark without even their phone lights to guide them. Very slow.

Delaney kept waiting for Matilda's heavy sword to drop. She had to be getting tired, but she didn't show it, and the sword stayed clutched in her hand.

"Southeast," Delaney said.

"What?"

"The creek runs southeast."

"That's not good news."

It was definitely not, with the wind at their backs. "The fire is gaining on us."

Leo shouted at Matilda. "You have to drop the sword. It's time to run."

She didn't even look at him.

Delaney said, "Matilda. We can come back for the sword. If we don't run, the fire is going to catch us."

Matilda snarled at her with Shirleen's face. "Traitor."

Again, Delaney wondered how this woman could not be her friend Shirleen. She looked enough like her to be her. Or at least her sister? Twin, maybe?

Something hit her in the back. The searing pain was so intense that she fell to her knees. Matilda leapt at her with the sword drawn, but Leo yanked the woman back.

"Sorry," Delaney said, gasping. "An ember. It hurts. It must be burning through my clothes."

Leo drew his gun. "Move back."

"What are you doing?"

"She has to drop the sword so we can all run."

"Don't shoot her."

"I won't kill her. Matilda, drop it now, or I'm going to shoot your wrist."

Matilda screamed and kicked at him.

A horn honked.

Delaney looked in the direction of the sound. A convoy of off-road vehicles emerged from the forest. The first in the line stopped. A wiry man in thick fire gear jumped out. Leo kept his gun pointed a Matilda.

"Sheriff Palmer? Deputy Pace? I'm Jonas Myerson of the Smokebusters from the Wyoming Honor Conservation Camp over in Newcastle. My crew was out here working ahead of the fire, and we got the call you were in distress. We need to get you out of here pronto."

Delaney knew exactly who this crew was—inmates working forestry management. On occasion, that included fighting wildfires.

"Great to see you," Leo said. "We've got a problem with our prisoner."

Myerson was eying Matilda like a grizzly with a paw in a trap. "I can see that."

"Can someone take my side?" Delaney said. "I can get it out of her hand."

Jonas walked up and grabbed the cuff from Delaney like it was something he did every day. "Like this?" He gave it a little pressure.

Matilda spat at him.

"That's perfect." Delaney walked in front of their prisoner. She tested the wind and had the men adjust their positions, so it was blowing against her back and Matilda's face. "I'm going to ask you to drop that sword one more time, Matilda."

Matilda began to pray in a language that sounded Italian to Delaney, based on one month listening to Italian lessons on CDs a lifetime and an ice road ago.

"Forgive me, Father," Delaney said. She took out her pepper spray, pointed it at Matilda. "Please drop the sword." Matilda's eyes were wide, but she shook her head. "Gentlemen, prepare yourselves."

"Ready," Jonas said, angling his body away and covering his eyes with one hand.

Leo did the same.

Delaney released the contents, then closed her own eyes and backed away.

Matilda's scream was out of a horror movie. Her body bucked, then she fell to her knees. The sword clattered to the ground.

"Move her away from it," Delaney shouted.

The men dragged Matilda away.

Delaney picked up the sword. "Got it."

Jonas shouted, "The fire has advanced to the east on our north side. We're close to getting surrounded. We have to go."

"I'll cuff her," Leo said.

"Okay." Jonas let go of Matilda's wrist.

Delaney wanted to scream *NO* but it was too late. She knew Leo would have wanted Jonas to walk Matilda's wrist over to him. With animalistic quickness and ferocity, Matilda whirled on Leo and swung the loose handcuff at his head.

"No!" Delaney leapt toward them.

The thwack of the cuff against the side of Leo's skull was audible even over the howling fire. He went down. Matilda kicked him in the stomach—over and over—until he released the other cuff. She turned, her eyes on the sword, which Delaney had tossed to the side.

Delaney was almost to Matilda. "No! No!"

Delaney dove for the sword, but Matilda had the angle and was closer. She scrambled across the ground and grabbed the hilt. Delaney caught one of Matilda's ankles as she turned to run. She held on for several steps until the woman stopped, raised the sword, and swung it down in a ferocious chop.

Delaney jerked her arm back and rolled away. She scrambled to her feet and pulled her gun, expecting Matilda to continue her attack.

But Matilda was running. Running straight for the rock ledge that extended over the burning forest. She turned once. "Tell my sister I'm sorry."

If Delaney didn't fire, Matilda was going to leap off the other side, into the fire. Even if she waited too long, the force of the bullet would carry Matilda over. An ugly memory of her brother Liam falling over a cliff up in the mountains took hold of her mind for a split second.

She whispered. "No. No. No. Don't make me do it."

Matilda kept running.

Delaney raised her gun and took aim, center mass, even though she wanted to shoot to injure. A leg. A foot. A hand. Something nonlethal to slow her down. *Never shoot in the back.* But wasn't the exception to that rule, *Except when a serial killer will possibly get away by throwing themselves into a fiery abyss where no one can follow?*

"Fire, Delaney," Leo screamed.

She pulled the trigger.

Delaney parked her Chevelle at Mark and Clara's house. Smoke still hung heavy in the air, but the fire was now significantly contained, thanks to a torrential rainstorm giving the firefighters an assist. The forecast favored continued progress, too. The community was breathing a collective sigh of relief.

Clara had been released from the hospital with a clean bill of health, despite being dosed with deadly nightshade and bruised by the hay bale. She'd already given a full statement to officers at the station.

This was a social call.

Leo waved from outside the front door where he was waiting for Delaney. By mutual agreement, they'd taken the two days since the events at the old Stiles ranch to sleep and catch up with their families. This was the first time they'd seen each other. Delaney was nervous. Shy.

"You look beautiful." Leo's blue eyes were shining neon. His wide smile split his cheeks.

She smoothed the front of her top. It was just a white blouse and jeans, but she knew he liked to see her girly toenails, so she'd worn sandals. Winter would curtail that before long.

"Thank you. You look great yourself. How's your head? And your back?"

"I'm no worse than usual." He touched her elbow. "Lunch after this?"

Leo asked her to eat with him frequently, but this time his request turned her knees to jelly. Going on a public date was a big step. "I could eat."

"Good."

"Does Clara know we've arrived?"

"Not yet." He turned and knocked. "Is that Shirleen's car out there?" He gestured toward a white SUV with a plethora of social justice-themed bumper stickers.

The door opened. Clara and Mark stood before them, holding hands. In all the times Delaney had seen them together, she couldn't remember that happening.

Clara opened her arms and threw them around Delaney first, pulling her in tight. "You did what you had to do with Charli. Thank you for saving me."

Charli. That was the real name of Clara's other daughter. Shirleen and Charli, the twins she'd never known she had. Tears sprang to Delaney's eyes. She'd been afraid that would happen. She hated shooting her gun at a human, seeing the bullet impact a living body. Luckily, her shot had stopped the woman from jumping into the fire, but Charli was still in the intensive care unit at the hospital in Billings. Delaney was on mandatory administrative leave while her discharge of a firearm was being investigated.

"Thank you," she tried to say. Not much sound came out. She cleared her throat and repeated it. "Thank you."

Clara hugged Leo next, while Mark welcomed Delaney.

Clara beckoned them inside where Shirleen was sitting in an overstuffed chair holding a mug of what smelled like coffee. She had clearly been crying as well. Greetings were exchanged again. Seats were taken on the L-shaped couch and two cowhide armchairs. The hairs irritated Delaney's legs through her jeans. She appreciated the ranch furniture, though, which matched the Western paintings of cowboy scenes and aged tools and bric-a-brac on shelves and the hearth about an enormous stone fireplace.

"It's been a bittersweet day." Clara stood next to Shirleen and took her hand. "I don't know how to take it all in."

"I hate to ask you to repeat yourselves, but we'd love to hear about it," Leo said. "First, though, I should update you on a few things."

"Please," Mark said, as Clara nodded.

"I apologize for bringing bad news. Anna Petrov's body was found in a ravine on the far corner of the Planter ranch, staged like the others."

"Another sword," Clara said, with a shiver.

"Yes. We expect we'll find she was poisoned with deadly nightshade, based on the results of our search in Charli's rooms in your basement, Shirleen, although we're still waiting on definitive toxicology reports for Anna as well as Genevieve and Anong."

Along with the one recovered from Charli at what used to be the Stiles ranch, that made four longswords. Genevieve, Anong, Clara, and Anna. Leo had told Delaney they had a possible match on a murder in Wisconsin involving a longsword that had come from Drew's FBI contact. That would account for the five Charli had purchased from Infiniquity.

Shirleen paled and clutched her stomach. "Oh, Charli, Charli."

Clara chewed her lip. "We expected as much, but it's hard to take in."

"Shirleen, you've probably heard that since we didn't know about your twin, we thought the killer was you." She wasn't the only person they'd wrongly suspected. Trey. Drew. The Planter brothers. Even Robbin Hood, who, it turned out, had slept with a married co-worker. The woman was married to a professional wrestler who threatened Robbin, so he'd high-tailed it out of town.

"Yes, I had," she said.

Delaney said, "I'm sorry I doubted you."

"Only because of evidence. It's okay. It's your job."

Delaney inclined her head. It was true. She believed with religious fervor in following the evidence. In this case, even the DNA evidence might have implicated Shirleen, though, as the piece of fingernail found under Anong's body, if Charli's, would match Shirleen's DNA as well. They'd know soon enough when the results came in.

Clara said, "Where are my manners. Coffee, you two?"

Leo said, "Please."

Delaney shook her head. She was nervous enough about her upcoming lunch date without coffee jitters. "No, thank you."

"I know how you take it," Clara said to Leo as she headed out of the living room.

Delaney said, "Why did you keep Charli a secret?"

Shirleen scooted forward on the cushion. "Habit, I guess. Experience, too. You've seen we're identical, but it's only skin deep. I've never had the mental health issues she has. Since our teens, she's struggled. First it was just bipolar disorder, but she's become delusional as she's gotten older. She goes in and out of treatment, then she shows up on my doorstep and I take her in. It's fine as long as she stays on her meds, then she inevitably quits taking them and everything degrades. She always ends up back in a facility. It's exhausting. I thought it would be easier to skip the explanations and introductions this time."

"Where was she before Kearny?" Delaney thought she knew the answer to the question but wanted the whole story.

"Wisconsin. A town called Appleton. I'd been living there, too, before she was involuntarily committed—courtesy of me, trying to save her life. I'd been searching for our birth mother for years, and when I found Clara, I decided to move out here." She made a self-deprecating face. "When I got here I was too scared to approach her. Anyway, Charli was released from treatment, and she followed me here. I let her in my basement to give her privacy."

"I've heard Charli was working as a hairdresser in town."

"To say she was working as a hairdresser is stretching it a little. I referred her a few clients she saw at my place. She promised me she'd keep a low profile. I tried to keep her busy in the house so she wouldn't get out and into trouble. For a while, I thought everything was fine."

Leo said, "Only it wasn't."

"Correct. You've got to understand the dynamic. I went to college, married young, lost a child—which I told you about, Delaney—then divorced and started graduate school. Charli has been following me around from town to town since we got out of high school. Probably because she couldn't live the normal life I had, she basically started consuming mine. She dressed like me. She called herself 'us' instead of 'I' or 'me.' When I was working on my Ph.D. in Medieval Studies, I came down with mono. She went to my classes in my place and took notes for me. I would have had to miss a semester without her. Looking back, I think the separation of our identities by then was very hazy in her mind. Anyway, I stayed home and worked on my thesis."

"On Matilda of Tuscany?" Delaney had done some research when she couldn't sleep over the last two days. Matilda of Tuscany had been a real Countess in Italy during the Middle Ages and one of the most amazing women of that era—a warrior and defender of the Pope.

"Yes." Shirleen sighed. "And Charli became even more obsessed with her than me. The background is important. After my adoptive father died, my adoptive mother married the father of my husband, making my husband—after the fact—my stepbrother. Sounds very *Modern Family*, I know. Because of that and other things, Charli fixated on the parallels she thought existed between Matilda and me, or 'us' as Charli called it. Being married to a stepbrother, losing a baby, our family's devout Catholic faith, which I lapsed from, but Charli did not. Those things lined up with Matilda, I guess. And, when Charli isn't at her best, she can't keep the two of us—Charli and me—separate in her mind."

"We found a Basilica of the Sacred Heart crucifix at the Planter ranch. Do you know anything about it?"

"Oh!" Shirleen's face crumpled. "I gave that to Charli. She was wearing it when she... did what she did? That's awful!"

"I'm sorry," Leo said. "When did you come to suspect Charli might have killed the women?"

"It was gradual. I didn't realize Charli even knew them. Then I heard that the swords used on the bodies were suspected to be medieval replicas, and I got a really bad feeling."

"Why didn't you tell me?" Delaney said, her voice gentle.

Shirleen's voice cracked. "I wanted to. I'd spent so many years protecting Charli, though. I had to know for sure she had done it before I told anyone. So, I confronted her. She denied it, of course. I guess I believed her because I wanted to. I mean, I shared a womb with her. She was the only blood relation I knew all my life until now." She sighed. "Then she poisoned me. Next thing I remember clearly was being in the hospital. I have flashes of feeling woozy and seeing her face, knowing something wasn't right. But she must have kept me pretty drugged."

"You're lucky you survived."

"She didn't use the belladonna on me. The surgeons think it was modern Valium, which she apparently hoarded and kept from her treatment stints."

Clara spoke from the doorway. "I can't help thinking that if my parents hadn't stolen the two of you away from me that none of this would have happened." With shaking hands, she gave Leo his coffee.

Shirleen shook her head. "No. Charli is sick. She has a long-documented history of mental illness."

"But she wouldn't have needed to avenge maternal desertion."

Shirleen stood and held out her hands to Clara, who took them. One so tall, the other tiny, but yet Delaney could see it now—something about the eyes and nose. They favored each other. "Then it would have been something else. Her memories of our childhood do not match my own. Our adoptive family was wonderful. My mother and her husband will love you. I hope you'll agree to meet them."

Clara looked at Mark who smiled at her and nodded. "And we can't wait for you to meet our daughter Josie."

Shirleen reclaimed her chair, and Clara went to sit with her husband on the couch.

Delaney remembered what Charli had said about ridding the world of their adopted father. She'd save that discussion for another day. Shirleen had faced enough horror at her twin's hands. She wondered, too, about the deaths of the uncle who had raped Clara and the aunt and uncle who had kept her at the Planter ranch until she gave birth. But sometimes it was just best to let the past stay buried. The thought made her stomach churn. There were certainly answers she'd received in the last year that she'd only thought she wanted.

Leo said, "Just a few more things. And I'm sorry, none of this is getting any easier. If Charli survives, she will be facing at least three counts of murder."

"Yes," Shirleen said.

Clara wiped her eyes.

"But there will be another case pending. The FBI is launching a massive investigation into the human trafficking and baby brokering that has moved into Kearny."

Shirleen said, "I am so glad to hear this!"

Delaney said, "Mika is under FBI protection and will testify against Albert Tuttle and other involved individuals."

"Is she going to get her baby back?" Clara asked.

"Maybe. We're told she's wrestling with that right now. The baby is with a wonderful family. It's a very difficult situation." The other person in a difficult situation was Sugar, who clearly had fallen for her co-worker Trey. She'd been devastated when he showed back up in town with a very young girlfriend, having lied to her about why he was leaving.

"I can't even imagine. I would have wanted my baby—babies—back, but even more I would have wanted the best for them."

Leo nodded. "In the end, what's most important to us is that you and Shirleen came out of this alive, Clara."

Mark put his arm around Clara. "I got my wife back. Our family has grown. I'm the luckiest man alive."

SIXTY-FOUR

Leo couldn't quit smiling at Delaney. They'd gone upscale at Palomino's Bar and Grill, where they were sitting at a high table by the picture windows facing Main Street. He wished she were beside him so he could hold her hand but taking her in from across the table was hardly a consolation prize.

"Has Kat recovered from you ruining her life after the fair the other day?" he asked.

"I've been forgiven in a haze of happiness about Freddy." Delaney dipped the last piece of calamari in aioli and popped it in her mouth. She wasn't a dainty eater. In fact, there was nothing dainty about her. She was bold, confident, and vibrant. Absolutely perfect.

"There's a lot of happiness haze at our place, too. Freddy, of course, and now my sister is in lust with Drew."

Delaney shook her head. "I wish I didn't know how that one had started."

"A week ago, Adriana was insisting she and Freddy were moving back to California. And that I had to go with them."

Little lines formed between Delaney's eyes. "But you're not, right?"

"My handler at the Drug Enforcement Agency told me they have a source in the cartel who says they've put finding me on the backburner. A fair number of their leadership was arrested in a massive sting. New leaders, new priorities—for now. But it's likely that if I ever pop up in California, I'm dead. So, no, I'm not even going back to take you to Disneyland. The Wyoming border is as far west as I want to be."

"That's good." Delaney's lines disappeared. "Mary is ecstatic that Adriana has agreed to come work with her at the Loafing Shed full time."

Leo groaned. "Please tell her not to hold me responsible for anything my sister does or doesn't do."

Delaney was laughing when her phone buzzed. "Do you mind?"

"Go ahead."

She made a face. "Grr. It's Clark Applewhite with the feds. I haven't heard from him in months."

"What does he want?" Leo took a sip of his Blacktooth amber ale, Bomber Mountain.

She read aloud. "*It didn't go well between you and I last time. I'd like a do-over. We still want to work with you. Let's meet up.*"

"He's direct, at least."

"Is this a coincidence?"

"What do you mean?"

"I get suspended, he reaches out?"

"I haven't talked to any feds, but word does have a way of getting around."

She looked back at her phone. "Oh!"

"What?"

"I missed a message earlier. From Skeeter."

"Is it about Freddy?" Leo put his glass down.

"No. It's about my mom." Her expression was pinched.

He reached across the table, palm up. She looked at his

hand. Looked at him. He wiggled his fingers. She put her hand in his. *Warm. Soft. Right.* "What did he say?"

"He found her. In Washington State."

"Has he talked to her?"

"No. I told him to let me initiate contact."

"So, it's not certain yet."

"No."

"This is good news, Delaney."

"It is, and it isn't. If she's alive and never called or came back for me after what I went through, that's kind of worse than if she died."

Leo squeezed her hand. "Talk to her. Let the evidence guide you. No assumptions."

She toasted him with her own Bomber Mountain. "Spoken like a cop."

"One who will be with you every step of the way, if you'll let him."

Color rose in her cheeks, but she nodded.

The server arrived with their meals. Leo released Delaney's hand, and she put her phone away. His burger was delicious and messy.

After a few bites, he said, "Joe's lawyer finally let him give his statement." Joe was suspended pending investigation like Delaney. The outcome of the two inquiries was sure to be quite different, however. Because of Delaney's suspension, she had not been in the loop.

"How did he spin it? Or did he admit he was trying to get rid of the competition?"

"He swears he mistook me for the suspect. He saw you rendering aid after and tried to call for an ambulance but couldn't get cell signal. He thought the best course of action was to drive a short distance until he could make a call out, then come back for me. According to him, by the time he made it back, we were gone."

"He's certainly gotten the media attention he's been craving from it."

"Not the kind he wanted."

Delaney was picking at her fettuccine Alfredo.

"Do you not like your food?"

She put her fork down. "I don't know how to do this, Leo." She smiled. "In a good way."

"Do what?"

"Be different with you than I was before."

He reached across the table again. This time she slid her hand into his without hesitation. "I don't want you to be different."

Her brows went up, then her tone grew serious. "I'm no picnic."

He busted out a laugh. "You don't lie."

She bounced his hand against the table playfully. "I don't do relationships well. I've been hurt. It's hard for me to trust."

"These are things I know. And yet here I am. It's me who's no picnic. I'm going to spend the rest of my life wondering if a cartel is going to execute me and everyone I love."

"I've seen pictures of the old Leo. You're completely different now. You've got that Wyoming beard, but I'd recommend a cowboy hat, too."

"Noted." He held her gaze for a few silent seconds. "I looked up the department guidelines, by the way. There's nothing in them prohibiting us from dating."

She shrugged. "That's because whoever put the rules together was a misogynist who lacked imagination."

"Maybe."

"The county commissioners will put a rule in place if we date."

"Probably."

"There are good reasons for the rules, Leo. Morale. Appearance of favoritism. We all need to be able depend on each other equally. You've heard Joe. He resents me because of... because—"

"Because of how I feel about you. And how you feel about me."

"That." Her cheek color returned.

"All of what you say is true."

"I don't want the drama from it, but I also don't want you to hate me later. This could hurt your career."

He jiggled her arm by the hand he was holding. "I need to be very clear about something with you."

"Uh oh. You're scaring me."

He looked deeper into her eyes than he'd ever looked into someone's before. She was beautiful. Not just the outside, but the gentle, caring warrior inside. "If I have to choose between being sheriff and you, I pick you."

"Leo—"

He held up their joined hands. "I will go to work as a security guard at a bank and pick you."

She ducked her face. Her checks turned a splotchy red. "Stop."

"I'll be the crossing guard for the elementary school and pick you."

"I get the point."

And just like that, he knew what he had to do. No, he knew what he *wanted* to do. All of it. He scooted his chair around the table until they were sitting knee to knee.

She laughed. *God, I love that sound.* "Leo, what are you doing?"

"I'm telling you what I'm going to do. Not asking you. Telling you."

"Ooh, you're going all tough guy on me."

"Nope. Just a guy who knows what he wants and isn't afraid to get it."

Delaney buckled herself into the passenger side of Gabrielle, feeling relaxed and confident with Carrie at the wheel. Back-to-school time was upon them. The summer's driving lessons were coming to an end. This was, in essence, a graduation. To celebrate, they'd packed Kat, a squirming and yappy Dudley, and Carrie's friend Victoria in the cabin. It was a violation of safety rules and a bad precedent, but they weren't going far.

"Promise you won't say a word about my driving," Carrie said as she let the engine warm up.

"Unless it's absolutely necessary."

Carrie turned to Victoria. "She always says that to leave herself an out."

Delaney harrumphed. "Kat, can you get your dog to shut his yapper?"

"Probably not. Can you not be gross and weird and date Freddy's uncle when he finally likes me?"

Delaney bit back her smile. "Probably not."

"Freddy and his mom are moving out of Leo's place anyway. So, whatever. I'm just happy Clara's okay. And that my first rodeo is this weekend. Is everyone coming?"

They all assured her they'd be there.

Carrie cleared her throat. "I shall now commence driving Gabrielle."

Victoria and Kat cheered.

No one but Delaney had ever ridden with Carrie, and Delaney realized the girl was nervous. Carrie put the tractor in reverse and swung it around, so the nose was facing down the driveway.

When she was chugging past their house and toward the gate, Delaney said, "A little less stressful without the trailer?"

"Just a little. Last time was scary in a lot of ways."

Victoria said, "I think it's totally wild that all three of the women killed were from other countries. In Kearny!"

"Watch out, Wyoming. The world is coming for you," Carrie said.

Delaney froze. That. That was exactly what had been eating at her. The world was coming for Wyoming. Whether in the hordes of visitors in buses to Yellowstone, the people slowly exploring the state in Sprinter vans on their grand American vacations, those that then chose to move to one of the last great wild places in the world and make them less wild, or even those that moved here through no choice of their own, like Genevieve, Anong, and Anna. Wyoming's problems weren't just the small town, Wild West issues anymore.

Their home was a mix of the Wild West and the big bad world now.

Delaney had tried so hard to figure out the *why* of it all when the murders first happened. Why in a state not known for attracting international residents had there been homicide victims from three different countries in little Kearny? She'd strained to make the international angle make sense. To make their deaths *because* of it. In the end, where they had come from had been irrelevant to the killer. Because of their gender, youth, and poverty, they'd been vulnerable to a trafficker and had their babies taken from them and sold. And that had caught the attention of a psychopath.

The more things changed, the more they became the same. The strong imposing their will on those weaker than them. Her own mother had been forced into a religious cult by an overzealous family who wanted to subdue her wild side. She thought of Igor Salazar—the perpetrator in one of hers and Leo's big cases—who had been cut loose by the feds in their grand wisdom, even though he preyed on girls. Of her own brother who had never been confirmed dead, who killed anyone who got in his way. They were criminals that should have been incarcerated. How many more were out there, beyond her awareness? In her mind, she pictured legions, and it terrified her sometimes.

Please, Lord, help me protect my daughters.

Carrie turned onto the paved road, shifting as she accelerated. She really had a good instinctual feel for the gears. Many good instincts, really, and not just about driving. About life. She would be all right. She had to be, as did Kat.

Okay enough to hear all the truths.

"Girls, I have something to tell you," Delaney said.

"In front of Victoria?" Kat asked.

Dudley barked to emphasize her point. Kat clapped her hand over his mouth. He barked through her fingers.

"Victoria is with us so much she's practically family."

"Thanks, Delaney!" Victoria said, smacking her gum.

"What is it?" Carrie asked. "Are you and Leo having a baby?"

"Whatever gave you that idea! No!" Delaney laughed, but the comment gave her pause. A serious relationship. There would be decisions ahead. Big ones. "You know how I thought your grandmother—my mom— was dead?"

"Yes," Carrie said.

"She's not?" Kat asked. Kat had been down this road with her own parents and jumped right to the possibility.

"Well, I had Skeeter looking for her because I got a tip she might not be dead. And he thinks he's found her. I just need to call her and see if it's really her."

Carrie frowned.

Kat said, "If she's alive, why hasn't she ever called you?"

"A valid question, and one I will ask, if it's her. I just wanted you guys to know before I contact her."

"Can we be there when you call?"

"I'll think about it." The moral support would be nice, but she couldn't guarantee they'd see and hear the best in her. "Now, Carrie, you're about to get on the highway."

"Duh." Carrie rolled her eyes. "I'm ready for it." She downshifted her way to the intersection with her blinker on and turned right. "Did I pass your test?"

"Nicely done."

They drove in silence past the Loafing Shed and toward town. On their right was the Kearny Women's Club. It was the site of primary voting for, amongst other offices, Kearny County Sheriff. Today was voting day.

Carrie said, "Should I just drop you off on the side of the road and wait for you there?"

"Better than going in that crowded parking lot. Be sure you pull *all* the way off, though. And leave your flashers on."

"Yes, ma'am."

"Kat, did you hear her beautiful manners?"

"Whatever," Kat said.

When the vehicle was in park, Delaney opened the door. "See you guys after I finish my civic duty."

"Next election, Victoria and I will get to vote, too!" Carrie said.

Delaney climbed out and walked toward the little building. The line was lengthy, and she passed the wait time chatting with fellow voters. Several mentioned that they'd seen the interviews Leo had been giving and read articles and social media posts where he was quoted urging people to write-in a vote for Clint Rock-Below for sheriff. The party had refused to remove Leo from the ballot even after he'd told them about his intention to pursue a relationship with her. And, of course, Joe remained on since the investigation into him shooting Leo was ongoing.

When it came her turn to vote, she took her ballot into the booth and filled it out for every office except sheriff, which she saved for last. She read the names. Joe Tarver. Leo Palmer. The line marked Other for a write-in. She sat in the booth for a long time, thinking. She finally made her decision and filled the section out, then deposited the ballot in the box, feeling good about her choice.

Her happy group made the short drive back to the Loafing Shed where the number of cars in the lot and people at the outdoor tables made it clear that the nearby voting location was good for business.

"Looks like you can park over to the side here," Delaney said, pointing.

Carrie stopped the semi in exactly the right spot. "Yes, Melaney."

"Melaney?"

Kat stuck her head between them. "Do you like it? It's like Mom and Delaney mashed together. We thought about Maunt Delaney but that was just weird."

Delaney rolled her lips inward. She was too overwhelmed to speak, but she threw her arms around Kat and pulled Carrie into the hug with them. Dudley narrated the tender moment with frantic yaps.

"I love it. And I love you guys," Delaney said.

"Yeah, we're pretty awesome," Carrie said, pulling back and breaking up the group hug.

"Ha. Thanks." Delaney wiped her eyes and jumped out. The others followed.

Leo was waiting for her in front of the patio holding a sign that said, WRITE IN CLINT ROCK-BELOW FOR SHER-IFF. When she reached him, he said, "Do you know how hard it is not to kiss you?"

His words warmed her insides. "Yes, I do." She waved at his sign. "You know one of us is going to get fired eventually, no matter who wins."

"It's going to be worth it. Besides, I got a call this morning about a job."

Her heart revved up. "In Kearny?"

"I won't be entertaining offers outside the area. I have ties." He winked at her. "I've been asked to put my hat in the ring when Mara Yellowtail resigns."

"Oh, my God. What happened?"

"Melanie Whats-her-face used her time here to dig up dirt on more people than just us."

Delaney threw her head back and laughed. Then she looked at the crowd eating their Loafing Shed breakfast, a few with libations because it was five o'clock somewhere else in the world and drink o'clock in Wyoming.

"Oh, what the hell," she said.

She stepped up to him, put her arms around his neck, and planted her lips on his. Patrons began to cheer, at first tenta-tively, then louder and louder, including some wolf whistles and woos that sounded a lot like her daughters. And she kept kissing him, until she couldn't hear anything over the wild pounding of her own heart.

A LETTER FROM PAMELA

Dear Reader,

You're here! At the end of *Her Burning Lies*! With all the choices for and demands on use of your time, I am honored that you spent hours of yours reading it.

If you would like to receive email alerts of all my latest releases, just sign up at the following link. Your email address will never be shared, and you can unsubscribe at any time.

www.bookouture.com/pamela-fagan-hutchins

It has been such a thrill to read your reviews of the first few books in the series and share my love for Delaney and her world with you. I can't believe I get the privilege of continuing her stories. In a crazy twist of fate, I've been writing this series in Denmark, the UK, France, and California, far from my home base in Wyoming or even our family cabin in Maine. This particular book was written in Martigues, France, one thousand meters from the Mediterranean Sea on Le Côte Bleu. Writing Delaney here has made me both more and less homesick.

I hope you enjoyed *Her Burning Lies* and if you did, I would be very grateful if you could write a short review online. I'd love to hear what you thought about it, and reviews make such a difference helping new readers discover one of my books for the first time.

Writing is a solitary experience, and I am somewhat of a

hermit anyway. I split my time between two rustic homes—when I'm not traveling the world. The one in Wyoming, on the face of the Bighorn Mountains, and the other on a remote lake in Maine. No matter where we are, my companions are my husband and our sled dogs, with visits from our adult children and grandchildren.

So, I *love* hearing from my readers out there in the real world. You can get in touch with me via my Facebook page where I am fairly active, through Instagram, Goodreads, or my website. I also so very greatly appreciate follows on Amazon and BookBub.

Thanks,

Pamela Fagan Hutchins

www.pamelafaganhutchins.com

 facebook.com/pamela.fagan.hutchins.author
 instagram.com/pamela_fagan_hutchins

ACKNOWLEDGMENTS

When the idea for *Her Burning Lies* first came to me in early 2024, I never dreamed this book would hit so close to home!

There were two key elements: the twisty plot that brought in a medieval sword and people from outside the borders of Wyoming and a late summer fire. Little did I know that by the time I started writing this book in August of 2024 an enormous wildfire would have engulfed the area where the book is set and where my husband and I make our home, while we were living five thousand miles away in France. The remnants of the Middle Ages all around me in Europe felt eerily reminiscent of the plot and undoubtedly influenced the book it became. But the Elk Fire back home in the Bighorn Mountains was a downright *spooky* parallel to the book. Luckily, the Elk Fire was ultimately contained before it could damage many homes or spread into towns, but it will be decades before the mountains and forests return to their former glory.

Our eternal gratitude goes out to the hot shot crews and firefighters who prepped our home in case the fire came for it. It was close, but the seven-mile fire line built by professional crews, volunteers, and neighbors held.

A few years ago, my husband posted that we were giving away rusty, fire-damaged barbed wire. One of the takers was Daisy, who showed up with her family to claim some to use for a project. We soon learned that she'd given up oil field trucking in North Dakota—and a side gig as a reality star—for taking over the family homestead, raising her second daughter twenty years after her first, and being a service to others through philanthropy and her physical labor. She was a key player in organizing one of the largest agricultural relief efforts in the history of the United States through a huge convoy of truckers, donors, and volunteers after historic fires devastated America's Midwest. She and her family raise (and butcher) a large flock of turkeys every year to feed three hundred-plus people at a free community Thanksgiving dinner. Daisy's the one you want as your second in a knife fight, who could have been a model or actress instead of a rodeo star and extreme trucker, and she's the friend you can knock back a cold one with or take to meet your pastor (after you've done your best to prepare them for the encounter). If by some small miracle you find her in a church, you won't see her sitting in the pews... she's the one standing in the back. She was forged in the kind of volcanic upheaval that can result in smoking rubble or beautiful rocky mountain ranges. Daisy, through character and force of will, is the latter. If you enjoy Delaney as much as I do, it is because of my friend Daisy. Daisy, thank you for agreeing to let me reshape you in fiction.

When it comes to creating a fictional law enforcement world, you have to start with the real thing. I am so lucky to have Police Chief Travis Koltiska of Sheridan, Wyoming, in my corner for this. A fourth generation native of Wyoming (with his kids the fifth generation like Delaney), Travis is a bit larger than life. I know him as the generous guy with the heart for his family and animals, a big laugh, and endless stories, but trust me that you would *not* want to be the perp who faces him! Which is ironic since we met him through his wife after my husband accidentally broke into a house she was listing for sale. (It's a long story that ends in years of friendship, and I swear, it was an accident!) I've included anecdotes, quotes, history, and ideas from Travis in many books. I even have a Deputy Travis who shows up from time to time in several interconnected Wyoming series. This time, he took it a step further and acted as my beta reader and coach. Any mistakes are mine alone. He improved the book immeasurably and put up with dumb questions in texts all hours of the day and night. Please email Travis some love through me as I am praying he wants to continue in this role! Thanks, Travis, for your friendship and your help.

Huge thanks to my creative, firm, encouraging, brilliant editor Helen Jenner for her patience and collaboration. Thank you for your confidence in me. Helen, you've pushed me through walls I didn't know I'd built to shelter deeply buried writing fears. I'm very lucky to collaborate with you on Delaney and her world. I hope there are many more to come.

Thanks also to the wonderful team at Bookouture. As a rugged individualist/indie since 2012, I didn't think there was a publisher I would ever be willing to work with. Nimble, lean, flexible, strategic, mission driven, and reader centric, Bookouture is everything I was looking for, and I appreciate them taking a chance on me. The support has been incredible, in every step of the process.

Thanks to my husband Eric for brainstorming with me, dreaming up ways to exhibit Delaney's superpowers and mechanical prowess, encouraging me endlessly, beta reading, and much more despite his busy work, travel, and workout schedule. And, most importantly, for putting up with my obsession with horses and sled dogs! Our life in the last two years has been the best of times and the worst of times. Mud huts on the beach, my love—anywhere as long as it's with you.

Thanks to our five offspring. I love you guys more than anything, and each time I write a parent/child relationship like the ones Delaney has with Kateena and Carrie, I channel you.

Finally, to each and every blessed reader: I appreciate you more than I can say. It is the readers who move mountains for authors, and you have done so for me, many times over.

Proofreader
Liz Hurst

Marketing
Alex Crow
Melanie Price
Occy Carr
Cíara Rosney
Martyna Młynarska

Operations and distribution
Marina Valles
Stephanie Straub
Joe Morris

Production
Hannah Snetsinger
Mandy Kullar
Ria Clare
Nadia Michael

Publicity
Kim Nash
Noelle Holten
Jess Readett
Sarah Hardy

Rights and contracts
Peta Nightingale
Richard King
Saidah Graham